An Unwavering Trust

L.L. Diamond

An Unwavering Trust
By L.L. Diamond

Published by White Soup Press
Copyright ©2015 LL Diamond

Cover and internal design © 2015 L.L. Diamond
Cover design by L.L. Diamond/Diamondback Covers

ISBN-10: 0692406719
ISBN-13: 978-0-692-40671-7

Facebook: https://www.facebook.com/LLDiamond
Twitter: @LLDiamond2
Blog: http://lldiamondwrites.com/
Austen Variations: http://austenvariations.com/

To my friends and betas, who generously give of their
own free time without complaint and ensure my
books are better than I could do on my own
—Thank you!

Acknowledgements

First of all, I have to thank Jane Austen, whose timeless works have inspired me, and others to re-imagine her unique and beloved characters into countless scenarios. She had a talent for words few possess.

I owe a huge thank you to many people, but my first (after JA of course!) goes to Lisa Toth, Kristi Rawley, Suzan Lauder, and Janet Foster who have spent their free time pouring over, critiquing, and correcting these chapters. Their hard work helps make this suitable for reading!

I would like to thank those who run and frequent the JAFF forums, especially A Happy Assembly and Darcy and Lizzy. You have provided me a launching pad for my work and helped me become a writer. I appreciate the support of those who comment and leave me feedback as well as the community itself. Your support has meant a lot!

I would like to thank the ladies and gent at Austen Variations for welcoming me this year. I still have to pinch myself at times that I am included with such company.

Despite her death over ten years ago, my mother played a huge role in my Jane Austen addiction by introducing me to Sense and Sensibility when I was about nineteen. I miss you every day, Mom! I love you!

Lastly, I have to thank my family. They may roll their eyes at the mention of Jane Austen, Pride and Prejudice, or sometimes Persuasion, but they support me daily, and tell me they are proud of me.

When I first began this journey, my husband could not have explained the intricacies of fan fiction, but recently, he did so to his office staff. He surprises me all of the time, and I know that when this book is released, he will make just as big a fuss as he did when I published the first.

Lastly, I would like to thank everyone who bought a copy of one of my books. You make it possible for me to write and make it worth the time and effort of multiple rounds of editing. Thank you!

Chapter 1

27 April 1810

Fitzwilliam Darcy stood before the full-length mirror in his comfortable rooms at Pemberley while James, his valet, brushed down his topcoat as he adjusted his sleeves. Satisfied with his appearance, he caught James' eye in the mirror.

"Please have my trunk packed and ready to depart at a moment's notice. I would also appreciate you notifying my driver to prepare the carriage and my horse." James nodded, his expression unaffected by his master's request for an abrupt departure from his ancestral estate.

"Of course, sir. Since, you mentioned that it was unlikely we would remain long, I took the liberty of leaving the bulk of your trunk as it was, only removing what was necessary. I could have you ready to leave in half an hour, at most." His valet's knowing expression made him relax somewhat. "I hope I am not being too forward when I say that regardless of the decision you make, I will wish to remain in *your* employ, sir."

James had been his valet since he was young and was still employed by Darcy's father. The servant's request and loyalty was an honour to him. "I appreciate that, James, but let me ascertain for certain why my father has summoned me."

His valet softly cleared his throat, an indication James was aware of information he had yet to share.

"There is talk below stairs then?" The staff knew more than he did, as usual.

"Yes, sir. The talk, which is very credible—both your father's valet and steward were present—was of his intent to force you into a marriage to a woman of his choice."

Darcy shifted his weight, his shoulders tensing. "My cousin?"

The valet nodded. "Yes, sir."

"I had suspected, but was not sure. Thank you for keeping your ears open on my behalf."

"Of course, sir," responded James, obviously pleased with his master's praise.

He exhaled heavily, blowing his breath in front of him as he pulled at the base of his coat to straighten it. "Into the lion's den it is," he muttered under his breath as he headed for the corridor.

James opened the door. "Good luck, sir."

Darcy took note of every detail he could as he passed through the hallways in the direction of the study, and committed them to memory. When he had received his father's letter demanding he present himself at Pemberley, he had suspected why but had hoped he was incorrect.

Pemberley had been the seat of the Darcy family for several hundred years, and Fitzwilliam was the last and only Darcy heir—however, how long would he remain the heir?

Before he was prepared, he stood before the door to his father's study. His hand lifted, almost of its own accord, and rapped on the sturdy oak, only turning the knob when his father's voice called for him to enter. As he stepped into the room, his father, George Darcy was seated behind his desk, and his childhood playmate, George Wickham, was settled in a chair before it.

"Ah, Fitzwilliam, I am glad that you responded to me so promptly. Would you please excuse us, George? I have some business to conduct with my son."

The sly smirk plastered onto Wickham's face was familiar, but Darcy did his best to ignore it. Wickham had been a favourite of his father's for years, and while Darcy did not like it one bit, he had learned to accept it. His father glanced up from his paper and quill as Wickham closed the door behind him.

"Please, take a seat. We have much to discuss."

Darcy sat opposite to where Wickham had been seated and waited for his father to place his quill on its customary resting spot. "I hope you had a pleasant journey?" His father's tone was congenial so far, but he could not let down his guard.

"The roads were dry and the weather was pleasant. I enjoyed the ride."

The elder Darcy nodded and leaned back in his seat. "How are things at Sagemore?"

"Very well," he responded.

"Did you have any problems with the spring planting?"

"No, everything was completed as planned."

His father always expected updates on Sagemore, as though that estate were a part of Pemberley. The prying for information had never bothered him in the past, yet today, the tension in the room implied he desired more information for some purpose of his own.

When it was clear nothing further would be offered, Mr. Darcy sat forward and leaned his forearms upon his desk. "I asked you here because we need to make arrangements for your upcoming wedding."

Darcy behaved as though he were ignorant of his father's wishes. "I have asked no lady for her hand, and I am unaware of any contracts. I am at a loss as to why you believe I am to be married."

"Do not be daft, Fitzwilliam." His father's tone was testy and his expression echoed the annoyance in his voice. "You are well aware that I expect you to marry your cousin, Anne."

He straightened himself taller in his seat, determined not to back down. "I am well aware of *your* wish, sir. The last I was aware, the choice of whom I wed was mine."

"I do not know where you came by that nonsense, but I have always had a say in who you take as your wife since it affects the Darcy name *and* the future of Pemberley. The shades of Pemberley cannot be polluted by some social upstart like the sister of that tradesman you befriended." The elder Darcy rolled his eyes. "If nothing else, think of your sister's prospects when she comes of age."

"And what of Anne's health? "

"What of it?" His father's response should not have surprised him, but it did.

"Do you honestly think she would be of the constitution to run Pemberley and Sagemore? What of an heir? She has always been so delicate and sickly. I am sure one confinement would kill her."

With a casual shrug of one shoulder, his father leaned back in his chair. "Then you would be master of Rosings as well, and we would find you a bride more suitable for providing an heir after your mourning period is complete. The addition of Rosings to your holdings should allow you to choose a wife with even better connections than Anne."

Darcy continued to breathe evenly to help disguise his irritation. "Anne and I have discussed this dream you and Lady Catherine perpetuate regarding our future marriage. She has no wish to marry me, much as I have no wish to marry her."

His father inhaled audibly, indicative of his anger at that moment. "Anne will do as she is told."

"Because Lady Catherine will browbeat her into submission."

"She will do her duty, as you *will* do yours!" exclaimed Mr. Darcy, his face reddening with ire. He often attempted to intimidate with his incessant stare, so Darcy returned the gaze as steadily as it was given, refusing to submit.

"Even if I were inclined to marry Anne, I would not go against *her* wishes. I will not bring about her demise any sooner than God has intended."

"You would deny the greatest wish of your mother!" The elder Darcy slammed his fist upon his desk with obvious fury.

Darcy stood abruptly and towered over his still-seated father. "My mother told me of her wishes concerning my future marriage, and indicated it was *my* choice. Do not attempt to manipulate me." His voice had dropped to a steely tone. How dare his father attempt to sway him with the memory of his mother!

"She told me of how insistent Lady Catherine was, speaking of the alliance. How it would unite the great estates of Pemberley and Rosings. Mother would smile and say that it was an agreeable thought." He brought his hand up and pointed at his father. "She would never attempt to force my hand in this manner, and she would be horrified by your argument."

"This is your grandmother's influence!" George Darcy bellowed, as he rose. He leaned forward on his knuckles and glared at his son.

"My grandmother simply continued what my mother taught me as a boy." He defended his position with conviction but never yelled as his father had.

"I knew I should have cut you off from her influence."

He laughed. "Cut me off? From the Dowager Countess of Matlock? You know whilst my grandfather was alive, he would have never allowed it, and you can be certain my uncle would interfere now that he is the earl."

"Are you insinuating that they hold power over me?"

"They are exceedingly well-connected, and you know it, father. You would have found London a very unfriendly place had you defied them. Am I right to say it is the reason you never tried?" The expression that suddenly crossed his father's face indicated he had indeed hit his mark.

His father then levelled his son with an unrelenting gaze. "Nevertheless, you will present yourself at Rosings within a fortnight and propose marriage to Anne." He opened his mouth to speak, but his father anticipated him. "If you defy my orders, I will travel to London myself to announce your betrothal in the society pages. You would never allow Anne to be shamed."

He had not anticipated his father's move. The man had always been a formidable opponent at chess, and this manoeuvre revealed why. George Darcy straightened and smiled, confident in his victory. The younger Darcy bristled.

"I will take what you have to say under advisement."

"You have no choice, Fitzwilliam. You will do as I say, or I *will* take action. Keep in mind that there is also Pemberley and Georgiana to consider."

"Pardon me?" he responded incredulously. Would his father forbid a relationship between him and Georgiana if he defied his orders?

"Your ability to reside at Pemberley as well as to see your sister is contingent upon your marriage. You will not return until you are wed to your cousin."

He clenched his hands and jaw before turning to swiftly exit the room. A happy tune was coming from the pianoforte in the music room and the sound coaxed a reluctant smile. James stood in the door to the servant's hallway, so he strode over to stand before him.

"We will be leaving within the hour." James nodded and disappeared down the stairs.

Darcy took a deep breath and exhaled, attempting to calm himself before he spoke with his sister. She tended to know enough of what was going on within Pemberley, and he did not wish to upset her with anything of which she was unaware.

Once he had tempered his anger, he made his way to her favourite room and opened the door with care. He could not help but grin as he watched her brow crinkle at a more difficult passage while he silently closed the door behind him.

His thirteen-year-old little sister, Georgiana, had grown several inches since the last time he had laid eyes on her. She was tall for her age; her blue eyes and dark chestnut hair made her a striking young lady.

As he listened to her with pleasure, he realised how much she had improved. He waited until she released the last chord of the piece and clapped. She startled as she jumped up from the seat.

"Fitzwilliam! I had no idea you had come in! You nearly frightened me out of my wits!" He chuckled as she came around to embrace him. "You arrived too late for me to greet you last night, and I know you are already planning on leaving us again." She gave a small pout, prompting a bit of guilt for how little time he had spent with her, as they both took a seat upon a settee to one side of the room.

"I am sorry, Georgie. Sagemore is my estate—my responsibility— and it was necessary that I be there for the spring planting."

She studied her fingers in her lap while he struggled to think of something to say that would help. The last thing he wanted to do was to tell her he might not be allowed to see her again. His thoughts were interrupted by the sound of her voice.

"I know, but I miss you when you are away." Her gaze returned to his face, and she placed a hand over his. "Please tell me you are not going to capitulate to father's commands."

He sighed. "I do not see how I have any choice. He has threatened to post an engagement announcement in the paper. People already question why Anne is not a part of London society. Could you imagine if I publicly jilted her?"

"Poor Anne," commiserated Georgiana. "She is really a sweet person once you get to know her."

"I know she is, sweetling, but neither of us wishes to be married to the other. If I were to defy father, you know I would not be welcomed back at Pemberley?"

Her eyes widened. "Did he say that?"

"Yes," he affirmed, nodding. "Which means that I would see you less than I do now."

Rising from her seat, she paced back and forth for a minute before she abruptly turned to face him. "I would not have you sacrifice your happiness for me. One day you may resent me for it."

He leapt to his feet. "I could never resent you!"

She shook her head and tears welled in her eyes. "You must do what makes *you* happy, Fitzwilliam. Neither you nor Anne would be happy in that marriage. You should find someone and marry her before father can announce the betrothal."

With a small choke, he dropped back into his seat. "You want me to find someone and wed within a fortnight?"

"Why not?" she exclaimed. "Would it not solve the problem for both you and Anne? A betrothal announcement for someone who is already married would not be taken seriously by anyone."

"Father would never allow me to return to Pemberley, and we would likely not be in company again until you come out or are wed yourself."

"But we can write letters," she said in a hopeful tone.

"You do not think he would prevent that?"

She waved her hand dismissively. "Mrs. Reynolds and Taylor sort the post before he sees it. I doubt he would ever know." She wore a wide grin, and he worried what thought had come to her mind. "Even if he did, you could have Grandmamma send them inside hers."

"He blames Grandmamma for my refusing to go along with his wishes. He could attempt to sever your relationship with her as well if I openly defy him."

She snorted. "As if she would ever allow that!"

Chuckling at something so similar to his own opinion coming from her mouth, he grinned while she took her seat once more. "So I am to find a bride in a fortnight? That does not sound like it would bode well for my felicity."

"When you put it like that, Fitzwilliam, no... it does not. But what if happiness in marriage is entirely a matter of chance? If the dispositions of the parties are ever so well known to each other, or ever so similar beforehand, it might not advance their felicity in the least. Perhaps it is better to know as little as possible of the defects of the person with whom you are to pass your life."

He regarded her sceptically and she shrugged with a smile. "Or perhaps Grandmamma will have an idea. You will just have to think hard during your return to London." She reached forward and grasped his hands. "You secure your happiness, and Anne's, and one day, perhaps Father will come around."

"I will consider what you have said, but I think you are mistaken when it comes to our father."

"You shall not take my hope away." Tears welled in her eyes again, one dropping on to her rosy cheek.

"I would never wish to, Georgie." He reached over and pulled her into an embrace. "I have no idea what the next fortnight will bring, but no matter what father says, please remember that I love you, little sister." Her shoulders shook and she released a small sob.

"I love you, too." She pulled back, her tear-covered cheeks breaking his heart. "I understand what will happen, but please do not marry Anne merely because you feel you have no other choice."

"Do you really think she would enjoy being jilted?"

Georgiana shrugged. "She has no wish to ever marry, so she might appreciate the scandal. You know that Grandmamma, Uncle Henry, and Aunt Elinor would ensure society knew the two of you were never truly betrothed. I doubt she would suffer any more than she does living with Lady Catherine."

"Behave, Georgiana," he scolded.

"You act as though you do not agree." Her tears had stopped, and she had perched her hands on her hips.

"I may agree, but I do try not to say it."

She giggled and reached over to hug him once more. "You should go before father finds you are still here." He drew back and placed a kiss on her forehead.

"I will expect a letter from you at Grandmamma's soon after my arrival."

He pulled away and left before he lost control of his emotions, hearing Georgiana's faint "Goodbye, Fitzwilliam" before the door closed behind him.

James had anticipated him, as always, ensuring the carriage and his horse waited just outside of the front door. Darcy quickly mounted and began riding while his valet and trunk followed behind.

Riding had always helped to soothe his mind when he was upset, and this instance was no different. He rode ahead allowing Homer to have his head at times, enjoying the feel of the wind on his face; however, the idea of tiring his mount so early in the trip was not a sound one, so he eventually pulled up and set a slower pace.

He had no wish to be estranged from his sister, but his father was not giving him an easy choice. He was fortunate to have been left an estate by his uncle, Nathaniel Darcy, right around the time he came of age. Nathaniel's only son and heir had some dissolute habits, primarily drinking to excess and gambling, which led to his death a few years before the father's. His uncle had felt his son's lack of occupation had led to his downfall, so left his estate to Darcy, giving him an occupation while he waited for Pemberley.

Sagemore was not as grand as Pemberley, but it still brought in six thousand pounds per annum, and besides, Darcy's father had continued to provide an allowance, so he had not needed to delve into those funds. Instead, he had been saving and investing for the future. If that future was imminent, he had no idea, but he was thankful to have the resources if it was.

That evening, he had dinner in his rooms while he continued to ruminate over his situation. He may have only been sixteen when his mother passed, but Darcy remembered his last conversation with her clearly.

"Fitzwilliam, come sit here by me," Anne Darcy said softly, gesturing to the edge of her bed.

She was paler than he had ever seen her, but he still thought she was lovely. He took a seat where she indicated, and she grasped his hand, giving it a small squeeze as she often did. He returned the gesture carefully so as not to cause her pain while he brought his other hand to cover it. Her fingers were so chilled, and he wished to convey some of his warmth to her.

"Your father has spoken with you?"

He made a valiant effort to control his emotions, but it was for naught as he broke down before her.

"Oh, my sweet boy," she crooned, gathering him into her arms. "I do not want to go, but it seems God has other ideas."

Darcy pulled himself away, took out his handkerchief, and dried his eyes. "I apologise. I should not have wept as I did."

She smiled gently as she tucked an errant curl away from his face. "You sound like your father. He has the ability to love deeply, but do not closet away your emotions as he does. There is nothing weak about expressing your feelings."

15

Nodding, he enclosed her hand between both of his. "I promise to take care of Georgie," he blurted. He did not want to speak of her condition, but he simply could not think of anything else to say. Her smile widened further, and she gripped his hand.

"I know you will, and I am so proud of you. You are a wonderful brother, and have become such an honourable young man." She tilted her head down and studied him. "You must not forget that your father will also be here for her. What I wish is for you to promise me that you will take care of yourself."

"I do not understand," he said with a furrowed brow.

*"I love your father, but he is far from perfect.
I believe he has grand ambitions when it comes
to your future marriage."*

His eyebrows lifted. "Mother, I have no expectations of marrying anytime soon."

She chuckled and traced her fingers down his cheek. "I understand... but I want so much more for you than an arranged marriage. Your father forgets that he married me for love, and that my connections and dowry were not his main inducement to propose."

With a heavy sigh, she glanced towards the windows and the blue sky outside. "Then there is Catherine." Her gaze returned to her son, steady and sure. "I do not want you to propose to Anne unless it is the deepest wish of your heart. Catherine has often indicated that she is desirous of a marriage between the two of you. 'Uniting the great estates of Pemberley and Rosings' was how she put it." Anne Darcy shook her head. "I have never agreed or stated that was my wish, Fitzwilliam. I have only said that it would be lovely were you and Anne so inclined."

Her voice faltered, and he leaned forward. "If you are too fatigued, I can return another time."

"No... I am as well as I can be." She squeezed his hand a bit, and he noticed that her expression had changed. "Please promise me. Your grandmother and your uncle will come to your aid should you have need of them."

Her eyes were imploring him, and he could not refuse her, not now. "I promise, Mother... I promise."

He remained that day until his mother fell back to sleep. She died that very night. His father had never been a very affectionate man, but what little tenderness George Darcy possessed died along with his beloved wife.

Darcy retired to his room that evening, struggling to devise a reasonable solution in which he could honour his promise to his mother and not lose his sister. He tossed and turned the entirety of the night. When he rose the next morning, he was no closer to an answer than he was when he left Pemberley.

As he resumed his journey towards London, he prayed for an epiphany before he was forced to break the vow he had made all those years ago.

Chapter 2

Darcy pulled back on his reins at the local inn. This particular establishment had never been one of his stops in the past, but Homer was tired and required rest. He handed his horse over to one of the stable hands along with a coin, and glanced around the small town as he made his way to the door.

The solitude of a private dining room appealed to him but the public rooms were not crowded so he decided to dine there. He took a seat and was looked after by the innkeeper and his wife; however, just as he was finishing his meal, two men took seats at the table behind him.

He was situated back to back with the strangers, but the dining room was packed so tight with tables that he was able to hear every word they said, despite their lowered voices.

"Do you have the money?" asked one voice, desperately.

The second voice did not take long to respond. "Did you not listen the last time? I have given you everything I have."

"I must pay back more of the debt, or Grayson will have me hanged, drawn, and quartered."

"Then you should not have been in business with the man," hissed the tablemate.

"I had an excellent return off of the last ship that made it to port; Grayson was thrilled with his return. We had no way of anticipating that the navy would seize the next one."

Darcy rolled his eyes at the man's stupidity. The capture of a ship smuggling goods from France was big news before he had left London. Could this be the ship they were speaking of?

"Smuggling is illegal; you knew it when you began the operation. Moreover, you should never have involved someone as cutthroat as Grayson. I cannot afford to continue covering your loss. Edith knows none of this, but she will if there is no money to purchase necessities."

"Then you will sign over Lizzy's money."

"We go through this every time. *I will not do that.* We support her now, but you would deprive her of her dowry and any chance at a good match."

"You do realise I was serious when I said I would trade her to Grayson to cover my debt. He blames me for his loss and will not stop until he recoups his money." The voice had once again taken on a desperate note. "I require her inheritance."

"You are despicable, Gardiner, trading your niece to pay off your debt."

Darcy was astounded. This poor girl's situation was unthinkable.

"I will never sign the paperwork required to release her inheritance to you, regardless of what you do."

"Philips! I swear by all..." the man whispered furiously.

"You will not take her. I will see to that."

"How would you prevent it? We were both named guardians in Bennet's will."

Someone released a heavy exhale. "That is because he had no idea what you have become. If he did, I can guarantee he would never have entrusted his favourite daughter to you."

"You act as though she will one day marry. No man around Meryton will want her, despite Sir William Lucas pronouncing her one of the 'jewels of the county.' Bennet ensured her spinsterhood when he educated her."

"There may be men who would appreciate her intelligence. I hoped she could join Sir William Lucas and his daughter Charlotte when they travel to London for the next Season. Perhaps, she might have some luck there."

Gardiner snickered. "Well, standing her by Charlotte Lucas could only help her. Lizzy would appear a stunning beauty beside that plain little thing. There is *another* spinster in the making."

Phillips was resolute. "You will not trade Lizzy for your debts. God only knows what that man would do to her." There was quiet for a moment before Philips whispered in a resigned voice. "Do what you will with me, but I will do everything I can to protect Lizzy. She does not deserve to pay for your mistakes."

"I shall return tonight during the assembly. Lizzy is still in mourning; she will remain behind whilst you and my sister attend. You *shall* ensure your wife is not in the house when I arrive. I will not hesitate harming her or you, should either of you attempt to interfere."

"You are insane!" gasped Philips. "Lizzy will never cooperate."

"Then I will just have to make her cooperate."

A chair scraped across the floor, and Darcy assumed Gardiner was rising to leave. "I am warning you, dear brother. Do not stand in my way."

Footsteps receded towards the door and Philips groaned. "Good God!"

The conversation he had just overheard left him stunned. The poor girl! Whatever situation he found himself in by his father's hand, it could be nothing to hers. Philips had said she would not cooperate, which he could understand.

A part of him wished to walk away and pretend he had never heard the whisperings at the next table, but he would never be able to live with himself. Perhaps she had other family, and he could help her find sanctuary there? In the meantime, how would he approach this man Philips? He was her uncle, was he not?

Throwing some coins on the table, he rose. The chairs behind him were empty; Mr. Philips must have gone while he was contemplating a way to help. There was still time before his horse would be rested enough to continue, so he exited the front of the building.

Several men loitered on the street, but only one stood out. He was walking with his head down, rubbing his forehead, and appeared as if he bore the weight of the world upon his shoulders. Following behind, he caught up with him as he neared the front of the local solicitor's offices. Offices that, according to a placard on the door, belonged to Mr. Philips.

"Pardon me," he called as Mr. Philips reached out to open the door.

The man turned and regarded him warily. They had never met before, so Darcy assumed that was the reason for his expression. He approached, and removed his hat.

"Good day, Mr. Philips," he began with a quick bow. The man made no effort to correct him; his supposition had been accurate. "I hope you will forgive me for approaching you in this manner, but my name is Fitzwilliam Darcy. There are some matters I would care to discuss with you… if you have the time. I do understand this is very sudden, but the nature of the business is rather urgent."

Mr. Philips nodded. "Of course, sir. I would be happy to help in any way I can." He opened the door, and gestured into the building. "Why do we not step inside?"

"Thank you," he said. Was he really going to such extremes for a stranger?

He followed Mr. Phillips to his study, which was located to the back of the small building. The solicitor offered him a seat before walking around to take his own.

"I apologise if I have forgotten, but have I made your acquaintance prior to today, Mr. Darcy?"

"No," he answered. "To tell the truth, I took a chance."

With a puzzled look upon his face, Philips leaned forward in his seat. "Then do you require my services?"

He shook his head, stood, and paced a few laps before he returned to face Mr. Philips. "I am unsure of how to approach this, so perhaps I should just be out with it." Philips nodded, his eyebrows still furrowed. "I was seated behind you and a man you called Gardiner in the Bird in Hand."

Mr. Phillips face blanched as he began to splutter. "Y… y… you were listening?"

"The infraction was not intentional; the sound carried between the tables quite easily. I had even contemplated rising and leaving, but then Gardiner mentioned his plan for your niece."

"Now, look here," Mr. Philips interrupted, his voiced raised to almost a shout. "I want nothing to do with that plan!"

"Please do not make yourself uneasy, sir. I know you do not approve and wish to prevent him from his scheme." Philips was angry and would be defensive, yet he still had to try. "I would like to help you, if you will allow it," he blurted when Philips opened his mouth to speak.

The man stood and leaned against his desk. "For what reason? Why would you want to help someone so wholly unconnected to you?"

He was startled when Philips raised an arm and pointed forcefully at his chest.

"What could you possibly hope to gain?"

He had to remain calm, but it had become difficult to remain unaffected in the face of Mr. Philips' suspicion and anger. "I would gain nothing." He made his way to his chair and dropped into it. "I can sympathise with her being in a position where there seems to be no other choice."

Philips appraised him carefully. "How could you help?"
Straightening, he crossed his arms over his chest. The position was a
conditional reprieve—he would be fine as long as he was honestly
attempting to help.

"I am passing through town today, headed to London, and thought I
could transport your niece to family this Gardiner is perhaps
unaware of. You could send a maid or a friend with her to ensure her
safety," he added quickly, before Philips could protest.

"If only it were that simple," Philips replied with a defeated air.
"Elizabeth is the last surviving member of her immediate family.

"Seven months ago, an axle broke on their carriage as they were
returning to Longbourn from church. The horses spooked and
bolted, taking the fork in the road much too quickly. You see, it
curves rather steeply on the other side. We think when the horses
took that bend too fast, the carriage fell on its side and slid over the
edge of the road where there is a very sharp drop to the river below."
He took a deep breath and exhaled long and slow.

"When we found her, she was between the bodies of her family, and
gravely injured. To be honest, those of us who discovered the
wreckage were amazed she was alive. I believe the protection her
family afforded was the only way she survived."

Mr. Philips shook his head as if he was trying to rid himself of the
image of the accident, and Darcy could not help but wince at the
terror the young woman must have faced. "Her sister, Lydia, was
thrown free of the equipage but succumbed to fever and infection
within a fortnight. Another sister, Mary, did not even make it that
long.

"So you see, her immediate family is gone. She has an aunt, my wife,
and an uncle, who is the Gardiner you heard in the inn."

"Perhaps your family, then," suggested Darcy. "Certainly they would
not wish to see her harmed?"

"I am a younger son, Mr. Darcy. My elder brother and I were never
close. As children, we were always in some fight or another. When
we both went to school, he never cared to be in my company, and
even ensured he and I had no friends in common. I am fortunate my
father lived long enough to see me finish my education." Philips
returned wearily to his seat and ran a hand along the back of his
neck. "My brother ensured I was never hired in a London firm, so I
found a place here with Horace Gardiner. I fell in love with his

daughter and, from there, my life seemed to fall into place. But, as you now see, that is the extent of our family."

"So, there is no one." It weighed upon him just to say it.

Mr. Philips shook his head. "You see my quandary then? There is also the possibility of him discovering her location. By law, Gardiner and I are both her guardians, and he has every right to remove her from her situation. The only solution I have been able to divine is for her to marry." He chuckled ruefully. "But to accomplish it before my brother returns this evening is impossible."

An unexpected idea shot through his brain: she was the answer to his dilemma! But it was preposterous—he had not even been introduced. The motivation for his next idea escaped him: meeting her might provide some insight into a possible solution.

"I regret to say I am unsure of what else we could do. I do think it is necessary to alert Miss…"

"Bennet."

"Miss Bennet of the situation. You cannot allow her to be taken unawares this evening." He was surprised to find her uncle nodding in agreement. "I believe I heard Gardiner say she has some intelligence. She may have some notion of what to do."

Mr. Philips stood and came around to the side of his desk. "I suppose it should be done sooner rather than later. If we were to require your assistance, you might be on your way to London by then."

"I am certain you wish to have a private conversation with your niece, so I will return…"

He was standing to leave when Philips interrupted. "Under more normal circumstances, I would agree with you, but I would appreciate your presence as a witness. I do not see why she should doubt me, but the entire situation seems so unreal to me that I cannot fathom her accepting it from one source.

"Of course," responded Darcy.

The proposal had merit, but to witness this young lady having her world unsettled disturbed him. He prayed there was some way to save her from what appeared to be a distressing fate.

He followed Mr. Philips out of his office and through a small garden to a small, well-kept home to the side of his business. As they entered, a servant bustled up to take their hats.

"Mrs. Philips is off visiting with Lady Lucas, sir. She mentioned calling on Mrs. Goulding and Mrs. Long as well. Miss Bennet decided to remain behind. She sits in the parlour."

"Thank you, Lucy."

Philips was attempting to smile but the gesture was just not right. The weary looking uncle stopped for a moment and wrung his hands together as if he were being forced to do something distasteful. How uncomfortable this conversation will be! What a thing to have to impart to your niece! It was no wonder he was at sixes and sevens.

He placed a hand on the man's shoulder to impart some kind of consolation, and Philips' expression offered his apology. "Shall we go in?" he appeared to ask. Darcy could never remember feeling as much pity for a man as he did at that moment.

Mr. Philips reached forth a shaky hand and turned the knob, opening it to reveal a comfortable room. A young woman was perched in the window seat, her head cocked slightly to the side as she read from a book that rested in her hand. Darcy paused and stared, speechless. In profile, her figure was light and pleasing. Her hair was the darkest of dark browns, piled in an arrangement of curls upon her head, and she had a slight crease between her eyebrows as she concentrated. She was the lady Gardiner wished to trade for his debts?

Fury welled up within him at the idea of her being handed over to some reprobate. God only knew what would happen to her! She would most certainly disappear from all good society.

She startled and placed a hand to her chest. "Uncle, I did not hear you come in."

"It is no bother, Lizzy. I apologise if we have interrupted you at an inopportune moment."

She laughed and raised an eyebrow, giving her a mischievous air. "No, I was not reading anything that will not wait."

Her face now in full view; he was able to study her in more detail. She had a creamy complexion with a slight tint of pink on her cheeks. Brown doe eyes sparkled with amusement, although they seemed a bit peaked. She must have been having problems sleeping since the accident.

"Lizzy, allow me to introduce Mr. Fitzwilliam Darcy to you," said Mr. Philips, shifting to the side. "Mr. Darcy, this is my niece, Miss Elizabeth Bennet."

Miss Bennet stood and gave a curtsy as he bowed. "I am pleased to meet you," they both said, almost in tandem.

Mr. Philips gestured to a chair, which Darcy took as the young lady seated herself on a small sofa across from him, smoothing the lap of her grey muslin gown. Mr. Philips was the last to sit, taking the seat to Darcy's left.

"You seem so grave, Uncle. Is there something amiss?"

Mr. Philips sneaked a glance at him before taking a deep breath and exhaling. "I am not sure how to explain this to you. I…"

Darcy's attention moved to Miss Bennet as her expression fell.

"Please just tell me," she said, her voice shaky. "I can see by your demeanour that what you have to say is not good."

"I am sorry, Lizzy. I have tried, but I do not know how to hold him off anymore."

Miss Bennet was becoming more alarmed, so Darcy leaned forward to catch Mr. Philips eye. "Perhaps you should start from the beginning. The business endeavour?"

Mr. Philips bobbed his head in agreement. "Your Uncle Gardiner, against my advice, began a smuggling operation last year." Miss Bennet's eyes widened, but she remained silent, allowing her uncle to continue his recitation. "Besides it being illegal, the money he invested in the ship and crew was excessive. The ship was old and not very fast, and I felt he was overpaying the men. He brought in a partner hoping to ease the burden on himself financially, but he did not research the investor before taking his money. Now, as a result, he has found himself in quite the predicament."

"I do not understand. What has happened that has him at odds with this man?"

She was regarding Darcy with wary eyes, as if she thought he was a representative of Grayson.

"The ship they were using was captured by the navy as it brought its load back from France. They lost all of their cargo and even the ship itself was confiscated. The business has not been traced back to your uncle, but his partner has demanded Gardiner compensate him for his loss.

"Your uncle had already taken his profits from his one successful run to put a down payment on another ship, so he had very little funds to give the man."

Miss Bennet's brow furrowed. "This man did not understand there were risks in such a venture?"

"I am certain he did, but he claims your uncle should have purchased a better ship. Grayson places your uncle at fault and has threatened him with bodily injury should he not reimburse his investment.

"Surely Uncle Gardiner does not expect you to pay for his mistake?" she questioned incredulously.

"I have aided him as much as I am able," her uncle answered, "but I do not have the funds to help him pay back the entirety. Gardiner has come up with a plan to rid himself of the debt to Grayson, but I have refused to help him with it."

Miss Bennet appeared worried as she shifted in her seat. "Is it really so bad, uncle?"

Mr. Philips rubbed his hands up and down his thighs, as if he were attempting to ease his nerves. "He intends to hand you over to Grayson in exchange for the alleviation of part of his debt. Then he wishes to withdraw the five thousand pounds of your mother's settlement, left to you, to pay the remainder."

She gasped. "But that is impossible. Uncle Gardiner would never…"

As it seemed the time to attest to the veracity of Mr. Philips statements, Darcy sat forward in his seat. "I am afraid Mr. Philips is telling the absolute truth, Miss Bennet." Her attention snapped to his face. Could she see he was in earnest? "I happened to be in the Bird in Hand a short time ago and quite unintentionally overheard all of Mr. Gardiner's plans."

Her hands reached up to cradle her face as she let out a sob. He was intruding now, and made to rise and remove himself from the room. But a hand on his arm stayed him.

"Please do not leave, Mr. Darcy. We may still require your aid yet today." Philips' eyes pleaded with him to remain.

"I had not planned to leave, only to give Miss Bennet time to collect herself." Something garbled came from across the room, where the lady was drying her face with her handkerchief.

"Please, Mr. Darcy," she said, as she attempted to control her emotions. "If there is some manner in which you can render us aid, then please stay. I apologise…"

26

He shook his head. "Your response is perfectly natural—and warranted. I see no reason for you to apologise."

"Thank you." She faced her uncle with a heartrending expression of fear. "Do you have a plan for me to avoid this?"

"I am afraid I do not. Mr. Darcy and I have both considered various solutions, yet there are problems with every idea thus far. We decided to include you, in the hopes you might have some thought as to what we could do."

"There is no possible way for me to remain with you and Aunt Philips?" she asked with a tremor in her voice.

"Miss Bennet, Mr. Gardiner has threatened your aunt and uncle with physical harm should they attempt to prevent him removing you from this house." Her eyes bulged, almost making him regret mentioning it.

She rose and walked to the window, staring out for a few minutes before turning back to them. "Would it be possible for me to access my mother's settlement without marrying?"

Mr. Philips gave her a puzzled look. "Not really. The legal requirements are either proof of marriage and one signature, or both my and your Uncle Gardiner's signatures."

"Could we not forge his signature?" A desperate gleam appeared in her eye.

"Lizzy, what are you thinking, child?" her uncle implored.

She crossed her arms over her chest in a manner that resembled insecurity, as though she was not comfortable with what she was preparing to say. "With the money, I could travel to London and arrange passage to one of the Canadas."

Philips shot out of his chair and stepped towards her. "Alone! That is madness!"

"Not necessarily alone," she countered. "Hattie Smith has no means of support since Mr. Collins did not require her services at Longbourn. She could accompany me as my maid."

"I do not think this is the wisest choice," Darcy interceded. "I admit you would be outside of your uncle's reach, but even traveling with a maid, it would be a dangerous journey. If you were robbed, you would be at the mercy of anyone for a bed or food. You and this Hattie both would."

"I do not see any other alternative." Tears were once again streaming down her face, while she gazed at her uncle and pleaded, "You must let me go."

Mr. Philips appeared weary and ready to agree, but Darcy was roiling. This was not a journey that should be undertaken by a young gentlewoman—not at all. There had to be another solution. He just had to think! What could he do to prevent her ruination?

"I could marry you," Darcy said out loud to himself before he really thought about it. Miss Bennet was so visibly shocked her tears abated. Mr. Philips turned to him as wide-eyed as his niece.

"I beg your pardon."

Somewhere beyond where he stared unfocused, Miss Bennet walked forward and dropped back in to her seat. "Mr. Darcy, I am flattered, but…"

"No!" He snapped back from his thoughts. The proposal had been said for all to hear, whether it was unintentional or not, so he was obligated to continue. "It would solve a dilemma for both of us. You would not have to risk your life sailing for Canada, and I would not be forced to marry my cousin."

Mr. Philips cleared his throat and stood in a position where he could view Darcy. "Perhaps you should explain your predicament before we consider this as a possible avenue to explore." He stepped over to his niece and took the seat beside her, taking her hand in a comforting manner.

"I…" he stuttered, trying to decide where to begin. "My aunt decided when I was very young that she wished to have me wed her daughter, Anne. She often mentioned it to my mother, who always thought it was a lovely idea, if we were both so inclined. Anne was never a healthy child, frequently suffering from fevers and influenzas. A few years ago, I was visiting my aunt, Lady Catherine de Bourgh at her estate when I had the opportunity to speak to my cousin without my aunt's interference. Anne has no desire to marry, let alone marry me. I think of her as a sister, and her sentiments towards me are likewise."

"Then why are you speaking of having to wed her regardless?" asked Mr. Philips. "Was there a contract signed?"

"No, there was never a contract. In fact, my mother told me on her deathbed that she did not wish me to marry Anne unless it was my choice. She wanted me to find someone who would make me happy." Darcy stood and walked around the chair, propping his forearms on the back.

"My father has his own reasons to wish for our alliance, not that he has shared those with me. I believe that Anne would likely die in childbirth, and he has, apparently, already factored in that eventuality."

Miss Bennet gasped and placed her free hand over her mouth.

"I cannot knowingly bring about my cousin's demise. My sister has begged me not to give in to my father's demands, insisting I find someone to marry within the fortnight—the time my father gave me to travel to Rosings and propose. I realise this may not be a realistic goal with the ladies of London society."

He paused and looked down between his arms at his feet for a moment, taking a deep breath. "I have not the talent, which some people possess, of conversing easily with those I have never seen before. I cannot catch their tone of conversation, or appear interested in their concerns, as I often see done."

"You seem to have had no difficulty today, Mr. Darcy." Miss Bennet arched her eyebrow; the gesture and her challenge made him smile.

"I assure you today has been quite unprecedented."

Her cheeks pinked, and they both gave a chuckle.

"But sir," Mr. Philips interjected, "you do not even know if you are compatible!"

Miss Bennet smiled with mischief in her eyes. "I might actually be a very excitable creature, complaining of my nerves and calling for my salts."

"Really, Lizzy!" Mr. Philips turned and looked at her with admonishment. "You should not tease Mr. Darcy in such a way. You also should not make sport of your mother."

Her grin fell, and he was sad to see its departure.

"I believe a bit of levity would be beneficial with the stress of the situation."

A glimpse of a grateful expression was his reward as one corner of her lips quirked upward. "Thank you, Mr. Darcy." She tilted her head. "You mentioned a sister?"

"Yes," he answered. "Georgiana turns fourteen in June. There are no other siblings, so we are very close."

"Do you not worry that an alliance with someone who is not your father's choice would cause a separation between the two of you?"

Her face reflected true concern, and he appreciated her all the more for it. "It most certainly would, but she has still encouraged me to seek a wife elsewhere. One day we shall see one another again. I am certain of it."

"So, you marry your cousin, or you lose your sister and father. You sound like Odysseus attempting to steer between Scylla and Charybdis.¹"

He could not prevent the hint of a grin upon his lips. "Eventually, I will have to face one monster or the other? Of course, I am referring to the circumstances, and not you, Miss Bennet.

She let out a bit of a giggle before she managed to restrain herself. "I understood, sir. Please do not make yourself uneasy."

"Perhaps not quite so dramatic a choice, though, Lizzy," Mr. Philips interjected. She shrugged with a slight lift to her lips.

"I heard you mention your aunt as Lady Catherine," said her uncle, returning to the topic at hand. "I would have you know that whilst Lizzy is a gentlemen's daughter, Longbourn is a modest estate, and she does not have any grand connections to boast of."

"Sir, I am a gentleman, she is a gentleman's daughter, so far we are equal."

Mr. Philips raised his eyebrows in surprise at Darcy's liberal statement. "I would imagine you are heir to your father's estate? How will you support yourself if you are cut off irrevocably?"

"I became master of my uncle's estate upon his death a few years ago. It is called Sagemore and lies in northern Oxfordshire."

"Is it a prosperous estate?" asked Mr. Philips.

"Uncle!" Miss Bennet was appalled by the question, and he smiled at her.

"The question is reasonable. Should you agree to this scheme, I would be responsible for providing you a settlement as well as supporting you for the remainder of our lives." She relaxed and nodded in acceptance.

30

"To answer your question, the estate profits approximately six thousand pounds per annum. There is also a house in town, but since I frequently stay with my father or grandmother whilst in London, I have it leased. I have never been a spendthrift or a gambler and often have funds left over from the allowance my father has continued to provide, which I invest. Since becoming master of Sagemore, I have saved all of the yearly profits from the estate as well." He motioned as if pointing outside.

"My carriage with my trunk and valet should be here by now. I can furnish my account book if you feel it necessary."

Philips responded with a nod. "Should we reach an agreement, then I would care to see it—simply to verify what you say is true."

"If I were to leave with you today, where would you take me?" asked Miss Bennet.

Her voice was so cautious, and he blinked for a moment. In his haste, he had not considered it. He supposed his grandmother would be willing to have guests.

"I know my grandmother intends to spend the summer in the country, but her last letter indicated she was still in town. We would go to her house in Mayfair. From there, I would apply for a license, and we could marry as soon as possible." She nodded, but there was still some wariness in her eyes. "You would be welcome to have the Hattie Smith you mentioned accompany you."

"Hattie was the maid who attended my sisters and me before the accident. Mr. Collins had no need of her when he took over the estate, and she has had difficulty finding work ever since." She wore a hopeful expression, which made her request even more impossible to refuse.

"You would be welcome to keep her as your ladies maid, if you wish. I am certain my grandmother's abigail would be able to teach her any extra skills should she require it."

With that Miss Bennet grinned, and he allowed himself to hope for the first time since he had left Pemberley.

"Would your grandmother be accepting of a union between us?" asked Miss Bennet.

"My grandmother married my grandfather after the death of his first wife. It was a love match, unlike his first marriage, which was to the daughter of a baronet. Grandmamma has much more liberal views than my father or my aunt, who is the child of my grandfather's first wife. She would not be pleased with my father and aunt forcing this betrothal on myself and Anne."

He paused for a moment before pointing to the book resting on the table beside her. "May I ask what you were reading when we came in?"

"Oh, I was re-reading Shakespeare's *Much Ado About Nothing*. My uncle admits to not having much of a library, but he does have a good selection of Shakespeare."

Mr. Philips chuckled and nodded his head. "She is partially correct. I have a large number of books on the law, but I fear I have failed in collecting much else."

"It is understandable," he said, before returning to Miss Bennet. "You enjoy reading then?"

"Very much. I mostly read poetry, dramas, and histories, but I do enjoy many different subjects." She lifted an eyebrow as she smiled. "What think you of books?"

He was amused by her arch manner. "I take great enjoyment in reading. My uncle kept a small library at Sagemore, and I have added to the titles since taking over as master. I hope to have quite a collection one day."

A chessboard on a table against the wall captured his attention. Standing, he made his way over to view a game that appeared abandoned.

"My niece and I had to pause our game this morning, so I could tend to business. She is quite the formidable opponent."

He raised his eyebrows with a grin. "I shall look forward to challenging you, then."

"What do you say, Lizzy?" asked her uncle. "I will venture that your chances with Mr. Darcy seem more promising than a harrowing trip to Canada." She bit her bottom lip as she held Darcy's gaze.

"We could be the solution to each other's dilemmas."

"That will not necessarily bring about felicity in our relationship, sir. My parents spent much of their time apart, my father in his study, and my mother complaining of her nerves. I have never wished for the same."

"I could never imagine such a marriage," he responded earnestly. "When they were not busy with estate or household matters, my parents spent much of their time together. And I find I am more comfortable with you than with most ladies of my acquaintance. I do not see spending time with you in the future as being a hardship."

She pinked as she muttered a soft "Thank you."

He enjoyed discomposing her, especially when she became flustered. Her soft blushes were very alluring. Perhaps this marriage would not be such a duty after all.

With a sigh, she tilted her head to the side as she appraised him. "I still have issue with the fact that I have only just met you."

"As I have only just met you."

"I wish we had more time, Lizzy, but we do not. Your uncle will return this evening, and you need to be as far from Meryton as possible."

Her gaze returned to her uncle, so Darcy rose and stepped over to where she was seated, dropping down on his knee.

"I promise to do my best to make you happy. I am by no means perfect." He took her small hand and encased it between his own. "I will probably say or do the wrong thing quite often, but I promise to always treat you with respect." Her gaze met his, and the determined look in her eye told him she had decided her fate.

Chapter 3

"I believe marriage to Mr. Darcy may be my best option," Elizabeth said in as strong a voice as she could muster. Becoming betrothed to a complete stranger was in no small way disconcerting, to say the least, but she was determined to choose her destiny rather than have one forced upon her.

Mr. Darcy smiled, yet there was something like regret in his eye. Could he be having second thoughts? "If you should change your mind, sir, I would hope you could tell me."

Her uncle gave a look of surprise as Mr. Darcy's attention snapped back to her. "Elizabeth, do not be rude!"

"I simply do not wish for him to have proposed on a whim, and then upon reflection, finds he does not wish for the connection."

His eyes sought hers, holding her gaze with sincerity. "I assure you. I have no such intentions."

"I apologise if I misread your expression. There seemed to be a sadness…"

"I do not think either of us rejoice in the manner of our betrothal," Mr. Darcy responded honestly, "but I do believe I am more likely to find happiness with you than with many of the women of my acquaintance."

She imagined those women must be rather insipid for Mr. Darcy to find them so unappealing. "What a glowing commendation!" she exclaimed as she chuckled.

"Lizzy! You should learn to have more respect for your betrothed."

"Mr. Philips, I have no issue with Miss Bennet's teasing. As I said earlier, I do believe it helps to relieve the seriousness of the discussion."

Shaking his head, Uncle Philips rose from the sofa, and relocated to the writing table in the corner. "Mr. Darcy, we should discuss the details of the settlement, so I can draw up the document." Her betrothed rose and made his way over to sit alongside her uncle.

"Lizzy, does Hattie read?"

"Yes, Uncle. I taught her years ago."

He set to writing, occasionally asking questions of Mr. Darcy. She could not say it bothered her to be left alone for the moment since she took the occasion to study the stranger, her betrothed.

He was certainly handsome: crystal blue eyes, dark brown curls atop his head, and tall—very tall. He was at least six feet and had the most impressive broad shoulders. He carried himself in a proud manner, and had been very serious in the short time of their acquaintance. In all probability, she might have found him disagreeable at first sight, had she not been introduced as they had. Who knew a gentleman of means and education could be uncomfortable—even shy—with strangers?

She took a deep breath, attempting to settle the fluttering in her stomach. Goodness! She would turn into her mother if she continued with the nerves!

The thoughts of her family caused her eyes to well with tears. For probably the millionth time, she wondered why they had all perished, leaving her so alone. Of course, her Aunt and Uncle Philips were dear to her, and they were welcoming, but it simply was not Longbourn. Perhaps marriage might allow her a place where she belonged. She hoped it to be true. The sensation of being a perpetual visitor was not to her liking at all.

She also had the impression that her Uncle Phillips had been using his savings to prevent the scheme of her Uncle Gardiner's. Shaking her head, she sighed. As it turned out, Uncle Gardiner was not much of an uncle, yet he had always been so amiable when he visited Longbourn! Who knew he could be capable of such treachery?

She could not have even imagined Jane's reaction. Her dear sister had never wished to see fault in people, and this infraction would have been impossible for her to accept.

"Lizzy?" Uncle Philips called, startling her from her thoughts.

She turned to where he was now rising from the escritoire and suppressed a grin. He looked so peculiar seated at his aunt's writing desk.

"I believe your aunt had a long day of calls planned?"

"Yes, uncle. She mentioned several ladies, but she also indicated a stop to see if Mr. Blake had any new fabric in stock." The calls and shopping her aunt had planned would keep her occupied for a few hours, which was why Elizabeth had remained behind—to enjoy some peace and quiet.

Her uncle nodded as he set down his quill. "I require materials that are in my office. I have penned a letter to Hattie, and I will send Lucy to deliver it. When I have finished the documents, I will return." He rose and made his way to the door, turning back as he stepped across the threshold. "I believe it would be a good time for the two of you to become better acquainted. The door will remain open for propriety's sake, so please keep in mind what topics you discuss." He gave them a look she easily understood and strode from the room.

"Is gossip a problem?" Mr. Darcy asked, as he took a seat on the other end of the sofa.

"I have never heard of his servants gossiping, but my aunt quite enjoys tittle-tattle. She will return later with all of the chat from the neighbourhood."

"Ah, I see." He was thoughtful for a moment before shifting in his seat. "Unless it pains you, I would enjoy hearing more about your family," he began carefully. "Perhaps you could tell me with whom you had the closest relationship, and let things grow from there?"

"I appreciate your consideration, Mr. Darcy. I do miss them immensely, but I have found speaking of them is becoming easier with time." She clasped her hands together in her lap in attempt to disguise her nervousness. "I would have to say that I was closest with my sister Jane."

"Were the two of you similar in looks?"

"No." She smiled as she shook her head. "Jane and I were as different as chalk and cheese. We were similar in height, but she was fair-haired and had blue eyes. She was considered the beauty of the county, and was a favourite of my mother's." Her gaze, which had been on her hands in her lap, moved to his face where his look of understanding calmed her anxiety. "She was compassionate and very kind. I do not believe I ever heard a disagreeable word from her lips. There was never an ill thought for anyone. Jane believed everyone to be inherently good."

"She sounds a bit like a friend of mine," he said in a pleased manner. "Bingley and I first met at Eton, but he is four years my junior. We did not become friends until years later when we happened upon one another in London. He always finds everyone and everything pleasing. I have rarely found him to be in any mood other than jovial and smiling."

"He seems a very agreeable friend."

He nodded as he leaned towards her a small fraction. "Your uncle indicated you were very close to your father."

His attempt to help her through the conversation was kind, and she smiled in appreciation of the gesture. "My father enjoyed his library above all other places. He was content to spend the entirety of his days in his beloved chair with no other occupation but reading. I was fortunate enough to be his favourite, and he taught me literature, mathematics, languages, chess…"

"What languages do you speak?"

"I speak French and some Italian. He attempted to teach me German, but I never took to it as I did the others." She picked a piece of non-existent fluff from her dress. "My mother felt it was a fool's errand, especially as I became older. She often interrupted our lessons to insist I occupy myself with needlework or practicing the pianoforte."

"She did not feel books were appropriate?"

"Mama did not mind books," she clarified, "rather, she deemed learning to run a home and lessons to be a good wife more important to our circumstances." He appeared confused, so she continued. "My father's estate was entailed, which is why our cousin, Mr. Collins, inherited. My mother found it vexing that she might one day be cast from her home. With only five thousand pounds, she worried over her ability to sustain five daughters should it be necessary and was adamant that we would wed as soon as a suitor presented himself."

"Your uncle scolded you for making sport of your mother earlier. How did your comments resemble her?"

Her face became warm, and she looked away for a moment, embarrassed he remembered her insensitive remark. "I loved my mother, but I used to mimic her, especially to Jane, when my mother was being particularly trying. Jane would scold me, as well."

She paused as she relived the memory, her attention returning with a start when Mr. Darcy tilted his head to catch her eye. "My mother often complained of her nerves and the 'flutterings all over her and the pains in her head'. Mama would call for our housekeeper, Hill, insisting she required her salts." She expected to see censure, but instead, saw only compassion in his eyes.

"My grandfather was known all over for a 'harrumph' sound that he often made when he was displeased or even trying to get someone's attention. His friends would even make jokes about its volume and gruff tone." The corner of his lips lifted slightly as he told the story; he was once again attempting to put her at ease. "To this day, one often hears a loud 'harrumph' at family gatherings. When I was last at my uncle's for dinner, my uncle made the noise before announcing it was time to remove to the study for brandy and cigars. My grandmother has even been known to attempt the impersonation from time to time. The sound never fails to bring a smile to her face."

"Were they married long?" she asked.

"They wed two years after the death of his first wife and were married for five and thirty years."

"I would imagine she misses him greatly."

"She has confessed that she does, yet she does not dwell on it, insisting that my grandfather never enjoyed her sour moods." They both chuckled, and Mr. Darcy leaned back in the seat. "Where were we before I interrupted you?"

"Your story was no interruption. I enjoyed it very much, thank you."

He nodded, laying his arm across the back of the furniture, his fingers not quite reaching her shoulder. His strong hand draped across the top of the sofa drew her eye. There were a few calouses, which surprised her. A gentleman of his means would not be expected to have laboured enough to cause such blemishes.

Her gaze returned to his. "I believe we were at Mary."

"Was she older or younger?"

"The eldest was Jane, followed by me, and then came Mary. Mary was two years younger, enjoyed reading sermons—particularly Fordyce—and playing the pianoforte. Kitty came after Mary by a year. She was rather impressionable and was often found with our youngest sister, Lydia. They had no care for reading unless it was a novel, and my father often said they were some of the silliest girls in England."

His attention never wavered from her, and she pivoted towards him to be more comfortable as they spoke. "You mentioned a sister. Georgiana, I believe? Is she very accomplished?" His face transformed into a brilliant smile, which conveyed just how dear his sister was to him.

"She is indeed accomplished for a girl of thirteen. She studies the pianoforte quite diligently and plays and sings all day long."

"Is she much like you?" she asked. Perhaps she had the same eyes—marvellous, crystal blue eyes.

"We are quite alike in colouring. We both have dark hair and blue eyes, but where I am rather stocky, she is quite tall and slender for her age."

"I think that a very reasonable difference for a sister to have." Her voice was teasing, and he gave a chuckle, accentuating his handsome features.

"She plays and sings, but does she enjoy needlework or the outdoors?" She was taking great pleasure in introducing topics that made him smile, and by the time Mr. Phillips returned, they had discussed his sister at length. The conversation was moving on to horses, which Elizabeth was pleased to know a little about, when her uncle showed Hattie into the room.

"Hattie!" She jumped from her seat and rushed across the room to take the young woman's hands. "I do hope you are here to accompany me?"

"I am," affirmed Hattie. "But I must say that I am relieved to find you well again, Miss Elizabeth. The entire town was so distressed whilst you were ill."

She was in the process of thanking Hattie when Mr. Philips cleared his throat.

"Lizzy, perhaps you and Hattie should pack your things whilst Mr. Darcy and I complete these documents."

She curtsied to Mr. Darcy as she excused herself and Hattie from the room.

Elizabeth helped as Hattie made quick work of packing her belongings, retrieving her clothing from the wardrobe and dresser in the small room, while Hattie arranged everything neatly in her trunk.

"Did my uncle explain?" she asked, as they worked.

"He did. I also told 'im that I 'ave nothin' keepin' me 'ere. If Mr. Darcy would allow it, I would be pleased to be your new maid."

"Then I believe the position is yours."

39

Hattie beamed. "Thank you, miss. Your uncle did surprise me with his note. I had'n heard you were to be married."

Remembering her uncle's advice when he left her with Mr. Darcy, she stopped and caught Hattie's eye. "It is a long story that I cannot explain at the moment."

"I probably should'n be askin' anyhow."

She handed over the next dress, clasping Hattie's hand when she did. "I am not upset about your curiosity, Hattie."

"I know, miss. Mr. Philips told me Mr. Darcy is more 'n your father was, so I was needin' to be more proper, nothing more."

Her uncle was probably correct, so she nodded. "I had not looked on it in that way." Suddenly, the new society she would be a part of became clear, and she balked. How much would she have to change to belong?

Darcy and Mr. Philips finished the initial settlement contracts together and, with the help of the clerk, signed them, making everything legal. Mr. Philips was agitated and jumpy and his long sighs and nervous mannerisms showed he still questioned their solution. The man had to be feeling guilty as well, yet this outcome had to be an improvement over Miss Bennet's scheme to travel to the colonies. What a harrowing undertaking that would be for a young woman!

While Philips and his clerk were both working on the copies he had requested, he stepped out to confirm that his carriage had indeed arrived in Meryton. The task had not taken long, since he found his valet standing by the front door of the Bird and Hand.

"There you are, Mr. Darcy!" exclaimed James when he saw him. "They said in the stables you were still here, but no one knew where you had disappeared."

"I had some business with a local solicitor," he began, hoping there would not be too many questions regarding their new traveling companion. "How much longer before the team is ready?"

"They are almost done changing the horses as we speak, sir."

"Good. We will have a young woman and her maid with us for the remainder of our journey. Please tell the driver to pull the carriage up the lane behind the inn. It will lead to a small house to the rear of the solicitor's office. I will be waiting for you there."

"Yes, sir."

James' furrowed brow and questioning eyes showed his confusion, but Darcy was not inclined to discuss personal affairs in such open surroundings. He had no idea where Gardiner had gone, but he would take no chances that a name or destination might get passed along.

The valet, realising no further information would be forthcoming, gave a small bow and hurried off in the direction of the stables.

When Darcy returned to Mr. Philips office, they completed sorting and finalising the paperwork before venturing back to the quaint home, where, hopefully, his intended was awaiting him. He was not disappointed when he found her seated in the same sitting room, in traveling clothes. She stood to face him and her uncle.

"I hope these will do. They are the finest I own." Her hands trembled as she smoothed her skirt.

Taking her hand, he bowed over it while kissing it lightly. "You look lovely. I am sure the horses will be suitably impressed." Her eyes betrayed her surprise as she stared at him with an open mouth.

"I believe he can tease as well as you, Lizzy," Mr. Philips quipped, chuckling.

Her shocked expression transformed into a smile as she reached for her spencer, bonnet, and gloves, resting on a side table.

"I had not realised you possessed such a talent, Mr. Darcy." She lifted one eyebrow and gave an impish little grin that was very alluring before disappearing down the hall with a slight limp. Had her gait been affected earlier?

"Mr. Philips," he began carefully. "Does Miss Bennet still have an injury of which I should be aware?"

Her uncle exhaled. "Firstly, I think you should call me Philips since you will soon be my nephew."

"Only if you will call me Darcy," he responded.

Phillips agreed and gestured towards the door from where Miss Bennet left. "Her left leg was badly injured in the accident. The doctor believed it to be broken, but by some miracle, the bones were not displaced. She also sustained a bad laceration to the back of the thigh along with some terrible bruising." He turned to face the man who held his gaze earnestly. "In the seven months since the accident, she has mostly healed, defying the doctor's prediction that the leg would require amputation. As of late, she has said that the leg rarely pains her, but I have noticed she often limps like that just prior to a rainfall."

"Perhaps a trip to Bath to take the waters would be beneficial to her. My uncle has a house in Landsdown Crescent; we could take a wedding trip there. It might allow some of the furore from the wedding to subside on both sides."

With worried eyes, Philips took a step closer. "What if my brother's anger does not diminish with time?"

He rubbed the back of his neck. "I refuse to worry about that now. There is a proverb that says do not cross the bridge till you come to it. I think we should follow that advice in this instance."

"Are you sure it is wise?"

Darcy gave a slight shrug. "He will not know where to find her until the wedding announcement is in the paper. Even then, if we spend a month in Bath, he may decide vengeance is not worth it, or his partner may take care of the problem for us. There are too many contingencies."

Philips nodded. "I see what you mean."

"What are your intentions?" inquired Darcy. "You and your wife cannot remain here."

"As we speak, a servant is packing trunks for myself and my wife. She has always bemoaned the fact that I have never taken her to the seaside."

"I hear both Ramsgate and Brighton are very popular."

"I have heard that myself," commented Philips. "In fact, I had planned on heading towards Ramsgate as soon as my wife returns from making calls. My clerk will be visiting his family in Norfolk, so there will be no one here for Gardiner to hound for information."

"Your servants?"

"Mr. and Mrs. Mills are our only servants. Their daughter, Lucy, has only worked a bit since Lizzy came to stay with us. I will give them a false direction before we leave. That way, they can honestly tell Gardiner where they believe we are."

Miss Bennet returned with Hattie as Philips finished his statement. "I assume we are ready to depart?"

Darcy glanced out of the window to see that his carriage had pulled up alongside of the house while he and Philips were speaking. "As soon as your trunks are loaded, we can proceed."

Mr. Mills assisted James in carrying out Miss Bennet's trunk and stowing it with Darcy's, while Hattie's small valise was secured on top. Homer was tethered to the rear of the equipage, relieving Darcy of the need to return to the stable.

Her maid entered the carriage easily, but Miss Bennet stalled, staring with trepidation at the interior. "Miss Bennet, are you well?"

Tears welled in her eyes as she turned to fiercely hug her uncle. "Please tell aunt that I love her."

"I will," he responded softly.

"Thank you for taking me into your home. I know it was not easy for you."

Mr. Philips looked as though he might protest, but with a knowing look from her, he closed his mouth and nodded. The carriage received one more fearful glance as Philips placed his reassuring hand upon her back.

"I know it cannot be easy, but you will be well. Look at how many carriage rides you took before the accident."

She took a deep breath, gave a great exhale, and with one last glimpse at her uncle, she climbed hastily into the carriage. Her fortitude was amazing. The courage she exhibited would have impressed even his cousin Richard, who was not often impressed by much from a woman.

Philips extended his hand, which he shook. The older man then added his other hand to grasp Darcy's, holding him in place.

"Trusting Lizzy to you, a complete stranger, is by far the most difficult thing I have ever had to do," he said softly with tears in his eyes. "Please take good care of her; I beg of you."

To console the man as best he could, he placed his other hand on top of their clasped ones. "I promise she will be treated well, and you will always be welcome to correspond with her. I am certain Miss Bennet would enjoy hosting you at Sagemore, if you are ever in the area."

The worried uncle seemed placated by his response because he dipped his head. "Thank you," he responded in a somewhat relieved manner. "You should be on your way before my wife returns. She has been making calls for some time now, and I expect she should be returning at any moment."

"Of course." He took a step towards the equipage, but paused before climbing aboard. "Please keep me apprised of any information you have on your brother."

"I will!" Philips called after him.

He took a seat across from Hattie and Miss Bennet, who gave a teary wave to her uncle. Mr. Philips put up his hand and held it there.

Darcy hit his walking stick on the roof of the carriage, and when his valet was safely aboard and seated with the driver, they began to move forward. He peered back once as they distanced themselves from the small house. Mr. Philips remained, his hand still raised, as they veered back towards High Street and out of town.

Chapter 4

Once they were on the road towards London, Darcy examined Miss Bennet, who sat quietly crying. His first impulse was to offer her his handkerchief, but she was already using her own. What more could he do to comfort a virtual stranger?

"Miss Bennet, I hope you know that you may correspond with your aunt and uncle as often as you wish."

She turned from her blank stare out of the window to study him for a moment. "I appreciate your kindness, Mr. Darcy."

An almost hollow smile briefly appeared, and it suddenly struck him that she was rather pale. His eyes did not leave her, continuing to observe her more closely in order to determine the best way to be of aid, but it was not until he took notice of the pained expression upon the face of her maid that he began to suspect the problem.

A glance down confirmed poor Hattie's predicament. Miss Bennet was gripping the young woman's hand until her knuckles were white, and she was not relenting in the slightest. He leaned forward, propping his elbows on his knees to catch the eye of his betrothed.

"Is this the first time you have been in a carriage since the accident?" He kept a soft and calm voice.

Her head bobbed up and down as she took a deep breath and exhaled anxiously. "I do not remember being brought to Lucas Lodge, which was the closest home to the accident."

"When were you moved to your uncle's house?"

She paused and thought for a moment, a small wrinkle forming between her eyebrows. "I am not certain. I know the physician ordered that I should not be moved for almost two months. Then, I was still too weak and unable to walk, so I rode in a cart. My aunt has said a liberal dose of laudanum was administered, so the transport would not give me pain."

"I would imagine there is much you do not remember."

"I have no memory of the experience," she interjected.

He peered over to once again find her maid wearing the same pinched expression. "Miss Bennet, I know it is not considered proper, but perhaps you might like to take the seat beside me, so you could grip my hand rather than your maid's."

She whirled about to face Hattie as she released the fierce hold she had been maintaining. "Oh Hattie, forgive me!"

"It's no matter, Miss. I knew ya had ta be frightened. It was no bother, really."

Despite her words, there was clear relief on the woman's face. Miss Bennet glanced down at her maid's hand one last time, with a guilty look, then clasped her hands together. Her countenance was still strained, yet she remained in her seat until they made one last stop approximately halfway to London.

He ushered her inside to take tea to calm her anxiety. She did not drink or eat much, but her hands stopped shaking after a bit.

Once they finished their refreshments, she requested a walk about the village. They had time, so he obliged her and escorted her down the main thoroughfare. She delighted in the picturesque river on the outskirts, and a vibrant smile overtook her features as she praised the beauty of the prospect.

Upon their return, he took her hand from his arm to help her enter the equipage, expecting her to sit opposite him. But, to his surprise, she took the seat beside him instead! He climbed inside, took his place, and then offered her his hand. She took it in a firm grasp before turning to view the scenery outside of the window.

They recommenced their trip, and were not long out of the village, when Hattie leaned against the side of the carriage and began snoring loudly. Miss Bennet made a valiant effort not to giggle, but the temptation was too great, especially, when the maid gave a loud snort. She peered up at him, biting her lip, a hint of the sparkle that had disappeared with her uncle's revelations evident in her eyes.

"It is well you will not have to share her room, is it not?" he whispered.

It was impossible not to join her when she buried her face behind his arm and laughed. She muffled the noise as best she could but her close proximity to his ear allowed him to hear it all, and he found immense enjoyment in her mirth. The sound was not discordant or annoying, but instead, had a pleasant effervescent quality.

The moment passed, as it always does, and she resumed her former position, smiling in his direction before her gaze returned outside to the passing scenery.

A loud cry woke Darcy as he slumbered against the squabs, and he jumped in his seat before realising it originated outside the carriage. He took a long look at their environs, and the landmarks he recognised placed them near Mayfair.

They would soon arrive at Ashcroft house, the home of his grandmother, so he sat upright, and checked on Miss Bennet. She was reading a book in her lap, but her hand still held his, just not as firmly as when he first offered it to her.

"You did not sleep?" he asked, startling her.

"No, I watched the forests and fields for some time before I began to read."

He peered down in an attempt to see the cover, but could not discern the title. "That does not appear to be Shakespeare?"

"*The Lady of the Lake*." She paused to mark her page and close the book. "My father asked the bookseller in Meryton to procure him a copy, but it did not arrive until after the accident. My uncle paid for it and set it aside for when I was well." She released his hand and held the book between both her palms.

"Mr. Collins did not allow me to have any of Papa's books after he had taken over Longbourn." She again paused as she stroked the cover reverently. "I was very pleased that my uncle saved this one for me." She seemed to shake off a memory or thought then turned back towards him. "Have you read it?"

"I have. I enjoyed it very much." He began to straighten and brush at his coat until he noticed she was watching him intently.

"Will we be arriving soon?"

"Yes," he answered. "We are very close."

She placed her book next to her reticule, trading it for her gloves, which she must have removed while he had been sleeping. They appeared new, yet also a tad large for such a petite frame. He reached over and took one of her hands to confirm his suspicions.

"They are too large." He pinched the end of the glove above her index finger to reveal a small excess of material.

"Mine were too worn, and despite my aunt and uncle's protests that I was not a burden, I did not want to ask them for new ones." She gave a small shrug. "Mr. Collins did send trunks with my family's clothing. I have altered and dyed my sisters' dresses as I have needed new ones."

"Your uncle mentioned your gown was once Jane's, if I remember correctly?"

Nodding, she self-consciously smoothed her skirt. "Yes, in my opinion, it was an impractical colour for a traveling gown, since it is such a light shade, which is easily dirtied, but my mother insisted the grey would match Jane's blue eyes more than most of the darker fabrics."

She fidgeted with her gloves, adjusting them as best she could. "The gloves were Jane's as well. She was a few inches taller, and her fingers were longer than mine. But they match the gown."

Her explanation brought to mind her wardrobe. Most brides would have some sort of a trousseau, which, due to the circumstances, Miss Bennet's family could not provide. Some of her gowns might do for every day or if she enjoyed nature, but she would need some new, more stylish ones for social events—especially if they were to travel to Bath after the wedding.

As he mulled over whether his grandmother would mind taking her to a modiste and how long the task would take, the carriage pulled to a stop, shaking him from his thoughts.

"Mr. Darcy, did you perhaps send a note ahead? I would not like to take your grandmother by surprise." Could she be intimidated by the position of his family? Her brow was creased with worry.

"I did, so she should be expecting our arrival." He rested a hand upon hers. "My grandmother is a little contrary at times, but she is not unkind."

The door opened, and he exited the coach, turned, and paused, holding out his hand for Miss Bennet. She followed a moment later, and after stepping down, placed her hand in the crook of his elbow.

He proceeded towards the door with some inward trepidation. He had been honest, his grandmother was not unkind, but he was uncertain how she might react to his engagement. The note he had sent ahead merely stated someone would accompany him; he had not indicated it would be a lady, much less his betrothed.

They were ushered inside, where her spencer and their hats and gloves were handed off to the waiting servants before being shown to a drawing room. The butler announced them, then withdrew at once, closing the door behind him.

Elizabeth examined the woman who stood before her. She was close to seventy, based on her assumption of Mr. Darcy's age. Her silver hair was elegantly styled, and her dress was of the latest fashion, the pale lavender colour complimenting her grey eyes and hair. She did not have a stern countenance, but instead, was smiling at her grandson. As the woman moved towards them, Elizabeth decided it was not her appearance that was intimidating so much as her manner. She was noticeably self-assured and poised.

"Fitzwilliam!" the woman exclaimed as he stepped forward. He took her hand and bestowed a kiss upon her cheek. "I had not expected you in London so soon. And your note was rather vague, young man," she admonished. "I expect you to explain."

A hint of redness appeared on his cheeks. "Yes, ma'am. Though, I fear that some things were last minute and could not be well-explained in a letter."

His grandmother nodded and turned towards her. "Well, are you going to introduce us, or shall I attend to the matter myself?" Unable to stop herself, Elizabeth smiled as she heard Mr. Darcy chuckle.

"Grandmamma, this is Miss Elizabeth Bennet, my betrothed. Miss Bennet, I would like to present my grandmother, Rebecca Fitzwilliam, the Dowager Countess of Matlock."

She curtsied. "I am pleased to make your acquaintance."

The lady's eyebrows lifted, and she turned towards Mr. Darcy. "Well Fitzwilliam, you will be doing a great deal of explaining!" She then faced Elizabeth once more, but her expression was not one Elizabeth could identify. "You must forgive me. Until this moment, I was unaware my grandson was to be married."

"Of course! I would imagine it would be quite a shock." The humour in the woman's eyes gave her the courage to take a chance. "I know it was quite a shock to me when he proposed."

The dowager appraised her, and then her lips quirked up. "I shall look forward to hearing the story from your perspective. In the meantime, I am certain you would like to refresh yourselves." She pulled the bell and a servant came through the doors a moment later. "Mrs. Henderson, my housekeeper, will show you to your rooms. Dinner is planned for seven."

"Thank you, Grandmamma," said Mr. Darcy as they passed the grand lady.

"You know you are always welcome here."

He leaned in to kiss his grandmother once more upon the cheek, and then proceeded to accompany Elizabeth up the stairs behind the housekeeper.

Elizabeth became more anxious by the minute as they were shown through lavish hallways to their rooms. The house was richly furnished and very beautiful. How would she, a simple country girl, fit into this world? Would people scorn her and would she care if they did?

The housekeeper halted before a door, causing her to startle. "These will be your rooms," the servant announced as she opened the large door.

Her betrothed released her hand, and Elizabeth stepped forward past the servant, taking in every detail as she moved to the middle of the room.

"I believe I have never seen a room so lovely. Thank you."

The woman dipped her head and then held it high as she smiled with pride. "As my lady mentioned, my name is Mrs. Henderson. I am the housekeeper here at Ashcroft House. Please inform me if there is anything you require for your comfort."

With a nod, Elizabeth watched as the servant closed the only method of escape before her eyes. She shook her head. "No, this is your only escape, Lizzy," she muttered. Before more second thoughts could come to mind, Hattie bustled through the door with her best gown over her arms.

"Judging by the looks of this place, miss, I readied your prettiest gown, and we must alter more of Miss Jane's. Mrs. Bennet used to use finer materials on hers than the resta you girls, but I don't have better to work with than this one."

The pale blue muslin gown was draped over Hattie's arm. "But the colour is not suitable for half-mourning."

"No, but the grey one you wore earlier didn' have black trim like it should've either."

Elizabeth's head shook in dismay. "I could not bring myself to do that to Jane's new…"

Hattie lay the gown on the bed. "If you'll forgive me for sayin' it, I think Mr. Bennet and Miss Bennet wouldn' be wantin ya to stay so sad for 'em—especially Miss Bennet. She was always such a happy young miss, and never liked ta see anyone sad." Hattie bustled over

50

and began to help her unlace the back of her bodice. "I don't think she'd mind ya wearin' her things either."

She took a deep breath and released it. Her heart knew Hattie was correct; Jane would want her to live her life and be happy, and would have expected her to take her belongings and use them, or at least find someone who could.

While Elizabeth remained by all appearances quiet on the outside, inside she argued with herself about her decision to travel to London with Mr. Darcy. Had it been the best choice? She continued to ponder the issue, turning it over and over in her mind, as her clothes were removed and she washed up with the water and soft towelling provided. Hattie prattled on, oblivious to her lack of attention.

"If ya be wantin' to dress half-mournin,' I'll have another gown pressed and ready for ya on the morrow."

Elizabeth caught her maid's eye in the mirror and nodded. She was too preoccupied with her present situation to really argue whether she would wear the proper mourning clothes the next day.

Meanwhile, Darcy had refreshed himself and sought out his grandmother, who was discovered in her private sitting room reading.

"Grandmamma."

Her head snapped up at the interruption, and she closed her book and gave him her attention.

He spoke with firm conviction. "I know you wish for an explanation, but I should like to dispense with what I feel will be quite the ordeal."

"You would think I was a harridan by the way you speak."

"Now, now. Do you think I would ever compare you to Lady Catherine?" He held his gaze steady for a few moments, knowing his eyes were full of mirth, until a smile erupted upon her face.

"Touché," she said with humour. "But you must not make sport of your aunt in such a manner, even if she does make it quite easy."

He rolled his eyes and took a seat opposite her while his grandmother observed him. She did not say a word, but there was more happening in her mind than she voiced.

"I received a summons from my father almost a fortnight ago." He adjusted his topcoat and shifted in his seat. "It took a few days, but I managed to complete the more pressing business at Sagemore, so I could travel to Pemberley with haste. I had a suspicion as to why he demanded I report there so urgently, which was confirmed the day after I arrived. You see, my valet was privy to the conversations below stairs, and it seems the entire household was acquainted with my father's plans."

"Well, my suspicion is that he is pushing you to arrange your marriage to Anne, regardless of whether or not the two of you wish for the union."

"Yes," he said with a start. "But…" His grandmother's lack of reaction unnerved him. He could not imagine that she was a part of his father's scheme, yet she remained unperturbed by his revelation.

Then, the dowager chuckled. "Catherine came to me and your uncle, insisting we promote the match."

He sat a bit straighter as he waited to hear whether he would be on his own in the future.

"As you should have expected, we both refused to aid her request."

He exhaled in relief, knowing his mother's family would remain by his side. "My father was unusually insistent. He even threatened to publish an announcement in the papers to force my hand if I have not proposed to Anne within a fortnight."

"And yet, here you are, betrothed to a young lady I have never heard you so much as mention in passing."

He fidgeted once more in his seat, as he was still concerned over his grandmother's view of his hasty engagement. "Would you believe this is Georgiana's doing?"

"I am unsure if relying upon the advice of your thirteen-year-old sister is the best method of solving your dilemma, Fitzwilliam; however, if you must assign blame, then I am most interested to know how your sister is responsible for your betrothal."

He shook his head and smiled at her dry tone. "I must admit I rather blurted my way into the entire situation."

Her eyebrows rose, and she tilted her head as she regarded him with marked interest. "That is unusual for you."

"It is." He recounted the conversation between Elizabeth's uncles in the inn, followed by his inclination to assist. "I cannot explain why, but before I was conscious of it, I had proposed—in front of her uncle! I could hardly credit it, yet, I would never dream of rescinding the offer. Once the words left my tongue, I was honour-bound."

"I do not believe Miss Bennet or her uncle would hold you to your impulsive outburst should you express a strong desire to cry off, even though it will solve both your dilemmas. But are you prepared for the repercussions?"

"Do you mean society's or my father's persecution?"

She scoffed with a dismissive wave. "Not that you have ever given a fig about society, but as long as the Matlocks stand behind you, the old bats will not be an issue. Other than disowning you, your father could withhold Georgiana from you. I believe that punishment would be the most effective."

"I had a long conversation with Georgiana before I departed Pemberley. She and I discussed the possibility."

"You told her your father's edict?" his grandmother asked surprised.

"No, she knew of it from the servant's gossip and approached me. Finding a wife besides Anne was her idea."

"Ahhh, I see why you are attempting to place the blame with her." She stood and poured them both a small snifter of brandy, handing him his before she resumed her seat. "The notion may have originated with her, but I do not believe your impulsive action was born out of that scheme." Her eyes narrowed a bit while she took a small sip of her drink. "I want you to describe Miss Bennet."

"Well… but why?" he questioned. He could not divine the reason his grandmother wished this, but he scrambled for words to sketch the character of his betrothed in the event she pressed him.

"Humour me, Fitzwilliam. Describe your betrothed." Her tone was insistent, and she had a recognisable glint in her eye; he would be unable to avoid her interrogation.

"She is a gentleman's daughter."

"You mentioned that, my dear," she said, "when you told me about her accident. You recounted they were travelling to her father's estate." She spoke in a casual manner despite the seriousness of their discourse.

He tugged at his collar as it had begun to feel too snug. "She is fond of books."

"Do you know of her preferences? What types of books?"

"She has read some Shakespeare and Homer, and she mentioned a portion of *The Odyssey*. In the carriage, she was reading *The Lady of the Lake*. I also know she speaks French and a bit of Italian."

He now grasped for any detail he could remember, so he would not sound too pathetic. "Her father taught her many subjects, but her mother often attempted to redirect her efforts towards learning more household duties or practicing the pianoforte."

"Do you find her pretty?"

"Pardon?"

"You heard me," she answered. "This woman that you brought into my home, and that you intend to wed will be the mother of your heir. If you are to marry without love, then I hope you find her tolerable enough for bedding."

"Grandmamma!" His face was warm, and he was positive his cheeks were a bright crimson, but nothing could be done to relieve his mortification any time soon. "I will not discuss this with you!"

She laughed, and he raised his eyes to find hers were sparkling. "I have borne children, Fitzwilliam, as well as lived in society these many years. You will not shock me."

"I will not…"

"Very well. I will not press." She took her last sip and set the glass upon the side table. "You will make arrangements for the wedding, and I will spend time with her. I will ensure she is everything you require, and help her to select an appropriate wardrobe. That way, not only will she have a trousseau, but she will also be witnessed by others whilst she is about town with me. It will help her entrance into society."

A sigh of relief escaped his lips. "Thank you, Grandmamma. I appreciate any assistance you can offer." He swirled his brandy around the glass before he remembered another important detail. "Oh! Miss Bennet's abigail comes from service at Longbourn. She may be perfectly adequate, but could you have your maid take her under her wing?"

His grandmother nodded. "I will mention it to Sarah this evening. I do not believe she will mind helping."

"Thank you." He finished his glass just as the doors opened and a footman showed Miss Bennet into the room. She glanced around in an unsure manner.

"I hope I am not interrupting." Her complexion was flushed, and she spoke with a swiftness that left no doubt she was nervous. She had changed her gown, which was more becoming than the travelling clothes she had worn earlier. The cut highlighted well the light and pleasing figure he had admired upon their first meeting.

His grandmother stood and crossed the room to take Miss Bennet's hands. "Please do not be uneasy. Dinner will be served soon, so we expected you. After all, it is where the rest of us are." Nodding, Miss Bennet gave a small smile, but still appeared to feel out of place.

She touched a bit of the fabric on Miss Bennet's sleeve. "This is a lovely gown. The blue is very pretty."

The shade did suit her, and a warm sensation crept over his body as he admired the manner in which her bodice and skirt accentuated her curves. He turned to hide his reaction from his grandmother, who was certain to notice.

"Thank you, my lady."

His grandmother waited, perhaps in case Miss Bennet might say more, but when nothing further was offered, she led his betrothed to a seat. "I understand you lost your family seven months ago. I hope you have not put aside your mourning to accommodate us."

He scanned Elizabeth's attire, and his grandmother was correct; however, the blue was better suited to her complexion and was more elegant than the gown she had worn for their journey to London. She appeared very well indeed!

Elizabeth swallowed, determined not to let her trepidation show. Her courage usually rose with any attempt to intimidate her; hopefully, this instance would be no different!

"My maid prepared what she felt most appropriate."

The dowager' eyes showed no censure or malice, only concern; a realisation that provided some relief in Elizabeth's unfamiliar surroundings. "I have been wearing half-mourning, but not all my gowns are black-trimmed. Those that I wear most often have the appropriate modifications, but none of the rest have been altered."

"I do not wish to sound callous," Mr. Darcy interrupted, "but it may be a sound idea to refrain from wearing mourning for now."

The dowager regarded him with a critical eye. "And why is that?"

"Mr. Gardiner will, no doubt, return to London at some point. Miss Bennet will be easier to identify at a distance in gowns he is accustomed to seeing. Without mourning attire, recognition is less of a threat."

"Yet, London is a very large city." She straightened and stared her betrothed directly in the eye. "We could reside here for weeks and never cross paths with him."

"Whilst that is true," he agreed. "I would prefer to avoid any chance of a threat to your welfare."

The dowager studied her grandson for a moment before she returned her attention to Miss Bennet. "Wear what you like, dear." Her voice was gentle as she patted the young woman's hand. "I will send a message to my modiste this evening, and she will arrange the necessities, so we can order your trousseau. I assure you, we will be quite safe whilst we shop; I always arrange for two footmen to attend me."

Her grandson's displeased countenance was evident, and though Miss Bennet had seen it, she nodded. "Thank you, ma'am."

They had no further time for pleasantries, since they were called in to dinner. Fitzwilliam offered an arm to both ladies and escorted them to the dining room, where a footman assisted Miss Bennet to her seat. Once they were all served, she returned to Miss Bennet.

Though sympathetic to the young woman's plight, during the dowager's conversation with her grandson, she resolved to discover for herself whether Miss Bennet had the mettle to take on his stubborn nature. She was disposed to accept this young woman, but would the future Mrs. Darcy know when to pick her battles? She had suggested the young lady continue to wear her mourning attire, curious how Miss Bennet would negotiate the situation.

Her grandson was silent as he ate his meal and observed the two of them in conversation. Well, it was not accurate to say he observed the two of them; instead, he was staring unabashedly at his betrothed. She smiled to herself. The poor boy was smitten by a woman he had met this day!

It reminded her of George Darcy's initial reaction to her daughter, Lady Anne Fitzwilliam. He had been unable to remove his eyes from her much in the same way his son was now eyeing Miss Bennet.

She was inclined to like Miss Bennet from their short acquaintance, but prayed the young lady was what her grandson needed. Moreover, that they were both truly what the other needed. If they were ill-suited, how would their marriage survive?

Back in Hertfordshire, Edward Gardiner's fear and anger were overwhelming. He had timed his arrival for as soon as he could be assured that most of the village would be at the assembly, only to find his sister's home closed and locked tight, and no servants available to answer to where they travelled. His law clerk was not even working his usual late hours in the office.

A quick turn through the assembly, garnered him a few strange looks due to his lack of dress for the occasion, but no one would share any rumours, so he had been unable to discover anyone who could help him solve his problem.

His last attempt was the small house where the Philip's servants resided. Mr. Mills claimed the Philips had gone on holiday to Lyme. Lyme? Why would they travel all the way down there? Mr. Mills appeared to truly believe that was his brother and sister's destination, which indicated the Philips had lied to their servants.

"Damn you, Philips! Where have you taken Lizzy?" he grumbled under his breath. He could not tarry lest he be discovered by Grayson—he must return to London! He mounted his horse and set off bewildered and unfulfilled.

Somewhere, he must find a hiding place to shield himself from Grayson for as long as possible.

Chapter 5

Elizabeth awakened early the next morning. The excitement and nerves of the previous day must have caught up with her by the time she had lain in bed because she could not remember closing her eyes. Rather than rise straight away, she lay there for a time watching the light streaming in through the drapes.

A part of her wished she could remain cuddled with a book, shunning the world and her problems behind the door to the room; however, reflection and lounging in bed were not a part of the day's agenda.

Hattie bustled into the room with Elizabeth's usual grey mourning gown hanging over her arm.

"Hattie, I think I will wear something different."

Her maid's eyebrows rose as she moved back towards the dressing room. "Which gown would you like, Miss?"

"Do you think the blue one I wore to dinner would be too fine?"

"Based on the gown her ladyship's abigail carried this morning, I imagine it would suit, but what would you wear for dinner?"

Considering the dowager's and Mr. Darcy's words from the night before, she gave thought to the items they had packed. "Perhaps the yellow or the grey you are holding since I will remain within the house."

Hattie was about to return to the dressing room when she turned at the last minute. "Your bath will be ready in a moment. I can also bring ya... your tea if you like."

Hattie's speech was slow and measured, so unlike her usual manner. Elizabeth reached out and grasped her maid's hand. "Hattie, why do you speak with such care? Has someone been unkind?"

"Oh, no miss! Her ladyship's maid and I had a talk last night. She offered to help me, ya see... you see." She blushed a bit with her error. "Sarah... that's her name, suggested I should speak more formally."

"I have no issues with your accent, or the manner in which you speak..." She meant to say more, but Hattie was too busy defending Sarah to realise.

"She said I would reflect better on you and Mr. Darcy if I am to serve you when you travel."

58

"Hattie, please do not feel you must do this for me. You would never do anything to cause us shame."

"No, miss, I would never do so on purpose, but I would not want people to think poorly of you or your family because of me."

"But…"

"I have listened to Mrs. Henderson and the resta the servants here. I sound more like the scullery maid than an abigail or even a footman in this house." A determined look in Hattie's eye prompted her to let her maid be. "I do not mind. I want to be what is expected."

She sighed. "Very well. As long as it is what you wish, and not because you feel you must."

"Thank you, miss," she said, returning to her usual manner. "Oh, your bath only lacked a few buckets, last I looked, so it should'n be long."

She nodded and Hattie entered the dressing room, reappearing seconds later with the gown from the previous evening, which she laid on the bed. Elizabeth was fingering the fine, pale blue that overlay the white gown underneath when a noise in the next room caused her to regard her maid with puzzlement.

"Your bath is ready, miss."

"Ah, thank you," she responded.

She took her time, soaking in the water as she considered what the next fortnight would bring. Her life was about to take a dramatic turn, and she could not continue to suffer from nerves lest she turn into her mother—Lord, what a nightmare that would be!

Yet, she missed her mother, and so a part of her felt guilty for thinking so of her, now that she was gone. In the end, she needed to learn to adapt to the situation that now presented itself. The idea was easier in theory than in reality, but she was determined to succeed.

Once she was dressed, Hattie, with the help of some instructions scrawled on some paper, styled her hair. The coiffure was more elaborate than she was accustomed to for every day, but then everyday would now be different, too.

When she stepped into the corridor, she nearly collided with the dowager as she passed. "Miss Bennet, I hope you slept well."

"Yes, the room is very comfortable, thank you."

"Good... good, I hope you will be content to spend your day with me." She took Elizabeth's elbow and steered her towards the stairs. "Madame Lebrun responded to my message last night, requesting her first available appointment. She will accommodate us early this morning. I am an early riser, so if I require a last minute gown, she schedules me before most of society would venture out for shopping."

"I appreciate your help, my lady." She was cheerful as she spoke, but was taken aback when the dowager abruptly stopped and faced her.

"Now, I insist you call me something besides my lady. You will be my granddaughter soon, and I do not have family address me with such formality." She smiled mischievously as she clasped her hands in front of her. "I had thought to introduce you as my future granddaughter today whilst we were at the shops, but without mentioning which of my grandsons was your betrothed. That will set some tongues to wagging!"

She chuckled along with the stately grandmother. "I would not wish to be considered disrespectful, so I leave it to you to decide the name you would prefer me to use."

"Fitzwilliam will be my first grandson to marry," thought the dowager aloud. "Elinor, my son Henry's wife, calls me mother. Would you be comfortable addressing me as grandmother or even grandmamma like my other grandchildren?"

"I would not mind at all, but only if you will call me Elizabeth, or even Lizzy as my family does."

Despite their brief acquaintance, the dowager appeared open and accepting, which helped to ease her mind. Mr. Darcy had assured her that this side of his family was different than his father, but she had still been concerned he might have exaggerated to calm her.

His grandmother nodded. "I should like to."

She glanced around at the offerings on the table, but where was Mr. Darcy's place setting? "Does Mr. Darcy usually break his fast in his rooms?"

His grandmother glanced over to the empty seat as she took a piece of toast from the tray before her. "My grandson is almost always up and about quite early. Since his spot is empty, you can assume he has already eaten. I would imagine he wished to get a prompt start to the day. He will have a great deal of business to take care of this week. It would not do for him to be out and about dealing with those matters in the weeks that follow the wedding."

"Of course," she replied, disappointed.

She did grasp what his grandmother was trying to tell her, and she agreed whole-heartedly. Neither his father nor her uncle needed any ammunition to challenge the validity of their marriage. It was of the utmost importance that everything seem as though it was planned in advance, regardless of what rumours might be in existence. Yet, the two of them still required time to become better acquainted before they were wed.

During the meal, she answered questions from her future grandmother about her accomplishments, likes, and dislikes, and by the time they rose from their seats, she had promised to prepare a piece on the pianoforte for after dinner one night later in the week. She had much in common with her future grandmother, and they did not lack for conversation.

When she had sipped her last bit of tea, they both rose, and Elizabeth collected her shawl that had rested on the back of the chair while she ate.

"Lizzy," said the dowager, as she grasped the wrap, "did you embroider this?"

"Yes, although I used a tambour stitch rather than regular embroidery. Tambour stitching is faster, and I am never the most patient with my needlework."

"The design is lovely, dear. We should bring this and show it to Madame Lebrun. She may have some designs for gowns you could embellish. You do not have to of course, but I think you could make a very simple gown stunning with some embroidered trim work."

"I have never done so in the past, but if Madame Lebrun has a gown that would suit, I would be pleased to attempt it."

The dowager beamed with pleasure. "Wonderful!

She followed the lady to the entrance hall, where Hattie was waiting with her outdoor garments. Elizabeth began to put on the same fawn coloured pair she had worn the evening before, when the dowager glanced in her direction.

"Oh! Last night my grandson said to be sure to purchase you some new gloves—ones that fit."

Elizabeth shook her head and laughed. "I truly do not require new ones. These are still very serviceable."

"That may very well be, but if my grandson could discern that they are not correctly sized, then so will the spiteful young things he deemed unworthy. Do not give them something so simple to criticize."

She could not help but smile as she shook her head. "Yes, ma'am."

Coming from a small town, she was overwhelmed when she accompanied the dowager. They arrived at the drapers as they opened and were ushered inside straight away, where they were shown a multitude of fabrics.

Once they selected their purchases, the dowager steered Elizabeth to a counter with various gloves on display. She tried on several pairs with her future grandmother, who set aside those they would purchase. She attempted to object at the number, but the dowager insisted she would require several colours and styles and would not relent despite her protests.

The gloves were added to the fabric, with one pair being handed to her before they departed the shop. Having no intention of changing them right then and there, she put them in her reticule then climbed into the equipage to travel to Madame Lebrun's.

Upon their arrival at the popular modiste's, the footmen handed them both from the carriage and escorted them into the shop, where a young girl raced to the back calling for the Madame.

"Bonjour!" the well-known modiste exclaimed a few moments later as she entered the room. "I see you are on time as always, my lady."

The dowager smiled. "Madame Lebrun, I appreciate you doing us this favour at the last minute. I hope it was not too much of an inconvenience."

"Of course not! I am always very happy to add an appointment for you."

"As I said in my note, the appointment is for my future granddaughter, Miss Bennet." She motioned towards Elizabeth as she spoke, and the woman examined her from head to toe before returning to the dowager with a pleased expression.

"Bien sûr, Madame." Madame Lebrun's attention was drawn behind them, and she turned to find the footmen who had accompanied them with their fabric purchases. "Place those on the table, s'il vous plaît, and I will send one of my girls to bring them to the back."

"Ladies," she said, gesturing towards them. "If you will follow me, we will take Mademoiselle Bennet's measurements and then discuss the gowns."

They were shown to a private parlour where they were attended by the modiste and her staff. Elizabeth had never requested so many items at one time before! Not only did they order several gowns, but also new undergarments and nightclothes, which she had been accustomed to making herself. An entire new wardrobe would be hers by the time she was wed, with very little work on her part. Madame Lebrun would even have a pale ivory gown made first, so that she could embellish it with embroidery for her wedding gown.

As they were in the process of leaving, she leaned towards the dowager. "I could not help but notice that when you introduced me as your future granddaughter, no one thought to ask to whom I was betrothed."

She was taken aback when the older woman began to chuckle. "Madame Lebrun has the utmost discretion. I trust her implicitly, but the girls in her employ are another matter. I have been witness to her terminating one of her seamstresses for gossiping about her clients, but I still do not take chances with them." She stepped into the carriage and took her seat, waiting for Elizabeth to be situated before continuing. "Fitzwilliam will be paying for your purchases, so Madame Lebrun does know. She would never inquire as openly as you might think."

Elizabeth glanced out of the window at the storefronts as they passed. "Are we finished for today?"

"We are heading over to order you slippers and boots. Of course, we will also need to stop by a milliners." She glanced down to Elizabeth's hands and back to her face. "May I ask what you did with your new gloves?"

Her lip quirked up on one side. "My gloves are perfectly serviceable."

The dowager rolled her eyes with a smile. "That may be, but they must also fit!" The older woman pinched the empty tip of her index finger, accidentally pulling the glove off in the process. Both ladies began laughing as the offending article was handed back.

"I did not expect it slip off quite so easily."

Elizabeth withdrew the new pair from her reticule and swapped them for Jane's, which she placed carefully back within her bag. "I must confess that I had not either" When she had completed her task, she held up her hands. "Are they a vast improvement?"

"Quite," replied the dowager, as they made their way into the shop.

The last few stops were not as time consuming as Elizabeth had presumed, and she soon found herself with the dowager in the lady's favourite teashop, seated to one side of the room with them both facing the interior of the establishment.

The dowager leaned over towards her ear. "I hope you will forgive me for instructing you as to where you should sit. I do not care to have my back to those who are entering. There is nothing more dreadful than being ambushed by someone you do not like." She straightened back up, returning her hands to her lap. "I would much prefer some warning."

Smiling, Elizabeth repressed a chuckle. An unobtrusive servant's hand reached past her and placed their refreshments before them. "I am not offended, and I can easily understand your motive." She leaned closer to the older woman, much as the other had a moment before. "I would imagine it also makes it easier to whisper to me those secrets you do not wish the room to hear."

"You understand me perfectly, Lizzy," she said with a wide smile. "I do not generally care for gossip, and you do not seem the type to enjoy it either. Nevertheless, you will need to know some tittle-tattle to navigate society as Fitzwilliam's wife."

Her eyes widened and she glanced about the room. "Is he often the source of rumour?"

"Oh! No!" the dowager exclaimed. "I had not meant to give you that impression. He is the topic! Rumours have circulated for the last few years that speculate on who and when he would marry. You may find you are not received with the welcome you deserve by those parties."

Her tension eased, and Elizabeth reached for a small cake to place on her plate. "I would imagine anyone could encounter that regardless of who they wed."

"Very true, but I think you will find it a bit more cattish in town than in the country."

A bell on the door sounded, and Elizabeth's eye was drawn to the two women entering the shop. They resembled each other enough that she assumed they were sisters. The fabric and lace of their gowns bespoke money, yet, in her opinion they were a bit overdone.

"Ahhh, what a coincidence that she should appear today and this minute in particular," the dowager whispered.

Elizabeth turned towards the dowager with her eyebrows raised in curiosity.

The older woman shook her head. "You will not have to wait long. It appears they are headed this way."

The women had indeed spotted The Dowager Countess of Matlock and were walking in their direction, the taller of the two with a most affected smile upon her face.

"Lady Matlock!" The voice was so falsely sincere that it took Elizabeth aback. "I had heard that you intended to quit town. I cannot say how pleased Louisa and I are to have happened upon you here."

"I was unaware that I had announced to all of London I was leaving, Miss Bingley."

Elizabeth bit the inside of her cheek to keep herself from laughing.

"I must say, the gossip mill must be starving for a scandal if it is taking such a keen interest in the travels of an old woman such as myself."

"I would not say that." Miss Bingley tittered and her sister followed suit. "I just bumped into Miss Crawley and she was telling us that Lord Grantley was seen at the theatre last night with…"

"Lord Grantley is always with someone it seems," interrupted the dowager. She glanced at Elizabeth and gestured towards her. "I would like to introduce you to Miss Elizabeth Bennet. Miss Bennet, these ladies are Mrs. Louisa Hurst and her sister Miss Caroline Bingley."

The ladies each gave a slight dip to their chin and a small curtsy as she said their names. They were disinterested in her and wasted no time returning to their attempt to draw the dowager into more gossip. Elizabeth continued to sip her tea until a question caught her attention.

"Does Mr. Darcy return to town soon? Charles has not mentioned it, and Louisa and I would so enjoy having him dine with the family one evening."

His grandmother smiled. "I believe he intends to be in London soon, but to conclude matters in preparation for his betrothal and subsequent marriage."

Miss Bingley's eyes sharpened. "I had not heard he was betrothed."

"Unfortunately, I am unable to elaborate at the moment—I am certain you understand—but an announcement will be made soon. I assure you."

Miss Bingley peered towards Elizabeth, seeming to notice her for the first time. "Miss Bennet, I do not recall Lady Matlock saying where you hail from?"

"I am from Hertfordshire."

"Her father's estate is called Longbourn, I believe. Is that correct, dear?"

"Yes, Longbourn." Why did the dowager speak as if the situation was current? Still, she did not contradict the statement, as the lady would have some motive for speaking as she was.

Giving a sniff, Mrs. Hurst glanced at her sister and back. "I have never heard of it."

"Well, it is long-standing and respected, whether you have heard of it or not." The dowager' voice was dry, and her countenance conveyed her annoyance.

Miss Bingley, who remained oblivious, surveyed the table in the obvious and vain hope they might be issued an invitation. With no welcoming overture, it would be rude to continue on as they had, yet she tarried.

But soon, she peered around the room. "I suppose we should find a table." The two places that had been available when they entered were now taken, but she shuffled in that direction.

"It was lovely to see you again, Lady Matlock," said Mrs. Hurst with a much more practiced air and a brief curtsy. "Miss Bennet." She collected her sister, but they did not remain; instead, they departed through the front door and crossed the street.

The dowager leaned forward for a better view out of the window. "I thought they would never leave." She dabbed her lips with her napkin and placed it back in her lap.

"How are you acquainted with them?"

"Those two ladies have a brother—Charles Bingley. He is affable and never less than generous; I cannot find anything improper at all about the young man." She took a sip of her tea and swallowed. "Fitzwilliam and he became friends just after Mr. Bingley, who is younger, graduated from Cambridge. I think Mr. Bingley's sociable nature draws out my rather quiet and reticent grandson."

She smiled as she remembered Mr. Darcy's description of himself and his problems conversing with strangers.

"Fitzwilliam invited Mr. Bingley to Sagemore a few years ago, not long after he inherited the estate, but when Mr. Bingley arrived, his sisters were with him. The ladies, if you can speak of them as such, had not been included in the invitation, yet Fitzwilliam did not turn them away. Instead, I received a letter begging me to come and serve as his hostess for the month."

"Oh my," Elizabeth murmured. "How rude."

"How rude, indeed! I suppose, in hindsight, the only thing I can fault Charles Bingley for is not standing up to those sisters of his." The dowager sat back in her seat and spoke rather low, even though no one was seated close to them. "Miss Bingley has been a thorn in my grandson's side since she came out into society four years ago. At first, she wished to distance herself from her roots in trade by marrying a gentleman of a certain wealth, and was eyeing several prospects, including my grandson.

"Her ambition became worse after she was invited to travel to the Peaks with another young lady and her family the summer after her debut. They toured Pemberley and Miss Bingley realised that fine estate was Fitzwilliam's future. Her interest in him as a gentleman of some means became complete avarice."

Bewildered by it all, Elizabeth shook her head. "Yet her brother brought her along uninvited. I cannot understand how he remains unaware."

"He is aware, very aware," the lady answered. "He has told my grandson she wishes to marry him, and Fitzwilliam was very emphatic that he would never entertain the thought. She is not unlike a great many ladies of the ton, but with her brother being

Fitzwilliam's friend, she is convinced she has an advantage over any competition."

"Is Mr. Darcy pursued by so many?" The idea sounded daunting.

"Not truly pursued. There are few who would turn him down, but George still receives a great deal of attention since he is the current master of Pemberley.

Elizabeth nodded in understanding.

The dowager indicated they should gather their belongings. Once they were ensconced back in the carriage, the grand lady placed her hand upon Elizabeth's forearm.

"Due to Fitzwilliam's friendship with Mr. Bingley, you will cross paths with both of those ladies in the future. You should never trust Miss Bingley or her sister," she said emphatically. "I would imagine she will react to your marriage in one of two ways: she will either ingratiate herself to you in the hopes of maintaining a connection to the Darcy name, or she will become a perfect cat and show you every bit of her disdain."

Overwhelmed by it all, Elizabeth leaned into the comfortable cushion as she considered all she had learned that morning. "Is Mrs. Hurst often with Mr. Bingley?"

"I believe Mr. Bingley and Miss Bingley have rooms in Mr. Hurst's home. I feel for Mr. Hurst, but then he went into that marriage with both eyes open."

"Was it a love match?"

The dowager gave a brief laugh and shook her head. "Heavens, no. His father was a drunkard and the estate was in need of funds. Her twenty-thousand pound dowry helped keep them from dissolving into debt."

The dowager turned to the window and watched the buildings as they passed, so Elizabeth lost herself in thought.

Mr. Darcy deserved a good deal of pity. First, Miss Bingley had pursued him for her own mercenary purposes, and then his father attempted to betroth him to his cousin to assuage his own greed. So many only cared for him as a means to an end.

The dowager touched her hand, and she startled and glanced to the side where Ashcroft house stood. When had they arrived? She must have been so absorbed with her thoughts, she had not noticed.

"Good afternoon, my lady." The butler gave a small bow as they entered. "Lord Matlock awaits your return in the drawing room."

"Thank you," she responded. "Come, Lizzy, I will introduce you to my eldest, my son Henry." She looped her arm through Elizabeth's and steered her towards the room where they had met the previous evening.

She could not account for her anxiety until she recalled it was similar to the night before. Once again, she was walking into an unknown, where someone might send her back to Hertfordshire—throw her back to the wolves from which she was trying to escape. The door opened and a gentleman sitting in an armchair raised his head from the book he was reading.

"Mamma," he greeted as they entered. "We were supposed to walk in Hyde Park this afternoon; or did you forget?"

"Oh! Forgive me, Henry. Fitzwilliam surprised me by his arrival last night, and as a result, I have been out shopping with Lizzy most of the morning."

He had glanced at Elizabeth when they entered, but now that his mother had referred to her, he regarded her with interest.

"Would you care for some tea or refreshments? Lizzy and I have just come from my favourite tea shop, but I will order a tray if you wish."

He glanced back to his mother and shook his head. "No, thank you. I am very well at the moment. I take it this must be Lizzy then?"

She was comforted by the fact that his voice was cheerful as he asked and motioned towards her.

"Yes, she is, as a matter of fact." The dowager pulled her forward from where she had held back near the door. "Elizabeth Bennet, I would like to introduce you to my son, the Earl of Matlock, Henry Fitzwilliam."

She then turned back to her son. "Lizzy is betrothed to Fitzwilliam."

The earl's face expressed shock as he gave a small sputter. "When did Fitzwilliam become engaged? I have always thought we would have a huge row because George would try to choose his bride for him."

"You are not far from the truth, my lord," Elizabeth interjected as she curtsied. Lord Matlock flushed—he now realised he had not behaved as he should—and bowed.

"Forgive me, Miss Bennet. I should have greeted you properly before I began discussing my misgivings about your betrothal in front of you."

A glint in his eye reminded her of his mother, and his statement appeared to be his attempt to inject a bit of levity into the situation.

"It is quite natural for you to have some questions. I am not offended."

The dowager released her arm and took a seat on the sofa. Elizabeth sat in the chair opposite her while Lord Matlock resumed his place in the armchair.

"As for George, he *has* tried to force his will on Fitzwilliam. Nonetheless, he became betrothed to Lizzy after his father issued an ultimatum, which gave him a fortnight to appear at Rosings and propose to Anne. He intends to wed Lizzy before George travels to London to force the matter."

Lord Matlock closed his eyes and exhaled heavily. "I thought Catherine was simply spouting off as she does from time to time. I was aware that his father would attempt this eventually, and I warned George I would stand against forcing my nephew's hand. I had not anticipated he would press the matter now."

"He has not listened to us for some time, as you are well aware. Anne's passing erected a wall, and nothing gets through, it seems." The older woman looked more her age at that moment than she had appeared since they had met.

"Anne was my younger sister and Fitzwilliam's mother," clarified Uncle Henry.

His mother smiled wistfully. "Anne was the only person who could penetrate that haughty exterior and bring out the best in her husband. That was her way with everyone. She was so gentle and kind."

Her description would have fit Jane well. "She sounds lovely. I am sure it would have been a pleasure to meet her."

The dowager and her son gave small smiles at her words, but words could not bring Anne Darcy back. If Lady Anne were alive, she would not be betrothed to Mr. Darcy, she would be on a ship bound for the Canadas. In spite of this, she still would wish Mrs. Darcy to be with her family. She did not have it in her to be selfish.

"Lizzy," said the dowager. "I am sure you would like to refresh yourself from the day."

Of course the lady wished some time alone to speak with her son, and so Elizabeth was content to make her way to her rooms. "I must admit that I would."

"Then why do you not go on up, dear. You may as well dress for dinner."

Elizabeth caught a glimpse of the clock on the mantel and frowned. "It would be a little early, would it not?"

"A bit, but there is no sense in refreshing yourself only to have to return to change for dinner."

One corner of her lips curled up in amusement. "Of course. You are very wise to suggest such a plan."

"I am always wise."

Elizabeth's eyebrow lifted as a twinkle in the dowager's eye let her know the lady did not take offense to her teasing, and the wit she had been suppressing could not help but assert itself in response.

"The fool doth think he is wise, but the wise man knows himself to be a fool.[1] "

The lady gasped in mock indignation as Lord Matlock guffawed.

"You are very uncharitable, Lizzy!" The elder lady grinned. "A still tongue makes a wise head.[2] "

Lord Matlock gave a small snort. "I believe the two of you get along far too well. I do wonder how long you would go on if I gave you leave to continue."

Elizabeth chuckled. "Please send word when you are finished discussing me."

She rose, gave a quick curtsy, and closed the door to the continuing sounds of the dowager and her son still chuckling behind her.

The laughter slowly ebbed after the door closed behind Elizabeth. Lord Matlock turned to his mother and lifted both eyebrows. "I have never heard of her or the Bennet family. What do we know of her?"

She smoothed her skirt as she turned serious. "Her father had a small estate in Hertfordshire called Longbourn. According to Fitzwilliam, a horrific carriage accident claimed the lives of her family almost seven months ago."

"She was not wearing mourning."

"No, I believe that is to please your nephew." At her son's puzzled expression, she raised her hand. "I will explain, but allow me to finish before you interject." He nodded his agreement, and she took a deep breath.

"Lizzy's only remaining family are two uncles on her mother's side. One is a solicitor in the town near her home, and the other is in trade here in London." Lord Matlock's eyebrows rose again, but he remained silent. "The uncle in trade has made some poor business decisions and owes money to an unsavoury character. When Fitzwilliam was passing through Hertfordshire on his return to London, he happened to overhear the two uncles arguing. The one wanted to trade Lizzy for a portion of his debts and use the money left to her after her family's passing to help pay more."

"Oh, Good Lord," exclaimed Lord Matlock. "He wanted to save her. Fitzwilliam definitely has his mother's soft heart!"

"George is not without compassion, especially with his tenants," she defended.

"That is true, but he would never advocate marriage as a solution."

"No, he would not, especially with Fitzwilliam. He might have nominated that boy he dotes on so much," she said distastefully.

"Wickham?"

She nodded. "I have never liked him!"

"No, neither have I. But I had Arthur and Richard informing me of his every transgression against Fitzwilliam. They disliked the way Wickham treated their cousin immensely, and lost all respect for George due to his sponsorship of that wastrel."

"Well, that will be one positive aspect of this break. Wickham should not bother Fitzwilliam anymore."

"I am not so sure," Lord Matlock replied speculatively. "But back to the subject of Miss Bennet. Are we sure this entire situation is legitimate? Could it be a way to fraud my nephew?"

"I do not see how. The uncle drew up the marriage settlement, which Fitzwilliam is taking to his solicitor in town today. I am sure if there is anything amiss, they will bring it to his attention."

"Powell will definitely speak up. He is excellent." Henry stood and poured himself a small glass of port. "I was relieved to discover Fitzwilliam took my advice and retained him. I was concerned if there was a break between him and George that having the same solicitor was not a wise decision." He took a sip as he returned to his seat. "There will be no possibility of Fitzwilliam's business affairs being passed to his father this way."

"It was a wise decision," she concurred. "As for Lizzy, I do not see any deception in her. The poor dear was trembling in fear when she arrived last night, but she has slowly been showing some of her personality as she becomes more comfortable. I must say, I have enjoyed her company a great deal thus far. She is proving to be witty and quite intelligent."

Henry was sceptical. "I would wish to spend more time around her. I do not want to see Fitzwilliam ruined by a rash choice. I will have to insist Elinor invite her around for tea."

"Why do you not write Elinor a note and have her join us for dinner? Mrs. Haney has plenty of time to prepare something extra if she feels it is necessary."

"That is a splendid idea, Mamma. I will take care of it as soon as I finish my glass of port."

She rolled her eyes and rose, stepping over to her escritoire. "Do not put yourself out, Henry. I will take care of the matter."

Her son lifted his glass to her. "Excellent! Let us ensure this young lady is what she appears to be."

Glancing up from her letter, she paused. "I truly do not think there is anything to discover. I believe she is *exactly* as she seems."

"I know, but Anne inherited her compassionate heart from you. I simply wish to be certain you are not blinded by the tale of woe that has accompanied her."

She chuckled as she placed her pen back in the ink. "Tale of woe? You are being rather theatrical, do you not think?"

Lord Matlock stared into his glass of port with concern etched across his face. "We shall see, Mamma. We shall see."

1 Erasmus (1466-1536)

2 Shakespeare, As You Like It, Act V, Scene I

Chapter 6

When Elizabeth ventured back downstairs after refreshing herself, she was dressed in her best mourning gown. Hattie had objected, claiming the material was not fine enough for dining with an earl and his wife, but Elizabeth had stood her ground and insisted since she had eschewed her usual attire that morning.

As she approached the drawing room, the door was still closed, so she passed it by and entered the music room, intent on practicing while she had the time.

The pianoforte was by far the finest she had ever seen, and she drew her fingers across the finish as she made her way to where the music was stored. The dowager's collection was extensive, which allowed her to find several pieces she had played previously as well as a few that she wished to try.

She took her spot on the richly upholstered seat and applied her fingers to the keys, playing several pieces, even repeating specific lines or the entire work to master the fingering. She had just managed to make her way through the first stanza of a new sonata, when she was startled from her study.

"You are correct that you would play better if you practiced more, but for your first attempt at playing that piece, you did remarkably well."

She stood and turned, her hand remaining on the side of the instrument. "Thank you, I did not receive a message. I hope you were not waiting on me."

The dowager smiled. "No, we were just finishing and heard the pianoforte. We thought we would come to you instead."

Lord Matlock appeared at his mother's shoulder, accompanied by a woman. She was an attractive lady with auburn hair and green eyes. She was dressed richly, yet she did not have a conceited air. Instead, she was regarding Elizabeth with a warm, curious expression.

"Miss Bennet," said Lord Matlock, as he took a step forward. "I would like to introduce you to my wife, the Right Honourable Countess of Matlock, Elinor Fitzwilliam. Elinor, this is Darcy's betrothed, Miss Elizabeth Bennet."

The two ladies curtsied and Lady Matlock smiled. "I am pleased to make your acquaintance, Miss Bennet. I hope you do not mind that Henry and I are joining you, Darcy, and Mother for dinner."

It was odd how they were essentially asking her if she objected as it was not her home. "Of course not. I am certain Grandmamma is very pleased to have your company this evening." Lord and Lady Matlock's eyebrows rose and they both turned towards the dowager.

"I have already given Lizzy leave to address me thus."

They nodded and Lady Matlock took her arm and followed the dowager and Lord Matlock back to the drawing room. "Henry and I offer our most heartfelt condolences for the passing of your family."

"Thank you, Lady Matlock," she responded, seating herself to one side of the sofa.

"We shall be family soon enough and as mother said earlier, we are a family party. Please call me Aunt Elinor, and you may call my husband Uncle Henry."

She thanked Lady Matlock while she attempted to regain her equanimity. The last four and twenty hours had been quite a jolt to her. Just when she would begin to feel herself, someone new would appear and she felt as if she was beginning once again.

The dowager took a seat beside her and patted her hand. "I am certain Fitzwilliam will return soon. We shall be a very merry party this evening. There is really no other choice in the matter. I do not host bad dinner parties."

She smiled widely. "No party is fun unless seasoned with folly.¹"

"Erasmus?" asked Uncle Henry.

"I believe so, sir. My father read many of his works, but he particularly enjoyed studying characters and the follies of others. He used that quote often."

"Was your father a learned gentleman?" chimed in Aunt Elinor.

"He attended Cambridge but preferred to remain in his study with a good book rather than most activities."

Uncle Henry chuckled. "I believe I would enjoy that occupation as well, if Elinor would allow it." After a loving glance directed at his wife, his insistent gaze returned to Elizabeth. "May I ask what became of your family's estate?"

She blinked at the stinging of her eyes and cleared her throat. "Mr. Isaac Collins, a distant cousin of my father's was next in line to inherit. From what I understand, he appeared at Longbourn two weeks after the accident."

With a furrowed brow, Aunt Elinor tilted her head. "From what you understand, dear?"

"I was gravely injured in the wreckage and was still unaware of the happenings around me. I was not even at Longbourn when he took possession." Elizabeth fiddled with her skirt and shifted in her seat.

Uncle Henry repositioned himself in his chair. "Why were you not at your home?"

"The location where I was injured was closer Lucas Lodge, home of Sir William Lucas. He has been a great friend to our family for years, and his daughter Charlotte and I have always been close. He graciously opened his home to me, and anyone I required, during my illness."

"That was very kind," commented the dowager.

"Yes, Sir William is thought very well of in Meryton."

Their conversation ceased at the sound of the front door and Hobbes, the butler, entering the room. "Pardon me, ma'am, but Mr. Darcy has arrived. He wished me to convey his apologies for his late return. He will be down as soon as he is appropriately attired."

"Thank you, Hobbes."

"Yes, ma'am." He delivered a curt bow and exited the room.

The announcement did not completely quell the slight tremor of her hands, but it did much to diminish its presence. The dowager was friendly and no one had been unpleasant or rude, but another familiar face at the dinner table would be a welcome sight.

"Miss Bennet, may I ask what you know of your uncle here in London?" asked Uncle Henry.

Startling, she turned to look him in the eye. "Pardon me for not saying so earlier, but please call me Lizzy or Elizabeth. You have been gracious enough to allow me the privilege of addressing you informally. You should have the same."

She adjusted her shawl as Uncle Henry nodded. "I am uncertain of what information you would like to know. His name is Edward Gardiner. He once owned a home on Gracechurch Street, but I would imagine he has sold it to pay his debts by now."

Uncle Henry listened without interruption and leaned forward in his seat, propping his elbows on his knees so he could look her in the eye. "To be honest, I was considering hiring someone to locate him and discover his movements. It would be beneficial to ascertain whether he is searching for you or attempting to access your money."

"I am afraid I do not know where he is living at present or what establishments he may frequent."

"What you have given me is a start," he responded. "I will ask Darcy if he may know more."

"He was not always like this." Aunt Elinor and the dowager both appeared intrigued, so she continued. "At one time, he was a wonderful uncle. He brought us trinkets and treats from town, and each of us girls were given a length of fine fabric for a gown each Christmas. Uncle Gardiner, Papa, and I would have our own chess competitions."

A tear fell dampening her cheek, and her trembling hand wiped it away. "He was even betrothed. It has been over two years ago, now. Miss Margaret was a lovely lady. She and her father once travelled to Longbourn with my uncle to meet all of us." She paused in an attempt to compose herself, but she had finish the tale. They had to understand.

"If you will remember, there was an outbreak of typhus two years ago. Miss Margaret became ill and never recovered. My uncle was devastated and has been different ever since. I just had not realised how much he had been altered until recent events brought his nature to light."

She wiped another tear from her face as the dowager placed a comforting arm around her shoulders. "Your family has endured a great deal of loss in such a short time. I find it admirable you have not closed your heart to protect yourself."

"I do not believe I could do that, and my family would not wish it for me. I love and miss them dreadfully, yet I have always tried to think of the past as its remembrance gives me pleasure. I attempt to retain the precious memories of them and not how they left this earth."

The dowager squeezed her hand as Mr. Darcy entered, straightening his topcoat as he strode through the door.

"I apologise for my tardiness, Grandmamma."

Uncle Henry stood and strode forward to shake his hand. "Darcy! I have been making the acquaintance of your betrothed in your absence. We must have the two of you to dinner later this week."

"That would be agreeable," he replied, adjusting his cuffs. He glanced over at Elizabeth and cocked his head a little to one side, studying her expression. "I hope you are well this evening, Miss Bennet."

She nodded and stood as her red-rimmed eyes met his. "I am, thank you, Mr. Darcy."

His grandmother stepped beside her and took her hand. "Lizzy was just satisfying your uncle's curiosity regarding her family."

His uncle raised a hand. "I simply wish to investigate Gardiner. I am concerned he will not disappear from Miss Bennet's life, and instead, will make a nuisance of himself."

"Powell recommended a man who I met with this afternoon." Elizabeth tensed, and he would not countenance upsetting her more. "Although, perhaps we should discuss it after dinner."

Uncle Henry cast a look over at Elizabeth as well, and nodded. "From what Hobbes has told me, you departed early this morning and have been out all day."

As everyone resumed their seats, he found one of his own. "I had a great deal of business to accomplish. I applied for a license with the bishop at St. Paul's Cathedral. Then I dropped in on Mr. Blair at St. George's. He was happy to schedule the ceremony for Friday, a week from today at ten."

"It is fortunate you attend St. George's whilst in town," commented his grandmother. "Mr. Blair knows you well."

He leaned over to take his grandmother's hand. "I could not let you attend church on your own, Grandmamma. It would not be proper for a young lady such as yourself." He smiled, and so did she. She always pinked a bit in the cheeks when he teased her in such a manner, and this time was no different.

"You can be quite the flatterer when you wish, Fitzwilliam."

He caught Elizabeth's warm smile directed at him, and with a lift to the corner of his lips, his attention returned to his uncle. "The bishop's office indicated the license should be ready Wednesday or Thursday."

"And only a few days before you are supposed to present yourself at Rosings," interjected his grandmother. He nodded just as the door opened to Mrs. Henderson announcing dinner.

His uncle escorted his grandmother and his Aunt Elinor while he took up the rear with Miss Bennet. Her small hand took his arm, and every bit of the contact was discernible through his layers of clothing. What was it about this woman that made him so attuned to her every move and emotion? He was drawn to her in a way that was unfamiliar, and to him, disconcerting.

The meal did not help his disquiet. His eyes continually found Miss Bennet, and he discovered himself staring in her direction more often than naught. As everyone rose at the end of the meal, the ladies to the withdrawing room and the men to the study, he hoped his distraction had not been apparent to everyone.

His uncle closed the door behind him while he poured them both a snifter of brandy. "Darcy, I still have my reservations about your betrothed, but she is a lovely woman."

He handed his uncle a glass and took a sip of his own. "Thank you, Uncle."

"You mentioned that you went to see Powell today. Did he review the document you signed with her uncle?"

His uncle meant well, but he did bristle a bit at the question. It was too much like his father for his liking. "I did. He saw nothing to cause concern, and we made arrangements to modify my will and carry out the terms of the contract." Uncle Henry nodded as he ran his finger absent-mindedly around the glass. "He will also move Miss Bennet's money to a new account that will contain the remainder of her settlement."

"I am impressed, Darcy, and thankful you ceased using Graham and Smallshaw last year."

He ran his hand across the back of his collar. "I am, as well. Mr. Graham is very loyal to my father. I would not be easy with him handling my personal affairs at present."

"Will you run an engagement announcement?"

He shook his head. "I considered having one printed so close to the wedding that my father would not see it beforehand, but I think I will simply print the marriage announcement. We will then take a wedding trip to Bath.

"Lizzy appears to be very friendly," Uncle Henry commented, before taking a sip of his drink. "She also seems a bit wary, but one cannot fault her for that with all of the changes in the last four and twenty hours. You will be marrying her in a week. I would think you would want to break down some of those barriers by becoming on more familiar terms."

His eyebrows shot up as though they would reach his hairline. "Exactly what do you mean by 'more familiar terms'?"

Uncle Henry chuckled. "Relax, son. I noticed the two of you are still referring to one another as Miss Bennet and Mr. Darcy whilst we address her as Lizzy, and she addresses us as informally."

"I see things in a different light, I suppose. She is amongst strangers, betrothed to a stranger. I do not wish her to be pressured into an intimacy that she does not feel."

"If you are alluding to as much as I believe, I must stop you there. You must consummate this marriage, Darcy."

He glanced up to find his uncle leaning forward, an imploring expression upon his face.

"Eventually, when we are both more comfortable…"

"No, not eventually," Uncle Henry interrupted. "It may be awkward but you must. There can be no hint that your marriage is not legitimate, or Catherine and your father will pounce. They may not be able to accomplish much with the information, but they would make an attempt."

He squirmed in his seat and averted his eyes back to his glass. How awkward a subject! He had no wish to discuss this with anyone, much less his uncle. "I could never force…"

"I never said anything about forcing your will."

Shocked, his gaze met his uncle's.

"I believe she will be rather practical about the situation. You cannot forget she faces the same possible issue with her relations." His uncle grasped his forearm. "You should spend as much time with her this week as you can. The more familiar you are with each other the less distressing the entire event will be."

"I understand your argument, but please give me some time to think on it. There has to be some way I can give her time to become accustomed to all the changes in her life."

"You will have a great many changes as well."

He was doubtful. All he could see was Elizabeth's sacrifices and her point of view.

"I never said it would be as many as she has—especially with her family's passing—but becoming a husband is acquiring a new way of life. You will need to consider her and her wishes when you make certain decisions, then there will be children. Your life will not be the same either."

His stomach churned, and he set down his brandy. He would have to marry, regardless of who the woman was, but his uncle was correct: he had not considered how much would be different. Uncle Henry's laughter brought him out of his panic as he glanced up to find him placing his hands on his shoulders.

"Take a deep breath, son. You are turning green. You know I like Anne, but she is not the young lady for you. The two of you are both rather quiet people, whilst Lizzy appears more gregarious and cheerful. I believe you need that."

Darcy gulped hard. "I made arrangements to wed her today; however, I cannot but think how I am to marry a stranger in a week."

Uncle Henry chuckled some more. "You will not be the first or last person who marries a stranger. I daresay you will live." He stood and patted the younger man on the back. "With that said, I think we should join the ladies. One of the advantages of a wife is having a lady to spend time with after dinner."

Shaking his head, he stood and followed his uncle. When they reached the hall, the harmonious notes of the pianoforte were coming from the music room, so they followed the sound. His uncle entered straightaway, but Darcy paused in the doorway, enchanted by the sight of Elizabeth Bennet sitting at the pianoforte singing.

Elizabeth stretched as she yawned, still not accustomed to waking in such a luxurious bed. Rolling to her back, she turned to face the sun streaming between the drapes and sighed. What had happened when the men arrived in the music room?

By the end of dinner, the Fitzwilliams were all friendly acquaintances. Aunt Elinor and the dowager had conversed about music and novels, which were two subjects Elizabeth could discuss without much effort. Before long, Aunt Elinor persuaded her to play and sing. The lady must have wished to assess her skill, so she tried her best; even though, her performance had to be lacking.

Mr. Darcy had become the enigma. He had not spoken much during dinner or after his arrival to the music room, yet he stared at her so—and for the entire evening! She had no idea what to make of it!

She lifted herself to sit against the headboard, and Hattie entered a moment later, setting a tea service on the table and pouring a cup.

"Good morning, miss," she said, handing the drink to Elizabeth. "Her ladyship's maid said you would be goin' to Lady Matlock's today. I wasn' sure what gown to press, but Lady Matlock, herself, sent one over this mornin'." She hurried back into the dressing room, returning with a pale peach ensemble very similar to something she would have selected. "I daresay the colour will be very becomin' on you."

"She mentioned sending over one of her daughter's gowns." She placed her teacup on the dressing table, reached for the skirt, and traced her fingers down the folds. "I suppose we should see how it fits. I do not want to be late because of alterations."

"Yes, miss." Hattie hastened to retrieve the necessary undergarments, and returned promptly to help her mistress don the gown.

As it turned out, the bodice only required a few small tucks, which were accomplished while Elizabeth finished her tea, and she was soon headed downstairs to the dining room.

"Lizzy," greeted the dowager, as she entered the room. "You do look lovely this morning."

Mr. Darcy stared with an unusual, surprised expression upon his face. "You are not wearing mourning attire?"

"As you see, Mr. Darcy. I did not wear my grey gown yesterday to the shops either. I only wore it within the house." She held his questioning gaze. "I did heed your counsel, sir."

"Thank you," he responded softly. "I may be being overly cautious, but…"

"I understand your concern. Please do not think I ever took it lightly."

With a nod, the discussion was over, and she turned to find the dowager regarding them with interest. She wore a slight smile, prompting an eyebrow to be raised in her direction. The older woman shook her head and continued to eat as Elizabeth placed some toast on her plate.

Mr. Darcy was just as much as a mystery now as he had been the previous evening. He held the paper before him, but she had caught him staring at her several times over the top corner. His reaction was to return his attention to the paper as if he had only looked up to catch a glimpse while she spoke with his grandmother.

The dowager placed her napkin beside her plate. "Do you have plans for the day, Fitzwilliam?"

He startled and folded the corner of his paper down. "Uncle and I are meeting at the club. After we discuss whatever he has planned, I believe I will pay a visit to Bingley."

His grandmother bit her lip. "I should probably tell you that yesterday I *may* have hinted to Miss Bingley and Mrs. Hurst that you were preparing for your betrothal."

Hinted? Elizabeth stifled a snort. Her statement to Miss Bingley had been exactly that—a statement, not a hint. She almost reminded her of her little sister Lydia confessing to something she had done, but for which she was not really sorry.

His hands did not release the paper as they dropped like a rock to the table and he groaned. "Grandmamma! Please say you did not do that!"

The woman did not look the least bit remorseful, a smirk adorning her face. "I could not resist. She has always been so smug as if she were certain to be the next mistress of Pemberley."

"Yes, well, what she has thought and what exists in the world are not the same. I have never had any intention of offering for her. That is one woman my mother would be appalled to have replace her."

"That she would," the lady agreed with a sharp nod. "If you and your uncle finish your business at the club, you should join us at Matlock house. Lizzy is going to receive callers with us."

She forced smile as he turned to her, perusing her as if in study. Did he not want her receiving calls?

"I suppose I will be thrust upon the Ton unless you do not wish it."

The servant removed the plate from in front of the dowager, and she shifted forward, her expression very serious. "Lizzy, Catherine will spew venom upon your reputation and intelligence when she learns of your marriage to Fitzwilliam. It is important that you are at least introduced to a few select people first. I also intend to take you with me on calls early next week. Some of these women are notorious gossips and will be thrilled to have first-hand knowledge of your character.

"You are also being accepted into Lady Matlock's house for the day. That will not go unnoticed. The association will help to dispel the vitriol that is spread."

Elizabeth's stomach began to churn. "Why is she so determined to have matters as she arranges?" All of the character assassination and rumour mongering was not to her liking at all!

The dowager sat back in her seat and sighed heavily. "Catherine has always been difficult. She was eight when I married her father, and already a spoilt and unruly child. Her mother, who had passed almost two years prior, had indulged her. She also resented me for replacing her mother, not that I ever tried to fill that role with her. I did try to befriend her, but Catherine was adamant she would never accept me."

The older woman's eyes glazed as if she could see her memories before her eyes. "My husband married his first wife according to his family's wishes. It was by no means a love match. He had hoped they could at least be friends, but Lady Charlotte despised him, and reared Catherine to be a younger version of herself. Poor Gerald had been miserable married to that woman and was broken hearted to see his daughter emulate her to such a degree."

"Did he ever attempt to reverse the damage?"

"Yes, he tried to spend time with her, taking her on picnics and horseback riding, but he was always disheartened by the time they returned. When she came out into society, she set her cap on the wealthiest of the ton, but she was obvious in her machinations and many of the mothers did not like her.

"After she had been out almost four years, Sir Lewis de Bourgh approached Gerald as a prospective spouse for Catherine. His family required a portion of her dowry to save Rosings. The estate had had several years of poor crop yields, and it had threatened their solvency." She snapped from her reverie and turned to Elizabeth. "Gerald arranged the marriage and Catherine never forgave him."

"At least Sir Lewis managed to bring Rosings back before he died," interjected Mr. Darcy. "And Lady Catherine's steward is competent. He manages to maintain Rosings despite Lady Catherine's arguments when money is required for tenant issues or repairs."

The dowager gave a small snort. "She only notices that when it takes away from her plans within the house."

"But why would she be so adamant that her daughter marry Mr. Darcy?"

"Do you not see, dear?" she asked gently. "Fitzwilliam has an estate left to him by his uncle, where he is already master. In addition, he is the sole heir to Pemberley, which is a larger, grander estate than Rosings, and he would gain Rosings by marrying Anne. The amount of wealth he would possess would rank him rather high amongst the Ton in regards to income. His wealth could also garner him the attention that could gain him a title as well."

She looked over to find Mr. Darcy perfectly still, but appearing as if he would rather be squirming in his seat. She took pity on him.

"Grandmamma, I thought Aunt Elinor requested us to arrive just after nine."

The dowager turned towards the clock and rose. "I honestly do not understand why. No civilized person will call before eleven. Fitzwilliam, remember to join us if your business with Henry is concluded in time."

Biting her lip, Elizabeth followed while she glanced back at Mr. Darcy. He was exhaling a deep breath and rising from the table himself. Their eyes caught and he gave her a half-hearted smile with a nod, which she reciprocated with a small wave just as she disappeared out the door.

Elizabeth might not have alerted the dowager to the time had she known why Aunt Elinor had wished them to arrive so early. Upon their arrival, Aunt Elinor pulled out the last weeks' worth of newspapers and insisted they review all of the gossip columns. Elizabeth would have preferred to pull out her fingernails one by one than listen to the rubbish she was being exhorted to learn, but remained polite as she attended—well, she could not help but roll her eyes from time to time.

"Darcy is not disposed towards a fondness for society, but the two of you cannot make a habit of shunning the Ton," lectured Aunt Elinor. "And just because you are aware of the latest rumours does not mean you must disperse them as much of our sex will do."

She nodded as she listened to all of it, but it made her discomfited. How much of this drivel could really be true, all of these people denoted by initials and supposed exploits? Married men and the women on their arms at the theatre—was she their wife or their new mistress? Young men and their supposed liaisons with certain daughters of peers. Who was seen where. The amount of balderdash was astounding! Did people have nothing better to do with their lives?

The time before calls seemed to plod on and on, but it did end, and she was now seated with The Dowager Countess of Matlock, Lady Matlock, and her daughter, Lady Grace. Together, they faced their guests, Lady Winifred Burke, Countess of Bletchley and her mother, Lady Eudora Burke, The Dowager.

"I was at the theatre, you know," Lady Bletchley tattled proudly as her mother tittered. "She was always so smug when she married Lord Harrington, but I suppose she has had her comeuppance."

The dowager leaned in with her eyebrows raised. "You were at the theatre last night?"

Lady Bletchley appeared bewildered but answered regardless. "Yes, we have a box and attend on a regular basis."

"I wondered how you found the performance."

Elizabeth bit her cheek to prevent herself from laughing at Lady Bletchley's continued bafflement, as well as the Dowager Countess of Matlock's questions.

"Oh," exclaimed Lady Bletchley. "To tell the truth, I did not watch much of the performance."

Aunt Elinor clasped her hands in her lap. "Such a pity! I had heard this production of *A Midsummer Night's Dream* was not to be missed."

"Had you?" Lady Bletchley's wide-eyed surprise and confusion was tempered by her mother, who leaned forward in her seat.

"My daughter enjoys Mrs. Radcliffe as opposed to Shakespeare," her mother clarified. "I must admit, I did not watch much of the play either. Donkey heads and fairies do not appeal to me in a story. I would much prefer if they did away with that load of tripe."

"If we shadows have offended,
Know but this and all is mended.
That you have but slumbered here,
While these visions did appear,
And this weak and idle theme,
No more yielding, but a dream.[1]"

Elizabeth recited the lines with confidence, which prompted the dowager to smile before she turned her attention to the elder Lady Bletchley.

"Miss Bennet brings up an excellent line. Shakespeare himself gave the viewer a way to dismiss the entire happenings of the play as a dream if they wished. Tis a shame you do not enjoy the work."

With a smug grin, Lady Grace dipped her head a notch in Elizabeth's direction. "I find there are few writers I prefer more."

Lady Bletchley glanced over at the mantel as she brushed off her skirt. "I believe it is time for us to take our leave. We hope to call on Lady Wheaton before it is too late."

Aunt Elinor stood with her guests and stepped to the side to pull the bell. "Ah, please give Lady Wheaton our best. I do so enjoy her company."

Lady Bletchley and her mother departed, and those remaining at Matlock house released a deep breath.

"Lord, what fools these mortals be[2]!" muttered Elizabeth, breaking the silence.

Lady Grace sputtered and laughed while her mother turned a surprised eye.

"Lizzy, for shame!" Aunt Elinor's face was scolding, but she was unable to hold the expression, and broke down into chuckles of her own.

"Are you going to admonish me as well, Grandmamma?"

The dowager grinned. "No, dear I will not. As it pertains to those two, I believe you have made an accurate assessment of their characters."

"I find it difficult to believe that Lord Bletchley married a woman as witless as his mother." Aunt Elinor was shaking her head. "Perhaps so she would not have the intelligence to discover when he visits his mistress?"

"Does he really?" Elizabeth's eyes bulged in surprise.

"You will find it is quite common, Lizzy," said the dowager.

By now, she had questioned her decision to marry Mr. Darcy dozens of times, and once again, began to doubt herself.

"You do know you should not have anything to worry about in regards to my cousin's integrity?"

She started at Lady Grace's voice, and their eyes met. She had warmed to Lady Grace almost the instant they were introduced: she had such a happy disposition and witty sense of humour.

"He has always been the most loyal of cousins. This betrayal of his father's wishes is really quite the aberration."

Her grandmother shook her head. "Not when you consider he is following the wishes of his mother, Grace. He was always closer to Anne than George."

One side of Aunt Elinor's lips quirked up. "She drew him out of his quiet nature, much in the way she did her husband."

His grandmother then focused on Elizabeth. "I should think you will have much the same influence on Fitzwilliam." She smiled and tilted her head to the side a bit as though she were studying her. "From what he has said of your first meeting, he had to have been more talkative than is his wont. I am certain you will be beneficial for him."

Her cheeks warmed as the ladies smiled at her. It would be a relief if she could prove to be a good wife. If only she could forget she was about to wed a stranger.

Lord Matlock remained once Darcy left the club. They had met with the investigator Darcy had hired the previous day, learning the man had not unearthed anything other than what they already knew, so Darcy had departed in the hopes of catching his friend Bingley while his sisters were either out making calls or receiving calls of their own.

He chuckled to himself at his nephew's plotting. He could not blame him for wanting to avoid that Bingley woman, and since he was not yet a "gentleman" Bingley could not join White's, which meant Darcy was forced to brave Miss Bingley.

Surveying the room, he determined he was not yet desirous to venture home. Entertaining callers was not a preferred activity, and most days, he tried to hide in his study while the women took care of their business. The last thing Henry Fitzwilliam wished was to make small talk if he happened to encounter those women as they were leaving.

Cards were a pastime he did not indulge in, except upon rare occasions, but today, the game was preferable to venturing home for the next few hours. He rose and made his way through the dark masculine-decorated rooms to the gaming den. Serious gambling was not available before evening, but a few friendly games could sometimes be found during the day.

His attention was soon drawn to a back corner where two men he knew, Mr. Reginald Grey and Viscount Hayes, were playing cards with a man unfamiliar to him. He approached the table, waiting for the hand to come to completion before interrupting.

"Grey, Hayes, may I join your game?" The two men grinned at him, and Grey pushed out a chair with his foot.

He took the seat, and while Hayes shuffled, he shifted to observe the stranger of the group. "And may I be introduced to the fourth person at our table?"

Grey sat forward. "Lord Henry Fitzwilliam, Earl of Matlock, this is Sir William Lucas, of Meryton, in Hertfordshire."

Since he recognised the name, he examined the man with interest. "Hertfordshire, you say?"

"Why yes." Sir William was jovial as he spoke. "Are you familiar with Meryton?"

"I have heard of it." He watched the cards as they hit the table, triumphant even before he had begun to play: providence had smiled upon him. "We passed through there, I would say seven or eight months ago, and saw the remains of a terrible carriage accident—appeared to have slid off the edge and down a ravine."

A grave expression came over Sir William's face. "I wish we had been able to pull the wreckage out sooner," he lamented. "There had been too much rain and the ground was much too wet for my team to gain enough traction. It was a horrid, horrid tragedy, sir."

"Oh?" His act needed to appear genuine, even though he lacked the skill to take the stage at Covent Garden.

"Yes, dreadful. One of our most prominent families was in that carriage—only one of their five daughters survived.

"That is most tragic!" He did respond in earnest. The plight of Elizabeth's family was indeed everything dreadful.

His mind then turned to his next question. Sir William Lucas did not hesitate to speak, and at that moment, Henry Fitzwilliam had no issues prompting him to keep speaking. A great deal could be learned from this gentleman, and he would not depart until he was certain he had learned it all.

1. *Shakespeare, A Midsummer Night's Dream, Act V, Scene II & Act III, Scene II*

Chapter 7

Sunday morning, all of the Fitzwilliams, Mr. Darcy, and Elizabeth attended St. George's for services before they spent the afternoon at Matlock house. Elizabeth made the acquaintance of Arthur Fitzwilliam, Viscount Huntley, the eldest son of Uncle Henry and Aunt Elinor. A tall gentleman with sandy brown hair and blue eyes, he appeared a much younger version of his father and had much the same sense of humour as well.

How the beginning of the week had flown by! The dowager countess kept her busy making and receiving calls, appearing for another fitting for her gowns, and receiving the ensemble she would wear for the wedding. She was now embroidering her wedding gown in every moment of spare time she possessed, and when she was not attending dinners at either Ashcroft or Matlock House.

Elizabeth was also becoming more comfortable amongst the members of what would be her new family—with the exception of Mr. Darcy. That gentleman, who had spoken without difficulty in her Uncle Philips' drawing room had been replaced with a quiet observer. He watched her, offered her his arm when necessary, and joined a bit in the conversation around them, but it appeared he no longer retained the ability to converse with only her.

A serious concern was that Mr. Darcy no longer displayed any intention of them becoming more than acquaintances, and that they would live as polite strangers. It was disconcerting, yet confronting him on the matter was not an option. They were always together in company or in the same room as a servant, situations not conducive to a private conversation.

"Grandmamma," called Mr. Darcy, as he entered the drawing room. "I am to see Bingley this morning. He sent a message to inform me his sisters would be out of the house. After that, I will meet my uncle around one at White's."

Elizabeth glanced up from her embroidery frame in response to the sensation of being watched. Mr. Darcy shifted his gaze to his grandmother, who set down the book she was reading. She looked to Elizabeth, who had resumed her work because it could not appear as though his leaving frustrated her.

"Have you been to the bishop about the license?" Her tone was casual, yet there was a glint in her eye that gave an impression of displeasure.

"At the earliest, it was supposed to be ready Wednesday."

"Which is today, Fitzwilliam." Her voice held a hint of censure in its tone. "I do not think it wise to be left to the morrow, if it is ready."

He clenched his jaw, but did not argue as one might expect. "Very well, I will stop at St. Paul's."

Bristling, Elizabeth continued her needlework in an attempt to again hide her frustration. Instead, she made a concerted effort to concentrate on the repetitive movements of the tambour stitches in order to ignore the conversation before her.

"I think the two of us must have a conversation this evening," continued the dowager.

"I cannot think why."

She peered up as he tugged his sleeves and adjusted his expression to be more neutral than it had appeared just a moment prior.

"That is exactly why."

Elizabeth's exasperation overwhelmed her, and she bit her lip in an attempt to prevent an angry tirade. He gave a farewell and brief nod to them both and strode through the door.

She set down her needle as her hands began to shake. Tears began to well in her eyes, so she leapt up and rushed towards the door. "Please excuse me. I shall return soon."

The sound of her name could be heard from the drawing room upon her exit, so she picked up her pace, almost running up the stairs to her chambers, breaking down once she was safely within the room and out of sight.

Her wedding was to take place in two days, and she knew him no better today than she did almost a week ago. The thought frightened her, but at this point, she was too involved in his family to simply ask for her and Hattie to be taken to the docks to board a ship—and that plan certainly had its drawbacks!

The mattress sank under her weight, as she laid upon it, allowing her tears to flow freely. Her emotions required purging or she would not have the willpower to continue holding them inside while in company. After almost five minutes spent crying into the counterpane, she resolved to no longer wallow in self-pity, rose to a seated position, and was drying her face when a soft knock startled her.

"Lizzy," called the dowager through the door. "May I come in, please?"

"I will return in a few moments, Grandmamma."

"Elizabeth Bennet!"

Her lip quirked up to one side at the use of her name. Her father did much the same when he was alive.

"It was obvious you were holding off tears when you left the drawing room. You will not be the first person I have seen cry, nor I daresay the last. Now, open this door at once."

With a sigh, Elizabeth crossed the room and pulled the knob.

"Oh dear," she said upon seeing Elizabeth's face. "I know he can be frustrating when he closes himself off, but it is never permanent."

The older lady placed an arm around Elizabeth's shoulders in a one-armed embrace, leading her to a sofa near the fireplace where they both took a seat.

"Mr. Darcy spoke to me the day we met, and in the carriage during the trip to London. He indicated his behaviour at my Uncle Philips' was not typical, but I never dreamed he would be so aloof."

The dowager took Elizabeth's hands. "I am going to be dreadfully forthright. I hope it does not offend."

"I would much prefer honesty than the alternative." She spoke matter-of-factly, drawing back her shoulders.

"Both of you jumped into this solution without having the time or courtship expected with any engagement. *You* have handled all of the new people and situations with aplomb."

With a heavy exhale, Elizabeth gave a rueful chuckle. "If you only knew how anxious I was at the beginning."

The dowager brushed a curl from Elizabeth's face. "Since I have spent more time with you, I am aware of how uncomfortable you were that first day or two, but you made a concerted effort to do what was necessary. I am remarkably proud of you."

She nodded and embraced the older lady. "Thank you. I would not have been able to manage this week were it not for you."

The dowager drew back and gave a lop-sided grin. "Having known Fitzwilliam since he was born, I can say with certainty that he is having a colossal case of nerves."

She raised an eyebrow. Could that truly be his problem? The theory was plausible; she suffered the same doubts and fears, yet she had no choice. She had to trust him.

"The boy proposed on a whim."

"We would never have expected him…"

"Oh, I know dear, but once he blurted his proposal, he would never have rescinded the offer. There is so much that happens in that head of his, he gives no thought to how his behaviour affects you."

"He keeps staring at me, Grandmamma," she whispered. "Every time I happen to glance his way, he is observing me… as if he looks to find fault. I keep expecting to find gravy on my lip or a third eye on my forehead."

His grandmother giggled and relaxed against the back of the seat. "I believe that is the one normal thing he has done since bringing you here."

"Pardon?"

"He is just like his father. When George Darcy met my Anne, he could not remove his eyes from her, just as his son cannot remove his from you." Elizabeth's eyes widened and the dowager laughed some more. "Dear, he is attracted to you! That is a good thing."

"I do not know him! How can I…?"

His grandmother reached up to cradle her chin. "Take a deep breath, Lizzy. Neither of you can afford the speculation that would come from not consummating your marriage. At the very least, the two of you should share a bedchamber."

Elizabeth's mouth gaped. She could not be serious!

"It is by far the best solution. The rumours that would arise amongst the staff would quell any suggestions of your marriage not being a real one." The dowager stood, and deftly changed the subject. "We should return to the drawing room in the event someone decides to call. You can continue your work on your gown. It is coming along beautifully."

"Thank you, although, I am not certain what more I can add."

"I think it will be lovely with the one large spray of flowers on the bottom of the skirt. You can always continue to add to it, if you wish."

"I believe I will. I considered adding some small flowers around the neckline and at the base of the sleeves."

"A smaller bouquet to each side of the one you have almost completed would be nice as well."

Elizabeth allowed the dowager to lead her back to the drawing room while she resolved to give more thought to the lady's advice regarding her betrothed, yet she would not have a free minute to do so until it was time to retire. If she was lucky, Mr. Darcy would begin conversing with her before then. That development would certainly make things easier!

Darcy surveyed the room, finding his uncle seated in a far corner with a paper held loosely in his hands. He appeared to be staring at the words before him, oblivious to the goings on—until Darcy took the seat across from him and pulled the paper down.

"Hello, uncle."

Henry Fitzwilliam startled and set down his paper. "You gave me a fright, boy."

"What was so interesting?"

"I was not actually reading." He folded the paper and turned his attention to his nephew. "I became lost in thought."

Concern crossed his features. "There is nothing amiss, is there?"

"No, nothing out of the ordinary." Uncle Henry glanced around him, and he followed suit, curious at his uncle's worry of being overheard. When he appeared satisfied, he tilted forward with his forearms on the table. "I met someone interesting in here Saturday after you departed."

Furrowing his brows, Darcy situated himself to the side of the plush chair with his elbow on the armrest. "I can think of very few people of importance with whom you are not acquainted."

"I would not say this gentleman was of significance to anyone but you, me, and your betrothed."

His eyes widened and he leaned forward. "Exactly whom did you meet, uncle?"

"Relax, son. I had no desire to return home and run the gauntlet of the entrance hall with the ladies coming to call, so I ventured into the card rooms. Astley and Grey were playing with a gentleman unknown to me, and I joined their game, only to discover the stranger was Sir William Lucas of Meryton in Hertfordshire."

The information took a moment to register, but when it did, Darcy ran a shaky hand across his mouth and swallowed hard. "Did you indicate that you knew Miss Bennet or her location?"

"No, I daresay I am a tad brighter than you think." His uncle's tone was sarcastic, which conveyed his affront. "What kind of dullard do you take me for?"

"I did not mean it in such a manner."

"Yes, you did, Darcy." His uncle sat back from the table and glared. "You know I had doubts I felt compelled to dispel."

"You have always been so polite to her. I assumed you had decided to accept her story as we explained it."

Henry Fitzwilliam chuckled, shook his head, and laughed. "I would not cause a rift between us over doubts. I had hoped that investigator of yours would have turned up more on her uncle by now, but the man must have an exceptional place to hide. Her neighbour's appearance did give me the opportunity to confirm her story."

"And how did you accomplish your task without him discovering your acquaintance with her?" His gut churned and his morning coffee rose from his stomach to burn his throat. It was a mere two days before his wedding. Their plans could not unravel now!

"I told him I happened to pass through Meryton and saw the wreckage. The man is loquacious, to say the least. Once I had him talking, the conversation was easy to maintain. A question here or a comment there, and he went on for two hours, until he mentioned how Miss Bennet and her remaining family disappeared the night of the last town assembly."

Darcy sank back into his seat. "He never questioned why you brought up the subject at all?"

"Sir William seems a good man, yet not the most intelligent. Mr. Philips whisking his family away to Lyme on holiday has put him in mind to do something similar."

His eyebrows rose and his uncle chuckled. "Only, he does not wish to travel so far. He is considering Ramsgate or Brighton. Do you not see? He would not wish to make that distance, yet he believes Mr. Philips did."

"You mentioned that he told you they disappeared?"

"Oh, that? He found it unusual they would depart that particular afternoon. Mrs. Philips had told his wife they would attend the assembly, so Sir William believes Mr. Philips owes someone money, and that he is hiding from the debt."

Giving a snort, Darcy's heart began to stop its incessant pounding. His uncle had returned the fright when he had mentioned the interview. Thank goodness this Sir William proved to be somewhat of a simpleton!

"So, now you believe Miss Bennet?"

"Yes, whole-heartedly. Her entire story from prior to your overhearing the uncles in the pub is legitimate." Uncle Henry reached forward and held out his hand to his nephew. "I congratulate you on your betrothal to her. I believe she will be the making of you."

He took his uncle's hand and they shook. "I am unsure if I appreciate the sentiment. I am not a miserable failure."

His uncle guffawed, drawing a look from one or two curious men on the other side of the parlour. "No, you are not, but she will have an influence on you. Do you think I am the same person now as I was before I wed Elinor? I would say I am an improved version."

"But would she agree?" Darcy asked with a wide smile.

"I doubt it." His uncle sighed and shook his head. "She would probably say I still require a great deal of work."

Dinner that evening was a quiet one. Lord and Lady Matlock and their family attended a dinner party, and the dowager, Darcy, and Miss Bennet remained. As usual, Darcy kept catching himself as he stared at Miss Bennet, but this time he was puzzled. Some aspect of her was different.

She was attired in the same grey and black mourning gown she had worn several days ago. Her abigail had been trying different ways of styling her hair, but tonight's coiffure had been worn before, so that was not it. He racked his brain, but he could not put his finger on what was out of the ordinary! She was even seated in the same blasted chair!

His grandmother carried the discussion during dinner. She described their day: the ladies who came to call and the gown delivery from Madame Lebrun. He had no interest in much of her conversation, but pretended to listen politely. Ladies' pursuits and gossip were not the most interesting of topics, yet she was prattling on throughout the entirety of the meal. It was not to be borne!

By the time they arrived in the withdrawing room, his grandmother had him quite vexed. Feigning a headache was an attractive option, but she could follow him to his room and continue her inane prattle until he fell asleep.

Miss Bennet must have found the evening as dull, because she offered to entertain them on the pianoforte, prompting him to all but fly from his seat to offer to turn the pages.

Yet, it would have appeared ridiculous to attempt to stare at Miss Bennet while seated beside her, so instead, he admired her slender, graceful fingers as they moved across the keys. She played, but did not sing. As he continued his occupation—if one could call it that—he found he would enjoy hearing her sing. Her voice was lovely, and he missed the sound accompanying her playing.

He paused to consider the entire evening. *That* was what was different! Miss Bennet had been quiet—not just quiet, but silent for a great deal of the time. She provided a few brief answers to his grandmother, but had not contributed to the conversations during dinner or even the short time they were together before the meal.

But why? Had he offended her in some way? Was she missing her family? His agitation grew as he speculated on the myriad of reasons she could be out of sorts. His grandmother's eyes shifted from Miss Bennet to him, which brought on a shift in her countenance as well. She had been content to enjoy Miss Bennet's playing, yet her jaw clenched when her eyes met his.

Darcy returned his attention to the music and turned the page so Miss Bennet could finish the piece. He should speak to her, try to understand her silence, before he escorted her back to her chair, but the moment she finished the last note, she stood and faced his grandmother.

"Grandmamma, unless you have need of me, I wish to retire."

"Of course, dear. I know this has been an exhausting week."

Miss Bennet nodded and stepped forward from the seat. He would need to act now if he wanted a private word, so he offered her his arm, intending to use the walk to her rooms to discover what was amiss.

In an odd move, she peered down at his arm and back up to his face. "You wish to escort me to my rooms?"

"If you do not object."

Elizabeth raised her eyebrows. "Do you plan to retire now, too?"

Why did it matter? He almost grumbled out loud. "No, but..."

"Then do not leave on my account. I can find my way to my rooms admirably. Thank you."

A slight snort came from his grandmother's direction, and his face burned at having her witness his betrothed's rejection. He was not just mortified either—he was angry. Elizabeth turned and took a step towards the door. In turn, Darcy followed and placed a hand on her elbow, halting her progress.

He kept his voice low. "I thought we could speak."

"There would not be adequate time since it is not a long distance to my rooms—very little could be discussed much less solved. Also, I am also not equal to a conversation at the moment. Please forgive me." With that, she pulled away and departed from the room.

Darcy stared at the closed door before him. Disbelief, anger, and frustration warred for dominance within him—disbelief that she had rebuffed him in that fashion, anger for the insult he perceived from her words and dismissal, and frustration for not knowing how he could fix the issue. His hand reached out to tear open the door in front of him, when a knowing voice called him back and made him pause.

"I would imagine you are enjoying her dismissal as much as she has enjoyed yours over the past week."

He turned to regard her incredulously. "Pardon me?"

"I love you, Fitzwilliam, but you can be just as thick-headed as your father at times."

His jaw clenched and his hands tensed into tight fists on their own accord. "I am not my father."

She rose to face him and shook her head. "No, you are not, but you do remind me of him from time to time. *Now* is one of those instances."

In his anger, he looked away, but she moved so she remained within his line of vision.

"Lizzy has done everything asked of her, has made every effort to become a part of our family—*your family*—yet you have not bothered to extend the same courtesy to her."

"I do not understand your meaning, Grandmamma. I met her Uncle Philips, and for reasons I should not have to enumerate, I have no wish to further my acquaintance with her Uncle Gardiner."

She exhaled heavily. "That was not what I meant."

"Then explain yourself, because I am in no humour to…"

Her hand raised with her index finger pointed in his direction. "You watch your tone with me, young man. I will brook no disrespect from you. Do you understand?"

He gave a curt nod, but started when her arm flew out to point in the direction of Miss Bennet's chambers. "That child has virtually no family left. Once you marry, *you* will be her family. *You* will be her constant companion and the one person she must rely on." She gave a rueful chuckle. "By the law, you will *own* her, and yet you are a stranger."

"I know her no more than she knows me!"

"By your own choice!" Her finger whipped back around in his direction, and he fisted his hands tighter, resisting the urge to push her hand back down to her side.

"Because of the circumstances! A betrothal to a marriage within a week does not give time for a proper courtship!"

"No, it does not, but it does not mean that you should abandon the attempt. She has attended every dinner and been present in the withdrawing room every evening. You could have taken a seat beside her and spoken of anything. Goodness knows, I tried to introduce topics during dinner so you could ask Lizzy more about them, but you did no more than sit there and stare at the poor girl."

"Poor girl? Why do you say that?" he retorted. "Even if I am disinherited from Pemberley, she will still marry far and above what she would have before."

"Do you believe that arrogant nonsense you proclaim? You sound more like George Darcy than Fitzwilliam! I am ashamed of you."

"Why? I am not ashamed of the feelings I related. They were natural and just. Could you expect me to rejoice in the inferiority of her connections? –to congratulate myself on the hope of relations, whose condition in life is so decidedly beneath my own?"

"I meant nothing of her status or connections; I meant that she has no idea what to make of you! I also doubt your conceit and selfish disdain for her origins are the true obstacle. They are no more than an excuse to hide your true feelings." His grandmother shook her head. "You must have been rather personable when you met, or I doubt she would have accepted your proposal. Your subsequent behaviour has left her to wonder to whom she is truly betrothed: the gentleman who rescued her from Meryton, or this silent haughty man who has replaced him.

"Have you considered what it must be like for her? How she must feel?" She paused, and when he did not answer she rolled her eyes. "In less than two days, she will stand before God and commit herself to you. She will be subject to any whim you may have."

"I would never harm her!"

"I never claimed you would, but you must try to see things from her point of view! You have made no effort whatsoever to further your acquaintance with her this past week! In all likelihood, she is wondering whether or not you will continue to ignore her once you are wed—whether you will only find time for her when you wish to relieve your needs or try for an heir, and as soon as you have accomplished your task, leave her to her own devices once more."

His blood boiled. "What kind of person does she believe me to be— do you believe me to be? I offered her rescue from a situation that would be more like what you describe. I would never demean anyone, much less my wife in such a way!"

"But you have! You have dismissed her at every turn by your refusal to engage in the simplest of conversations! Is she to believe you will change for no other reason than the two of you becoming married? Because a ceremony occurs?"

"This is absurd!" He spun around and strode towards the door.

She grabbed his arm, halting his movement.

In a low voice that bespoke of her ire, she said, "I sat with that young lady whilst she cried this afternoon. She is confused, wondering who you are, and scared. You need to cease thinking of yourself and put yourself in her position. You must speak with her in the morning."

"I have business meetings on the morrow." He avoided her eyes and feigned interest in a book laying on the side table. He was not lying. He was supposed to meet with Bingley, but one could hardly call that business.

"Very well." His grandmother released his elbow and took a step back. "Then whilst you are taking care of that *business*, you can go to St. George and cancel with Mr. Blair for Friday."

His eyes met hers and he could see a steely determination rather than her usual humour. She would not sway from whatever plan she had concocted in her head. "Why would I cancel with Mr. Blair?"

"Because I will contact your uncle in the morning. I believe he still owns a small estate in Ireland. I will accompany Lizzy there to ensure she is well and happy. She has suffered enough misfortunes without counting a marriage to you amongst them."

His heart dropped and his eyes widened. Never had he dreamed his grandmother would take Miss Bennet's part over his. Never had he thought she would leave him vulnerable to the plans of his father.

"You would have me marry Anne..."

"No, Henry could handle your father, and I do not think Anne would mind being publically jilted. She would likely find humour in the experience."

"I... I... " He stammered. "You would take Miss Bennet's part?"

His grandmother stepped forward and held his face between her hands. "No, Fitzwilliam, I would do this for both of you."

He furrowed his brow at her sorrowful demeanour.

"If you do not care enough to make her at ease, then she is not the young lady you should wed. Your marriage would be a miserable one for both of you, and that would break my heart."

He placed his hands over his grandmother's, eased them off his face, and held them clasped within his own for a few minutes, while he attempted to the find words for what was in his heart. In the end, he could only kiss her on the cheek before walking out the door.

Chapter 8

Darcy departed the withdrawing room and headed straight for his chambers. He slammed the door behind him and paced back and forth in front of the fire.

"I am *not* arrogant or conceited!" He made a particularly sharp pivot. "I cannot believe Grandmamma…" he began again, before his rant was interrupted by his valet.

James stood in a timid fashion just inside the dressing room door. "Pardon me, sir, but I presumed you might require assistance changing for the evening."

He cast a quick look at his evening attire. "Yes, of course."

As he disrobed, no care was taken, no attention paid to how the articles landed once they were shed. His topcoat and waistcoat were thrown on the bed, and Darcy yanked and pulled at his cravat, but the confounded thing would not yield in the slightest.

"Blast!"

"If you will allow me." His valet's voice came from behind him.

He took a deep breath and exhaled while his man worked at the knots he had tightened in his frustration, and soon enough, was freed from the constricting cloth. He rubbed his sore neck for a minute before he pulled roughly on the closure of his shirt. James stood to the side, nervous and out of sorts.

When he handed off the last of his clothing, James gave a quick bow. "If you require any further assistance this evening…"

"You may retire; I can fend for myself."

"Very good, sir." The valet then strode out of the door.

Darcy stared in the direction of the dressing room. His valet's brevity was strange, and had to indicate there was talk below stairs.

He could call James back to report on what was being said. No, that would not do. His grandmother had a very loyal house staff, and without a doubt, they would side with her. The last thing he could stand to hear was that he was incorrect.

He continued to pace, but with a freshly poured glass of brandy. He had been wronged. Not so much by Miss Bennet, although, if she had had a problem, she could have let him know. He had no idea what was in her mind, after all!

His grandmother's words kept echoing through his head.

"You have dismissed her at every turn by your refusal to engage in the simplest of conversations!"

"You sound more like George Darcy than Fitzwilliam! I am ashamed of you."

"Your subsequent behaviour has left her to wonder to whom she is truly betrothed: the gentleman who rescued her from Meryton, or this silent haughty man who has replaced him."

He took a long drink from his glass and squeezed his eyes shut as if it could stop the voice in his head.

"I am nothing like my father." He dropped into a chair facing the fire and stared straight ahead past the flames as if entranced. He remained thus, engrossed in thought, for several hours. His mind whirred, the brandy left forgotten.

Every encounter he had with Miss Bennet was dissected and analysed and then analysed again. At one point, he leaned forward and attempted to remember the conversations instigated by him since their arrival in London. There must be... but he could not think of a single one. Sure, he had been witness to many instances where she had spoken and laughed, but those had all been due to questions or discussions begun by his family.

With this, he conceded he had not made any effort to get to know Elizabeth. The revelation resulted in further questions. Why? He had been in company with her every evening, and sometimes in the morning, for the last week. His eyes found her often enough. Could he be avoiding her?

Something inside him screamed he had indeed found the answer. Avoiding her kept her distant, reason enough to change their fate; yet, he had been deeply unsettled when his grandmother announced they would not wed. He groaned aloud, set his glass on the side table, and rubbed his hands up and down his face.

All week, planned meetings kept him away, and if not, other reasons were found to avoid the house during the day, but the evenings were unavoidable. Elizabeth was always there, her eyes sparkling as she spent a pleasurable evening with his family.

Had he not figured it out the day before, the reason for staring at her so?

It was her eyes. They were wide, doe-shaped and brown, which was not necessarily eye-catching, so to speak, at a glimpse. But when one took one's time and observed Elizabeth, they were striking. She had the most brilliant, expressive eyes—full of life, full of laughter. One could not help but stare into them, attempting to discern the mischief that lay in their depths.

Sighing, he dropped his head against the back of the chair.

Elizabeth.

He had never allowed himself to think of her so familiarly, and she had never attempted to become on more familiar terms with him, so he had let things be.

He rested his elbows on his knees as he stared into the fire. Had he attempted to erect a barrier for himself? His mother on her deathbed begged him to marry for love, but what good had it done for his father or even his Grandmamma, who after all these years still mourned her husband? She was devastated upon his death, not as altered as his father, but he caught her from time to time in front of his grandfather's portrait, usually shedding a tear or sometimes quietly weeping.

Despite that barrier, Elizabeth still continued to garner his attention without even trying. A part of him worried about becoming too close to her, a rather absurd thought when one considered it, yet what if she never felt more than appreciation for him?

An unequal alliance was another legitimate fear. What if he fell in love with her, but she was never able to return his affection to the same depth of regard? That could be a miserable existence, too.

"Blast!" He lifted his head and downed the last remaining dregs of his brandy.

At that moment, a light knock drew his attention. Who would still be awake at this hour? He strode to the door where his grandmother stood just outside in her nightclothes.

"I was passing and heard you swear." Her voice was soft so as not to disturb anyone nearby.

"I apologise if I offended you."

"It would take more than a silly word like that to offend me."

He gave a small snort in amusement.

"Would you care to speak of it?"

Darcy moved aside, allowing her to pass, and she took a seat on the sofa. He returned to his chair, but sprang back up almost immediately. "I was partaking of some brandy. Would you care for some?"

"Yes, I think I would. Thank you."

Once they were both situated with their glasses, she turned to the side and drew her legs up under her gown. "I assume you are worried over having to marry Anne or whether your uncle can handle your father."

He furrowed his brow and shook his head. "No, I was thinking of Miss Bennet... Elizabeth." Her eyebrows rose as she took a sip of her drink. "You do not have to look so surprised."

"But I am. I still think it best that I take her to Ireland."

"Perhaps I do not want you to do that."

She propped her elbow on the back of the sofa and rested her head on her hand. "Really? Why is that?"

"There are a multitude of reasons. The first, and probably foremost, I made a promise to her uncle that I would care for her. I would be going back on my word if I allowed you to take her. That would weigh heavily upon me." He shifted forward, his forearms on his knees, cradling the glass in his hands. "Second, I still think our best chance is with one another. And lastly, I feel drawn to her in a way I have never experienced before. I have caught myself wondering if I was supposed to overhear her predicament, if I was supposed to offer for her in order to save her." His head dropped down and he stared into his brandy. "It was as if God had put us both in that time and place for a reason."

She tilted her head and watched him intently for a few minutes. The examination was just beginning to annoy him, when she broke the silence.

"I never thought you one to believe in providence."

He released a laboured breath and shook his head. "That is true, but as much as the idea of this marriage frightens me, the thought of breaking my promise terrifies me—and not just due to father's ultimatum."

"Is that why you shut yourself off from her this week?"

"I do not know. I thought I would be relieved if a change in circumstances occurred, and we were no longer required to wed, but when you announced you would not allow the marriage to occur..."

"You were not relieved."

Relieved? No, he was frantic that Elizabeth would be taken from him. She would no longer be under his protection.

"No, and my first thoughts were not for myself; they were of concern for her."

"So you are frightened of a future with her and also frightened of a future without."

He grimaced. When had he become so chicken-hearted? "I think so."

She chuckled. "I have never known you to have so many fears."

His head shot up as his arm dropped to his lap. "I have never been so confused! I was scared when my mother died, but that situation was different. I was not this conflicted."

His grandmother stood and made her way over to him, taking his face in her hands as she had earlier, and tilting his head back so their eyes met. "If you think you can care for her—love her—then do not hide from it."

"What if she never feels the same? What if we wed, and I fall in love with her, and she never has any affection for me?"

"Lizzy has such a big heart, Fitzwilliam. I do not think that will happen." She brushed a curl back from his temple and smiled. "Look at the way she has accepted the mad Fitzwilliam clan. I daresay she will even be fond of Richard when she meets him."

His lips quirked up on one side in amusement, and she gave him a kiss on the forehead before she released him to resume her seat.

"I have not had a letter from Richard in some time." His cousin's lack of correspondence was always of serious concern.

"Neither have Henry and Elinor. His communications are rare with us whilst he is away with his regiment, so I must assume he is well."

Darcy remained quiet. He agreed with his grandmother and deep down, hoped she was correct.

"I believe I will retire." She rose to place her glass on the side table.

"I was surprised to see you at my door this late." He went to her side, holding out his arm to escort her.

She placed her hand near his elbow. "I was not sleepy after our argument and was heading to the library for a book when I heard you. The light streaming from under the door was greater than just the fire, so I knocked. I do hope the interruption was not unwelcome."

"No, Grandmamma. It was not unwelcome."

She patted his cheek and stepped through the doorway. "I will see you in the morning, dear. Perhaps you would join Lizzy and I when we break our fast?"

He grinned and nodded his head. She may have had a plan for Elizabeth, but she must still have some faith in him. "Yes, ma'am. I will be there."

"Good night, Fitzwilliam."

He wished her the same and ensured she arrived to her rooms without incident. When the door clicked shut behind him, he surveyed his bedchamber and sighed. He was not tired.

A copy of *The Lady of the Lake* lay on the table beside the bed where he had left it the night prior. He took his usual spot, settling under the bedclothes before opening the cover.

He was not aware of when he fell asleep, only of how he awoke the next morning, still half-sitting up with the book laying open, face down upon his chest.

Elizabeth awoke the next morning determined to begin the day anew. Perhaps Mr. Darcy would wish to speak to her as he had the night before.

She did not hear Hattie bustling around in the dressing room, so she picked up her copy of *The Lady of the Lake* from the table beside her.

Hattie happened to arrive around the time she finished the last few lines. "Good mornin', miss. I hope you slept well."

"Yes, thank you. I believe I was in great need of it, too."

"Well, from what is said downstairs, you missed quite the argument between Lady Matlock and Mr. Darcy."

Her eyes grew wide, and she leapt up so she was face to face with her maid. "Please say the disagreement was not over me."

Though the dowager was upset with Mr. Darcy over his behaviour towards her, she had not wished for her to scold him for it.

"Yes, miss. The yellin' could be heard in the dining room where the maids were finishing up the cleaning from supper."

Perhaps she could feign illness and remain in her chambers for the entire day... no, it would not solve anything. Hattie brought a jug of water in and placed it in the ewer, before bustling back to gather her clothes.

Elizabeth poured some of the warm water into the basin and began wiping down her face, neck, and arms. "Hattie? Did they say below stairs whether Mr. Darcy was *very* angry?"

"Well, his man was down rather quickly after goin' up to tend to him, though he is pretty tight-lipped, that one. He never said a word."

She closed her eyes in dread. What would she do if he was upset with her when they wed? That would not do. She would have to find some way to make amends.

Hattie chattered on about this and that while she helped Elizabeth dress and styled her hair. When she was ready for the morning meal, she reluctantly stepped out into the hall, took a deep strengthening breath, and left the safety of her rooms to brave the ire of her betrothed.

The food had not yet been laid out on the table and so she ventured to a conservatory she had found a few days prior. A small bench sat to one side, surrounded by plants and flowers, and she took a seat, admiring the dowager's orchids in planters along the far wall.

Elizabeth enjoyed the warmth, especially on dreary days. That morning happened to be sunny, which made the room significantly warmer. She had just closed her eyes and tilted her face up to bask in the pleasant warmth when a distinctive deep voice brought her back.

"I am sorry to disturb you, but I hoped we could speak," said Mr. Darcy with a small bow.

"Of course." Her voice wavered and her cheeks became heated. Why did her nerves have to assert themselves now? She shifted over and gestured beside her. "Would you care to sit?"

"I would. Thank you."

"My maid informed me this morning of your argument with your grandmother, and I am mortified to be the cause. I had no idea she intended to..."

"Please, do not make yourself uneasy. Nothing was said that I did not deserve. My behaviour to you over the past week must have been confusing, to say the least, and I do owe you an apology. I had not considered you as I ought."

His countenance bespoke of his remorse, and she could have cried in relief. He was not angry with her. The gentleman who she first met in Meryton seemed to have returned.

"Perhaps we should begin again?" she suggested tentatively.

His lip quirked up to one side. "I think that is a splendid idea, Miss Bennet." He was silent for a minute as if unsure of what to do next. Elizabeth was just turning to ask him a question when he abruptly stood, circled outward a bit, and approached from directly in front of her.

"I apologise for the impropriety of approaching you without a formal introduction, but my name is Fitzwilliam Darcy."

She swallowed back a chuckle and stood. "I am pleased to make your acquaintance, Mr. Darcy. My name is Miss Elizabeth Bennet." He gave a brief bow and she curtsied. He gestured back to the bench, and she resumed her seat.

"I must ask your forgiveness once more, you see. I overheard a conversation recently, and I understand you to be in quite a pickle."

She could not hold her amusement in anymore and burst into gales of laughter. Once she had calmed, she gave him a look of mock reproof. "And do you often make a habit of eavesdropping, sir?"

He wore a small smile as he shook his head. "No, this one was heard quite unintentionally. I assure you."

His hand appeared before her as if he planned to assist her to stand, so she placed hers in his palm. Instead, he dropped to one knee, his hand still clasping hers. "I find myself in the position of wishing to offer myself as a solution to your problem. If you would have me, that is. Miss Elizabeth Bennet, would you do me the great honour of accepting my hand in marriage?"

She rarely found herself speechless, but she had seen so little of his sense of humour. Her heart lightened and she placed her hand on her stomach, pressing the butterflies that had suddenly taken flight within. "I would be honoured to be your wife, Mr. Darcy."

The words came out at little more than a whisper, but the look of pleasure he wore when she uttered her agreement indicated he had indeed heard. He placed a small kiss on her hand, and her face became aflame as the warm sensation rushed all the way up to her shoulder.

Mr. Darcy rose from the floor and took the seat beside her once again. He turned the hand he held palm up and placed something in the centre. When his fingers moved away, a ring with a pink stone flanked by two diamonds stood out against the pale white of her skin.

"It was my mother's. She gave it to my grandmother to hold until the appropriate time."

She brought it closer and fingered the fine gold band and the middle stone. "It is lovely. Is there a story that goes along with it?"

"How did you know there would be a story?"

"There usually is, is there not?"

He smiled and took the ring from her. "If you ever see a portrait of my mother, she had a very pale complexion and faint rose cheeks. My father claimed he picked the centre stone, a pink topaz, to match her complexion."

While he spoke, he placed his other hand under hers, spreading her fingers slightly as he slipped the ring onto the ring finger of her right hand. The fit was not quite right, so he moved it to the middle, where it fit well.

"What of the diamonds on either side?"

"I believe they were simply there as accents." Mr. Darcy rubbed his hands on his thighs in a nervous manner before facing her once more.

"Now, I have been thinking."

"Is that not a dangerous occupation, sir?"

"Pardon?"

At his incredulous expression, she began to laugh. "We became betrothed after you had been thinking…"

Mr. Darcy shook his head and chuckled. "I believe that was more from a lack of thought."

"I do not know if I should be offended or flattered!"

"I would take it as a compliment," he responded.

"Very well, I shall. Now, what has your mind occupied this time?"

"I have begun to think it inappropriate that you are on such familiar terms with my family, but not me." Her eyebrows raised, and she was certain her surprise was evident. "I feel we should perhaps emulate my aunt and uncle. They address each other formally when in a social or public setting, but use each other's given names when in private."

"So, you wish me to call you Fitzwilliam?" He gave a nod and she smiled. "Do you wish to call me Lizzy?" He shook his head and her eyebrows furrowed again.

"My entire family addresses you as Lizzy, but I would wish to have a name all to myself. I would prefer Elizabeth." She felt her face warm once again and looked the other way in an attempt to hide it. "Would that bother you?"

"No." She caught his eye through her lashes. "It would not bother me at all."

He grinned and began to open his mouth as if to say something further when the sound of a door opening startled them both.

"There you two are," exclaimed the dowager. "I thought I might find Lizzy here, but I am happy to discover you here, too, Fitzwilliam."

"Nothing had been laid out in the dining room yet when we arrived. Hobbes informed me that Elizabeth had just ventured in here, so I decided to join her. I hope she was not too put out by the interruption."

She laughed. "No, I was not *too* put out." His grandmother was studying their interactions, and this time her cheeks burned.

"Would either of you care to join me in the dining room now that the food is laid out and waiting?"

Darcy stood and offered Elizabeth his hand. "Shall we go?"

She placed her hand in his. "By all means, lead the way."

He offered his Grandmother an arm as well, and they walked to the dining room. Once they were all seated, his grandmother served the tea, but when Elizabeth reached to take her cup, the elder lady reached for her hand.

"I see Fitzwilliam has finally given you your betrothal gift."

"Betrothal gift?" She frowned as she tilted her finger to better see the ring.

"Is something wrong?" Darcy asked with a furrowed brow.

"I suppose it makes sense." Her voice remained light. The ring was the most beautiful thing she owned. It would not do for him to believe she was disappointed by it. "I assumed it was to be my wedding ring. I hope that does not sound too silly of me?"

"Elizabeth." He tilted his head in order to catch her eye. "If you wish for that to be your wedding ring, I can see if a jeweller can have it adjusted to fit you before tomorrow; however, I planned on purchasing you a more traditional set of rings."

"I do not expect you to buy me anything more. You have been more than generous so far, and I do not require anything extravagant. I am unaccustomed to wearing a great deal of jewellery."

Darcy stood and rounded the table to sit in an empty seat beside her. He took the hand wearing the betrothal gift, and immediately drew her gaze. "I am not purchasing you wedding rings because it is expected of me. I do feel I must do it, and I intend to tell you why."

Her mouth opened to protest, and he shook his head. "Let me finish, Elizabeth."

He looked down to her hand and reached over to take the left, holding them between both of his own. His thumb traced over the third finger of her left hand, and she watched and waited for his explanation.

"We are both rushing into a wedding out of a mutual necessity. I would like to say I behaved admirably for the last week and did my utmost to make both of us comfortable with that fact, but instead, I was selfish and withdrew into myself. It was not what you deserved."

He paused for a moment obviously searching for the correct words. Her betrothed had, for the most part, appeared so serious and this time was no different. "Had we met under different circumstances... if your family still lived, and we happened to meet, fall in love, and become betrothed, you would have had a betrothal gift, a trousseau, and a wedding in the chapel you attended your entire life, surrounded by those you love. You deserve as close to that experience as can be managed."

"We both should have had that." Her voice broke as a tear trailed down her cheek.

He gave her hands a light squeeze. "I suppose, but I would look terrible in a gown. I do not think the modiste would fancy fitting one for me either."

She could not help the burst of laughter that erupted. His eyes shifted to stare at the ring on her finger. Could it be his nerves that made him avoid her eyes?

"I know I have been a horrible betrothed this past week, but allow me to make up for that—allow me to give you as close to what you deserve as possible." He looked up and their gazes locked. "I hope neither of us will one day think back upon our wedding and have regrets. If I am adamant about you having a ring for an engagement gift and wedding rings, it is because I will not give you something less due to the manner of our betrothal."

He could certainly speak eloquently when he tried, and gave a lot of thought to what was said. The concentration had all been in his eyes and the way his brow would sometimes furrow as he hesitated for a brief moment. Darcy stood and placed his handkerchief in the palm of the hand he still held.

"Thank you," she said in a quiet tone for his ears alone.

His grandmother cleared her throat. Elizabeth pivoted and avoided the dowager's gaze in embarrassment; although, the dowager's mischievous smirk was not missed.

Darcy rose and returned to his place, and the remainder of the meal was passed in companionable conversation.

When they had finished, Darcy expected to adjourn to the drawing room together, where they would receive callers for the day. But his grandmother looped her arm through his.

"Lizzy, would you mind if I have a word with my grandson?"

"Of course not. I will practice on the pianoforte in the music room until you send for me."

She smiled warmly and exited the room, while his grandmother tugged him towards her favourite drawing room. Once they were inside, she released him and turned. Her hands were fidgeting, and he was unsure what she was about until she placed her wedding rings in his palm.

"Your father has Anne's, which I am certain she would have liked for you to have, but I know he would never relinquish. My fingers were always a bit smaller anyways."

Darcy furrowed his brow. "I do not understand."

She rolled her eyes in exasperation. "Tomorrow, I want you to give these to Lizzy."

He stopped and gawked at the precious keepsake he held in his hand and began shaking his head. "I cannot accept these, Grandmamma. I know how much they mean to you."

"I have other rings your grandfather gave me. I can wear one of them in their stead."

Despite her words, tears were in her eyes. "I would prefer that Lizzy have my rings rather than any of the young women your cousins might marry. She will have a greater appreciation for what they have meant to me, and what I want them to mean to her."

"For that reason, she may refuse to take them from you." Perhaps his grandmother would change her mind. In his heart, he appreciated the gesture and loved her for it, but did not wish her to miss something that was so much a part of her.

"Then do not tell her where you obtained them." He opened his mouth to protest, but she placed her hands around the one that held the rings.

"I want Lizzy to wear these. I want her to eventually pass them on to one of your grandsons for his future wife." He opened his mouth to object further, but she never gave him the chance. "I will not give way on this. You may as well take them and say thank you."

The gleam in her eye was a familiar one. He had seen it in many family squabbles, and recognised it for what it was—a determination that he would not overcome. She would not change her mind. "If you ever wish for them back…"

"Then I will take comfort seeing them on Lizzy's finger, where they belong."

He sighed in resignation. He had the most recalcitrant grandmother in all of England. "Thank you, Grandmamma. I know she will take very good care of them."

"I have no doubt or else I would not entrust them to her." She removed her hands from his and reached into her pocket, removing a small velvet pouch. "For you to keep them in until tomorrow." She took a deep breath and straightened her shoulders. "Enough of this sentimental drivel!" she exclaimed. "We have gossip columns to pour over before the callers begin arriving."

Darcy groaned and followed her towards the music room to fetch Elizabeth. It was going to be a long day!

Chapter 9

Fitzwilliam George David Darcy stood, a glass of wine in his hand, to one side of the drawing room at Ashcroft House, his attention focused on his wife of less than an hour. She was standing across the room conversing with his grandmother, his Aunt Elinor, and his cousin, Grace. Her laughter floated across the room, and he smiled.

"Aaah," teased his cousin, Viscount Huntley, who had just leaned against the wall beside him. "You are staring and smiling at simply the sound of her laugh? You are besotted, cousin."

Darcy rolled his eyes as he glanced over at the one who interrupted his reverie. "I can enjoy a pair of fine eyes and a pretty face without being besotted."

"You might watch your teasing, Arthur, or you may find yourself on the receiving end one of these days." Uncle Henry took a position beside his son with a smirk.

A laugh erupted from Huntley's mouth. "Me? Besotted? I will never moon over a woman the way he is. Whenever they are in the same room, his eyes follow Elizabeth the entire time."

"A man can admire his wife." Darcy spoke with care as he stole a glimpse of Elizabeth. "It is preferable to marrying a woman who is unpleasant and unattractive. My wife is one of the handsomest women of my acquaintance."

"As opposed to Caroline Bingley, who told all of her friends she would be the next mistress of Pemberley?" Huntley rubbed his hands together with glee.

A shudder ran down Darcy's spine while Uncle Henry gave an amused snort. "The only way she would become mistress of Pemberley is if she manages to ensnare my father."

"I would love to be a fly on the wall when she discovers you have wed," Huntley mused. "She will not leave any survivors by the time she is through."

Darcy's lip curled in amusement and after a quick glance to his uncle, turned towards his eldest cousin. "Now that you mention it. I *am* a letter in Bingley's debt. I will be happy to convey your warmest regards to Miss Bingley when I next write to him. She will, no doubt, be overjoyed to know you were thinking of her."

Uncle Henry guffawed when Huntley paled and lost his smug expression. "That is not even funny, Darcy."

"I believe she would not find it difficult at all to transfer her affections to you. Just think, Lady Caroline Fitzwilliam, Viscountess Huntley."

"I think I will go join the ladies," Huntley pouted. "Perhaps *they* might not treat me so unfairly." He stalked off and made his way to stand beside his mother.

Uncle Henry watched his son converse with the ladies. "Do not let him fool you. He is jealous of your good fortune."

Darcy's head whipped around to his uncle. "He considers my father's ultimatum and Elizabeth's circumstances good fortune?" Huntley would never wish to be in a similar predicament. "Perhaps you should have him evaluated for Bedlam."

His uncle laughed, but then, his tone became serious. "Your father may have forced your hand, but you managed to find a lovely, intelligent young woman who happened to need assistance in much the same fashion you did. You were quite lucky. You could have had no choice but to beg Bingley for his sister's hand."

"Huntley needs no help in exacting revenge."

"No, he does not," responded Uncle Henry. "He has joked quite enough this week that he intends to scour the countryside for an honest, witty young lady to marry."

From across the room, Elizabeth happened to catch his eye, and gave him a shy smile. "You believe my cousin to be serious?"

"Only time will tell, but if he is, I credit the change to Lizzy. His glances towards the young ladies in London are rare—he overhears too many of their conversations." Uncle Henry peered over when he heard his wife giggle and grinned. "Did you make all of the arrangements for your trip?"

Darcy swallowed the sip of wine he had just taken and nodded. "Yes, we will remain here tonight, leave for Sagemore in the morning, rest there for Sunday, and depart for Bath on Monday."

"I assumed as much. The house will be open and ready when you arrive Tuesday evening."

"I appreciate you giving us use of your house."

His uncle waved off his thanks. "Do not thank me until you have seen it. Elinor cannot abide Bath, and so we have never been. It has been closed up since father became too ill to return."

"But you have had a staff in place?"

"We do, but I would welcome your opinion of its condition, and I am certain Elinor would like Lizzy's assessment. We have thought about leasing it, but since we are not certain of its state…"

He nodded in understanding. "Would you not be better off selling it if you have no intention of using the property?"

"I have considered it, but Elinor and I will give the property to Richard when he returns. We hope he will resign his commission, but I fear he is not one to remain idle. He may not have a long career in the military without being injured, and perhaps a house of his own will allow him some relief when he must settle down."

"In the meantime, the property will be his and leased for an income." His uncle's plan showed a great deal of wisdom. Richard often joked of marrying with concern for money, but it was doubtful he ever intended to find a bride.

"Precisely. Due to his allowance, he does not require it to sustain himself, so I plan to invest the profits for him until he returns."

"He will be fortunate that you considered his future when the time comes." His uncle appeared pleased with his assessment, yet now was an appropriate time to change the direction of the conversation. Otherwise, with his cousin Richard away, his uncle might become mired down in his worry.

"I have thought to terminate the lease on my house in town in order to free it for my own use."

Uncle Henry shifted from the appearance of wool-gathering back to attend to Darcy. "Why? Have you some reason to dislike the family?"

He frowned. Had he indicated anything amiss? "No, not at all. I just thought it would be preferable, now that I am married, for us to stay there when we are in London."

"I would discuss this idea with your grandmother." Uncle Henry's head tilted so he levelled a stare over his spectacles. "She delights in your company, and frankly, I am more comfortable when I know that you are here. She is so stubborn about not hiring a companion."

"She is independent," he defended, "gets around very well, and you know that whilst she may call herself old, she will rebel against anything that would label her as such."

"Young ladies have companions as well," her son groused. "Why does she have to be so inflexible?"

"She has a loyal, devoted staff, who will notify you and take care of her every need should something ever happen, but I will speak to her before we depart. We can discuss whether she would prefer us to stay in our own home."

"Just consider the option," his uncle persuaded, "and do not forget the money you can put aside from having it leased."

"Elizabeth has a decent settlement, and I still have some savings. I do not even use all of my income as it is."

"You might want to consider saving for daughter's dowries." Uncle Henry patted him on the shoulder as he grinned. "Daughters are not an inexpensive endeavour and if your wife follows in the footsteps of her mother, you may have quite the brood."

Darcy gave an almost imperceptible snort. "We will not have to worry about that for some time. Not all babies are conceived immediately."

"No, they are not, but you should begin considering it now rather than later." He laughed and nudged Darcy in the side. "You know, Elinor's mother used to say that the first baby could come at any time, after that, it takes nine months."

"At least we will not have to worry about the gossip an early baby would bring."

"Speaking of gossip," Uncle Henry chuckled, "Elinor and I would have appreciated some warning yesterday."

Darcy gave him a questioning look.

"We had no idea you were going to introduce Lizzy as your intended. Lady Selwyn appeared in our entry hall directly after calling upon Ashcroft. She appeared as though she had run the entire way, she was panting so hard."

Giving a bark of laughter, Darcy set his empty wine glass on the table next to him. "No gossip or rumour could have reached my father in time for him to stop the wedding, so we thought it better to introduce her as my betrothed."

"Lady Selwyn was under the impression you had asked for her hand some time ago."

He smiled. Their plan had proven successful. "That was Grandmamma. She implied the arrangement between Elizabeth and I had been of some duration and was delayed to accommodate as much of the mourning period for the Bennets as possible."

Uncle Henry shook his head. "My mother is truly diabolical. Selwyn did not marry that woman for her intelligence that much is certain."

"Lady Selwyn does not give a care for accuracy," interjected Aunt Elinor, as she stepped beside her husband. "She only cares that she has the latest tittle-tattle."

"Which is why she was so useful yesterday." The dowager smirked as she stepped into their group. "She was easily led to believe that Fitzwilliam and Lizzy had been betrothed since before her family's passing. She even supposed that we kept the entire affair quiet because of the mourning period."

Huntley snickered, drawing everyone's attention. "I attended school with her son. He is much the same: a cloying gossip."

"As is the father," chimed in Uncle Henry. "He is forever attempting to ferret out information to hold over people for political gain."

Aunt Elinor rolled her eyes with a distasteful expression upon her face. "I do not wish to discuss Lord and Lady Selwyn. We have been here all afternoon and it is time we return home. I am sure your mother did not plan dinner for all of us tonight."

"No, I did not," agreed his grandmother, "but I am certain we could accommodate you should you care to join us."

"Thank you for the invitation, but I will not inconvenience your cook with a sudden change to a dinner for seven when she expects three."

Offers of congratulations and joy were offered to the newly married couple, and soon, just the three of them were standing in the entrance.

Elizabeth broke the silence. "I would like to refresh myself before dinner."

"Yes, of course, dear," agreed his grandmother. "I will do the same after I see to a few household matters."

His bride nodded and ascended the stairs. She went out of earshot when she turned to head down the corridor, and his grandmother grasped his arm.

"We need to discuss your wedding night."

He groaned and attempted to wrest his arm back without injury to her. "I have already had this conversation with my uncle, and I will not have it with you."

She pulled him back into the empty drawing room and shut the door.

"Then I will repeat what I assume he has already told you. You must, Fitzwilliam. I have even told Lizzy this."

His eyes flew wide at her presumption, and he tugged his elbow from her. "I cannot believe you broached this subject with her!" He clenched and released his jaw to steady himself. "She will have the time she requires. I will not force anything upon her."

His grandmother made a noise, resembling a growl, and he balked.

"You can be so stubborn!

"At the very least, the two of you should share a bed. I doubt anyone would dare to challenge the validity of your marriage when gossip of that makes the rounds."

"I do not want our sleeping arrangements to be fodder for society to bandy about!" He rubbed his face roughly and took a few steps away. "I do not care to discuss this any further. Like Elizabeth, I wish to refresh myself before dinner. Grandmamma, I implore you not to bring this up during the meal."

"When have I ever been so indiscreet?" she exclaimed. "I may have discussed the topic with both of you, but I was not so indelicate as to do so with you together."

"Thank goodness for that!" He exited, and headed up to his new suite of rooms. His grandmother felt his former accommodations were not suitable for a married couple, so he and Elizabeth had been moved down the hall to two rooms that were joined.

Movement could be heard within Elizabeth's chambers, and he wondered what she was thinking. His grandmother's conversation must have unsettled her as much as it unsettled him—more so, he suspected.

James hurried in with warm water, and he decided to not give the matter any further thought for the moment. He would have to make a decision soon enough.

For Darcy, soon enough came much quicker than he anticipated. His grandmother did not join them for dinner, instead, she sent a note to inform them she would take a tray in her rooms. Elizabeth initiated a conversation on books and the rest of the evening progressed at a swift pace.

Now, he stood in his nightshirt and dressing gown before the door that connected his room to Elizabeth's. Should he change his mind? What did Elizabeth think? Those questions turned over and over in his head until he became annoyed with himself.

"Blast," he muttered. He rapped upon the hard oak before he could second-guess his resolve.

Her musical voice called for him to enter, so he reached out a shaking hand and turned the knob, opening the large wooden door at a snail's pace. When he noticed his bride, he stopped.

She stood beside the bed in her dressing gown, her hair in a long braid down her back. At another time, he was certain he would have been studying her robe, the curve of her hip, or even attempting to catch a glimpse of her ankle, but tonight, his attention was caught by her wide eyes. No, he would not press.

"I would desire us to be more comfortable with one another before we…" Try as he might, he found himself tongue-tied and opened and shut his mouth twice before deciding to skip ahead. "It has been brought to my attention that we should at least share a bed for the night."

Elizabeth's shoulders relaxed and she nodded. "The same has been mentioned to me." She clenched her palms together nervously. "Do you favour a particular side?"

"No." He peered at the side tables. "Do you read before bed?"

"Sometimes, but I had not planned on it tonight." She blew out the candle on her dressing table, and he followed her lead until the only candle left was on his side of the bed.

At some point, she must have taken advantage of his distraction, because she was already in the bed with the coverlet pulled up to her neck. He climbed in to the place left for him and curled to his side, facing her.

"Good night, Fitzwilliam."

"Sleep well," he replied.

He lay for some time, attempting to sleep, but his body would not cooperate. Elizabeth was quiet—too quiet. She was not moving a muscle, and even in the dim light of the room, her form could be distinguished all the way on the far edge of the bed. She was unlikely to be sleeping, and he hesitated to wake her in the event that she was. The situation was awkward, and he did not wish her any more discomfort than she endured already.

The next morning Darcy startled from his sleep for no reason that he could discover. The morning seemed as any other with the exception of the woman curled up close to the opposite edge of the mattress. The only clue that she had moved during the night was the arrangement of the bedclothes. The night before, they were tucked up around her chin, and now, they were down around her knees.

Her shift, on the other hand, was bunched around the tops of her legs, drawing his attention to a jagged scar that began about mid-thigh only to disappear under the hem of her nightclothes. The injury still had a pinkish hue, indicating it had not completely faded in the months since the accident.

He studied the mark for some time, taking in her entire leg, foot to hip. She had smallish pretty feet. He had never considered before whether feet were attractive or unattractive, but Elizabeth's were not large and her toes were proportional to the rest of the foot. Her ankles appeared delicate, yet she had confessed herself partial to long walks, which could be credited for their strength, as well as the shape and tone of the remainder of her legs.

Biting back a groan, he turned his head away from what she had bared. He had awakened in much the same state he did most mornings and his perusal of Elizabeth's body was not helping matters. Things had only intensified and had become painful. He shifted in an attempt to press that matter down from where it was tenting the bed covers.

Elizabeth could not see him in that state—at least not yet, so he gingerly rose to sit on the side of the bed, facing away from her. He remained there taking deep breaths until he could walk comfortably, allowing himself one last glance as he donned his dressing gown, and slipped through the door to his chambers.

Elizabeth remained still when she woke not long after her husband's hasty exit, debating whether he was still in the room for almost ten minutes before becoming frustrated. "This is ridiculous," she mumbled as she rolled to her back. A great deal of relief, and to her surprise, a small bit of disappointment filled her; her husband no longer remained within her room.

They would be traveling to Sagemore, and Fitzwilliam wished to be off as soon as weather or light would allow. He must have arisen early in order to ensure they were ready to depart on time.

Her maid was as efficient as ever, and was putting the finishing touches on Elizabeth's hair when a knock came from the door to Fitzwilliam's room. They looked at one another with astonishment before Elizabeth gave a giggle and called for him to enter.

He was handsome in his choice of apparel for the day. "I thought I might escort you to the dining room, if you are ready."

Why was she blushing? "Yes, I believe Hattie was just finishing. Were you not?"

"Yes, ma'am," she replied. "I only have to put a few final things in your trunks. If you would set aside what you would like in the carriage, I will ensure it is there when you leave."

"I will place the items on the bed."

"Yes, ma'am." Hattie curtsied and wasted no time as she departed to the dressing room.

She glanced at Fitzwilliam. "It will only take a moment."

"Of course." He reached over to the table beside the bed and picked up a book, extending his arm to hand it to her. She thanked him and set about gathering odds and ends, which she stacked on the end of the mattress.

"Is that all you require?"

"Yes, I do not have many books I can keep with me whilst we travel."

He offered her his arm, which she took so he could lead her out of the room.

"You should have a look through the library at Sagemore before we continue on to Bath. The trip is longer, so you will require more to occupy your time."

"Is there a large library at Sagemore?"

"No, my uncle was never a great reader. I have added many books since I took over the estate, and I have considered expanding the library."

She smiled, pleased her husband was as fond of books as she was. They seemed to have a great deal in common. She was perhaps a bit more open and animated than him, but he might allow her in more, with time and familiarity.

The dowager was already seated and sipping her tea when they entered. "I hope the two of you found your suite comfortable?"

"I had no issues with the rooms," her husband answered. "I believe we both found them acceptable."

Elizabeth nodded while she placed a piece of toast on her plate. "I found my bedchamber to be quite comfortable. I am particularly fond of the view of the back garden."

"Splendid," the older lady exclaimed. "Those shall be your rooms whenever you come to town in the future." She gave Darcy a look as if she did not approve of something. "Your uncle mentioned last night that you had thought to begin using your own house. If you would not mind, I would prefer you continue to stay here when you travel to London."

Her husband appeared somewhat taken aback. "I simply thought there might be a day when you would like us to be in our own home."

"I have always enjoyed your company, Fitzwilliam, and I adore Lizzy. There is no reason you should not stay here."

Fitzwilliam opened his mouth as if he were going to speak, but he glanced at his wife, and gave a casual shrug.

"Very well, Grandmamma."

His grandmother grinned widely, and Elizabeth stifled a chuckle at her husband bowing to his grandmother's wishes. He could be very considerate when he wished to be.

The three of them discussed the next few months while they partook of their tea and toast. The dowager intended to close the house and remove to her home at Matlock for the summer. They had a standing invitation to visit her there if Uncle Henry and Aunt Elinor did not issue an invitation.

They were just finishing their meal when the butler entered, shooing the footman back to the kitchen. He leaned over and whispered something in his mistress' ear, prompting her to grin.

"Good," she said aloud. "Thank you, Hobbes."

The servant gave a slight bow and stepped against the wall where he remained. Elizabeth's curiosity had the better of her, and she observed the butler and her new grandmother in an attempt to discern what was happening."

The lady only laughed. "You will bore a hole in either my head or Hobbes' if you continue staring at us in that manner."

Elizabeth started and reached for her teacup. "I apologise."

His grandmother shook her head. "No, I should not have had Hobbes inform me whilst at the table, but I asked him to alert me at once, should a little plan I implemented this morning succeed."

Her husband's head whipped around to face her. "What have you done?"

"It was done and done for the best. Your father and Lady Catherine cannot attempt to claim that your marriage is a sham."

The shocking news caused a piece of toast to become lodged in her throat, and tears came to her eyes as she choked. Questions flew through her mind she could not ask. What had she done and what had this plan entailed?

The dowager moved her teacup in front of her, and when her coughing subsided, she took a large sip of tea, her face crimson.

"What exactly has been concocted to prevent such claims?"

"I simply had my abigail remove your bed linens and put them in the full laundry tub before the regular maids entered the room to clean. In addition, my new housemaid also noted that Fitzwilliam's bed has not been used and announced it before the kitchen staff and the delivery boy for the butcher."

Heat radiated from Elizabeth's face and her husband came around the table to take a seat beside her. "Do not let it bother you," he said softly. "I doubt a butcher's boy is the origin for much gossip in town, and I am certain such a source would not be taken seriously."

"Sarah has told me quite a bit of gossip from that young man, which I hear bandied about at the next ball or tea a day or two later. You might be surprised."

Fitzwilliam closed his eyes in apparent exasperation. "Grandmamma," he groaned. "It was in the event my father or Lady Catherine appeared at this house or Sagemore—not for you to circulate around town."

"It is so much more effective this way." She placed her cup on the saucer. "Do you not see? Your father would no more believe a servant loyal to you or me than he would your testimony. However, if all of society knows you share chambers and have since you were married, he cannot refute it."

"I am unaccustomed to having such personal information dispersed as gossip." Elizabeth swallowed in an attempt to not feel ill.

"Please do not make yourself uneasy, Lizzy," his grandmother interrupted. "It will have long blown over by the time you return to London. I thought it important that when George comes to town, which he will very soon, the gossip should still be circulating."

Anger welled inside her at the dowager's blasé attitude towards the business. "I do not want the details of our lives to be circulated! What happens behind the closed doors of our bedchambers should not be bandied about for the amusement or derision of others! It is private!"

She turned to her husband, and he took her hand, clasping it between his.

"Do not worry. Some scandal will crop up that everyone will decide is more interesting than us sharing a bedchamber, which is not completely unheard of."

"I do not care if the gossip will wane; it should have never been dispersed!"

He leaned in and placed one hand to her back. His reassurance was effective and appreciated, causing her to sigh.

I would simply like to forget that this information ever left our chambers." She glanced back to her husband. "To think of the past only as its remembrance gives me pleasure."

He chuckled and stood, pulling her up with him. "Perhaps the best way to start is to leave the past behind us? Hobbes, have you any word on our carriage?"

"They were hitching the last of the horses when I came upstairs, sir. I am sure it is ready by now. Your servants and trunks have already departed."

Fitzwilliam peered down to her place setting. "Are you finished?"

She placed the napkin in her free hand beside her plate. "I am." His elbow appeared before her.

"Then shall we?"

She held his eyes while she placed her hand on his arm, her eyebrow arched and a mischievous smile upon her lips. She followed his lead to the entrance hall, where Hobbes and a maid met them with their gloves and hats.

"Have you decided to ignore me for my penance?" his grandmother asked from behind them. "Or are you simply too busy flirting with your wife to say farewell to your poor, old, and decrepit grandmother?"

"Do not use the poor, old, and decrepit act with me, Grandmamma!"

The pink blush that now was spread across his face gave Elizabeth a great deal of amusement, and she bit her lip to prevent herself from making a sound.

"You have always enjoyed me calling myself poor, old, and decrepit."

"Because you have never resembled that description." He stepped over to her and took both of her hands. "Thank you for all that you have done for us this past week—well, almost all that you have done."

His grandmother shook her head with a chuckle. "I enjoyed it. I only hope I will be around for the fireworks when your father and Lady Catherine come to call!"

At that, Elizabeth relinquished control and allowed an unladylike burst of laughter.

Her husband's lip quirked in amusement as he shook his head. "As long as I am not part of that confrontation."

"Safe travels." The dowager's face straightened into an earnest expression. "And do not forget to send me a note now and then." Fitzwilliam kissed his grandmother's cheek, and she had him escort her the few steps to Elizabeth.

"I will expect you to correspond with me as well. How else am I to know if he is telling me the truth?"

Elizabeth grinned. "I will be pleased to write." She leaned forward and kissed the older lady on her cheek, taking her hands. "Thank you for all your help. I do not know if I would have made it had you not been there for me." The dowager opened her mouth to respond when Elizabeth interrupted with an impish grin. "Even if I could have done without this morning's help."

The lady squeezed her hands. "I only want what is best for you and my grandson. I would have never exposed something so private if I had not felt it necessary."

"The carriage just pulled around front," said Fitzwilliam, holding out his arm.

His grandmother gave her a quick hug before she and Fitzwilliam made their way outside. He handed her into the equipage, took the seat across from her, and rapped his walking stick on the ceiling.

"Grandmamma never mentioned you having problems in the carriage around London. Will you be well for the day in here?"

"The idea may be nonsensical, but during a short trip, it is much easier knowing you will make your escape in a few minutes."

He smiled and swapped seats to sit alongside her, with his hand resting open and upward upon his leg. "My hand is yours should you require it."

She placed her palm atop his and smiled. "Thank you."

With an expression of genuine pleasure that she accepted his offer, he entwined his fingers with hers. "Shall we go home, Mrs. Darcy?"

"By all means, Mr. Darcy. Lead the way."

The music room at Pemberley had always been Georgiana's favourite room. She often spent hours playing her pianoforte while her father worked on estate business. This morning had been no different, until a crash from outside the room resulted in an inadvertent strike of a discordant note. Another crash followed, emanating from her father's study.

She leapt up and hurried to the entrance hall as her father stormed through. "I want my carriage readied! I am leaving for London at once!"

"Father! What is the matter?"

"Your brother has defied me—has made a colossal error. I must travel to London as soon as possible to salvage the situation."

"Might I go with you?" It could not hurt to hope. "I could work with my piano master and possibly see Fitzwilliam. The last time he was here, he had no sooner arrived than he had to leave again."

"No, of course not! I forbid it! You are to have no further contact with your brother unless I inform you the circumstances have changed. Do you understand?"

She cast her eyes to the floor. "I understand Papa."

Fitzwilliam must have defied their father regarding the marriage to their cousin. He would not have been so furious otherwise.

"I will return as soon as I can, Georgie. I promise."

She hugged her father and sighed. He would never accept that Fitzwilliam had no desire to wed Anne, but she could not fathom his demand for the betrothal in the first place. Her father had deeply loved her mother. Why would he not desire the same for his son?

He strode from the room in long, angry strides, and at the close of the door, Georgiana exhaled with a great puff. She returned to the pianoforte, took a seat, and began to play again. Between songs, the carriage pulled around to the front of the house, and with a shout from the coachman, it departed.

Almost ten minutes after her father left, Mrs. Reynolds bustled into the room. She closed the door behind her, and rushed over with a letter in her outstretched hand.

"Fitzwilliam?"

"Yes, Miss. I delivered one to your father earlier, and after his reaction, I felt it best to hold this one until he had gone."

Georgiana's grin covered her face as she took the proffered note and her arms flew around the motherly housekeeper. "Thank you, Mrs. Reynolds!" Georgiana held her tight as tears flooded her eyes but did not fall. "Thank you!"

Mrs. Reynolds chuckled as she pulled back. "Well, I for one am curious as to what news he sends. Your father swore, and did not give one hint as to what his contained."

Georgiana broke the seal, poured over the first few lines, and let out a squeal.

"Well?" asked Mrs. Reynolds.

The young girl cleared her throat, but did not stop smiling as she read,

"*My dearest Georgiana,*

My apologies for not writing sooner, but I hope you will forgive me when I tell you how my time has been occupied at every moment for the last fortnight. There is much to explain, but first, I must tell you that I will not marry Anne. By the time you read this, I will be married to Miss Elizabeth Bennet of Longbourn in Hertfordshire."

"Thank goodness!" exclaimed Mrs. Reynolds. The two ladies hugged and twirled around laughing. "Thank goodness."

Chapter 10

The pump room bustled with activity as people gathered with their glasses of water, mingled, and traded gossip. Elizabeth stood to one side with her husband, observing all and sundry as they passed or stopped to greet an acquaintance.

They had been in Bath for a few days, but one day in public was all she needed to ascertain how very uncomfortable Fitzwilliam was in public settings. The couple happened upon several acquaintances of his, and each time, he was stiff and formal, hiding his true self behind an adherence to propriety; however, Bath, despite her husband's reticence, was diverting. Elizabeth enjoyed their walks in Sidney Gardens, as well as the performance they had attended the night prior. The soprano's voice was divine, and well worth the effort her husband had made to procure the tickets.

Overall, she had no cause to repine. Her husband had been very solicitous of her since their arrival, even ensuring that she tried the women's baths, which had not been comfortable, yet she had been willing to make the attempt in order to improve the ache in her injured leg. She was simply not comfortable bathing with a number of other women in a large and scalding hot pool of water, even with the dark coloured flannel she wore.

Her husband had also insisted they venture to the pump rooms twice a day to take the waters, since they were considered part of the treatment as well. She finished the last of the glass she was drinking and shuddered. Fitzwilliam took the now empty glass and placed it upon the end of the bar beside him.

"Would you like more?"

"No." She cringed and attempted to swallow the remainder of the foul flavour. "I have never before tasted anything so revolting."

"If the baths helped your hip more, perhaps we should concentrate on those and not bother with drinking the waters."

Elizabeth wrapped her hand around his arm and raised an eyebrow. "Perhaps we should procure some of those biscuits we heard mentioned yesterday.[1] The gentleman who spoke of them claimed they removed the bitter flavour."

He nodded with a smile. "I will send out for some when we return to the house, then."

They were about to make a circuit about the room, when they heard a familiar voice behind them.

"I cannot understand why we *had* to travel to Bath. It is the end of the season, and all of the best families are leaving for their country estates, unless they are aged or infirm."

"You never listen to a thing Charles says, do you? When Mr. Darcy's wedding announcement was in the paper, he slipped, and mentioned Bath."

The other woman scoffed. "Charles had no idea to travel here until you pushed for the holiday."

"No, he would not. But do you not see? Mr. Darcy brought his new wife here on their wedding trip."

"Caroline!" her companion reproached in a loud whisper.

Of course! Miss Bingley and Mrs. Hurst! The poorly concealed reprimand was reminiscent of her own mother, who had never been the model of propriety in public.

"Please tell me that you did not berate Charles into this trip because you wanted to follow Mr. Darcy!"

Disdain dripped from Miss Bingley's tongue. "No, it was because I wanted to see the little trollop he chose over me."

Elizabeth was not troubled over the jealous musings of Miss Bingley, but her husband must have been, since Fitzwilliam's hand covered hers. She peered up to see him watching for her reaction, and rolled her eyes, which prompted him to give a tight smile.

Mrs. Hurst continued, "You met her in London, or did you not pay attention when the Dowager Lady Matlock introduced Miss Bennet that day in the tea shop? She even indicated Mr. Darcy was in London to prepare for his wedding, but you were resolved that he would arrive on our doorstep any day to ask for your hand.

"His family must have sanctioned the match. Between the rumours about his betrothal to his cousin, Miss de Bourgh, and now his marriage to Miss Bennet, you never had any possible chance of becoming Mrs. Darcy. Charles tried to tell you…"

"Charles is useless," seethed Miss Bingley. "He could have persuaded his friend if he was not such an imbecile."

"Well, that useless imbecile brought you to Bath when you demanded it, and we are fortunate he had friends who were not using their home, else we would have been relegated to an inn."

Fitzwilliam moved as though he might lean down to speak, but before he could open his mouth, the women began to bicker once more.

"You cannot attempt any untoward action related to either of the Darcys, or consider shunning his wife. Charles requires Mr. Darcy's help to purchase an estate. He has no idea how to manage a property and all it entails. You would also offend Lord and Lady Matlock, as well as the dowager countess. You would alienate us from society!"

"But I must see them together for myself, Louisa! Did you hear the story Mrs. Grey heard from Lady Selwyn?"

"Which rumour was this? The one where Lady Catherine de Bourgh travelled to Mr. Darcy's estate in an attempt to annul the marriage, or the one where his new wife is the bastard daughter of Lord Matlock?"

Elizabeth's astonishment was so great as to almost overcome the bounds of decorum. She held back a guffaw, and gave a rather unladylike snort in the process. It was difficult to keep herself from burying her head in her husband's shoulder in order to laugh uproariously. The entire notion was preposterous! Aunt Elinor and Grandmamma would have found an enormous amount of amusement in such a rumour. What a pity they were not present, so they could giggle and ridicule it together!

"No!" blurted Miss Bingley. "I meant the fact that they shared a bedchamber for the entirety of their wedding night."

"That, I would imagine is not so uncommon, Caroline, especially, if he desires an heir straight away."

"I would call any woman who puts up with such behaviour a wanton, one who has no place in good society."

"As if *you* were familiar with the marriage bed!" Mrs. Hurst muttered under her breath.

Fitzwilliam could hear them speak of her this way! Elizabeth bit her lip in mortification.

"What did you say, Louisa?"

"I told you, Caroline, that Mrs. Darcy is obviously familiar with the marriage bed."

Elizabeth's face was aflame. She was riveted to the spot as she listened to every last word until Fitzwilliam led her away. She almost faltered, but fell in step with him as he steered her towards the doors.

"Caroline Bingley is finished!" Her husband was so furious he walked at a faster and faster pace as he led her in the direction of the booksellers. "I would have *never* asked for that harpy's hand!"

"Fitzwilliam," she called, out of breath, "can we perchance take a slower pace?"

He glanced behind him and made an abrupt halt, so she could take an extra step to catch up. "I apologise. I have *never* liked Bingley's sisters. They are the ones who do not belong in good society.

"Hurst required his wife's dowry, and I hope someone will come along who requires Miss Bingley's—for that is the only way her brother will ever rid himself of her. Otherwise, she will continue to be a lead weight attached to his foot, dragging him down into the depths."

Elizabeth began to giggle and Fitzwilliam regarded her in puzzlement. "I am astounded by the creativity of some of the rumours. I mean, me, a child of your uncle's? Anyone who has observed him with Aunt Elinor knows that he is besotted, even after all these years. Not to mention, I do not resemble any of the Fitzwilliam clan in the least."

Her husband nodded and one side of his lips curled in amusement.

"I am also embarrassed to know that people have, indeed, gossiped about our wedding night, but do remember, it was your grandmother who ensured our sleeping arrangements would be bandied about. Just now, we heard the fruits of her labours."

Fitzwilliam stared at her for a moment before they both began laughing. "The fruits of her labours? I do not know if I would put it that way."

"But you laughed, did you not?" She sang in a triumphant voice. He placed her hand upon her arm, and began to stroll along once more.

She had restored his temper, which was what was important. There was no use allowing such ridiculousness to ruin their day. Caroline Bingley would not spoil their time in Bath!

"That I did, love. That I did."

The Dowager Countess of Matlock was seated in her favourite drawing room when there was a commotion in the entry, followed by the face of a harried Hobbes peeking in the door.

"Mr. Darcy, Lady Catherine de Bourgh, and Miss Anne de Bourgh, ma'am."

She groaned in irritation and stood, her body complaining as well. Of course, they would make an appearance, sooner rather than later, but why that evening? Hobbes stood to the side as Lady Catherine pushed George Darcy and her daughter out of her path to enter first.

"Madam," Lady Catherine began, with no attention given to a greeting or even a curtsy—no adherence to formality. "You can be at no loss to understand the reason of our journey hither."

"You have come to make peace, so we can be friends at last." The dowager spoke with cheerful optimism in her voice for a simple reason: it would anger her husband's eldest child.

"Rebecca," reprimanded the elder Darcy with a stern demeanour. "I do not think your sarcasm is necessary. We must know where to find Fitzwilliam."

"I am sorry, George. He and his bride are entitled to their solitude."

Lady Catherine struck her walking stick on the rug; however, the pitiful, dull thud could not have been the impressive sound she expected. "That woman is not his wife! You are well aware that, from their infancy, he and Anne have been intended for each other. It was the favourite wish of *his* mother, as well as of hers!"

"Which would be why my Anne counselled him to follow his heart and marry for love before she died."

"She what?" gasped George Darcy.

Rebecca almost took pity at the shock displayed on his countenance. Had he listened to her after Anne's death, rather than close his heart to matters too painful for him, he may have been aware of more than his own grief.

She placed her hand on the back of a chair as she regarded him with empathy. "Anne asked for Fitzwilliam to be brought to her the day she died. I escorted him to her bedchamber and remained in the sitting room while they talked. He was with her for over an hour, and later, confided that he had waited for her to fall asleep before he left her side. She ensured he understood that she wanted him to marry for love and no other consideration."

"Anne was spineless." Lady Catherine was unmoved by the revelation, but no one had expected her to become any more sympathetic now than in the past. "No doubt because she was your daughter. Everyone these days claims to marry for love, but no one does so in truth, because love has no place in marriage."

She shook her head and faced her husband's daughter. "You missed out on a great deal, Catherine. I pity you."

"I do not require your pity!" roared Lady Catherine.

A smaller voice came from behind Lady Catherine, and Rebecca shifted to the side to find Anne, who struggled to be recognised by her mother. "Mama, I have no wish…"

"You will be silent, Anne. You do not know what is best."

The dowager rolled her eyes as she stepped forward. "Anne is four-and-twenty and a bright young lady. When will you allow her to express her own thoughts?"

Lady Catherine sniffed dismissively. "Nonsense. She will think the same as her mother until she marries, and then she will think as Darcy tells her."

"My son has forgotten what he owes to himself and to all his family," interjected George Darcy.

His words pained and disappointed her. Had he forgotten Anne's wishes so soon? "Your son wished to make his own decision, which he did admirably, if you ask me. He and Lizzy are well-suited."

Anne smiled from where she was partially obscured behind her mother. She was so intelligent and could have had so much more if Henry had raised her. Instead, she had been coddled and suffocated by her mother. The concerned grandmother could not remember a time when she appeared as sickly and weak as at that moment. Her guilt struck her to the core for not insisting Henry remove Anne when Sir Lewis died.

"She is of inferior birth! She is not worthy of him!" Lady Catherine dropped into one of the chairs and lifted her nose a bit higher in the air.

"Anne, would you care to have a seat, dear." The dowager gestured towards the sofa. "I would be happy to ring for some tea."

"Anne requires nothing from you! You, who have paid no attention to the tacit engagement between Fitzwilliam and her; you are lost to every feeling of propriety and delicacy!"

Anne rolled her eyes. The dowager stifled a grin; she had always liked her eldest granddaughter.

The dowager resumed her seat where she could observe both Lady Catherine and George Darcy as she spoke. "You both did as much as you could in planning the marriage; its completion depended upon others. If he was neither by honour nor inclination confined to his cousin, why should he not make another choice?"

"Because honour, decorum, prudence—nay, interest, forbid it." The elder Darcy emphasised his statement by pounding his fist upon the back of Lady Catherine's chair. "He was to do his duty to his family."

"Yet, he is married before God and witnesses. It cannot be undone."

"The marriage can be annulled!" shouted Lady Catherine.

"On what grounds? The entire Fitzwilliam family attended the ceremony, and marriage contracts were signed by Mrs. Darcy's nearest relative."

"We could claim she refused to consummate the marriage."

The dowager laughed at Catherine's enthusiasm for her own flawed proposal. "You are well aware of how seldom that ploy is successful, but that is neither here nor there, since it is obvious you have not heard the latest gossip in town?"

"What are you blathering on about? We arrived just yesterday. Where would we find the time for making calls or entertaining?"

Darcy exhaled and closed his eyes. "What are you so eager to tell us?"

"Merely that it is well-known that Fitzwilliam and Elizabeth shared a bedchamber in this house—once they were wed, that is."

Lady Catherine's face turned a brilliant shade of crimson and she sputtered in a most unladylike manner. "Well, that proves she is nothing but a strumpet and has no place in decent society."

"Perhaps that proves theirs is a marriage based on affection rather than money and connections."

"Love is an illusion." She stared into the dowager's eyes with malice. "It is nothing but the arts and allurements of a woman who has drawn him in just as you did my father."

"If you had ever experienced the emotion, you would not say such things." She did not let Lady Catherine's bait rile her, and remained in her seat, holding the haughty woman's steady gaze. "Your father did not wish for another marriage such as the union he had with your mother."

"He had no reason to find another wife after my mother."

"He required an heir, Catherine."

She sniffed haughtily and again, lifted her nose in the air. "He had me."

"You could not have inherited the earldom, the properties associated with the title, nor the additional entailed property. Your father required an heir for the Fitzwilliam name to retain any kind of prominence." She was not tall enough to once again catch Lady Catherine's eye, but did not let it deter her. "You would not be the sister to an earl if he had not married me." She disliked stooping to Lady Catherine's manner of thought, but this old argument was becoming wearisome.

"You were beneath him. You had no dowry or connections of which to speak. I was in the park with my governess and heard the women as they gossiped about the country girl Lord Matlock had married. How they tittered!"

She shook her head with a sad smile. "They did not titter for long. I had what none of them did, a husband who valued me—loved me. They soon realised I did not care about their gossip or innuendo because I had that bond. While their husbands passed their evenings in brothels and visiting with their mistresses, my husband came to my bed. He never strayed."

"None of that matters anymore." Lady Catherine's voice was spiteful and full of venom. "Will you tell us where to find Fitzwilliam?"

"I will not."

"This is your final resolve! Very well. I shall know how to act." Lady Catherine rose and strode to the door, where she rotated back with a whirl of her skirts. "I came to try and talk to you. I hoped to find you reasonable; but depend upon it, I will carry my point. Come, Anne."

George Darcy stepped forward. "You cannot stand by and allow him to make a mockery of this family. He must be found and made to see sense. You *must* know that." He spoke with sincerity and urgency, but her heart remained unmoved.

140

"This young woman that you and Catherine are so set against will be the making of him. She is precisely what he requires in a wife, and there is nothing you can say to me or to Henry that will persuade us otherwise."

George shook his head and followed Lady Catherine, passing by Anne, who still stood near the chair her mother had vacated.

"He is happy?" she whispered, as she glanced back at the door.

"I believe he is, yes."

The young lady revealed a brilliant grin. "Good. I do not know if I can manage a letter to him; Mama intercepts anything I attempt to send. Will you wish him joy for me?"

With a wistful smile, she stepped forward and took Anne's hands. "Of course I will."

"ANNE!" came a bellow from the front door.

"We love you, Anne. If you need either your uncle or myself..."

"Mother would never allow it." She turned towards the door as she released one of her grandmother's hands. "But thank you."

A wave of sadness washed over her as the frail girl moved away with her arm outstretched, releasing her hand at the last minute. Anne glanced back and gave a small wave that would not be noticeable to anyone who stood near the front entrance.

"You should have followed me directly." Lady Catherine's strident scolding echoed through the entrance hall.

The dowager closed her eyes and gritted her teeth, unable to help Anne escape the harsh treatment.

"That woman should have never had a child," she muttered under her breath.

Once the carriage departed from Ashcroft house, George Darcy rubbed his hands across his face.

Anne had spoken with their son the day she died? Why, oh why did she conceal it from him? Could she have believed he would object to one last visit with their son?

He had loved his dear Anne, but he also had the good fortune to fall in love with a woman whose status and connections helped elevate the family name. His father had made a list of families with whom he approved a connection, and the daughters of the Earl of Matlock were near the top.

If Fitzwilliam had come to him and indicated he had fallen in love with the daughter of a peer, he might have considered it, but he was doing him a favour. By arranging a match without affection: his son would never know the heartbreak that comes with the death of a beloved spouse. In fact, Anne's poor health was not a negative quality in his eyes. Fitzwilliam would be spared since he would not have the time to become attached to her companionship, not if she lived for as little time as he suspected.

Most would find his way of thinking cold, but it was the least a father who loved his son could do. With the marriage, they would gain Rosings, resulting in a substantial elevation in their status. Fitzwilliam could then wed any young woman of means and connections he wished.

"That woman is of no relation to you." Lady Catherine carried on as she continued to fuss at Anne. "You are not to acknowledge her again in the future. Do you understand?"

"Yes, Mama."

He started when Lady Catherine struck her walking stick on the floor of his carriage. "Now, we will go to your solicitor's office and have the paperwork to disown Fitzwilliam begun. Pemberley can pass on to Georgiana's first born son."

He glanced at the floor of the carriage, where a small dent from her stick remained, before his eyes bore down on the imperious woman. Lord, she could set one's teeth on edge!

"You will most certainly not accompany me on *my* business. Pemberley and the Darcy properties are none of your concern."

"Of course, I will accompany you," she insisted. "I am almost the nearest relation you have in the world, and am entitled to know all of your dearest concerns. I also insist you send Georgiana to me this summer. She will benefit from my, and Anne's, example."

He tilted his head to the side and marvelled. How could she believe the sun, moon, and stars revolved around her and her whims?

"But you are not entitled to interfere in my personal or business affairs, nor will you have such a profound influence on my daughter." He shuddered at what a summer at Rosings would do to his sweet, docile Georgiana.

"Your son was supposed to marry my daughter and he married a nobody—a harlot without a name! So unless she was from a wealthy tradesman…" Lady Catherine shuddered. "It is highly unlikely she had any fortune. Anne will be a laughingstock!"

He lost all restraint. Rosings would have been a boon to the Darcy wealth, but all patience for Catherine had dissipated long ago.

"If she is a laughingstock, it is because you have made her one. You have boasted for years that she would marry my son without a contract or a binding agreement from me, or him for that matter."

"I do not mind…"

"Anne, be quiet." Lady Catherine returned her attention to him. "How dare you, Darcy! I am the daughter of an Earl with connections to some of the cream of society. I can ruin you!"

He chuckled. "Think over those connections you boast of as you return to Rosings. Most of your intimate friends are either dead, or they would give you no importance since you have hidden yourself away at Rosings these past twenty years."

The grand lady's eyes bulged until he became concerned one might pop out and strike him in the forehead. He pursed his lips to keep from smiling at the vision in his mind. The equipage stopped, and he glanced out the window to see her Mayfair home.

She leaned forward in an attempt to intimidate him. "I expected you to be more reasonable. But do not deceive yourself into a belief that I will ever concede. I shall not go away till you have given me the assurance I require."

"That I will disown my son?"

"Yes! That pretentious upstart should not be mistress of Pemberley."

He gave an exasperated sigh. The day and her incessant bickering had left him weary. "Allow me to say, Lady Catherine, that the arguments with which you have supported this extraordinary application have been as frivolous as the application was ill-judged. You have widely mistaken my character, if you think I can be worked on by such persuasions as these. How far my son might approve of your interference in *his* affairs, I cannot tell; but you have certainly no right to concern yourself in mine."

Catherine began to puff up her chest, but his niece distracted him. "It was good to see you, Uncle George."

Anne was rising to alight from the carriage, and he held out his hand for her to use until she could reach the footman awaiting her outside. "Yes, it was good to see you too, Anne. I am sorry we did not have more time to talk."

Once the young lady was being escorted into her home, his attention returned to Lady Catherine. "I have more information to collect before I make any decision; however, you will *not* be privy to my final resolution."

"I am most seriously displeased. You will hear from me on this matter. I will not disappear." She stepped out and bustled through the door, prompting him to take a deep breath that he exhaled audibly.

Unbeknownst to Lady Catherine, he had arrived the day prior and had already been to his solicitors. A better understanding of his son's assets and the marriage articles had been his motive for the appointment, but Fitzwilliam had moved his business to another firm six months ago. The answers he received in regards to the entailment on Pemberley, as well as the legality of the marriage, were not promising.

Pemberley could not be passed through Georgiana. The sole way he could bypass Fitzwilliam was to remarry and father another son, which he had no intention of doing. No woman could replace his wife—his Anne, and he refused to even attempt it. Regardless of his actions, Fitzwilliam would inherit Pemberley; however, he would never tell him so long as he was married to this young woman.

The solicitors at the firm were even aware of the rumours, which had circulated about his son's new marriage. The widespread belief around town was that his son had been betrothed to this girl for some time. She had the full support of the Matlock earldom—that much he knew was true. No one knew of her family or connections, but he intended to investigate those on his own. The announcement in the paper gave him that information, at least.

He would make arrangements to travel to Meryton on the morrow. George Darcy would go to Longbourn, and maybe, just maybe, he would find some way to correct this travesty.

Music drifted from the balcony above and across the lawn to where Fitzwilliam Darcy gazed at his wife as she closed her eyes and absorbed the melody. She had been excited at the prospect of tea at the Sydney Hotel, and so he had arranged to have them seated in one of the dining boxes while an orchestra played from a balcony of the hotel, the music filtering its way to the park below.

She opened her eyes, and he started when she discovered him staring. "This is lovely. Thank you for thinking of it."

"I am glad you find the orchestra enjoyable. If you would like, we can walk around the park when the performance is concluded." They spoke in low tones so they would not disturb anyone else who cared to listen to the music.

Her face lit with happiness, and he basked in the glow of her approbation. "That would be delightful." Elizabeth turned back to face the musicians.

"Have you ever seen fireworks?" The distraction was deliberate, to make her focus on him for a moment.

"Pardon?" she asked, turning her attention his way again.

He should encourage her to smile more often. She was so beautiful when she smiled and her eyes sparkled. "I asked if you had ever seen fireworks."

Her eyes widened, and he grinned at the child-like excitement in her expression. "No, I have not."

"I have been told a grand gala for the King's birthday will be held a few days before we return to Sagemore. There will be a concert, illuminations, and fireworks. Would you care to attend?"

"If you do not mind the crowds."

He shook his head. "I am not fond of them, but I am willing to brave them if you will be at my side."

She beamed at him and bit her lip as her face was overcome with a becoming blush. "I would love to attend with you."

Fitzwilliam had studied their location and the people nearby for the first portion of the performance. If he took her hand in his, no one would be in a position to see his lapse of decorum. Now that she was so happy and pleased, he extended his hand, wrapping it with care around the small fingers resting in her lap. Her lips gave a small lift to one side, and she peeked down as her other hand left the table to cover his.

Her eyes flitted in his direction from time to time, but she gave most of her attention to the remainder of the performance while he enjoyed every subtle emotion and reaction the music evoked in her.

A mouse scurried across the floor and into a hole in the wall of a dingy room in St. Giles. The disgusting creature disappeared and Edward Gardiner pounded his fist on the filthy table in his room. He was furious with his brother, who had vanished and left him with nothing. He was forced to live in squalor due to Philips' actions!

His hands curled around a worn copy of The Times he had stolen from a pub earlier. How a paper made it to this part of town was a mystery. After all, how many in this neighbourhood could read?

He stared at the words and clenched it tighter in his fists. His eyes scanned the page, yet over and over, they were drawn back to the lines that stoked his ire immeasurably.

Mr. Fitzwilliam Darcy Esq. of Sagemore, Oxfordshire to Miss Elizabeth Bennet, daughter of the late Mr. Thomas Bennet Esq. of Longbourn, Hertfordshire.

How did his brother find someone for Lizzy to marry so quickly? Had this been planned before, and Philips did not mention it to protect her? He gritted his teeth and scratched his new beard as he contemplated his next move.

He had no money, and Grayson was looking for him with men stationed at all his normal haunts in Cheapside. All Gardiner wanted was work so he could pay his debt, but their presence made it impossible to move.

The announcement crumpled within his hands as he took out his frustration on the brittle paper on which it was printed. Grayson would never consider Lizzy for any kind of repayment now—part of the deal had been that she was guaranteed untouched. He seethed as he contemplated methods of retribution for his traitorous brother and his niece. Gardiner doubted his annoying, upright brother ever told Lizzy of his plan. Not that it mattered. She had abandoned him just as everyone else had, and he had nothing and no one left to lose.

---

1 Refers to Oliver biscuits which were invented by William Oliver, a physician who treated patients at Bath

Chapter 11

A loud thud echoed about the room, and a sharp pain shot through Elizabeth's hip. With a groggy groan, she pushed her upper body up from the unyielding floor.

"Elizabeth, are you well?" She glanced up to see the dark shadow of her husband peering over the edge of the bed.

Her voice was dazed and shaky, and she grimaced as she attempted to move from her side to her back. "That was not a pleasant way to be awakened."

The bedclothes rustled followed by the sound of the drapes opening before he appeared before her. "I am not surprised you fell. I have oft times wondered how you remain balanced on the edge of the bed in that manner." He aided her to stand, and she leaned against one of his arms and massaged her bad leg. "You did not reinjure it, did you?"

"I do not believe so, but I did land on that hip."

Her head was bowed, and she caught sight of his long legs in the light of the moon filtering in from the window. Elizabeth could discern that they were covered in hair as her eyes followed them down to a pair of rather large feet. How had she never noticed how enormous his feet were compared to hers? He was a tall man, at over six feet, with broad shoulders, so they were in proportion to the rest of his body, but she hoped he would never tread on her toes while they danced.

A knock sounded on the door to the hallway. "Mrs. Darcy?" The voice of the footman stationed outside carried through the heavy wood. "Are you well? It sounded like someone may have fallen."

Her head down, in conjunction with the dark, was a blessing as her husband had likely not caught her as she blushed or as she stared at his toes.

"Yes," she called. "I am well, thank you."

"Are you sure I cannot awaken someone for you?"

"That will not be necessary, Matthew," Fitzwilliam called. "I am helping Mrs. Darcy."

There was a long pause, and she glanced up and arched her eyebrow at her husband, who grinned at the humour in the situation.

"Oh… very well, sir."

The footman's footsteps retreated along the corridor as she breathed a sigh of relief. "I was worried he would enter."

"I imagine he would hasten to fetch me or the housekeeper. I do not think he would enter without permission."

Relief coursed through her, and she nodded. Her hip no longer ached, so she put her full weight on her injured leg. There was a bit of a twinge, but there did not appear to be any further injury.

"Is it still painful?" He took her free hand and placed it on his shoulder.

"I think it will bruise, but I do not believe I have reinjured anything. I expect I will be sore for a day or so."

"I would imagine it is much like falling from a horse."

Their eyes locked and her stomach fluttered. "Yes, precisely. I have always been sore for a few days after a good tumble from horseback."

"You like to ride then?"

"I do! My father kept a mare, so I could accompany him as he rode the property at Longbourn."

"I have several horses at Sagemore. We could see if one would suit, and you could go out with me some mornings… If you would care to, that is?"

The last was said with such a boyish expression and hope for approval that she grinned. "I believe I would enjoy riding your estate with you."

She yawned, and he started as if all of a sudden, he remembered his surroundings. "I almost forgot that it is still the middle of the night."

"Despite the fact it is still dark?"

He chuckled, and she closed her eyes at the deep rumble she had come to enjoy. One of her favourite occupations since becoming Mrs. Darcy had been eliciting a laugh or chuckle from her husband.

He had been nothing but solicitous since they were wed, and tonight was no different. He pulled the bedclothes back and insisted on holding her hands while she took a seat on the mattress. When she was comfortable, he climbed in on his side and turned towards her.

"You cannot keep sleeping on the edge or you will fall again," he chided softly. He reached a hand over and trailed his knuckles down from her temple to her chin.

How was she breathless from the mere touch of his fingers to her face? The sensation radiated through her body, and she shivered.

"You are captivating, did you know that?"

If there had been enough light, her face would appear the colour of a beetroot as she shook her head. She was spellbound as her husband rose on his elbow and wrapped his other arm around her waist, gently pulling her towards him.

"I promise I will not bite."

An anxious laugh escaped her lips as she held her body stiff. He did not remove his hand; instead, he began to caress her side with his thumb, which brushed along the underside of her breast.

Her eyes did not leave his. They could not. She was both entranced and anxious about what she saw in their depths.

Darcy had allowed Elizabeth to set the pace of their relationship in the fortnight since their marriage, but whatever progress was made during the day evaporated at night when she curled as far from him in the bed as she could. Their amiable conversation was satisfying, it was evident his wife enjoyed holding his hand, but she appeared to waver between contentment and discomfort in his presence. He wanted more between them.

There was not much light in the room, but she had physically responded to him: her chest rose and fell with an increased tempo, and her tongue peeked from between her lips to moisten them.

He dipped down and brushed a kiss as soft as a whisper against her crown. She made a swift inhalation, and he smiled as he bestowed kisses to each of her closed eyelids. Her eyes fluttered open, and she bit her lower lip in a hesitant expression. He pressed forward and claimed her lips with his own.

When he drew back, she licked her top lip just before he lowered to kiss her again, this time her lips attempted to move with his.

Fear prevented him from an attempt at more; he could not push her beyond the pale. That would make them both uneasy; her because he ventured too far and him because he waited too long to stop. She made a small high-pitched noise and he pulled back.

"Are you well?"

"Yes," she replied.

He lifted his hand and again, ran his knuckles along the side of her face. She closed her eyes, which was understood as a silent permission to trace his fingers across her forehead, down her temple, against her lips. Her skin was so soft and her mouth opened a bit with his touch, but he stopped and lay back against the pillow.

"We should get some rest. I had thought to go book shopping on the morrow."

She curled onto her side, a slight smile upon her countenance. "You think you have found the way to my heart, Mr. Darcy?"

He chuckled. "I am fairly positive, my wife." He lay his arm across the pillow and gestured her to move closer. "I believe I should hold you close to me, so you do not take another tumble from the bed."

"I will have you know that I have not fallen from bed since I was a little girl." Her voice held a note of humour at his tease, an almost mock affront.

She hesitated with a wary expression, so he rolled onto his back and pulled her the remaining distance. Her head found a place to rest upon his upper chest as his arm wrapped around her back and his hand cupped her shoulder.

He inhaled deeply in an attempt to remain calm. Her pliant body pressed against his own was much too pleasurable, and his body's urges were not the priority—her comfort and ability to trust him were too important.

"Goodnight, Elizabeth."

"Goodnight," she whispered, as she placed her small hand on his stomach.

To help himself sleep, he closed his eyes and attempted to block out the sensation of her against his side, but the remnants of her orange blossom scent teased him. Her breast was pressed to his ribs, and she lifted her knee so it lay on his hip. God help him!

His every muscle and nerve fibre was attuned to the sound of her breathing; her chest expanded and contracted as her small

150

exhalations warmed his chest. The awareness of her unnerved him, but it allowed him to determine when she slumbered once more.

If she was at ease enough to find sleep within his arms, perhaps, she had begun to feel something for him. He dare not label the emotion, but he smiled in contentment just before he dozed off.

"It was most deceitful of you to promise book shopping when you intended a trip to the modiste, Mr. Darcy." Darcy laughed in delight as Elizabeth regarded him with teasing eyes. Unable to resist touching her, he covered her hand with his while continued their walk to the booksellers, the earlier part of their morning spent at the local seamstress.

"Grandmamma mentioned you were not fond of shopping for gowns, but you did not purchase many in London. You will no longer be wearing half-mourning in another few months."

"I have gowns from before the accident, and also Jane's. They will require a few minor alterations, but they are still quite serviceable. My mourning gowns can be re-trimmed with white or perhaps a pretty ribbon, and continue to be worn."

With a broad grin, he shook his head. How had he become so lucky as to marry a woman who would not spend all her pin money at the modiste? "You will also require a new gown for the gala."

"I had thought to wear my wedding gown. I will have it embroidered the way I had hoped by then."

He attempted to catch her eye, but she took in their surroundings with great interest. "You may, of course, but I would take great pleasure in seeing you wear the pattern I selected."

"You selected all my gowns, sir. I must inquire of other wives to see if their husbands take such a prodigious interest in their wardrobes!"

He paused and angled his body towards hers. "I was in earnest when I said you could change any of the patterns you wished. I would not have you purchase something you dislike."

She shook her head and placed her hand upon his chest. "I was teasing! I did not mean to imply that I was unhappy with your selections. They were all very fine."

"You are quite certain?" He searched her eyes for any hint of displeasure, and was relieved to find none.

"I assure you. I am delighted with your choices. They are exquisite, and I am certain they will suit me admirably."

He continued on in his previous direction, with Elizabeth on his arm. "I do not wish to overstep. I hope you are aware that my sole desire is your happiness."

She tugged on his elbow, so he allowed her to pull him out of the path of the people on the pavement.

"I am happy, Fitzwilliam—truly. I have no cause to repine."

"Truly?" Until that moment, he had been unaware how much he needed to hear those words from her.

With one arched eyebrow, she grinned mischievously. "Well, we have not yet been wed a fortnight, so you could one day give me reason, but yes, truly."

His shoulders relaxed, and he released the breath he held.

"Perhaps we should have this conversation later, when we are not on a busy street."

He glanced around and chuckled. "You are correct, of course."

They had not taken many steps along the pavement, when they almost collided with none other than Charles Bingley.

"Darcy!" he exclaimed, his jovial countenance brightening. "It is good to see you, man. I knew you were in Bath, but I was unaware of the direction to your lodgings."

There had been a specific reason for withholding the information, but regardless, he smiled out of politeness, and gestured towards Elizabeth.

"Bingley, may I present my wife, Mrs. Elizabeth Darcy. Mrs. Darcy this is Charles Bingley. We have been friends since we became reacquainted in London several years ago."

Elizabeth curtsied and Bingley gave a bow.

"I have heard much of you, Mrs. Darcy; I am glad to meet you at last."

Darcy had to bite his lip to prevent himself from guffawing as Elizabeth lifted that one eyebrow. She may not have laughed aloud, but she most certainly laughed.

"I have heard much of you as well, Mr. Bingley."

"Really?"

She nodded and squeezed Darcy's arm. He could not fathom why until she began to speak again. "Yes, Mr. Darcy's grandmother mentioned you on multiple occasions as we prepared for the wedding. Then, from your sisters, when we met in London, as well as when we happened upon them here."

"I was unaware you had met my sisters." Bingley's tone was wary, but he could not be blamed with sisters such as his. "They have not mentioned such an encounter."

Bingley's brow creased in deep concentration. He was probably thinking in detail as to when they could have come across Miss Bingley and Mrs. Hurst since their arrival in Bath.

"I believe you first made their acquaintance in a tea shop," Darcy interjected.

Elizabeth desired Bingley to be made aware of his sister's activities, and while Darcy had planned a more private locale, he saw no reason to delay if it could be done without causing affront. Bingley despised confrontation, so it was doubtful he would cause a scene.

"Yes, Grandmamma and I had a nice discussion with them that morning. My husband and I also caught a glimpse of them in the pump room."

Bingley had an apprehensive expression as he nodded. "They have never mentioned that they were introduced."

"I do not believe they were aware of our presence," added Darcy.

Bingley cocked his head to the side, and Darcy sighed. The poor fellow was like a lost puppy. It was no wonder his sisters could manipulate him as they did.

"We were visiting the pump room a week ago when we became aware of Miss Bingley and Mrs. Hurst whilst they gossiped behind us."

Bingley's face blanched. There was a certain satisfaction derived as they informed him but allowed him to discern the remainder on his own.

"Do I dare ask what they said?" Bingley's voice echoed the trepidation on his face. One had to pity him. His friend had not chosen his sisters, and he had always tried to be the best of brothers. His sisters did not share a similar obligation, which was unfortunate.

Darcy extended his hand as if they had just approached one another and Bingley took it, shaking hands while he prepared himself for what had been long overdue.

"Bingley, you will always be welcome to visit Sagemore, but your sisters will never again be welcome into one of my homes."

Bingley nodded. He accepted the news better than Darcy had expected, so he took a deep breath and steeled himself again. "If you ever betray my trust again, our friendship will be at an end. Do you understand?" Darcy's voice was low so no one nearby could hear.

"But I did not!" cried Bingley. A few passers-by glanced in their direction and Bingley started and shut his mouth.

Leaning forward, Darcy continued in the same low voice, "Miss Bingley informed Mrs. Hurst that you mentioned Bath during a discussion of my wedding announcement. She insisted you bring her here because she understood this to be where we are staying."

Bingley's eyes widened. "I did not realise."

"That is part of the problem, Bingley, you never do." Darcy placed a hand on his friend's shoulder. "You would do best to find Miss Bingley a husband as you did Mrs. Hurst. Otherwise, she will continue unchecked as she has for the last few years."

"She cannot be so terrible." His friend's voice was laced with desperation.

Darcy shook his head, willing him to understand. "Miss Bingley is disliked amongst most members of the Ton. Some receive her calls for the gossip she manages to bring, but they would not seek her out should she lack the information they desire.

"She has also set her cap too high and will make a fool of herself attempting to obtain her goal. She will ruin you in society before you can even purchase an estate."

A shrill voice sounded behind them, where Miss Bingley threatened to bear down upon the three of them.

"We will not associate with her, Bingley. I will write to you when we return to Sagemore."

"Good day to you, Mr. Bingley," Elizabeth said with a curt nod, as Darcy propelled her forward and around the corner with him. She had to work hard to keep up, but in this instance, likely did not mind. Soon, they arrived at the next corner and their destination.

A bell sounded upon his opening the door, and a portly man looked up from behind the counter. "Good day to you sir, madam."

They wished the man good day as they stopped, and surveyed the room of shelves before them. "Did you wish to find anything in particular?" he asked. The poetry section was straight ahead with the novels further down the row.

"I am unaware of which books you have at Sagemore. I would not wish to purchase what you already own."

"We own," he corrected, "and do not worry; if I remember we have a copy, I will let you know. You may also buy your own copy for the shelves of our sitting room. I keep many of my favourites there and would be happy to share the space with you."

"Do you have any of Mrs. Radcliffe's books? *The Romance of the Forest*, perhaps?"

He groaned and she giggled. "You are going to fill my library with novels?"

"I was under the impression it was *our* library, sir, and I can always keep them in *our* sitting room."

He feigned disappointment. "And here I thought we had similar tastes in books."

He led her to the poetry section, where she stepped down the aisle from him. He spotted the sign that designated novels, and he quirked a side of his lips upward. She, no doubt, searched for novels by Mrs. Radcliffe, so he pulled a volume from the shelf, perusing its pages until she drew him from his musings.

"For the most part, I believe we do read similar subjects, but on occasion, I dearly love to read a novel." She beamed in his direction, and he had no wish to refuse her anything when she was so happy.

"You may buy every edition in the section if it pleases you."

She pulled out a volume of poetry. "Perhaps not every one but maybe just one or two by Mrs. Radcliffe."

"Have you never read them?"

"No, I have, but I enjoyed them so much; they are like an old friend. I like to go back and visit with them from time to time." She traced the front of the cover with her fingertips while she spoke, and he stared at the movement. If only she would touch him in such a fashion!

"My books were at Longbourn with my father's, and if you remember, Mr. Collins only allowed us our clothing and personal effects."

Darcy's attention snapped away from her fingers as he registered the information she imparted. He stepped over and covered her hand with his.

"Buy any books you would like. I will not mind."

Her expression became hopeful. "You will tell me if you already have a copy?"

He took her hand from the book and pulled her closer, so they were face to face. "I am unconcerned if you happen to purchase a spare, Elizabeth. As I said, if you are taken with a particular text, you are welcome to keep it in our sitting room."

Her eyes were a bit teary as she nodded, but her expression indicated she was more touched than distressed. He turned back to study the titles before him, but not before he saw her hug the book in her arms to her chest.

After an hour, both had chosen several books, and he held out his arm to take Elizabeth's selections as they made their way to the counter. One by one, he placed their purchases on the hard, wooden surface where he read through each of the titles. He laughed softly as he flipped through Elizabeth's. She had chosen two of Mrs. Radcliffe's novels, as well as poetry by Wordsworth and Byron.

"We have the Wordsworth and the Byron in the library," he mentioned softly. "We can purchase these for our sitting room if you like, or we can move the copies we already own upon our return to Sagemore."

Her eyes were wide with concern. "What if you would like to read them?"

He took her hand and gave it a gentle squeeze. "I believe I will know where to find them,"

"Oh," she said with a start. "Of course."

She lay the two volumes of poetry in front of her and studied them. "I have never read this particular work of Byron's, but this collection of Wordsworth is one of my favourites. I would like to keep a copy in the sitting room at Sagemore if you do not object. I can wait until we return home to read the Byron."

He nodded, separated the books accordingly, and paid, requesting them to be delivered rather than having to carry them while they walked about town.

As they stepped out of the shop, he leaned towards his wife. "Now, about that orange scent you wear?"

She withdrew with a concerned look upon her face. "Do you not like it? I thought it pretty, but I can find something different if you prefer."

He shook his head and placed a finger over her lips. "I find it enchanting and hoped to ensure you would not find yourself without it in the future." The pink that imbued her cheeks brought him immense pleasure. He loved to make her blush.

"I purchased the bottle whilst shopping in London with Grandmamma. I am certain it would not be difficult to acquire more."

Nodding, he offered her his arm, which she took as he began to walk towards the house. "Good. I find that it suits you well—very well indeed."

When they returned, a few hours remained until dinner, so Darcy escorted Elizabeth to their suite, where she deposited a few packages they had purchased on the way home upon the bed, giggling. "I would not have thought you liked to shop."

He grinned. "I do not enjoy shopping unless it is for books."

"You shopped for more than books today."

For a moment, he appeared as though he was about to say something. His smile became soft, his eyes met hers, and they shifted to her mouth. After a moment, when not a word passed his lips, she stepped forward.

"Fitzwilliam?" He started and turned crimson at being caught wool-gathering. "What has you so preoccupied all of a sudden?"

"Nothing," he blurted, as he unwrapped the package that had awaited them when they returned.

"It has to be something. Will you not trust me?" She attempted to decipher the expression now upon his face. He was clearly embarrassed, and she was dying to know what it was.

Her husband took a step closer, and she took a step back. He grinned, and she raised her eyebrow. "What are you doing, Mr. Darcy?"

He had turned the tables on her, and she was not certain she liked it. Another step forward by him led to another back by her, and so on until the back of her legs were pressed against the side of the bed.

Less than a half-stride more brought him directly in front of her, and her heart thumped in her chest at his proximity. She swallowed and was about to speak when his hand reached out to touch her side and slid to her lower back. He pressed her to the solid plane of his body, and his head dipped down until she closed her eyes. His warm breath fanned across her face a moment before the velvet softness of his lips caressed her own.

Her stomach fluttered madly, and she grasped his lapels in the event her knees refused to maintain her weight. After the previous night, his kisses were not as unexpected, but the sensations that accompanied his attentions were disconcerting.

She was clumsy as her lips attempted to move against his, but it did not take long before they moved in tandem, just like before. His hand at the small of her back bunched her gown, and she lifted onto her toes in an effort to reach him better. Her body urged her to be closer to him, but why?

Her own gasp startled her as much as the sensation of her feet leaving the floor as Fitzwilliam lifted her. He laid her back on the bed where he loomed over her, supported by one arm while he continued to kiss her, caressing and parting her lips to touch his soft tongue to hers. A whimper of surprise escaped from her, and he broke the kiss to gaze into her eyes in a silent question as to whether she was well.

In order to reassure him, she lifted her head and placed her hand on the back of his, the pressure of her lips giving him an unspoken message that she wished to continue. She was soundless when he deepened their kiss, but found herself amazed not so much by the action, but by her desire that he do it again.

Before her marriage, Elizabeth had entertained fantasies of the man she would marry, but they had never included feelings like these, the ones she experienced with Fitzwilliam. His hands stroked her body as his lips clung to hers, eliciting an intense awareness of his nearness and an ache for something she could not identify.

Her husband threaded his fingers into her still-styled hair and pulled her head back to expose her neck, where he pressed a warm kiss just under her ear. Gooseflesh erupted down the back of her shoulders and her arms, and she grasped his curls, her fingers tugging at his dark locks as he began to trail his lips down her neck to her chest.

His hands had not remained idle and were leaving trails of heat wherever they touched: her back, her stomach, her breasts were all grazed, while his mouth worked its way to the tops of her breasts.

He even buried his nose in her cleavage and just breathed, the damp warmth of his exhale sending a shiver throughout her body. She could not catch her breath, and closed her eyes.

But what would her husband do if she touched him? Her eyes shot open, and she studied him as he loomed over her. Until then, one of her hands had been in his hair and the other bunched the counterpane to her side. She had been too timid to try touching him any more than she already had.

Fitzwilliam glanced up, catching her eye, and she pulled his head back to her lips. She began to kiss him with abandon, letting go of the inhibitions that had held her back. Her hands made their way under his topcoat to the rigid muscles of his stomach, and she received a groan in response to the first contact of her fingers to the thin lawn separating her from his flesh.

His vocalisation was accepted as an approval of her actions, so she pushed at his topcoat in an attempt to remove it. Breaking the kiss, he lifted enough to allow her to remove both topcoat and waistcoat before he settled upon her once more.

The pressure of his body against hers was nothing short of heaven. The strong muscles of his chest flexed and moved against hers, and her leg instinctually lifted to wrap around his hip, as she pulled his shirt from his trousers.

Her hands moved under his shirt and traced through the smattering of hair on his stomach to his ribs. His breathing was as laboured as hers and a hand to his chest confirmed his heart pounded as intensely as her own.

He grasped her thigh just above her garter and pulled her closer. A rigid and hot part of him pressed against her through his clothes, and she groaned at the intense ache growing between her thighs. Everything in her body screamed for him to touch her there—his touch alone could alleviate the want that continued to intensify.

159

Just as his fingers brushed against that part of her body, she moaned, masking the sound of the dressing room door as it opened; however, she could not miss Hattie's voice as she called her name, the high-pitched gasp, or the door slamming shut.

Her husband sprang from her body as if he had been singed, and made haste to stride through the doorway to his room. His young wife remained splayed on the bed; her hair a wreck, her skirt bunched up around the tops of her legs, and with a throbbing ache between her thighs that begged for relief.

Elizabeth pulled her skirt down, rolled to her side, and curled into a ball, where she remained as she attempted to bring herself once more under regulation. Her breathing, over time, returned to normal, as did the beating of her heart, but that ache, while diminished, would not disappear altogether.

After she felt more in control of herself, she groaned and stood, smoothing her skirt as much as she could. When she caught her reflection in the mirror, she gave up, since her dismal efforts would not go far to righting her appearance.

When she opened the door to the dressing room, Hattie bustled through, blushing to the roots of her hair.

"Mrs. Darcy, I beg you to forgive me."

"Do not fret," said Elizabeth. "I am not angry, but in the future, both of us might be spared this mortification if you knock before entering."

"I had already determined to do so, ma'am." Hattie nodded and gestured towards the dressing room. "The housekeeper thought you might be wanting a bath after being out all day. She has footmen bringing up the water now."

"A bath would be lovely." She smiled in an effort to put her maid at ease. "But perhaps we could get my hair taken down and combed out first?"

Hattie beamed as Elizabeth took a seat before the dressing table. "Yes, ma'am. I'll get your pretty curls combed out in a trice!"

Meanwhile, Darcy was sinking into a bath of his own. He deserved a solid tongue-lashing for pushing Elizabeth. Although he had meant to do no more than kiss her, her response urged him further. The little pants in his ear, her vocalisations, her removal of his coat; all indicated she had not been frightened or averse to his advances.

The problem was that he had fallen in love with her. After considering the situation, he discovered it was useless trying to figure out how it had happened. Bewitched from the beginning with her beauty, her wit and her honesty had drawn him in further. She was so unlike anyone—any woman—he had ever met before, and the emotions had simply crept up on him. He was in the middle before he had been aware he had begun.

The night before, he had taken a step towards advancing their relationship, but still denied deeper feelings than friendship for her. What a farce!

Now, he needed her to love him in return. Ever since his grandmother had knocked sense into him, he had courted her. But what if it did not work? What if she never felt more than gratitude?"

He groaned and sank further into the tub. They had not been married long; so it was far too early to concede defeat. The courtship would continue until she loved him. Hopefully, it would not take months or even, god forbid, years.

He groaned again and sank below the water. She had to care for him at least a little.

Chapter 12

Darcy was seated at his grandfather's desk as he sorted his correspondence and the papers he had received since their arrival in Bath.

His grandmother had sent several letters, which included one with the details of the visit his father and Lady Catherine had bestowed upon her before she departed London. He had even received a similar letter from his uncle, who chronicled his confrontation with Lady Catherine. Uncle Henry had refused to argue with her and had his butler show her to the door.

The missives were gathered and set together with notes from Georgiana that had been included in his grandmother's correspondence. She had been thrilled when she received word of his marriage and was insistent she would meet Elizabeth one day.

The last letter was from Bingley. It had been a fortnight since they happened upon his friend on the street, and Darcy had been shocked when a messenger arrived the day after their impromptu meeting to deliver the missive. He had never provided Bingley with the direction, but Bingley was more industrious than he presumed. He opened the page, and scanned it one more time.

18 May 1810
Camden Place, Bath

Darcy,

Caroline's machinations truly astound me at times, and dear friend, I owe you an apology for not seeing through her latest scheme.

I swear to you my slip was entirely accidental. I seem to have muttered it under my breath, and she somehow heard what I said. That is beside the point now, and I can do no more than remedy the situation I have caused.

I was gobsmacked when you told me why she insisted on passing the month in Bath, but her motives were clear when you departed with such haste. She was furious at the perceived slight and blamed your wife for the public cut. You and I are both aware she is mistaken, but Caroline has always viewed matters from one perspective, and attempting to convince her otherwise has proven to be a fruitless endeavour.

Tomorrow, we depart for the north. I will be taking Louisa and Hurst to his estate in Warwickshire on my way to Scarborough. Unless Caroline wishes to remain with the Hursts, we will return home for the summer. She is angry, to say the least, and has sworn she will never forgive me. Somehow, I believe I will survive her disapprobation.

Last night, I also informed her I would accept no further excuses to reject calls from potential suitors. She must find a husband by the end of the next season, or she will be sent to serve as a companion to my great aunt in Yorkshire.

I do hope this will alleviate any concern that she might confront you in the future. I would not wish to mar the joy of your wedding trip with her antics.

I will be in touch further once I have reached Scarborough.

Regards,

Charles Bingley

Darcy sighed and threw the letter, along with a few invitations to which Elizabeth had already responded, into the grate. They had not attended many functions since their arrival in Bath and had avoided the remaining balls of the season, instead frequenting concerts and theatre performances. Their last public outing was to be the next evening at the Gala in Sydney Gardens in honour of the king's birthday.

He took great pleasure in the look of child-like wonder that graced Elizabeth's eyes when he mentioned fireworks. Her reaction to viewing the spectacle for the first time would, no doubt, give him great pleasure.

Thoughts of his wife brought back memories of the interrupted encounter between them only a few days prior, he had been so concerned matters would be awkward between them, yet when he ventured to her chambers to escort her to dinner that very evening, Elizabeth put him at ease with a becoming smile and her teasing manner.

"I hope I did not offend you earlier," he began as soon as Hattie departed the room. His hands were clenched before him as he awaited her answer.

Before he finished speaking, she began shaking her head. "No, I was not…"

"I also owe you an apology for leaving so abruptly. I had not expected your maid to interrupt."

She laughed, and his fingers relaxed their grip as his tension eased. "I had not either. I believe she was as mortified as we were." She glanced towards the door to the dressing room and back. "She will knock before entering in the future."

"I should have a similar conversation with James."

"I do not think your valet will burst into my room."

She wore a mischievous expression that he wished to kiss, but instead, he chuckled and shifted on his feet. "No, but one day, we may try to spend a night in my bed, and I would not wish him to barge in as Hattie did today."

He enfolded her in his embrace and his lips caressed her forehead. Darcy sighed in contentment when her small hands came to rest upon his waist.

"I was concerned things would become awkward between us after the... interruption."

She nestled closer to him. "I had been, too; but we cannot be awkward for the remainder of our lives."

He smiled and smoothed a loose lock of hair over her shoulder. "You are a very practical woman, Mrs. Darcy."

She giggled and stretched up to give him a brief kiss on the lips. "Well, it is fortunate one of us can see sense." His mouth opened in a stunned expression as she backed away towards the door, laughing. "Shall we go to dinner, Mr. Darcy?"

He admired the way her eyes sparkled and beamed in pleasure. "I believe we should."

"Fitzwilliam?" He turned to where the object of his musings entered with a letter in her hand. "I received a note from my aunt and uncle. They have returned to Meryton."

"How long since their arrival?"

She scanned the paper and shook her head. "He never mentions, but their house was in shambles. It seems someone searched for a clue as to their destination."

Concern was evident in her eyes and, more than anything, he did not want her to worry. "The investigator has been unable to locate your uncle. Gardiner has not shown at any of his usual haunts, and Mr. Simms believes he is hidden somewhere in one of the poorer neighbourhoods in London. I doubt he has the money for travel to Meryton."

"But we have no way of knowing for certain." Her voice was soft but anxious, so he stood and closed the door for privacy, then drew her into his arms.

"No, we do not, but the man I hired is excellent. I believe his instincts to be correct." He trailed his hand up and down her back until she relaxed and wrapped her arms about his waist. "He has seen Grayson's men watch these places too as they wait for your uncle to appear. He wants this debt he thinks he is owed, and he wants it badly."

"My uncle would be a fool to show his face, then."

He bestowed a kiss to her hairline. "He has hidden himself well. I do not believe he will emerge from his refuge willingly."

She nodded with a relieved air. Then she caught his eye and raised her eyebrows, which he had learned indicated a desire to kiss him. He loved that expression. It was rivalled only by the dreamy look she had after a kiss.

"You do not wish to discuss your uncle anymore?"

"No, for it is worrisome, and I should much prefer something pleasant to occupy our time."

"Do you wish to play cards?" he asked with mock innocence.

A mischievous smile lit upon her face, and she shook her head.

"We could play chess or backgammon?"

She blushed to the roots of her hair. "Kiss me, Fitzwilliam."

He grinned and drew her closer to touch his lips to hers. He deepened the kiss and Elizabeth responded by pressing herself against him, soon finding themselves quite entangled.

She had one hand in his hair, while the other was pressed against his lower back. His lips had long since left hers and were poised at her bosom while he pulled her as close as possible.

How he had refrained from taking her in the last fortnight was beyond his comprehension. She had slept in his embrace every night, but he had managed to limit their interludes to kissing.

A loud groan erupted from his chest, and he gathered her up into his arms, taking a seat on the sofa with her astride him. His shaky fingers caressed a wisp of a curl from in front of her fine eyes. Every facet of his bride's appearance was stunning—face flushed, lips slightly swollen, hair falling from its pins. If only a portrait could be painted of her like this—but he could never abide another man seeing her in such a state.

Elizabeth leaned forward and brushed her lips against his, while she stared into his eyes. The body that lay beneath her clothes beckoned to him, and the pull was too intense to ignore. He reached back to unbutton her gown and pushed the garment away until it was bunched at her waist. Her stays were removed and tossed to the floor, the delicate ribbons of her chemise were loosened without care, and the thin material wrested to the side revealing one flawless breast.

He was entranced by the part of her that had been, until that moment, a mystery to him. His hand rose to gently touch, but Elizabeth began to work loose his cravat before his fingertips could meet the soft, exposed flesh. He helped her remove his topcoat as well as his waistcoat; however, before his fine lawn shirt could be pulled over his head, she stopped and stared, tracing her fingers down his neck to the indention of his collarbone where she threaded them through the hair that peeked out of the opening.

His lips claimed hers without restraint as he ran a hand into the opening of her chemise. His palm cupped her breast where he began to knead the firm flesh with his fingers.

He did not need to gaze upon her to know she was perfect. Not that he did not want to memorize in detail every inch of her like she was a fine work of art. Whatever scars or imperfection she had did not mar her in his view. They were a part of her—a part of her beauty.

"You are exquisite." His lips moved to her neck as his thumb brushed the soft peak. At the sound of her sharp inhale, his arousal heightened.

They had barely begun anything, and she had already made things impossible for him with her constant shifting. Her small vocalisations were another problem. She had to have no idea what they did to him. How could he possibly stop? The door was not locked, and they were not even in the vicinity of their rooms. What if someone entered?

He peeked at her face and her eyes met his. Holding her gaze, he reached over to bestow a small kiss to her nipple. No objection escaped her lips, so he gently suckled. Her expression was one of surprise, but her hand tightened until she had a painful grip in his hair, which prompted him to continue his explorations. He received a throaty moan, in response, which was music to his ears, and he rejoiced as she pulled his head closer to her chest.

He pulled away and pressed a small kiss to her mouth. "Does that feel good?"

She nodded as he ran a hand down the side of her face. "If there is something you find objectionable, then you must tell me. I want you to always be honest with me." He spoke low, but she was attentive to every word.

"You have always been a perfect gentleman. I trust you to be honest with me, too—especially, in this."

Her voice was uneasy as she spoke, so he paused, aware she was relying on him to guide her. Most young women had a mother or aunt to talk with them before their wedding. Elizabeth had no one.

"You have no reason to be uncomfortable." He brushed her hair back from her face, and his lips caressed her temple until they reached her ear while she angled her head to bring him closer. "Nothing pleases me more than hearing the noises you make when we are like this."

Heat radiated from her cheek, and he nuzzled his way to her collarbone, then further down to her chest. Her chemise was shifted to reveal her other breast, so he could repeat the attentions he gave to the other side.

Elizabeth was panting heavily, a small high pitch sound coming with every exhale. When he released her nipple and buried his face in her cleavage, breathing deeply, she was still clinging to his head.

The pain of her tugging on his hair was nothing, because in all his memory, he had never had an erection so painful, and as much as he wished to release it and finish what they had begun, he knew he could not. Elizabeth deserved better.

He had just reached to bestow one last soft kiss to her lips, when a knock interrupted him. They both startled and stared at one another.

Elizabeth's eyes were like saucers, and he had to restrain his amusement while he began to tie the delicate pink ribbons on her chemise. "Who is it?" he called loudly.

"It is Mr. Shaw, sir. A letter was delivered for you." Darcy withheld a groan of disappointment.

Elizabeth lifted herself from his lap to grab her stays, wrapped them around her, and turned so he could lace and tie them.

"Mr. Darcy?" they heard the butler call through the heavy oak of the door.

She looked frantically over her shoulder, and he gestured to his still present erection. "I cannot open it," he whispered.

Her eyes darted to his trousers. "Neither can I, but is the door locked?"

"Mr. Shaw, please slide the letter under the door." The statement was made in as normal and in as usual a voice as he could muster, but Elizabeth bit her lip as she tried not to laugh. He pulled and tightened the laces—*please do not let me lace them incorrectly!* The last thing he wanted was for his wife to be embarrassed when her maid helped her change for dinner.

"Oh... Yes, sir," called Mr. Shaw. The letter appeared on their side of the door as it slid underneath.

"Thank you!" Darcy collected the missive, noting it was from his sister, and placed it in his pocket; he was not in the proper frame of mind at the present moment.

He turned his attention back to Elizabeth, who had been unable to hold in her mirth any longer, and burst into gales of laughter. The sound of his amusement soon joined hers and they both took seats on the sofa. As they brought themselves under control, Elizabeth drew out her handkerchief and wiped her eyes.

He gestured towards her skirt. "Would you like me to help you with your gown?"

"Oh, yes, thank you." She pivoted, so he could fasten the row of tiny buttons. When he was finished, she settled against the back of the seat and curled her legs under her skirt.

"Who sent the letter?"

He leaned his head against the sofa, and she began to brush his curls back from his face. He closed his eyes and simply enjoyed the sensation of her fingers as they ran through his hair. She continued her occupation, and he did not move or speak for fear she would stop.

"Fitzwilliam," she said with a giggle. "Who sent the letter?"

"Oh... Georgiana."

"You are not curious to know what she has to say?" How relaxed he had become with her touch! She had always enjoyed when Jane combed her fingers through her hair and it was clear her husband found contentment in it as well.

He fidgeted in his pocket and pulled the note out, presenting it to her. "I cannot read it whilst you are doing that. Perhaps you could read it aloud?"

"Are you certain?" she asked, surprised. "I would not wish to intrude."

"Georgiana turns fourteen this month. Her letters are usually about Pemberley, her horse, and the pianoforte. Besides, there is nothing I wish to hide from you."

She bit her lip as she beamed with pleasure. He had become so open with her lately, sharing so much more of himself. She had fallen in love with him over the course of their wedding trip, but had kept the knowledge to herself. A part of her was screaming to tell him, but what if he did not say those precious words back? She would be unable to hide the disappointment if he failed to reciprocate her adoration. Her only other option was to wait and pray that he would one day have the same passion for her.

The seal on the letter broke easily, and she opened the page, noting that his sister had a neat and even handwriting for one so young. He laid his head in her lap, and she laughed at the dimpled grin on his face as she stroked his locks with her free hand.

"28 May, 1810
Pemberley, Derbyshire

Dear Fitzwilliam,

I was pleased to receive your response to my last letter this morning. Mrs. Reynolds has been instrumental in ensuring I am able to post my letters and that I receive yours. Thus far, I do not think father suspects, but I do not believe we should enlist Grandmamma unless it is necessary. I would not wish to give father further reason to dislike her.

Thank you for describing Mrs. Darcy. She sounds delightful and accomplished. How I wish things were different, so I could meet her face to face! It would be so wonderful to have a sister to accompany me riding around Pemberley or to play a duet. Please do not think I am disappointed in only having a brother! I have always enjoyed your company, but I have longed for a sister for some time. I do hope she will like me!

"I cannot imagine not liking one as kind and agreeable as she is. I hope your father does not discover your correspondence. Would he be terribly angry?"

"Father will be angry, but his ire never lasts long towards Georgiana. I believe she reminds him too much of my mother. He is also aware of her tender heart. She rarely misbehaves, but when she does, it is usually for the best of reasons."

"Then she is very unlike me when I was that age."

He opened an eye to peek in her direction. "Were you forever in trouble?"

"No, not always. My mother was never sure how to make me behave like a girl—those were her words."

He frowned as he gazed at her. "You by no means resemble a boy."

"She claimed that girls did not climb trees or play swords with the boys."

His eyebrows lifted. "You fenced?"

"I stopped by the time I was Georgiana's age, but I still found great enjoyment in climbing trees." He nodded and closed his eyes as she continued to comb her fingers through his hair.

"Would you please request Mrs. Darcy pen a letter to enclose in your next correspondence? I would dearly love to know her in the event we are unable to meet in person for some time. Father has said he will bring me to London in October for the benefit of the masters, and I would like to spend some time with Grandmamma whilst I am there. Perchance you can travel to London in October or November?

I look forward to letters from you and Mrs. Darcy. I do so like receiving post!

Your loving sister,

Georgiana Darcy"

"She sounds charming, Fitzwilliam. When will you send your response?"

"I think once we have returned to Sagemore. I am sure she would like to hear of the gala."

"I am certain you are correct. I will be sure to write to her as soon as we return, too." She began to read through the letter once more on her own.

"Thank you."

She peered down to find him staring at her. "Why do you thank me?"

"For wishing to be acquainted with my sister."

She smiled, folded the missive, and placed it on the side table. "She is my sister now, as well. Besides, how could I not wish to correspond with her when she is so welcoming?"

"It is you who is kind." He spoke so earnestly that she blushed at his praise. "I am glad I happened upon you in Meryton. I have come to believe we were meant to meet that day."

"Do you?" she whispered.

His expression was so serious, so earnest it made her stomach flutter. "I do. I do not think I could be happy married to anyone but you."

Elizabeth clung to Darcy's arm as he escorted her towards the queue for their carriage. He had just had the most incredible evening! The gala in honour of the king's birthday had gone off without a spot of rain, and he was certain Elizabeth had never witnessed anything so spectacular.

He had reserved a private booth outside where they dined as the musicians played on the balcony of the Sydney Hotel. The performances they had heard prior were by far superior, but the illuminations and the fireworks had been worth the time spent listening to the mediocre music.

They had been sitting in their seats when a whistle blew to queue the simultaneous lighting of the oil lamps all over the garden. It had been a breath-taking sight, and Elizabeth had grasped his arm as she gasped in delight. Then, rather than listening to the musicians, he had taken her on a walk through the garden nearby, until it was almost time for the fireworks, when he returned them to their seats.

The fireworks had been his best idea yet! He chuckled whenever she jumped at the loud explosions they made, and she marvelled it was like nothing she had ever seen before. The evening had been a great success!

Elizabeth leaned against him as he spied the carriage make its way towards them. He was anxious to return to Landsdown Crescent so she could rest. The morrow would be dedicated to packing, and they would depart the day after for Sagemore.

Bath had been worth the social discomfort he had suffered, but Elizabeth alleviated a great deal of it with her outgoing personality. He did not mind the social whirl quite so much in her company, so they had attended musical performances and the theatre often. They did avoid the Upper and Lower Rooms. He had no wish to attend any of the dances, and she confided that, while she enjoyed dancing, she was content without that diversion. He made up for his aversion to the assemblies by taking her on frequent walks through Sydney Gardens and the various parks around town, where they both took great pleasure in nature and the pleasant weather.

At the moment, she was watching the people around them.

"Elizabeth," he said when the door to their carriage was opened.

She started. "Oh, I had not noticed it arrive."

He handed her inside and followed, taking the seat across as propriety dictated. Once the carriage pulled from the curb and turned a corner, he closed the blinds and shifted to his usual place beside her. Her hand joined with his, and their fingers laced together. He had been about to turn in order ask her favourite part of the evening, when her head rested against his shoulder. He loved her spontaneous gestures, her natural affection.

His mother had been similar, and, since her passing, Darcy had not had someone who made him feel as loved as Elizabeth did. He buried his nose in her hair, bestowed a kiss and closed his eyes as he caught the familiar scent of orange blossoms.

The evening had been magical. He had been to Vauxhall and had seen illuminations and fireworks before, but through Elizabeth's eyes, the experience became new once again. She watched the shows with such a wide-eyed wonder, and he enjoyed every minute of the evening in her company. The crowd had not even dampened his enjoyment.

She had also worn the gown he requested, a deep green silk with a silver embroidered trim that matched her complexion perfectly. With the jewellery Hattie found tucked in a drawer in Elizabeth's dressing room, they had even managed a coordinating emerald necklace and earbobs.

"Elizabeth?"

"Hmmm?"

"I just wanted to be sure you were not falling asleep."

He heard her soft chuckle. "No, not yet."

"Did you enjoy the evening?"

She lifted her head and looked with concern into his eyes. "Could you not tell? I felt as if I were a child at Christmas."

He laughed and put his arm around her, which caused her to have to adjust her head to become comfortable once more. "I suppose I just wanted to hear you say it—to tell me what part you enjoyed the most."

"I do not know if I have a favourite part. I enjoyed everything."

"But the music," he commented. "You do not always ask to go for a stroll whilst the musicians are playing."

"There were quite a few people who left to walk through the garden after the illuminations were lit." She glanced at him with a content expression. "But you are correct. We have heard performances that far surpassed tonight." She nestled back onto his shoulder and they continued in that attitude until they arrived at the house.

He anticipated joining his wife in her bedchamber that evening. She had not indicated she loved him, but she enjoyed the intimacy they had shared thus far. Would his wife object to him initiating more?

He took his nightshirt from James and then dismissed him for the night. The idea of finally making love to his wife for the first time had rendered him aroused, a sight he had no wish for his valet to witness. He rushed through his evening routine and donned his nightshirt and dressing gown, then when he was ready, he began pacing.

Should he try to speak with her first? Should he begin with simple kisses and let things progress from there?

He halted and muttered to himself, "What am I doing? Get to it, man!"

With a step forward, he knocked lightly, but his brow furrowed as he remained awaiting her call to enter. Surely, her sweet voice would have summoned him by now!

He turned the knob, pushed open the door, and peered around to ensure she was not still with her maid. Hattie was not present and his eye was drawn to the bed, where Elizabeth was curled on her side fast asleep, a book resting open on the bed beside her.

Sighing, he looked down to his tented nightshirt and dressing gown. "I suppose tonight is not the night."

He carefully removed the book from under her hand and marked her place as he set it on the side table. The last of the candles were extinguished, and he crawled into bed where he curled up to her back and draped his arm over her waist.

Sleep did not come easily, but eventually, his eyes began to droop.

"I love you," he whispered, as he slipped to sleep.

Chapter 13

Elizabeth's eyes flew open as she awakened with a start. The house was quiet, and a gap in the draperies showed it was pitch black outside, which indicated it was still quite late. The comfort of being wrapped in her husband's embrace was no surprise, since it had become their usual practice. But, what had caused her to awaken so abruptly?

Fitzwilliam moaned in her ear, and her eyes bulged as his hand at the junction of her thigh and rear, kneaded her buttock; his fingers curling into her flesh. He had awakened her!

Warmth radiated from him, permeating the bedclothes and heating her skin, and she yearned to remove the sheet and coverlet to cool; however, she would be exposed to him should he awaken. The problem was that his actions did not cease, but continued; his hand ran down the back of her thigh, then slid back up to squeeze her rear again.

She did not know what to do. If her husband continued on as he was she would never return to sleep!

The dream could not last until morning, could it?

She reached behind her to bring his arm back around her stomach, and he stopped for a few minutes—long enough for her to settle. His fingers then inched down under her shift, pressing her back to him. He groaned as he rolled his hips against her backside. The impression of his ardent touch and the warmth of his firm body along her back was causing a now familiar ache which was sure to prevent her from drifting back to sleep.

A serious dilemma was before her. If she roused him he would be embarrassed by his actions and she had no wish to cause him unease.

His hand began to search once more, rising up to cover her breast and squeeze. Her eyes closed as she gasped with a strangled vocalization, and his movement came to an abrupt halt. His fingers retreated from under her nightclothes before the bed shifted and her back cooled with the loss of him against her. He had rolled away.

She remained stunned where she was for a few minutes and then bit back a frustrated huff. Now, she was wide-awake, even though he had stopped! He could not stop! Not now! His caresses had her body demanding satisfaction, and despite her naivety on the subject, she would not be put off. She steeled her courage and rolled over to face her husband in the dim light of the fire.

He closed his eyes in mortification. "Forgive me…" he began in a whisper.

His apology was unnecessary; she reached out to grab his nightshirt near the collar, his words ceasing as she stopped them with her mouth.

Until now, she had used a little look to indicate her desire for a kiss, but after all of his touching and stroking, she was in no mood to wait for him—she had waited long enough! She even deepened their kiss before he did by grazing his tongue with hers. He groaned again and drew her closer as she ran her knee up his leg, wrapping her calf around his hips.

Fitzwilliam's response was immediate and by no means dispassionate. His hand left a scalding trail of heat up her leg until he reached her waist and pulled her flush to his body. Nothing could have prepared her for the onslaught of sensation he invoked when he drew her closer, but she clung to him, one hand bunching his nightshirt, the other on the side of his muscled stomach.

Taking her with him, he rolled on to his back and withdrew from their kiss; so they were a hairsbreadth apart. When she opened her eyes, he studied her as her legs slid down so she was astride him. The position was similar to when they were in the study, and the remembrance was enough to cause her heart to pound in breathless anticipation. Her husband's eyes sought permission, so she ever so slightly dipped her head and closed her eyes.

Darcy had not the words to ensure she was aware of his intentions. Her face tilted forward and he brushed her lips with his. The kiss began gentle, but she escalated their embrace by grazing his tongue with hers. He moaned out loud as he reached up to grasp her by the hair. His desperation for her was beyond reason, and he poured every bit of his longing and love into his worship of not only her body but her.

He had been waiting for this—waiting for Elizabeth his entire life. No woman was more perfect, more alluring than his wife, and with very little effort on her part, he was undone. Tonight, she was proving she wanted him—she desired him. It was more than he could have ever dreamed; yet she was here before him, casting aside her inhibitions. He breathed deep and steady in a futile attempt to calm himself.

The temptation of Elizabeth above him was too great, and he moved his hands to her hips, holding her in place as he ground himself into her overwhelming heat. Despite his nightshirt between them, the sensation was indescribable, but not enough, so he urged her hips up in order to pull his garment from beneath her. Once it was removed, it was hastily flung to the floor and forgotten. In the hopes of gaining some semblance of control, he paused to admire her.

She was so beautiful. Her shift draped to expose a portion of her chest and cleavage, her hair was loosened from its braid, trailing over her shoulder, and her lips were moist and swollen. Her eyes held his, unabashed and full of passion, as she pressed herself to his chest and claimed his lips.

He enjoyed the pleasure of her kiss while he skimmed his fingertips down her shoulder, marvelling in how soft she was to the touch. When her mouth parted and her small gasps fanned across face, his lips, following no rhyme or reason, tasted wherever they touched. He sampled her neck, her collarbone, and her ear as her panting increased until she sounded out of breath.

When he drew back to gaze upon her once more, her eyes were dilated, her jaw was slack and her lips reddened and parted open. His hand grazed her breast and stomach to her leg where her shift had bunched up around her upper thighs. Reaching under her gown, he clenched the sides of her hips and moved the material aside so they were skin to skin and again ground up. Her eyes fluttered closed and the incoherent noise that escaped her lips was the most incredible sound he had ever heard uttered.

Her hips began to undulate against him, and it was necessary to find an occupation to help distract from the exquisite torture she inflicted. He gently drew her head back by her hair, so he could claim her lips while he untied the ribbons at the top of her shift, the diaphanous material sliding from her shoulders with little prompting.

He touched his forehead to hers and peered down to find two of the most flawless breasts he had ever seen. Before, he had only had a glimpse through the opening of her chemise, but now she was completely bared to him.

She ceased her movement and bit her bottom lip.

"Elizabeth," he whispered, "open your eyes."

Wide, mahogany orbs met his and their gazes locked as he continued to stroke over her supple flesh. "Your beauty awakens my soul to act[1]."

He lifted his head from the pillow to worship her breasts, and a garbled sound rose from her throat as she grasped his head to pull him closer. With her enfolded in his arms, he rolled her underneath him. She squirmed at the lump her shift had created under her back, and he helped her to remove it, casting it to the floor with his nightshirt.

He gazed at her unguardedly, taking in every detail of her body before lowering himself on top of her. "Lift your knees."

"Like this?"

His kiss was unreserved as he caressed her sides and hips to ensure she was at ease. His heart ached at the pain he was about to inflict, but it could not be helped. He balanced his reluctance and desire and pressed forward as her barrier provided just enough resistance that there was no mistaking when it gave way. As she gasped, he was engulfed in such heat that he grit his teeth as he hastened to maintain control.

"Oh, Lizabeth," he gritted out. Though it was torturous, he remained still despite every fibre in his being screaming for him to bring them both to completion.

"Yes?"

"I need you."

She cradled his face and gazed at him with tears in her eyes. "You have me. I am yours."

He groaned in response and began carefully moving in and out. It was bliss! His forehead dropped onto her shoulder as he moved faster and faster, and she began meeting him stroke for stroke. Her legs gripped his hips as if she were trying to prevent him from bidding a hasty retreat, and her fingernails dug into the tender flesh of his sides.

Time was forgotten and everything around them blurred. It was impossible to focus on anything other than the exquisite sensation of making her his. The end barrelled upon him with force, and he clutched her to him as he made one last surge, a guttural cry escaping his throat.

His arms were like jelly and could not keep him aloft, so he collapsed on top of her. Pure joy overwhelmed him to an extent unknown before that moment. Being with Elizabeth was unlike anything he had ever known or expected—it was better.

His lips found the velvet soft skin of her neck, and he trailed along her flesh to her ear. Gentle kisses were then bestowed to her eyes, nose, and finally, her lips. He drew back and his eyes sought hers, searching for definitive proof that his experience and emotions were shared to the same intensity.

Her gaze was soft. She reached for his temple, brushed back a few damp curls, and skimmed her fingers down his neck to trace along the spattering of hair on his chest.

With great care, he rolled from her and pulled her to his side, sensitive to the possibility she might have some discomfort. She gave no indication she was even sore as she placed her head upon his shoulder while he wrapped his arm around her body. His free hand took hers from where it rested on his chest, and he caressed her palm.

After a few passes, she reversed their hands, taking his and rubbing a callous. "How did you get these?" Her voice was quiet.

"From working in the stables at Pemberley."

She propped her chin on his chest and furrowed her brow. "Your father expected this of you?"

"No… and it is not one of my favourite memories."

"Then I do not expect you to share it. I am sorry if I caused you pain by asking." She wore a look of genuine concern as she returned her head to his shoulder.

Darcy reached up to brush his fingers through her curls. He should not have avoided the question. Since becoming his wife, she had asked him for so little. How could he deny her wish to know him better?

"When I was a boy, I often played with the son of my father's steward, George Wickham. He was an only child and quite spoiled whilst his mother remained with him and his father; however, she deserted the family when he was five. No one knew to where she had disappeared.

"His father, with the help of a few of the tenants, managed as best he could. The absence of the mother appeared to correct much of the younger Wickham's temper, but the elder Wickham died when his son was thirteen, and matters changed in a drastic fashion.

"My father, as the boy's godfather, took pity on the young man. He gave him a room within Pemberley and promised to educate him as a gentleman."

"That was very generous of him."

Elizabeth once again watched him with her chin propped on the back of her hand. He had little pleasure in the current topic, but he could not deny the great pleasure he felt at such intimacy with his wife.

He again combed through her locks as he regained his place in the story. "It was quite kind, but I am afraid it altered Wickham." She frowned, and he traced the little crease that formed between her brows.

"How so?"

"We were sent to Eton together." As he recounted the tale, he continued to toy with her hair to ease the tension caused by speaking of Wickham.

"Wickham believed that as my father's ward, he was as good as a son—but the other boys did not see it as such. He became angry that they accepted me whilst he found only a select group of boys who would befriend him." He glanced back to her face. "Most of the boys who accepted me did so only because of who my father and grandfather are, not who I am inside. I was always polite, but I had few true friends, just as he did."

"He could not be upset with you? It was hardly your fault."

"But he believed it was, and when we returned to Pemberley during break, he ensured I was well aware of the fact that we were no longer friends, even at home." She furrowed her brow, so he tried to smile, but it came out half-hearted.

"He began plotting schemes which often resulted in my receiving punishments from my father."

"What sort of schemes?"

"Well, once he spilled ink on a book in the library. The rain that day prevented me from venturing outside, and the entire staff was aware I had passed the day within that room reading. When I returned to my chambers to refresh myself, he committed the offense and departed with haste. I was blamed."

"I admit to not being familiar with Pemberley's library, but could the book not be replaced?"

A heavy exhale left him as he gave her a sad smile. "Are you familiar with the Eliot Bible²?"

"My father once mentioned it to me. It was a version of the Bible translated into the Indian language in America, was it not?"

"Yes, it was, and my father received an edition of that book from the first printing in 1663, as a gift. He was furious when it was destroyed. There were other plots, but that was by far the worst."

She pressed her lips to his chest, and then leaned forward to bestow a kiss to his lips. "What else did Wickham do?"

"He ambushed me as I ventured around the estate either to fish or to the stables to ride. The first few times, he caught me by surprise and managed to throw some rather hard blows to my chest and stomach before I could escape him."

She lifted her head from where it rested; the horror she felt evident in her expression. "That is terrible! Did your father never discover Wickham's abuse?"

"No, George ensured his punches were always to the body and never my face. My father also enjoyed Wickham's company. I had no desire to disappoint him."

"But he injured you! Your father's first loyalty should have been to his son, not his ward!"

He shrugged. He had no desire to become angered about the past. Little could be gained by such resentment.

"The stable manager witnessed one of Wickham's attacks. He pulled George off and told him to be on his way, threatening to tell my father. Mr. Johns then took me aside and asked questions about how long Wickham had been assaulting me."

"Did he come to your defence?"

"After I confided in him, he suggested I spend time in the stables. He offered to teach me about horses, which appealed to me; I have always loved horses and riding. The occupation also kept me out of Wickham's schemes. The next time he attempted to cause trouble, I had Mr. Johns to confirm I was nowhere near the west wing of the house where the incident had occurred.

As it turned out, my father was very pleased I had taken such an active interest in the horses, and asked me to ride the estate with him."

"What became of Wickham?"

"Towards someone who is unaware of his true nature, he is very charming and manipulative, and he remains a favourite of my father's. We attended Cambridge together, and I know my father intends for him to take orders when an opening becomes available. I cannot think of anyone more poorly suited to become a clergyman."

Elizabeth placed another soft kiss over his heart. "Thank you for telling me. I know it could not have been easy."

He curled his hand around the back of her head and pulled her up to brush his lips across hers. He rolled them to their sides, keeping Elizabeth's body flush with his own.

"Elizabeth?"

"Hmmm?" she asked while kissing his chin.

"Do you think we could… I mean… I understand if you are sore and wish to wait."

She pressed her lips to his, and rolled to her back, pulling him along with her.

His body tensed in anticipation, but he paused and studied her eyes. Could she only trying to please him? "Are you certain?"

"Yes, I am," she whispered.

The equipage hit a bump, and Elizabeth jolted awake. She had not slept in a carriage since the accident, but her exhaustion must have overridden her fear. She shifted and peered up to find her husband still sleeping peacefully, so she nestled back against his chest.

By their surroundings, they were not far from Sagemore, and she closed her eyes, content they would soon be home. She had been to their estate the one time before, when they broke their journey to Bath; it was a lovely spot. The placement of the house and park—on an island in the middle of the Thames with stone bridges for access to the farmland and local villages—was idyllic.

Her husband had explained it was nothing to Pemberley, but having never seen his ancestral estate, she could not compare the two. She found her new home enchanting.

Beside her, her husband continued to doze. Even as he slept, he was a handsome man with his chiselled features and curly dark locks, but when he opened his crystal blue eyes, she was lost. Elizabeth was most fortunate that Fitzwilliam was also as good as he was handsome. He had proven himself time and again to be a considerate husband; one who valued her opinion and desired her comfort.

Who would have dreamed she could be so happy with someone she was more or less forced to marry? She loved him with her whole heart—if only she could hear those precious words from him!

He must have been tired. The night of the gala, they had made love a second time and then talked until they could no longer hold their eyes open. They had not rested much the two nights that followed either.

Matrons in her acquaintance spoke of marital intimacy as if it were a chore, and after their first time, it seemed possible it would be. Kissing and touching were enjoyable, but becoming one flesh had been awkward. A certain fulfilment came from his pleasure, so she could not deny him when he derived such satisfaction.

Another glance outside revealed they were passing through the village of Sonning Eye and would soon be at Sagemore. When her gaze returned to her husband, he was awake and observing her in much the same manner she had studied him earlier.

"We are in Sonning Eye."

"It appears we are." She lifted herself from his chest, and he straightened, likely stretching to alleviate the stiffness from being in such an uncomfortable position for much of the ride.

He shifted to the other seat, and they began setting themselves to rights. She adjusted any loose hairpins and put on her bonnet, while her husband buttoned his coats. As they both donned their gloves, the stones of the bridge rattled against the hard wheels of the carriage, and she shifted to the side so she could see the Magnolia trees[3] lining the road.

When they first travelled to Sagemore, the Magnolias had fascinated her. She had never seen one until that day, and she had walked amongst them, studying the dark, waxy leaves and brilliant white flowers larger than her own hand.

"You are taken with the Magnolias again?"

"There are more blooms than when we were here last. They are beautiful." A mischievous eye turned towards her husband. "But I am not as taken by them as I am the estate's owner."

His cheeks pinked, and she giggled; however, as they pulled up to the front door, her stomach clenched at the sight of the staff lined along the side of the drive. Of all this, she was mistress!

Her husband alighted the carriage and helped her down, beaming with pleasure. "Welcome home, Mrs. Darcy."

Elizabeth moved beside him and took his arm as she took in her surroundings. The house was not large by society's standards, even if it was larger than Longbourn, but her heart swelled at the sight of it. Young rosebushes forged their way up the outer walls of the house, hedges were neatly trimmed, large trees surrounded the periphery, and the wilder outer garden was in bloom. It was home—her home, and it suited her well.

They paused within the entry hall and handed their gloves and hats to Hattie and James, who had arrived before them. With a few steps forward, she stood under the crystal chandelier gazing at the small curved ceiling and painted trim that had attracted her eye during their first visit. It was one of several simple yet elegant details, which rendered the home a bit grander than it first appeared.

Mrs. Green, the housekeeper, stepped forward. "Mrs. Darcy, I hope you do not mind, but I took the liberty of ordering baths for you and the master. I have sent the footmen to begin carrying the water upstairs."

"That sounds wonderful, Mrs. Green. Perfect, I would say after two days of travel."

With a neutral expression, the housekeeper nodded, excusing herself to attend other matters. Thus far, she had accepted Elizabeth but acceptance was not enough. As the new mistress, Elizabeth would have to earn her staff's respect.

Elizabeth's attention was drawn to her husband's arm, and she allowed him to lead her to their suite of rooms. When he closed the door to the sitting room, her hand slid down until it was encased in his.

"I meant to ask you before, but why is there only a master's bedchamber?"

184

He glanced towards the bedroom and pulled her into a loose hold in his arms. "My uncle and aunt felt they would have better use of the smaller home if they shared a bed chamber. My mother indicated they expected a large family, but it was not to be."

He pulled her closer and kissed her softly. "If you would like your own chambers, we can move these furnishings and take the old bed down from the attics, or you can purchase new furniture should those not suit."

She shook her head. "I was curious, nothing more. I have no desire to change our current sleeping arrangement." He must have been concerned she now wished her own chambers since he relaxed when she shook her head. "Unless you now desire to remove to your own rooms?"

"No, I would like us to continue as we have been."

She stood on the tips of her toes and gave him a cheerful peck on the lips. "We should both take our baths before they get cold."

"I could join you," he whispered, gripping her waist. "Then we would only need one tub of water."

She laughed at his eager smile and deposited a kiss on his cheek. "I applaud your idea to save the footmen work, but the water has already been brought to our dressing rooms."

Thus far, she had been unclothed in the dark or with very little candlelight—he had yet to see her scars. What if he were to find them repulsive?

His frown displayed his disappointment, but he took her hands and drew them to his lips as he took a step back. "You are correct, of course. May I come fetch you in an hour? I thought we could take a walk around the park."

"Yes," she gushed. "A walk sounds lovely."

"Good, then; an hour it is."

He caressed her lips with tantalising slowness against hers, eliciting gooseflesh down the back of her neck. She grinned, and strode through the doorway to her dressing room. When she turned to close the door behind her, he was still standing in the same place, watching her go.

An hour later, Darcy knocked on the door to the mistress' dressing room. She called for him to enter, and he stepped through as Hattie exited to the water closet. "Are you ready?"

"Yes." She was beaming in happiness, and he could not help but take great pleasure in her joy.

He stepped forward, took her hand, and led her out of the house to the grounds. Walking his own property with her was an eye-opening experience. She noticed so many small details he had never given a second glance.

"So you approve of Sagemore then?"

She spun around with a startled expression. "Yes, very much so. I am sorry you are only now discovering how much I adore it. It is a lovely home."

"I was too concerned with estate business before our departure for Bath. We both spent that Sunday occupied with our own concerns."

Elizabeth stopped and placed a hand upon his chest. "Do not feel you did something wrong. You had not been here in over a fortnight and would be leaving again for a month complete. It was understandable you had business to attend."

"I suppose so." He entwined their fingers, and they began to walk towards the bridge that led to the farmlands.

"Where are we going?"

He could not restrain the grin that threatened to envelop his face. "Not much further. I have something I wish to show you."

A flirtatious look lit her face, and he laughed in delight. "Do not attempt your arts and allurements on me, Mrs. Darcy. You will discover where when we get there."

She pouted. "Most unfair."

"I have been anticipating this for quite some time. I will not spoil the surprise."

They continued along a path to the side of the road and soon found themselves in front of the rather large stables.

Clearly, Elizabeth was taken aback. "You wished to surprise me with the stables?"

"Not quite," he replied, as he pulled her inside.

She examined her surroundings as if she were unsure. She had spoken of riding several times since they made their initial acquaintance. Could she be wary, or perhaps, she suspected? He should not have asked her to ride with him while they were in Bath.

"I mentioned I spent a large amount of my childhood in the Pemberley stables. Mr. Johns taught me a great deal during that time. When I inherited Sagemore, I began breeding horses. My uncle had several from good bloodlines, and Homer has an excellent pedigree. I began there."

"Mr. Darcy," called a man, standing to the side, "it is good to have you back, sir."

"Johns, may I present my wife, Mrs. Elizabeth Darcy. Mrs. Darcy, I would like you to meet my stable manager, Johns."

Elizabeth must have recognised the name since she broke into a wide smile. "It is a pleasure to make your acquaintance."

Johns bowed. "Yours too, ma'am."

"Where do you have him?" asked Darcy.

Elizabeth glanced between the two men with curious fascination, and he implored Johns with his eyes to understand his request. Fortunately, the stable manager grinned and led the way to an older portion of the building situated to the back of the courtyard.

"I put what you specified back here." They turned a corner where he stopped at a stall and peered inside. He then nodded as he stepped to aside.

Darcy pressed his palm against the small of Elizabeth's back and guided her forward, so she could see inside the stall where a huge sorrel horse stood, chewing his hay. She gasped and looked to him with wide eyes.

"He is beautiful!"

"Do you like him?"

"Very much, but he is so large." Elizabeth regarded her husband with wary eyes. "You cannot mean for me to ride him?"

Johns chuckled and stepped forward. "This one's a big baby, he is, and one of the best horses we have. He's a good ride, but still gentle."

Darcy opened the door, and pulled her into the opening. "Page is perfect for you, but if you try him and do not like him, you can pick another horse."

Johns reached into his pocket and pulled out a carrot to hand to her. "Go ahead, give him this. You will see."

Darcy nodded and she held the carrot where the horse could see it.

She gave a few clucks. "Look what I have for you."

Page nickered as he stepped forward until they were face to face. He stretched his head out a bit, and she giggled as he moved his lips towards the treat, clamping them once or twice on air before grasping his prize. The entire carrot was worked into his mouth, and he began to crunch, stopping at times to nuzzle Elizabeth's hand.

When Page appeared satisfied he knew her, she ran her hand up the side of his face, gave him a scratch on the cheek, and beamed with pleasure when he twisted his head so her hand was in the soft indention under those cheeks.

"That's where he likes to be scratched ma'am," said Johns.

She made a few passes with her fingernails and the horse stretched his neck further to help her reach better. Elizabeth began laughing. "He is nothing more than a big baby."

"So, you will try him?"

"I will, but I make no promises. The mare my father had was much smaller. He would have never allowed me to ride a stallion."

Darcy nodded for Johns to leave them. When he was sure they were alone, he wrapped his arms around Elizabeth from behind as she continued to stroke the horse's large white blaze.

"He is a gelding, Elizabeth. I did not need any stallions with his bloodlines, but he had such striking markings with the small bits of his white socks that stretch over his hocks. He was also such an enjoyable ride I could not bear to part with him. I thought he would suit Georgiana well if she visited, so I kept him. Stallions can be unpredictable and unruly, so I had him gelded for my sister's safety. I wanted a horse I could trust.

"Georgiana saw him once when he was young and wanted to name him Knight. Johns and I felt Page Boy was more appropriate since he was gelded."

She arched her eyebrow. "You could have just said you named him Page Boy."

"I suppose, but I did not consider it."

She stroked back over his blaze following the white over the side of the nose. "His markings do make him beautiful. The little bit of white on his back leg looks a bit like a lick of fire."

"Do you mean over his hocks?" He gestured towards Page's back leg, and she nodded. "I think it looks like fire, as well." He wrapped his arm around her back. "So, will you ride with me tomorrow morning?"

She stopped petting the horse and rotated to face him.

With obvious pleasure, she nodded. "Yes, I would love to go riding with you."

1 From Aleghieri, Dante. The Divine Comedy

2 Eliot Bibles were published in the Algonquin language in 1663 in Cambridge, Massachusetts. There is a copy in the library at Blickling Hall in Norfolk.

3 Varieties of Magnolia existed in the UK during this time period. For example, a variety called 'Exmouth' was developed in the early 18th century by John Colliton in Devon. (http://www.telegraph.co.uk/gardening/howtogrow/8229745/How-to-grow-Magnolia-grandiflora-Exmouth.html)

Chapter 14

The early July sun beamed through the windows in the west drawing room—the best room, in Elizabeth's opinion, for needlework and reading. The west side of the house was a bit warm in the summer months, but opening a few windows allowed for a refreshing breeze to keep her cool as she worked.

In the month since their return from Bath, she and Fitzwilliam had been on their own. It had been a blissful time as their bond grew.

The few intrusions on their privacy included several callers, which Elizabeth welcomed graciously. She was pleased to meet people of the neighbourhood, and happy to find most of them welcoming. Some of the more affluent members of society were more curious to see the unknown young woman the younger Darcy had selected as his bride, but they were never rude. Regardless of the reason for their visits, she did her duty and returned every one.

Aside from the callers and the servants, their only other interruptions had been correspondence from family, which was not onerous by any means. Fitzwilliam's grandmother had sent several letters. The dowager mentioned she had extended her stay in town, but had been mysterious as to her reasons for the delay; although, her last missive told of her arrival at Matlock with Uncle Henry and Aunt Elinor.

Her husband had also received several diatribes in the form of letters from his father and Lady Catherine. Lady Catherine's were lit with a candle and tossed into the grate unopened. The elder Darcy's soon were set aflame as well, and their ashes joined the previous missives for the maids to clean later.

Elizabeth paused as her eyes studied the entire composition of her needlework. The last few stitches were not quite even, and she debated whether to remove them or leave them as they were. With a sigh, her shoulders dropped. No, they would need to be re-stitched. She began to tug at the thread but was interrupted when Knowles, the butler, entered.

"Colonel Fitzwilliam, ma'am."

She rose from her seat as a gentleman in regimentals entered behind Knowles. He came to stand before her and bowed as she curtsied.

"Mrs. Darcy, I understand."

Fitzwilliam told her of his cousin often, yet he never mentioned his or his regiment's return. Was her husband even aware of his visit?

"Yes, Colonel. I apologise; Fitzwilliam is not here to greet you, but an issue with a tenant required his attention. He felt it necessary to address the problem as soon as possible."

Knowles, who had not yet been dismissed, hovered nearby, so she faced him. "Please have tea delivered to this room, and see to it my husband is notified of his cousin's arrival as soon as he returns."

"Yes, ma'am," he responded with a bow. He made haste through the door, as she returned her attention to her guest, who was grinning, undaunted at being welcomed by a stranger.

"Please do not worry on my account. Darcy has always said I am welcome at my leisure, and I have become in the habit of arriving without warning. I do hope I have not inconvenienced you with my terrible manners."

"No." Her lip could not help but quirk up at his behaviour. "You are most welcome here. I am sure the arrangement you have with my husband still stands." She gestured towards a chair as she made herself comfortable on the sofa. "Would you care to have a seat whilst I have a room prepared? I am certain you would like to refresh yourself."

"Thank you."

The colonel situated his sabre as he sat, and she took the opportunity to study this unknown cousin. He was similar in age to her husband, perhaps a bit older. He was not handsome, but he appeared both in person and address a gentleman.

"Are you just returned from your duties?"

"I understand from the family that I arrived not long after you were wed. I spent over a week with my parents and my grandmother before taking a trip to Rosings Park in Kent."

"That is Lady Catherine's estate, is it not?"

"Yes, I wished to see how Anne fared in the wake of her mother's tirade over your marriage." He gave a small bark of laughter at his own joke.

"From what Grandmamma has told me, I would not be surprised Lady Catherine was unhappy with our marriage, but we have not opened her letters. Fitzwilliam relegates them to the grate before the ink is dry."

The Colonel gave a snort and shook his head. "I am not surprised. It does no good to argue rather, it is best to ignore what are her

191

attempts to intimidate you." He leaned towards the arm of the chair and adjusted his sabre once more. "I believe my father managed to silence her when she travelled to London. Then Anne took ill, and she hurried them back to Rosings, blaming the putrid air in town."

She tilted forward in her seat. "I do hope Miss de Bourgh is recovered. I know Mr. Darcy is very fond of his cousin."

Mrs. Green bustled in and placed a tea service on the table before her. "Pardon me, ma'am. I have the colonel's usual room being prepared, and Mrs. Thomas has been informed there will be three for dinner."

"Thank you," Elizabeth replied. The housekeeper bobbed her head in a curt manner and exited.

Her attention returned to the colonel. "Miss de Bourgh is well, then?"

"I do not know if you could ever consider Anne *well*. The fever has abated, but she has a lingering cough. Despite her ill health, she was pleased to hear of your marriage to our cousin."

She was taken aback. "She could not have been pleased to endure the resulting trip to London, where she became unwell?"

He held her gaze. "No, but Anne has been lectured her entire life that, despite her wishes, she would marry Darcy. She no longer has to endure her mother's insistent arguments, and is thankful to be free of something she always dreaded. Your marriage has made her very happy." He pulled several letters from his coat and placed one on the table. "She requested me to deliver this to you."

Elizabeth picked up the note and stared at the shaky script of her name. "I am glad to hear her fever has abated. I hope the cough does not linger for long."

The sound of the front door opening and the tell-tale steps of her husband's boots, striding through the entry caught her ear. Colonel Fitzwilliam must have recognized it too, since he stood and rounded the chair at almost the same moment Fitzwilliam entered.

"Richard!" Fitzwilliam exclaimed. The two men clasped hands and Fitzwilliam grasped his cousin's hand with both of his own. "We have heard nothing from you for so long! We quite feared for news of you."

"I have been well—only busy. You should know what a terrible correspondent I am by now.

Her husband chuckled, strode over, and placed his palm to the small of her back. "You have met Elizabeth, then?"

"I have met your lovely wife, cousin. She made my cup of tea whilst Mrs. Green has a room prepared."

"You will remain with us for some time, will you not?"

Her husband was so hopeful, yet perhaps the colonel would say no. The sentiment was terrible, but what if he stole Fitzwilliam's time away from her? Her husband would not forget about her now that his childhood friend was here, would he? The entire idea was nonsensical, but she had been Fitzwilliam's sole companion since their marriage. She did not want to be replaced, even if it was temporary. The colonel's answer returned her to the conversation at hand.

"I am required to report to headquarters in London in a fortnight, although I am unsure what my plans are after I speak to my commanding officer. I do hope I will remain in London for some time."

"That is excellent." Fitzwilliam beamed in her direction, and she reciprocated his smile. At least the gesture was not forced; she dearly loved to see his dimples. "We should celebrate with a drink. Elizabeth, do you mind if the two of us catch up in the library?"

"Of course not," she said with a cheer she did not possess. "You wish to visit. I will make certain the colonel's rooms are completed and send word when he can refresh himself."

"I am in no hurry, Mrs. Darcy. I daresay I am used to a bit of dust and the smell of horse."

Her husband strode forward and slapped his cousin on the back. "Come, I have an excellent bottle of brandy I have been saving for a special occasion. This most certainly qualifies."

They departed towards the library. "You are too good to me, Darcy." The colonel exclaimed in a cheerful tone.

Sighing, she resumed her seat and lifted the letter in her hands. There was no time like the present! She broke the seal and unfolded the expensive paper.

20 June, 1810
Rosings Park, Kent

Dear Mrs. Darcy,

I am so very pleased to address you as such, and that it is not someone addressing me as such. I pray you will not think me too forward by penning this letter, but I am eager to wish you and my cousin joy. If you know the desires of my mother, I am certain this note must seem very odd, yet I am determined to make those sentiments known to you.

My grandmother, during our recent trip to town, informed my mother and myself that you are a good match for my dour cousin, and I have not the words to express how pleased I am to hear this news. I welcome you to the family, dear cousin, for that is what you are to me now if you do not mind claiming the relation.

I wish we were able to correspond, so we could become acquainted. My mother would be incensed if she discovered evidence of this note, much less a long-time correspondence, so it is with regret that I will have to bide my time until we happen upon one another.

I must seal this letter since my mother will, no doubt, soon be here to assess my condition. I wish you and Darcy happy and fruitful lives.

Anne de Bourgh

She refolded the missive and traced the letters of her name. Anne de Bourgh's letter painted her a friendly young woman, despite her mother's influence. Perhaps, if things were different, they would be friends. As things now stood, she found it doubtful they would ever cross paths.

"Your wife is stunning," praised Richard when the door was closed behind him.

Darcy grinned with pleasure and gestured to a seat. "Thank you. I am quite fortunate."

Richard tilted his head to the side while he made an obvious study of Darcy. "Being aware of how your marriage came about, I am happy to see she is quite besotted with you. I would say as much or more so than you are with her."

A glass of brandy was passed to his cousin, and Darcy took a seat across from him. "You have seen our grandmother or your parents then?"

His cousin chuckled. "Both, and they all sang her praises."

He stared at the light as it refracted around the glass. Richard thought Elizabeth was besotted with him? Of course, she had feelings for him, but he had never allowed himself to hope she felt more than gratitude and friendship. Could it possibly be true?

"What has you so contemplative?" asked his cousin. "I hope I did not say something wrong."

"Oh… no… I just." He fidgeted and took a gulp of his drink.

"Spit it out, man. We have never had secrets between us… well, not many anyway."

"You said you believe…" He shook his head. "Pay me no mind. I am being ridiculous."

His cousin leaned forward so his elbows were upon his knees. "Say whatever is on your mind. You would not be stumbling so if it were not important."

He took another gulp of his drink. "You believe Elizabeth is besotted with me?"

Richard's eyebrows rose, and he appeared incredulous. "If anyone else had asked, I would have believed it to be a joke. I saw the warm smile she wore when you entered the room, and she barely removed her eyes from you during our conversation." He sat back and examined his cousin. "And, unless I am mistaken, she was jealous when I mentioned the possibility I could remain for a fortnight. Your wife was also less than pleased when we departed the drawing room."

He startled. "Jealousy? I cannot imagine why…"

"I would imagine it is because we would spend time riding or fencing, and our activities could take time away from her."

Surely, it could not be true! "But it would not be the same!"

Richard agreed. "No, it would not. Could she have reason to doubt you or your affection?"

He shrugged. "I have never spoken of my feelings."

"Good God man, but why not?" The shock on Richard's face was evident.

"I have feared since we became betrothed that one day, I would love her, and she would feel no more than gratitude or friendship towards me." He paused for his cousin to tease him or make some sarcastic remark, but he did not.

"I think you should admit to your wife how you feel. She may very well surprise you."

Could he allow himself to hope? "You believe she has feelings for me?"

"I would wager she is as in love with you as you are with her."

Fitzwilliam stood, walked to the window, and stared at the row of lavender blooming along the low wall near the kitchens. "I have searched for some alteration in her to indicate a change in her feelings, but I have noticed nothing different. I took it to mean she might be better acquainted with me or we might be friends, but I had no reason to believe she felt anything deeper."

"Darcy, if her attachment came on gradually, then you might miss whatever it is you think is indicative of a stronger attachment."

"I suppose…"

"No, do not suppose. Confess to her, and see if she admits hers in return. I would wager my horse she does."

He regarded Richard with amusement. "That is quite a wager! You love that horse."

"That horse is more reliable than any woman I have ever known, and has saved my life a number of times."

He laughed, and returned to his chair as Richard's face changed to a smirk. "Did you have any questions for Uncle Richard now that you are a man?"

Darcy rolled his eyes and felt his face become warm. "I believe I am doing well enough, thank you."

His cousin tilted his head and examined him for some time. "I understood why you remained celibate. Wickham would have exposed you if he had ever gotten any idea you had been with a woman."

"It was more than that." He grimaced, placed his glass on a table, and glanced towards the window where he could see Elizabeth as she walked in the garden. The mere sight of her did much to restore his humour.

"But you always told me…" came his cousin's voice from behind him.

"I cleaned up several of his messes," interrupted Darcy. "I decided early on not to be anything like Wickham. I would not ruin any woman's life in such a fashion. Whether she was a prostitute or a wealthy widow, there would be no possibility of me causing them any form of shame or derision. I would not abandon my illegitimate children to wallow in the gutters."

Richard stood and placed a hand on Darcy's shoulder. "I always understood. I may not have taken the same path as you, but it did not mean I belittled your choices or convictions. I envied you them."

Darcy was shocked. "You did?"

"I know I joke about requiring a wealthy heiress, but the truth of the matter is I do not foresee myself marrying or settling down. I have been in the military for ten years, and I am unsure if I could live another way. I dare not presume many heiresses of the ton would have me or be willing to put up with my nonsense."

"There might be someone."

"No, Darce. I spoke with Anne about my future during my visit to Rosings. She offered to leave me Rosings, did you know?"

He clapped his cousin on the shoulder. "That is wonderful! You can sell your commission. I am certain your father will allow you to remain with them until you can claim the estate."

"I refused her."

"You did what?" He was stunned. He would never wish to be sent off to war and could not understand why his cousin would reject such a generous gift.

"I have no idea how to run an estate." Richard raised his hand to stop him from interrupting. "I know you and father would help me, but I have no interest in being a landowner. I would feel trapped behind the desk, and would die of boredom."

"So, you could allow the steward to run things. Anne was entitled to take control when she gained Rosings from the trust at five and twenty, but she has allowed the current steward to oversee its management."

Richard shook his head and took a large gulp of his drink. "It is of no matter. Lady Catherine attempted to force Anne to change her will, but because I refused, Anne has insisted Rosings will be yours when she dies."

"Lady Catherine has always known and been furious that her settlement left her nothing more than the dower house and the sum grandfather set aside for her dowry. I am also sure she is aware that I would not allow her to remain at Rosings if I were to inherit. I am amazed she has not arrived on our doorstep to spout her vitriol against myself and Elizabeth."

Richard gave a loud guffaw. "I will have you know that you have Anne to thank. She did take ill whilst they were in London and asked to return to Rosings, which they did. Since then, whenever Lady Catherine makes a reference to travelling here, Anne feigns a relapse. She takes to her bed for a day or two. She and Mrs. Jenkinson have even discovered how to fake a slight fever."

"I never knew our cousin was so duplicitous!" Darcy chuckled. "I wish I could thank her."

"She is thinking of herself as well. Anne has no desire to be hauled to Oxfordshire."

Nodding, he peered back out of the window to find his wife had disappeared. He glanced towards each corner of the house in the hopes of catching a glimpse, but she was no longer in sight.

"I was in earnest when I offered to answer any questions," said Richard. "The situation would be awkward, but I might be able to offer some advice."

His cousin's offer was mortifying, causing his face to become warm; he shook his head. "Thank you, but no. Elizabeth and I will learn such knowledge on our own."

With a snicker, Richard leaned against the wall. "You heard enough at Cambridge and whilst we fenced in London."

He faced his cousin with a look of angry shock. "I would never demean my wife by treating her as they do their mistresses or the actresses they bed."

Richard angled his head towards him, making it hard to maintain his cousin's eye. "Perhaps if those, who were married, treated their wives as they did their mistresses, they might not be so dissatisfied at home. Those wives may not have gone looking elsewhere either."

He paused, disturbed by the idea. Could Elizabeth be dissatisfied with their intimacy? Her sounds and willingness indicated otherwise, but he needed to discuss it with her, regardless of the embarrassment the conversation would cause. "I will give it some thought."

198

A knock on the door interrupted their conversation, and he called for the person to enter. To his disappointment, Mrs. Green opened the door.

"The colonel's room is ready, sir. We also have water warming in the event you wished for a bath, Colonel."

"A bath would be most appreciated, thank you. If you could notify my man I will be there soon." The housekeeper gave a pleased nod and departed with haste.

"Before I forget, I have been charged with conveying these letters. I believe Grandmamma addressed hers to both you and your wife, but the remainder are yours. I delivered one to your bride from Anne earlier."

He started and looked up from the correspondence. "Do you know what it contained?"

"Anne wished nothing more than to welcome her to the family. Despite what her mother dictates, she is very happy for you, and ecstatic to not have to listen to her mother's incessant talk of her marriage to you."

The letters were placed on his desk as he groaned. "I have wished to write her a note to explain matters."

"Her mother would have intercepted it before she knew it existed," interrupted his cousin. "She understands. Read her letter. I believe she will absolve you of any guilt."

Darcy placed his fingers upon his correspondence. "Thank you."

Richard set his glass down beside the decanter. "I should be headed to my room; otherwise, the water may no longer be hot."

He followed his cousin to the stairs where Richard proceeded to his chamber. Darcy's first inclination was to seek out his wife; he was fortunate when the lady herself entered through the front doors.

She caught his eye and arched her eyebrow in the way he loved. "Is there something you required, Mr. Darcy?"

He ensured his voice remained formal in the event any servants were nearby. "I wish to speak with you a moment, Mrs. Darcy?"

His arm was outstretched before him, and she stepped forward to place her hand in his. He led her to the library, closed the door behind her, and quickly secured the latch.

"I should go exchange my boots for indoor slippers," she said softly.

He steered her to the sofa, and when she took a seat, he unlaced both shoes, removing them and placing them nearby. "They do not appear muddy today, but if it makes you feel better, they have been removed."

He sat beside her and traced his knuckles down the side of her face. He loved how her eyes closed and a look of bliss appeared! "I need to confess something to you."

Elizabeth's eyes opened to reveal a certain amount of worry in her countenance. "I am willing to hear anything you need to say."

He swallowed hard in an attempt to quell his nerves. "I…"

She entwined her fingers with his, and he bent down to kiss her knuckles but did not relinquish her hand. Instead, he held it before him, tracing his index finger across the top.

"I have realised…" He shook his head. "No, you deserve complete honesty." He was so ill at ease with confessing his heart he could not meet her eye. "When we were in Bath, I came to the realisation that I had fallen in love with you."

"You did?" Her voice was almost a whisper, yet it conveyed every bit of her surprise.

"Yes, but I never told you for fear you would not reciprocate those sentiments." He took a chance and lifted his eyes to her face.

She was biting her bottom lip, suppressing a smile. "But you would have heard them in return, because whilst we were there I had the same realisation about you."

"You did?"

"I did, and I had the same fears as you. I thought I would wait until I had some indication that you felt the same."

His palms cradled her face, and he claimed her lips with his. "I feel like such an idiot. I have been so worried you would never feel the same, that you might merely feel gratitude, but nothing deeper; I have deprived both myself and you of saying and hearing those precious words."

She returned his soft kiss and grinned. "Then we should not deprive ourselves any longer." Her lips met his again and she leaned her forehead against his. "I love you, Fitzwilliam Darcy."

In a futile attempt to control his emotions, he gulped hard. "And I love you, Elizabeth Darcy."

He again captured her lips; this time determined it would not be a short interlude. His arms wrapped around her to press her closer to him as his tongue darted between her lips. He could barely contain his joy when hers sought access to his mouth to caress his own.

He had to have more. As he pulled her astride his lap, her gown bunched around her thighs. He was inflamed and attacked the buttons on her bodice, wanting her to be as mindless with want as he was. Once her upper body was bared, he pressed kisses to the exposed flesh, relishing the taste and feel of her creamy skin against his lips.

She leaned away from him and tugged at his lapels. "Your coat."

He aided her in removing his topcoat, waistcoat, and shirt, groaning when she pressed her body to his naked torso.

The feel of her soft breasts pressed against his chest was incredible, and he ran his hands down her bare back, her hips, and her thighs. He wanted to imprint his love upon her body, so she never forgot that she was his or he was hers.

Her lips trailed kisses up his shoulder to his neck, and she brushed her lips under his ear, darting her tongue against the lobe, her warm breath burning against his neck. He hissed and dug his fingers into her hips as she began to suckle. She had become freer in their bed, but their confession seemed to melt away any remaining inhibitions.

His hands slipped into her hair where his agile fingers loosened the pins and pulled her face back to his. "I love you," he rasped.

His kiss was not gentle, but desperate, just as he had been desperate to hear those words from her. She did not back away or behave as if intimidated by his intensity, but met him as an equal, kissing him as ardently as he was her.

"I love you," she whispered when he released her mouth.

He scraped his teeth down her ear lobe and she whimpered. The familiar noise was not fear or pain, but one she made when aroused, which only served to excite him more. With the advice he was given fresh in his mind, his fingers inched their way up her thigh until he touched between her legs; she stiffened and pulled back.

"Do you trust me?"

Without saying a word, she nodded, so he brought her forehead to his where he maintained eye contact as he rubbed down and back.

He had no idea if his actions were correct until he stroked a spot that made her jump.

"There?"

She appeared alarmed rather than aroused. "I do not know what that was."

His thumb continued to brush the spot, and she began to make small vocalisations as her eyes fluttered closed. Continuing with his thumb, he inserted a finger and pressed around until her eyes popped open, and she gasped, followed by a deep moan.

"Shhhh, else all of the staff will know what we are doing." Her cheeks turned crimson and she bit her lip. She had misunderstood. "Please do not hold back. We will both need to ensure we do not become too loud."

"But…"

He began his ministrations once more. "No, I want you to be honest in your reactions. I want to know what you enjoy."

With a shaky breath, her eyes rolled back and closed as he watched, fascinated by her ardent response. Her face contorted as though she were about to cry, her lips were parted, and her body arched towards him. Her breaths came in uneven gasps, and her fingernails dug painfully into his sides.

She was so beautiful, so passionate, and she was *his* wife. He was so lucky to find her! She stiffened, made an inarticulate cry, and her head dropped to rest against his shoulder, Unsure if she was well, he ceased the movement of his fingers for a moment, but she shifted against them.

"Please do not stop yet," she mumbled. He chuckled softly and continued until she placed her hand on his arm, halting his movement.

His head dropped back onto the sofa as her heavy breaths filled the air. Could he do this while inside of her? The feel of her as she peaked had been incredible and inspired him to try.

A movement between them redirected his attention to where her small hands attempted to unbutton the fall of his breeches. The cool air of the room hit his bare skin, and he grasped her hand to place it in the opening.

Her hand, covered by his, stroked his length several times, and he moaned. "I want you now, Elizabeth. This only makes matters more urgent."

She drew back, stood, and pulled him up to stand. After taking a few steps back, she shed what remained of her clothing and lay on the carpet by the empty fireplace, holding up her arms and beckoning him to her. He removed his trousers and lowered himself into the warm cradle of her thighs.

"I love you." She murmured the words as she trailed her lips along his collarbone and neck, which incited gooseflesh down his back. Her hands reached up and pulled his face to hers where he answered her unspoken plea and claimed her lips.

Her hands slipped up his sides to his back as he slipped himself inside her. She had always felt warm, but today she was aflame. He fell into a rhythm, and unlike before, her hips surged to meet his while her hands moved down to his buttocks, where they pulled him further in with each thrust. Each puff of breath she exhaled, coincided with each swift movement he made, a small cry escaping her lips every time.

His satisfaction with their prior intimacy was surpassed as they continued; he had not been aware it could be like this. Elizabeth's legs wrapped around his hips, and he squeezed his eyes shut as he attempted to stave off his completion. She had to peak around him!

His angle shifted slightly and she gasped, digging her nails painfully into his skin.

"Did I hurt you?"

"No!"

Her tone provoked him to thrust harder and faster. She met him at every push, and he had no choice but to shout for joy when he heard her cry as she tightened rhythmically around him. The experience was more amazing than expected as his voice joined hers, echoing off of the wooden panelling.

He collapsed onto her warm, damp body. "So much for keeping the household unawares."

"So that is what was missing."

He propped himself on his elbows to take in her expression. "What do you mean missing?"

Her face paled, and she brought her hands up over her eyes. "I did not realise I had spoken aloud. Please forgive me." She removed her hands and put her palms to his cheeks. "Please."

"I am not angry, Elizabeth, though I am disappointed you found something lacking and never mentioned it."

"At first, I believe I was too sore to feel as I did today. When that disappeared, I attributed it to my own inexperience."

His heart dropped as his head fell to her shoulder. "How long was I hurting you?" he asked in a low voice.

"Only the first few nights. It has been awkward since then."

"Why did you never tell me?"

"Fitzwilliam." She pulled his face up so she was eye to eye with him. "I never disliked our intimacy. I loved kissing you and the manner in which you touched me. You were always so gentle, too." Her cheeks reddened as she held his gaze. "I also found a great deal of satisfaction in pleasing you."

He opened his mouth to speak, but she interrupted. "Did you not derive satisfaction in bringing me pleasure today?"

He nodded his head, and she grasped his face between her palms once more. "I know you did. I could see your joy."

"Yes, but…"

"No," she insisted. "I always enjoy the feel of you against me, I quiver inside as your hands caress my body, and I rejoice in seeing your completion."

"But you felt as though something were missing."

She released an exasperated exhalation. "There was always an ache that was temporarily assuaged when we joined, but when things were done, the sensation remained."

He began to roll away, but she tightened her legs around him. "You will not leave until we discuss this."

"I promise not to leave." He wrapped his arm around her and rolled them both to their sides. "Please forgive me."

She opened her mouth to speak, but he placed a finger over her lips. "I was just as inexperienced as you when we were first together."

Her eyes widened. "I have heard enough to know most men are not innocent upon their marriage. How?"

He brushed several curls back from her face. "I do not wish to go into detail, but one reason was so Wickham never had such information to use against me, and the other was that I had cleaned up too many of his messes. I never wanted to wreak the same havoc he did.

"Today, Richard reminded me of conversations about intimacy for which I had been present—other men joking, telling bawdy jokes, and speaking of their experiences. I refused to consider using anything I had ever heard—most of their stories did not include wives."

"And he changed your mind?"

"He suggested that perhaps those men would not have mistresses if they took the time to please their wives."

She chuckled and traced her fingers down his chest. "It could be valid to some relationships."

"I am sure it is." He ran his hand through her curls, and she tilted her head to brush her lips against his. She appeared upset with him, but when she returned his kiss she let him know without words that nothing was amiss.

"After we confessed our feelings to one another, I found I had more confidence to try. When you began to respond, I decided to go one step further. Your face when you began to enjoy it, was indescribable."

She blushed and averted her eyes. "I would think I appeared ridiculous."

"Far from it." He combed his fingers through her curls once more. "You were beautiful. Seeing you enjoy yourself, and the noises you make add to my experience." She blushed and buried her head into his chest as he grinned. "I am sorry I did not attempt more before now."

She shook her head. "You should not apologise. It means a great deal to me that you waited for marriage. We will learn together, which I imagine would mean at times, things may not work as well as others."

"I believe I married a very wise woman but promise me we will be more open with one another. No more concealment."

"I promise." She arched her eyebrow. What mischief was she about to impart? "Just do not forget I am so wise, dear husband, and I believe things will be well."

Fitzwilliam's happy laugh reverberated through the room as he rolled back on top of her. "You are a minx, wife." She giggled and pulled his head down for a kiss.

He made certain the master and mistress were not seen by most of the household until dinner that evening; however, Hattie's search for a salve for the mistresses back was bound to have raised more than a few eyebrows below stairs.

"We have been unable to locate Gardiner, sir." A man dressed in a suit similar to one worn by a tradesman stood in a lavish study while his employer puffed at his cigar. "I have men stationed near his rooms in Cheapside as well as the last places he found employment. He has ventured nowhere near his typical haunts. I have even remained in his usual pub every evening for the last month. He has simply disappeared."

"No one simply disappears," said the man behind the desk. He took a long drag on his cigar as he examined his employee. "Gardiner has no doubt eschewed his usual practices. You need to search the slums."

The man was taken aback. "You believe he would hide there?"

"It is what I would do rather than remain in the open where I could be easily found." He poured himself a glass of cognac and took a sip. "I want Gardiner. He will pay for being so careless with my money."

He swirled the amber liquid around the wide bowl of the glass, his last tumbler of French cognac until he found a new smuggler. Damn Gardiner and his ineptitude! He could not abide the pale, cheap versions most suppliers claimed were authentic.

"Men who cannot pay their debts do not deserve to live." He spoke in a casual tone, not as though he were speaking of someone's life.

"Spread out your search. Hire more men if you require them, but find Gardiner."

"Yes, sir," squeaked the employee, who rushed from the room.

Thomas Grayson sat against the back of his seat and smiled, his nature evident in his expression. "I know what became of the young woman you were to bring me, Gardiner." He stood and stared out of the window into the darkness beyond. "I made arrangements to sell her to a duke for a hefty sum based on her description. You now not only owe me a great deal of money, but you have also made me a fool."

Chapter 15

As she took a short-cut through the trees, Elizabeth looked over her shoulder to where her husband and Homer drew near.

"I wish you would not ride ahead," he scolded. "I do not like it when I cannot see you. When we have ridden longer, it may not bother me so much, but you have only been riding again for a few weeks."

"Long enough for me to get a feel for Page, and I only wished for a bit of a race." She gave him the mischievous look he favoured, and he shook his head.

They emerged from a copse of trees and crossed a field. Fitzwilliam rode ahead to a gate along the fence line and dismounted to open it, so she could pass through. She had not wished to go jumping yet, and he had confessed he was relieved since she had not been in the saddle for almost a year. As a result, their rides were planned accordingly, ensuring there were gates or ways around certain fields and pastures.

The roof of their beloved Sagemore was visible in the distance. Elizabeth looked back to ensure her husband was once again in the saddle and then urged Page forward, setting off for the small wood ahead. Homer's hooves pounded the ground behind her when she cornered her horse to disappear into the trail. She pulled back on the reins to slow within the trees, but was unprepared for when Page reared.

Gasping, she gripped the pommels with her thighs and leaned forward, as she had been taught, managing to keep her seat when his front legs landed back on the ground; however, he immediately lifted himself again and emitted a shrill whinny. She responded as before, but pulled back the reins when he began to lower in the hopes that asking him to reverse might halt his actions. He took a few steps back, stomping wildly, before rearing again. What had frightened him so?

Her husband yelled her name from behind, but she had no time to consider his alarmed tone or location. She was too focused on her attempt to rein in her horse.

The last rear unseated her, and she landed with a thud on the ground, her behind smarting when it made contact with the hard earth. She was too close to Page's hindquarters! She cried out as she scurried backward, not rotating to all fours in order to keep the horse within her sights, but strong arms wrapped around her abdomen and

208

pulled her from the ground. Her back was shoved against a tree and Fitzwilliam pressed himself against her while Page stomped and bucked before he took off up the trail.

"Page!" she cried, as she lunged after him.

"No!" Fitzwilliam grabbed her upper arm. "He will most likely return to the stable, and we do not know what scared him so."

"He is normally such a docile animal."

"I have seen Page buck but once, and his odd behaviour was due to a bee sting. Without a doubt, his actions are very out of character." He crept forward and picked up a stick from the brush as he came closer to where the scuffle had occurred. "An adder!" He picked up the dead snake with the stick and held it aloft. "It is no wonder he became unhinged."

"What if it bit him?"

"We will have to treat the leg and rest it, but he will recover. A creature as large as a horse does not have as severe a reaction to the bite as we would."

She nodded, still uneasy, and began to tremble.

"Elizabeth?" Her husband stepped in her direction and placed his hands on her arms. "You are shaking. We must get you back to the house. I can go ascertain if Page…"

"No," she interrupted. "I want to go to the stables with you. I have to be assured he is well."

"Are you certain?"

"Yes, I must know whether he was bitten."

"Very well." He placed his arm around her shoulders and held her to him as they approached Homer. His hands gripped her waist, he lifted her into his saddle, and he mounted, seating himself just behind the cantle. While in her husband's embrace, they made their way back to the stables. As they cleared the last of the trees, Johns hurried towards them.

"I was just goin' to send someone out to be sure Mrs. Darcy was not hurt," he called. "Did he bolt when you were not on his back?" Fitzwilliam pulled Homer to a stop and dismounted, helping her off after him.

"No, Mrs. Darcy rode ahead into the trees between the Randall and Benson houses. When I followed, he was rearing and stomping. We discovered after he fled that they came across an adder."

"I thought it odd he showed up without his rider. You are well, are you not, Mrs. Darcy?"

She nodded, still attempting to control the shaking she had been experiencing since the fall. "Yes, thank you, but I am very concerned about Page at the moment. We must inspect his legs for snake bites."

"Yes, we should," Johns agreed. He led them towards where the large gelding was tethered. He had been unsaddled, brushed, and was attempting to steal a few leaves from an overhanging branch.

"It took some time to get him calm, but Joe walked him around until he cooled and stopped blowing so hard." He bent over and ran his hands down one long front leg to the hoof, where he carefully ran his fingers through the hair. Her husband did the same to the other, and she held out her hand to Page's face.

"Shhhh, all is well, boy."

He smelled her hand, his warm breath fanning against her palm. She gingerly stroked his nose and then scratched his cheek. His head leaned into her palm, and her other hand joined the first, each on one side of his face.

She continued to pet him, keeping him calm until Johns and her husband both rose.

"I cannot find anything."

"Neither can I," replied Johns. "I will make certain there is no swelling before I lock up tonight. It might be best, ma'am, not to ride him for a few days. I do not think it will take long for anything to show if he was bitten, but we will not take chances."

"Of course; I would not want to cause him any harm." She leaned forward and kissed Page on the nose. "I will be sure to bring you a carrot tomorrow when I visit you." She said the words softly, but her husband chuckled.

"He was already a big baby, and now, you are going to spoil him."

"I am not," she said defensively. "He had a fright. It will not spoil him to coddle him a little." Both men laughed, and she gave a huff. "Please notify me if he shows any signs he was bitten. I believe I shall return to the house." She strode off in the direction of the bridge, and Fitzwilliam followed.

"Elizabeth, I was teasing."

"But you did not have to laugh."

He grabbed her hand and pulled her into his arms. "You had a fright as well, and I have been unable to coddle you."

"I am quite recovered from the scare; I assure you." Her insult from their amusement was disappearing by the minute. A part of her was frustrated she could not remain angry, but the other did indeed want him to cosset her.

"Please do not be upset with me."

"I am not upset with you. I am more annoyed with myself." His eyebrows furrowed, and she slipped her arms around his torso. "I did not heed your request and wait for you. If I had, this might not have happened."

Her husband put his finger under her chin and lifted her head. She raised her eyes to meet his, and his steady gaze comforted her. "The snake would not have gone too far in such a short amount of time. Page would have likely still espied it and reacted in the same manner, only Homer might have spooked as well. If that had happened, you could have been trampled when you fell."

"I had not thought of it in such a way."

"You have not been on a horse much in the last year, and I was hoping to keep you safe. When I came around those trees, I saw him rear twice before you fell. You managed him well, and you were attempting to bring him under control. No seasoned rider could have brought him around with a snake at his feet."

"You are in earnest?"

His eyes showed no humour, no sign he was placating her.

"Yes! I am amazed you stayed in the seat as well as you did riding side-saddle. Many women would have fallen the first time he reared."

"Well, men have an unfair advantage by riding astride."

"We do, but I would not want Johns and the men in the stable to see you in breeches. That is for my eyes only." Her face heated, and he took her hand, pulling her towards the house. "We should return and allow you to bathe and change. Are you sure you do not require a doctor?"

"I am well. I may be sore for a few days, and I will probably have a lovely bruise."

"I am anxious to tell Richard. He will be impressed."

She raised an eyebrow. Was her effort truly worth such praise? She tilted her head to the side, catching his eye. "Will he? Even though I fell?"

"Do not let him fool you. Even Richard has taken spills, and some of those tumbles were quite impressive." Fitzwilliam regaled her with several stories of his and Richard's, escapades around Pemberley until they reached the front door where they entered to find Richard himself preparing to exit.

"Darcy?" His eyes shifted from Fitzwilliam to Elizabeth. "Lizzy? I was just informed your horse returned to the stable without you. I was about to ride out to see if you required help."

"I am well, Richard, thank you." Despite her initial jealousy, which she confessed with ease after their encounter in the library, she and Richard had become fast friends and on familiar terms within the first few days of his arrival. "Page and I had a run in with an adder whilst we were riding in the trees."

Richard's eyes widened, and he glanced to his cousin as if verifying the story.

"Elizabeth was quite impressive. Page reared twice and stomped the snake, before he unseated her the last time he reared."

"Was he bitten? They can make a horse's leg swell significantly."

"Johns and Fitzwilliam both examined his legs and could not find evidence of any bites. Johns wants to watch him for the next few days to ensure he is sound."

Richard had a thoughtful expression while he nodded. "Johns has always been excellent with horses. I am glad you were able to steal him away from your father."

Darcy studied his cousin with a puzzled expression. "My father let him go without reference, and I *asked* him to come to Sagemore. I thought you would be aware of what happened. Your father and Huntley knew of the incident. I think you were at a training of some kind at the time."

"I do not think they ever told me."

"Wickham set Johns up as retribution for helping me. He took to sneaking in the stables at night and opening stalls so the horses would get out. One of his last escapades killed father's favourite stallion."

Richard's eyes bulged. "And you did not tell your father, did you?"

"We had no proof! I was visiting Pemberley for the summer to see Georgie when this happened. I went out every night for the last month Johns worked there to help ensure everything was locked as it should be. We still do not know how he got inside."

"It was lucky you could take him on here."

"I never liked my uncle's stable master. Johns returned with me, and I let the other go. I do not think he cared for me either because he seemed relieved to be leaving. He never could appreciate my involvement with the horses. He did not like capitulating to me when we disagreed."

"Fitzwilliam," she interrupted. "I wish to go to my rooms to refresh myself." She looked to Richard and gave a small smile. "If you will excuse me."

She had taken no more than a step or two before Fitzwilliam reached forward and grabbed her hand. "Richard, I want to ensure Elizabeth is well."

With a grin, Richard waved him off. "Go take care of your wife. I can fend for myself."

"You can stay and talk with your cousin if you like. I do not mind."

Her husband shook his head and placed a hand on the small of her back pressing her forward. "But I wish to go with you."

He ushered her up the stairs to their rooms, where he closed the door behind them. She removed her riding jacket, and his fingers went to work on the buttons down the back of her gown. When she was divested of everything but her chemise, he began to lift her skirt, but she halted his movement with a firm grasp of his forearm.

"What are you about?" They had both been nude before each other quite often in the past six weeks but there was rarely much light, and he had never seen her from behind.

"I want to be certain a bruise is the worst of your injury." He smiled rakishly as he gave her slip a small tug. "I bet your rear will be just handsome with all of those colours."

She shook her head vehemently and attempted to turn in his arms. "No."

His eyebrows furrowed, and he took her by the shoulders, which prevented her escape to her dressing room.

"What is it, Elizabeth?"

She avoided his steady gaze until he cradled her cheek with his hand and shifted her face until her eyes met his. "We promised no more concealment. Do you not remember?"

Her vision clouded with tears, so she averted her eyes, feigning interest in something on his cravat as her fingers fiddled with the folds. "I do not want you to see the scars."

"My love," he said gently. "I saw your scars for the first time the day after we were wed."

Her head shot up and he laughed. "How?"

"Your shift had ridden up around the tops of your thighs, and I could not help but notice when I attempted to see if you were awake."

"Oh." Her brow furrowed and she tilted her head. "All you have seen so far is my thigh?"

"I do know there is scarring on your buttock, but I was not about to lift your shift—despite how much I would have enjoyed the view. I would never violate your trust in such a manner."

She wrapped her arms around his chest. "I would have been horrified to find you peeking then. Now, I would not care—unless you were trying to see where I was injured."

He kissed her temple and angled his head to speak near her ear. "But those blemishes do not matter. I find everything about you stunning."

"My scars are not attractive," she stated frankly.

"They are a part of you, and that makes them attractive."

She rolled her eyes as she giggled. "You are wilfully blind, Mr. Darcy."

"You have a kind and generous heart, which is beautiful. I have received compliments on how lucky I am to have found such a handsome wife, so you are lovely." He took her face in his hands and gazed at her with imploring eyes. "Do you not see? The scars you carry may mar your skin, but they do not detract from you. They do not make you any less beautiful—especially to my eyes."

A wet tear cooled the swell of her cheek, and he skimmed it away with his thumb. She had felt loved by her family and friends her entire life, but she had never felt as loved and accepted as she did with Fitzwilliam.

She stood on her tiptoes, and brushed her lips against his. He eagerly reciprocated her kiss as his arms shifted to wrap around her body. He appeared puzzled, when after a few minutes, she drew back from the warmth of his arms.

Her fingers worked the pink ribbon of her chemise, releasing the tie that held the front together. Her heart pounded in her ears, and she could not control the slight tremor of her hands, yet somehow, she loosened the knots.

As she turned away from her husband, she glanced over her shoulder to find herself the subject of his intense stare. The gaze was familiar. She had seen it often since they had become intimate. He was definitely not looking to find fault.

She took a deep breath, pushed the straps from her shoulders, and then worked it from the remainder of her body. Her eyes closed as she waited for a reaction, but there was nothing for a moment. Her husband's hands found her waist as his breath caressed her ear.

"Lie down on the bed, so I can see it better."

He had shed his coats and his cravat, and the love that shown from his eyes was a relief to her anxiety. He smiled and kissed her on the tip of the nose as he pivoted her towards the bed. "Go on."

She stretched out on the coverlet, burying her face in the softness of the mattress. The wait was not long before his fingers grazed over her rear.

"You will bruise, but I do not see any scratches or abrasions." The sensation on her scars was different than on her skin. With a light touch, he ran his fingers down their length. When his lips caressed the marred flesh, she gasped. He then moved to the other cheek and bit softly.

"You once promised you would not bite," she scolded over her shoulder with an arch look.

His deep laugh reverberated through the room as he covered her with his body. "I lied," he said in her ear. The warmth of his breath against her neck caused gooseflesh to erupt down to her shoulders.

She gasped in mock indignation. "I thought deception of any kind was your abhorrence."

Fitzwilliam slid his hands underneath where he caressed her breasts and stomach, wreaking havoc on her ability to tease him. "In this case, it put you in my arms, so I cannot despise it."

His lips peppered kisses from her shoulder down her back and she moaned. "You cannot mean to… I smell like horse."

"My second favourite scent to orange blossoms." Her giggle joined his low chuckle just before his bare torso came skin to skin against her back, bringing all coherent conversation to an end.

Richard departed a few days after Elizabeth's fall in order to return to London. He had managed to retain his standing invitation to Sagemore, and it pleased Darcy that Elizabeth had become rather fond of him.

August brought long-awaited news from the investigators Darcy and his uncle had hired to find Gardiner. Grayson's men had withdrawn back from their usual posts and moved into the seedier parts of London, citing Seven Dials and Saffron Hill as the main areas of their search.

The investigators were not just watching the places Gardiner used to frequent, but also Grayson's men. They explained the strong likelihood that Grayson's men would lead them to their quarry—or at the very least, flush him out.

By September, Darcy was busy with the harvest, but watched his wife with the same care as the investigators watching Grayson's men. He had learned a great deal about women's cycles and bodies during the first month of their intimacy. Elizabeth was far too modest and mortified to answer his questions, but a handy medical tome in the library filled in the knowledge he lacked.

She had missed a month of her courses, and they were almost at the completion of the second month, but Elizabeth had not said a word. He suspected she was with child, but other than being a little sleepy, she had not complained of one symptom of the condition. She had even smirked when she blamed her fatigue on him keeping her from her much needed sleep.

He had just returned from a few of the tenants' farms where he had validated their yields so far, when he espied his wife as she wandered through the stable. He followed behind and watched from the door as she opened Page's stall with a carrot in one outstretched hand and a halter hanging from her arm.

"Hello, sweet boy," she crooned while the horse munched on his treat. "Do you want to go for a ride? We could go find Fitzwilliam and Homer." She was beginning to slip the halter around his head when Darcy came up behind her and stopped her progress with a hand to her arm.

"We have servants who can do this."

"But I do not mind. I took him out the other day by myself."

He nodded and took the halter from her. "Johns told me about that, but I am glad you allowed the groom to saddle him." Page pivoted his head and presented the bottom of his chin for a scratch, prompting a broad grin from them both. "I am also pleased you are so happy with him."

"He is wonderful," she praised. She began scratching, but Page soon decided he wanted more stroking down his blaze. Elizabeth began laughing when the horse rubbed his head down the front of her body and back up. She surveyed the dust and horsehair covering the front of her riding habit. "Hattie will not be pleased."

"Would you walk back to the house with me?"

"I planned to ride. Mrs. Green and I did not have any household matters to discuss this morning, and I wanted to take advantage of the free time."

"I have something I wish to discuss with you. Please."

He disliked the disappointment in her eyes, but she gave Page a peck on the nose. "We will do this another time. Be a good boy."

"You are going to make him a pet rather than a working animal. You already speak to him as though he were a lap dog." He chuckled as he stepped ahead of her to place the halter on a hook near the door.

"But he has so much personality. I have never seen a horse behave as he does."

He reached out to thread his fingers through hers and led her back in the direction of the house. Once they were over the bridge, he turned onto a path that trailed along the edge of the island, until they reached a bench. He took a seat and pulled her into his lap.

"Fitzwilliam," she exclaimed with a giggle. "Anyone could see us like this."

"The groundskeepers are on the other side of the island, clearing brush from the trees. We should have plenty of privacy."

She relaxed into his embrace and wrapped her arms around his shoulders. "Why do you not want me to ride?"

"What makes you think I do not want you to ride?"

"I noticed the expression on your face a few days ago when I arrived at the stable on Page. I assure you, a groom went with me."

"I know, and I appreciate that you did not try to elude him."

She bit her lip as she grinned sheepishly. "I did not want to make you so angry again."

"I was worried, Elizabeth. The groom returned to the stable without you, and then, for the next hour we had no idea where you were. My only consolation was that Page had not returned without you."

She stroked up his chest and kissed him tenderly. "I apologised then and I apologise now. I do not like having to ride with anyone but you, but I will not steal away again."

"Thank you." He hugged her to him and placed his lips against her forehead. "Do you realise you missed your courses last month?" He did not say the words too loudly, yet she heard, because she tensed.

"At times, they are a bit late," she prevaricated. "I am certain it is no cause for concern."

He turned her face so she could not avoid his eyes. "They are not just a bit late. If I have my calculations correct, then tomorrow or the day after, you are supposed to have them again. You have missed an entire month."

She sat up to regard him with curiosity. "When I first had them after we were intimate, you had no idea what courses even were, and now, you calculate when I should be indisposed?"

"There are several medical books in the library; I read everything I could find." Her cheeks were overcome with a vivid blush.

"I cannot imagine there was a great deal. Women have courses."

Anyone could see she was uncomfortable, but if she indeed suspected she was with child, it was important to be prepared. "Elizabeth, do you not know what it means when a woman's courses cease?"

His wife's face blanched, and she gave a nervous gulp. "No, but you are beginning to frighten me. Is it something serious?"

How could she be so naïve about the subject? She had refused to give him details when she explained she was indisposed and they could not be intimate. At the time, she had given every indication she was mortified rather than uninformed.

"Your mother never explained any of it?"

She shrugged her shoulders and stared as her fingers fidgeted in her lap. "My mother was rather brief on the subject." She made a face, took out her handkerchief, and began to wave it with the characteristic high-pitched trill she used to mimic her mother. "Oh, Lizzy, stop your crying! All women have courses! I suggest you become accustomed to the unpleasantness because they come monthly."

"Why were you crying?" he asked horrified.

"I woke up one morning, and I was bleeding. I am not one prone to hysterics, but I thought I was dying."

"Your older sister never mentioned them?"

Elizabeth shook her head and began to fidget with the folds of her skirt. "Jane and I were barely a year apart. I was the first of us to begin." She continued to run her fingers between the swaths of material, refusing to look at him, until she took a deep breath. "What does it mean?"

"According to what I have read, it is the first sign a woman could be with child." He hated that she never had another female to discuss this with her, so he spoke in as gentle and careful a manner as he could. Despite his tone, her head lifted and her wide eyes locked with his.

"A babe?" she squeaked.

"I have watched for other signs, but I have yet to notice any." She appeared terrified, and he took her hand, ceasing her fidgeting. "Nothing is definite until he or she quickens or moves."

"I am aware of what the quickening is. I remember Mama speaking of when Lydia moved for the first time." She shook her head and became teary. "I knew children came with marriage, but I had not expected it so soon."

He brought his hand under her ear to cradle her cheek. "You are not upset by the idea, are you?"

"I always thought they would come in a few years. I do not feel ready for this." Her eyes were fearful, and he ran his fingers from her temple to her chin.

"If you are with child, we have some time before it will be born. Please do not fret about an event we cannot control. We will simply take things as they come."

"You said you have been watching for other signs—what other signs?"

"Some women become sick to their stomachs and sometimes purge their meals." She shook her head, indicating she had not had any of it. "Sensitivity to certain foods and smells can be a problem." Again, she shook her head. "Moodiness can occur. One book cited that some women become more emotional." She looked to him and lifted her eyebrows. "I have not noticed you are any more emotional than usual."

He squirmed and glanced off to the side before his eyes caught hers once more. "Your breasts do not seem to be any larger, yet."

She became a vibrant red, and her arm tightened around his shoulder. "They will get bigger?"

He could not restrain the amused snort that escaped, and she stared at him incredulously. "I am sorry, love, but I see no problems with that particular symptom. I do love your breasts, and I feel they are very well proportioned, yet I will not mind if they get larger." During his speech, his eyes had wandered to her bosom, and she placed her hands on his cheeks to redirect his gaze to her face.

"Is there anything else?"

"Your breasts can become tender."

"My breasts have ached for the last week," she confessed. "Sometimes they become sore before my courses, so I assumed…"

"You assumed they were coming soon?" She bit her lip and nodded. "Will you do something for me?"

"What is it?" Her voice was soft, and she laid her head upon his shoulder. He kissed her soft curls and inhaled the comforting orange blossom scent in her hair.

"If you are with child, I would ask that you refrain from riding Page."

"Is that why you prevented me from going out today?"

"There could be more risk with a fall now, and I do not just mean the potential of losing a child. If something happened and you did lose the child, I know your kind heart would carry guilt, and I do not want that for you." She buried her face into his neck as he rubbed her back. "Are you willing to give way to me on this?" Her head bobbed against his chin and his lips lifted into a satisfied smile.

The satisfaction of having her in his arms was wonderful, so they remained as such until he had to adjust his legs for fear they would go numb. She must have noticed his discomfort since she moved beside him on the bench.

"Perhaps, we should return to the house. I would like to refresh myself and change into a gown not covered in horsehair."

After standing and stomping around to ensure his legs were steady, Darcy held out his hand for his wife. She laced her fingers with his, and they made their way towards the house, hand in hand, determined that whatever the future brought, they would deal with it together.

Chapter 16

As the carriage pulled up to the Mayfair home of his grandmother, Darcy kissed his wife's temple and held her a bit closer.

"Elizabeth, we have arrived."

One eye opened; she groaned and stretched her legs. The remembrance of how nervous she had been during their first carriage ride together brought a smile to his face. She had gradually become more comfortable, but now, her fatigue overcame what remained of her fears.

"How long was I asleep?" She donned her bonnet and gloves as the step was placed before the door.

"Other than when we had refreshments at the inn, you slept the entire trip."

She stretched her arms over her head, but her husband's interest was captured by the swell of her breasts when she yawned. With a kick to his foot, she startled him from one of his favourite occupations.

"*Fitzwilliam!*" Her remonstration was not loud, but she used enough emphasis to cause his line of vision to jump from her chest to her face. "The door is open."

Her bubbling laugh could be heard as he stepped from the carriage and held out his hand for her to descend. Upon her toes touching the pavement, she took his arm, and he led her into the house where Hobbes greeted them.

"It is good to see you again, Mr. Darcy, Mrs. Darcy," said the butler, as the staff took their coats, gloves, and hats. "If you will follow me, her ladyship is in the blue drawing room."

The dowager was standing when they entered, and rushed forward to embrace her grandson. "The roads must have been good and dry. I was not expecting you for another hour."

After their greeting, he grinned and stepped back so his grandmother could hug Elizabeth. "The roads were excellent, and we required no unscheduled stops. It was an easy trip."

His grandmother embraced his wife and then held out Elizabeth's arms with raised eyebrows. "It appears we shall need to go shopping for you, too."

Elizabeth reddened, which prompted a chuckle from him at her expense.

"I do have the gowns we purchased in Bath. Perhaps Madame Lebrun will be able to alter them. Hattie does well with trim and minor alterations, but a modiste might know better how to increase certain areas."

"We will bring those gowns with us then. Our appointment is for early tomorrow. I hope you do not mind that I scheduled it so soon."

Elizabeth shook her head. "No, I do not mind. I will be satisfied to have some of them adjusted."

"I am sure you will enjoy the ability to breathe freely once again," said his grandmother.

He could not help but laugh when his wife bobbed her head in agreement.

"Would you care for some tea before you refresh yourselves, or would you prefer to go up to your rooms straight away."

"Tea sounds lovely, Grandmamma." Elizabeth's face lit, animated at the mention of refreshments, so his grandmother rang the bell.

With a hand upon the small of her back, he guided her to the sofa where he sat close beside her. She turned and gifted him with a broad grin, prompting a chuckle from him.

Every week since they had discussed the possibility of a baby, she had exhibited more of the signs. To his immense relief, she had never become ill, but she had begun to find certain odours now offensive. He was thankful the orange blossom scent she used was not on the list of items that caused her stomach to churn.

Her emotions had not become as unpredictable as the book indicated, but he had noticed she shed a tear or two over certain poems or novels. She had never exhibited such a tendency in the past, so he was inclined to believe it was due to the babe as well.

One symptom he could not bemoan was the enlargement of her breasts. They had been perfect before, but now they were larger, fuller, and the nipple seemed a bit darker pink—they were enchanting. They captured his attention quite easily, and much to his chagrin, his wife had noticed.

Elizabeth placed a hand on his knee, startling him from his thoughts. "Are you going to join us, dear?" She bit her lip in an obvious effort to restrain her giggles.

"I had just asked Lizzy what you have planned for your visit," repeated the dowager with one side of her lips quirked up.

"Oh, we hoped to see Georgiana, of course. I would like Elizabeth to meet her. I know Elizabeth plans to do some shopping, and I would like to take her to the theatre and perhaps Vauxhall."

"*You?* At the pleasure gardens?" His grandmother feigned exaggerated shock and rose to pull back the drapes.

"What do you seek outside the window?" He was certain she was doing it for effect, and asked so he might hurry her along.

"I was searching for a hog flying about the skies of London."

Elizabeth gave an unladylike snort and erupted in gales of laughter; his grandmother joined his wife in her amusement as she returned to her seat. He shook his head. These two were going to tease him without mercy during the entirety of their stay.

As his wife brought her laughter under control, she placed a hand to her chest and placed the other upon his arm. "I apologise, but I did not expect her to say that."

The dowager directed the maid, who had just entered, to place the tea service before her. "Fitzwilliam did take me to Sydney Gardens whilst we were in Bath. He did not seem to mind."

"I was amazed then, too, because he has avoided Vauxhall for years. His willingness to go is due to you, Lizzy."

He lifted his wife's hand and placed a small kiss to her knuckles, chuckling when she would not look at him.

When they had their teacups, Elizabeth leaned over to search for shortbread amongst the selections on the tray. She found a few pieces to one side and selected the largest slice.

"So, when am I expected at Sagemore for the birth?" The dowager's gaze moved back and forth between the two. "I thought you might welcome a baby within the first eighteen months, but not the first year."

Concerned for Elizabeth, he shifted his hand to take hers. "It is not confirmed yet, Grandmamma."

She scoffed. "Have you taken a good look at your wife lately? Her glow is noticeable to anyone who is looking. She is also about to fall out of her bodice, her face is a bit rounder, and she has never before been so picky about the sweets on the tea tray."

"No one can say you are not observant." He shook his head with a smile.

"I have been with child twice, and I have seen others in such a condition many times. It is only a matter of a few weeks before the child within your wife quickens."

They both turned at the sound of a sniff to find Elizabeth with tears streaming down her cheeks. He was quick to wrap her in his embrace, as his grandmother moved to her other side.

"Oh dear," the dowager said softly as she took her hand. "I fear I have been too blunt."

Elizabeth shook her head. "It has all been so swift. Each time I begin to feel settled, some new distraction takes place. I was not prepared for this."

He pressed a kiss to her temple and opened his mouth to speak, but halted when his grandmother motioned for him to leave. "Grandmamma?"

The glint in her eye was familiar; he had seen it many times before. "Leave us for a while, Fitzwilliam."

"But…" He did not want to abandon his wife when she was so upset.

"I am sure Mrs. Henderson will have bath water for you. Go refresh yourself, and prepare for dinner. Lizzy will not be long."

He was hesitant, but Elizabeth gave a squeeze to his hand. "I will be well."

Exhaling heavily, he stood, handed her his handkerchief, and bestowed one last kiss to her hair before walking out of the door.

When the two women were alone, Elizabeth covered her face with the handkerchief and continued to cry. She had been honest when she said she was not ready. How ridiculous she must appear!

"I feel like such a half-wit," she groaned.

"You are far from a half-wit, Elizabeth Darcy, so you can stop your foolishness directly."

"No, I am!" She dropped her hands from her face and began to tug at her handkerchief. "I was unaware of what it meant when my courses stopped, but Fitzwilliam knew and had to explain it to me. I was so embarrassed."

The dowager's eyebrows raised. "And how did my grandson know? It is not as if he has ever been in a situation to understand."

"I was mortified when I had to tell him about my courses. He asked so many questions I could not answer—and did not want to answer. As it turned out, several books in the Sagemore library provided the information I refused to give him."

His grandmother chuckled. "That does sound like him." The dowager appraised her for such a period of time that she became uncomfortable. "Your mother did not prepare you much for marriage then?"

"I do not believe my mother was patient enough to explain matters."

The older lady sighed. "I owe you a great apology."

Shocked, Elizabeth placed her hand over their joined ones. "Whatever for? You have been of great assistance to me. I could not imagine you doing more."

"I wondered if you had been taught about the marriage bed, but given that your betrothed is my grandson, I was uncomfortable broaching the topic. It was one thing to insist the two of you consummate your marriage. An actual discussion of the act was not an idea I relished. I should have pushed my unease aside and thought more of you."

She shook her head. "Fitzwilliam is always thoughtful and kind. I have never had any reason to complain. I just felt so ignorant when he explained."

"The fundamentals were explained to me the morning of my wedding," explained the dowager. "Gerald's sister was embarrassed and tried to reassure me, but I was left with little understanding of specifics—besides how to know if I was with child." She covered Elizabeth's fidgeting hands. "There is no reason to feel as you do."

Her eyes lifted to catch the elder lady's gaze. "I know *nothing* of how to care for a babe."

The dowager furrowed her brow. "But surely, you have, at the very least, had some experience between your younger sisters and the tenants' children?"

"I have held a few when visiting tenants, but Lydia was not quite five years younger, so I remember very little of when she was a babe. Aside from how to hold a child, I was taught naught of how to care for one."

"Is that part of what troubles you?"

She nodded and sniffled, another tear trailing down her face.

"How much you need to know depends on how much you wish to do yourself. Mrs. Green is sure to have some knowledge, and you can hire a nurse. If you like, I can come for the birth and stay for a month complete."

She wiped her nose as a weight lifted from her shoulders. "You would?"

"Of course! This is my first great-grandchild. I have to be there to welcome him or her into the world."

Elizabeth gave a small smile, as she became more at ease.

"After all, this child must know who is head of this family. We cannot have it assume that it is Fitzwilliam, or God forbid, Henry."

She reached over to the dowager and embraced her. "Thank you."

"You should have told your worries to Fitzwilliam," she chided gently.

The censure in the older lady's expression prompted a sigh. "We discussed my feelings when a child was first mentioned, and he seemed so disappointed. I did not want to upset him any longer."

"I believe you stand to worry him more by not confiding in him, dear."

Elizabeth sighed. "I know. He was just so elated." She was unsure of the dowager's expression. Could she be upset with her? "Of course, I am grateful he is excited about the idea of a baby. I would be inconsolable if he was as apprehensive as I am, but I require time to come to terms with the change."

"Your feelings are just, but next time Fitzwilliam might know what to do or say to help."

Elizabeth snorted and covered her mouth and nose with her handkerchief.

The dowager pursed her lips. "You are correct. He would not."

She stole another piece of shortbread from the tray and stood. "I should go refresh myself before dinner."

"Here, Lizzy," called the dowager. She prepared her a fresh cup of tea, placed two more pieces of shortbread on the plate, and handed it to her. "Take this with you."

"Thank you," she replied with a grin.

"Are there any foods which make you ill? I will need to amend the menus for the next week."

"Please do not change your plans for me!"

"It will be as much for us as it will be for you. We cannot have you run from the room because the scent of mutton sends you to the chamber pot."

Elizabeth rolled her eyes. "You do not serve mutton."

"No, I do not. I detest it." The dowager remained in her seat, her face expectant.

"Most fish, above all pickled or smoked, tends to send me seeking fresh air."

The dowager gave a curt nod. "Thank you, dear. Those foods should not be difficult to eliminate from the menu." She reached over and rang the bell. "I shall see you at dinner."

After a quick bob of her head in acknowledgement, Elizabeth made her way to her chambers, noticing Mrs. Henderson appeared and knocked on the door to the sitting room as she ascended the stairs.

Darcy was seated in the library, waiting on the ladies, while he entertained himself with a book. He turned the page and jumped when he caught sight of his grandmother who stood just within the door.

"Forgive me for startling you."

"Please do not concern yourself," he replied. "I simply had not heard you enter, and was taken by surprise."

She took the chair across from him as he closed his book. Her expression indicated a lecture was forthcoming. What crime had he committed lately?

"You look as though you are about to give me a scolding."

She shook her head. "No, not a scolding."

"Then what have I done?"

His grandmother smirked. "Do you feel guilty about some transgression? Because I assure you, I have no intention of reprimanding you."

"I am unaware of any wrong doing on my part."

"Is Elizabeth coming down for dinner?" she asked.

He found the change in subject confusing, and furrowed his brow. "She claimed I was pacing whilst Hattie fixed her hair and ordered me to leave."

His grandmother shook with mirth. "I do like that young woman."

"Me, too." His voice was soft but full of warmth.

"I would say you more than like her," she retorted. "You do not stare as much as was your wont, but now you are always touching her in some manner. Do be careful when you are out and about in town."

He had been caught. "Yes, ma'am."

"You will be required to have a great deal of understanding over the next year. You may need to draw her out so she will speak to you of her feelings."

He frowned and rose to pour himself a glass of port. "I have, Grandmamma, but it is not so simple. She prefers to wait to see if the babe quickens before admitting she is with child."

The dowager reclined against her elbow, resting on the arm of the chair. "Her behaviour is, by and large, so mature; one forgets she is still so young. She has also had a great deal of change in the last few months, *and* she will need to make a numerous decisions before the babe arrives—the least of which will be what kind of mother she wishes to be."

He fixated on the liquid in his glass. "I had not thought of it in such a way." Would Elizabeth ever accept being with child?

"Do not fret, Fitzwilliam. She confided to me earlier that she does not know much about babies; I am inclined to believe she is afraid."

He was relieved her assumption was close to his own. "That was my belief at first, but over time, I became concerned it was more."

229

"Lady Bletchley's daughter, Lady Tabitha Dawkins has just begun to receive callers since the birth of her son."

He glanced at his grandmother with alarm and she chuckled.

"I know what kind of mother *she* will be; she and Sir James will desire to show off his heir. I also have no doubts that Elizabeth will be horrified by them."

"Yet, you plan to take her!" He was incredulous. "I was not left to the sole care of the nurse, and I never thought my children would be."

She leaned over and placed her hand over his. "Lizzy's heart is too big. She is incapable of such disinterest in someone she loves, but it is imperative she learn this now rather than later."

His pain must have shown in his expression because she implored him with her eyes. "I would say trust me on this, but really, you should trust your wife. You know her better than I, yet I know she would never be like Lady Bletchley's family."

"You are correct," he agreed with a sigh. "I know you are, but she has been so temperamental."

"You would be, too. Just you wait until she nears her confinement, and she cannot see her feet, and those feet ache. Oh! And the backaches!" She pointed to her grandson with a stern mien. "Then we will speak of her unpredictable moods."

The door opened to reveal Hobbes, who gestured Elizabeth inside. She thanked him with a beatific smile, and approached Darcy's outstretched arm.

"There you are, my love. If you had been any later, I would have sent up a search party."

"Did you think Hattie would hide me beneath my hair?" she asked with a teasing smile.

"Fitzwilliam, you are being silly." His grandmother shook her head, and he showed his immense pleasure when his wife took his arm, tucking herself to his side.

"No, but I did wonder if she would ever finish. You will not be presented to the Queen after all."

"I would sponsor her if the Queen were to hold a drawing room at St. James," commented the dowager.

"Would it be a necessity if she holds presentations in the future?" Darcy had no interest in whatever St. James had to offer and did not want Elizabeth subjected to the claptrap if it was unnecessary.

"Richard mentioned that Anne has named you master of Rosings after her death. The income from Sagemore and Rosings will make you a wealthy man."

"I wish she had left the estate to Richard," he complained. "I detest seeing him sent to war again."

Elizabeth squeezed his arm. "But he does not want it. He recognises his hopes for the future and his capabilities. Do not begrudge him that. It is admirable."

His grandmother gestured her agreement. "She is correct. Richard was always a realist. He has passed over Rosings, and in the process, offers a younger son of yours an estate."

"It is odd to think of Rosings for a second son since it is larger than Sagemore."

"But it is not larger than Pemberley." His grandmother wore an odd expression, but he was unsure of what it meant.

"I was certain I would hear from my father by now, but there has been little reaction. I received a few letters when I expected his unannounced arrival at Sagemore." Darcy shook his head. "He would never allow me to inherit Pemberley. I am certain of it."

"Your uncle and I discussed this last week when Richard mentioned Rosings, and we believe your father cannot disown you."

He stared at her.

"Oh, for goodness sakes, close your mouth, Fitzwilliam, before you catch a fly."

He clamped his jaw closed and sealed his lips into a line. He had not expected he would ever inherit Pemberley now. How would Elizabeth feel if one day they were expected to move there? She loved Sagemore, and he had no wish to uproot her from her home.

"Why do you believe he cannot disown me?"

"I remember when your father brought the marriage settlement to Gerald. They discussed Pemberley, and I am certain Gerald indicated to me that there was still an entailment. If you passed away and George had no remaining sons, a distant cousin would inherit, but he

231

could never disown you for a distant relative. Society would go rabid with the information."

He was astounded. "Father never mentioned it. I always assumed whatever entailment had once been in existence had been broken."

"Your grandfather Darcy started the entailment after his father sold off a good portion of the properties the estate owned to pay off debts. Your grandfather and father have done a great deal to find new properties to add to their holdings, to rebuild the legacy."

He was quiet for a while as his grandmother and wife watched his every move. Elizabeth caressed his arm with her thumb, but he moved her hand to his forearm where he could hold it.

"I apologise. It is a great deal to absorb."

"We understand, Fitzwilliam." Elizabeth's voice soothed him and he kissed her hair, even though his grandmother was present.

Dinner was a lively affair. Elizabeth and his grandmother were animated in their chatter while he observed and sometimes joined the conversation. Despite the dowager's sarcasm, the two ladies were near to identical in temperament, and he was pleased they were such good friends.

After the meal, they withdrew to the music room for an informal evening. Elizabeth played the pianoforte, even sang along with one of the tunes, before she took a seat next to him.

The dowager had poured a snifter of brandy for the two of them, and they were seated comfortably while Elizabeth spoke of the gala they had attended in Bath. She had just begun to describe the terrible performance when they heard the faint sound of the knocker as it echoed through the entry hall.

"Who could it be at this hour?" The dowager peered at the clock on the mantelpiece.

They listened as Hobbes greeted the caller. Darcy's heart dropped at the sound of the guest's voice.

"It is my father," he whispered.

"Now, how did he know we were discussing him?" his grandmother groused. "Were his ears ringing?"

Elizabeth's eyes were wide as saucers, and he took her by the shoulders. "My love, you must wait for me in our chambers."

Her eyes met his, and courage lit their depths. "My place is with you."

"I appreciate your loyalty, but I do not know why he has called, and I do not want you to be subjected to his anger. There is no reason for it."

"I agree with him, Lizzy. This is their first meeting since your marriage. Allow Fitzwilliam to handle his father, then later, he will tell all."

"I promise."

Fortune smiled upon him when she acquiesced and made for the door leading to the servant's hall. Before she could depart, he rushed forward to take her in his arms. "Thank you. I could not concentrate if I was worried for you."

She caressed her lips against his cheek and slipped through the door where she startled a passing maid. Somehow, the maid's presence soothed his anxiety. She would have help as she found her way to their rooms.

He had just returned to his seat when Hobbes opened the door, prompting him and his grandmother to rise to their feet. "Mr. George Darcy insists he must see you, ma'am and sir."

"I assumed as much," she replied. "You may show him in, Hobbes. We would like an expeditious completion to this call, if possible."

Hobbes stood to one side of the doorframe, which allowed the elder Darcy entry. The son stared at his father, who still appeared much the same except for the signs of fatigue etched upon his face.

"I was unaware you were here, Fitzwilliam" were the first words from his mouth.

"We have not corresponded of late, so I would be concerned about the trustworthiness of my grandmother's servants if you *did* have knowledge of our arrival in town." He made certain his voice was unemotional and even. He was his own man, and he did not answer to his father in any way.

"I had come to ask your direction from your grandmother. I dispatched a courier to Sagemore in late May, but he was informed the family was not home."

"No correspondence from you awaited me upon my return."

"No, I wished it delivered straight to your hands, so he returned to Pemberley."

Darcy took a step forward. He had no wish to speak in riddles, but desired the confrontation to be concluded with haste. "Let us not beat about the bush, Father. Why have you sought me out? You were unmistakeable in your ultimatum when I was last at Pemberley." His father's eye twitched. He had hit his target.

"I am pleased to know I was so clear. I had begun to think I had been ambiguous in some fashion since you did not conduct yourself in the manner I requested."

"You were told I would not bring about Anne's death. By marrying her, I may as well put a pistol to her head."

George Darcy scoffed. "Do not be so dramatic, Fitzwilliam. Besides, as things appear now, she would never have made it long. You would have sacrificed no more than a month or two to have Rosings and been guilt free, since that was such a concern to you."

"He will have Rosings anyway, George," interrupted the dowager. "Anne is not unhappy and neither should you be."

His eyes darted back and forth between his grandmother and his father. "What do you mean Anne would not have made it so long?"

"I never meant for you to be told this evening," she sighed. "You and Lizzy had just arrived. I wanted us to have a pleasant evening before we addressed those concerns, but since our plans have been disrupted—Anne took ill a fortnight ago. Her mother, instead of keeping her at Rosings and comfortable, brought her to London where she worsened. She foisted every physician and surgeon she could find on the poor girl until Henry removed Anne from Catherine's care."

He was appalled. "First she removes her to Rosings, then she improves, and now she sickens, which prompts Lady Catherine to return to town? She tends to make matters worse, in my opinion."

The dowager rolled her eyes. "Yes, but Catherine was never known for her presence of mind."

"Are you certain matters are so grave?" His heart may have rebelled against the notion of marriage to his cousin, but it pained him that she might be near her end.

234

"They almost bled her to death, dear. Catherine was not informing the incoming physicians of the treatments of the prior physicians. As a result, she is fragile."

He ran his hand across his forehead and combed his fingers through his hair. "Is there no other remedy?"

His grandmother indicated all hope was lost with a shake of her head. "I am afraid not. We have no choice but to wait and see what God determines."

"But she intends to leave Rosings to you?" asked his father.

He bristled and his posture became rigid. "That is Anne's decision, one she can still change. I will not rejoice if I benefit from her death."

His father gave a huff. "I never insinuated your conclusion. You were lucky she still named you as her heir; however, we must handle matters now before they become more complicated." His father had a calculating gleam in his eyes, and the son recognised it all too well.

"Handle matters?"

"I have found a man who can forge a marriage certificate for this woman you wed."

"I beg your pardon?" he asked, raising his voice a notch.

His grandmother replied. "He proposes to have your marriage voided by somehow producing a husband for Lizzy." The dowager's face was reddened. She was livid! "Your father seems to forget I was the daughter of a country squire once upon a time, filled the role of a countess with aplomb, and bore a daughter who became his beloved wife. He now scorns your mother's lineage with his ill-judged application."

"You accuse me of a judgement I have not made!" exploded the elder Darcy.

The Dowager Countess of Matlock stood tall. "You may not have made the statement outright, but you implied it. You scorn Lizzy and you have never taken the opportunity to know her!"

The elder Darcy took a step towards the dowager and lifted a satchel from his side. "I travelled to Meryton in an attempt to discover more about her. The estate was entailed to a cousin—who is an imbecile, by the way—after her father's death. Her uncle is the local solicitor! Whilst everyone in the area seems to have no less praise for her, she is not of our sphere!"

235

George Darcy proffered a document, which Darcy took. It was certificate of some kind, claiming his Elizabeth had married someone by the name of Christopher Hoskins.

It was utter rubbish; the date was one week after the horrific accident that claimed the lives of her family. The document also alleged the marriage had occurred in Wiltshire. Elizabeth would have been in no state to wed anyone at that time much less travel.

The notion of his father purchasing a forged marriage certificate astounded him. The most important question was: had he already presented it to anyone in the church? Had his father attempted to void his marriage?

"What have you done?" he asked through clenched teeth.

"What needed to be done."

His father was too at ease for his taste, and his heart began to pound, as terror filled his breast at the possibilities laid before him. He brandished the forged document before him. "Have you shown this to anyone?"

"What if I have? That woman cannot remain your wife!"

He rubbed his hand across his mouth and attempted to control the shaking of his hands before his father noticed. His grandmother appeared beside him and peered at the papers in his grasp.

"My God, George, what have you done?"

Chapter 17

The documents fluttered down as Darcy lunged forward and pinned his father against the wall behind him, sending a painting crashing to the floor.

"Fitzwilliam!" his grandmother cried over the din.

"Did you use this rubbish? Have you shown it to anyone?" he yelled. His hands bunched the fabric at the base of his father's throat as he pressed him against the solid plaster with force. "Have you attempted to destroy my wife?" Naught mattered but his own fury. His voice was rough and sure to carry throughout the house.

The elder Darcy tugged at his son's wrists in a futile effort to free himself. "I have done nothing wrong! I swear to you, I have done nothing as of yet." He gulped hard, his horrified expression proof he had not anticipated his son's outburst. "I wanted to see if you would return with me. I wanted you to accompany me to the bishop."

His hands relaxed against his father's clothing, but he kept him pressed against the wall. "I will never, ever void my marriage. I would never banish Elizabeth to Scotland. I shall never abandon her or give her up." He had stopped yelling, but he spoke through clenched teeth and in an ominous voice. Cool air rushed through his flared nostrils and a solid ache filled his chest as his heart pounded as though it would burst through his sternum.

"If you persist with any plot that dishonours either my vows or hers, I will never set foot in Pemberley again, and, as soon as I am its master, I will break the entail and sell it to my friend Bingley."

His father's eyes bulged. "You would not dare!"

"Fitzwilliam!"

A frantic voice emerged from beside him and broke through the haze of his anger. He glanced to his side where Elizabeth stood. She placed one hand on his arm and the other reached between him and his father to press her palm to his cheek. He released his father, took her in his arms, and grasped her to him.

"I love you," she whispered against his ear.

He drew back and scanned her eyes. How would she react to his utter loss of control? Would she be frightened, upset? His hands cupped her cheeks as he studied her expression; to his relief, no horror or revulsion was present, only concern.

Oblivious to his father and grandmother, he kissed her soundly, in need of reassurance she was still his, regardless of his father's machinations. She did not object to such a public display and even wore an amused smirk when he pulled away. His grandmother handed him the forged documents, and he peered down on them in disgust one last time before they met their fate in the fire.

"What are you doing?" His father made a futile grasp for the papers as his hand released them, but was too late. "Those cost a great deal of money!"

"Then you spent a great deal of money on ash," retorted the dowager. "I can think of no better place for them."

Emboldened by the truth of his wife's affection, he faced his father. "You claim to have travelled to Meryton, yet it is obvious you did not bother to learn much more than who Elizabeth's family was. The dates and location make it impossible to be a legitimate article, and I could present the entire town of Meryton to prove it a forgery.

He tugged Elizabeth to his side, her proximity providing support while he faced the uncertainty ahead. "You have always been fond of ultimatums, so here is mine to you." His father clenched his jaw, but remained silent, which surprised Darcy. "I have been advised that Pemberley is entailed, and it is impossible for you to pass over me as heir. So, my ultimatum is if you persist in your attempts to discredit my wife, I *will* see Pemberley sold to my friend Bingley, or, if he is not in need of an estate, some other tradesman, for whatever funds he has available to him."

His grandmother giggled, and they all turned to stare at her in astonishment. With a smirk, she looked to George Darcy. "You were adamant Caroline Bingley would never be mistress of Pemberley. I would wager she would be delighted to be labelled spinster in the hopes her brother becomes master of Pemberley."

Darcy shook his own head as he heard Elizabeth's laughter. The sound helped soothe his anger as well as his soul.

The elder Darcy stepped forward, furious. "You would defy your father in this manner? Your mother would be ashamed of you."

Darcy pinned him once again, but this time with an appalled gaze. "My father took me fishing and riding. He was strict, but he read to me as I sat on his knee. *That man* died the night my mother passed from this earth. The man, who stands before me, is no more than a simulacrum of the gentleman I once knew."

At a minimum, his father should have vented his anger with the son's revelation, but the man's eyes were more bewildered and hurt before indifference and a flash of ire masked the emotion. No further threats were issued, no angry retort voiced. He merely straightened his coat with a firm tug to the bottom, and strode out of the door.

With a collective exhale, the room relaxed at the sound of the front door closing, and Darcy grasped his wife by the shoulders, so she faced him. "I asked you to wait for me in our rooms, Elizabeth."

"I remained on the stairs due to my apprehension. When I heard Grandmamma's raised voice, I hurried to come to your aid. I presume he had documents to ruin me in some fashion, but I could not allow you to harm your own father."

His grip on her arms loosened as he drew her into his embrace. "I was attempting to protect you."

"I do not think your father would have harmed Lizzy," interjected his grandmother. "He may have blustered and badgered as we saw today, but he would not have injured her."

"I could not take such a risk." His palms cupped Elizabeth's cheeks. "I cannot lose you."

She placed her hands over his. "Regardless of what your father does or what society thinks, I would not leave. If he somehow brought an end to our marriage by law, I would know—we would know—it was a lie."

His grandmother gave a small snort and shook her head. "He would cause quite the scandal, but I imagine people would begin to question the validity of the marriage license when no husband appeared to claim his wife."

With a sigh, he entwined his fingers with hers as he brought their hands between them. "The date on the license was exactly one week after the carriage accident."

Elizabeth's eyebrows lifted. "I was not even conscious. I could not have been wed to anyone in my condition at the time."

"I doubt he knows the dates of the accident well enough to have taken it into consideration." His anxiety gradually ebbed as they spoke of the encounter. The discourse with Elizabeth in regards to the license gave him the confidence he required to put it behind him. "The wedding would have occurred in Wiltshire, too."

"So I was feverish and bedridden in Hertfordshire whilst I was being wed in Wiltshire? I must be quite accomplished to perform such a feat."

"Lizzy, you should not make light of it," the dowager scolded with amusement.

"I must, Grandmamma, else I will cry. The thought of him nullifying our marriage frightens me, and I can imagine how much it would pain me if my father were the one to attempt it."

Despite the company of his grandmother, Darcy wished to be alone with his wife. "If you have no objections, Grandmamma, I believe it is time for us to retire."

If she was amused or upset, she gave no indication, but his grandmother was almost impossible to shock. "Of course, I have no objections. I am certain you would much rather be alone after the events of this evening."

"Thank you." He gave his wife's hands a tug, and led her to their chambers.

He did not wish for interruption. In fact, he did not wish for Elizabeth to leave his side; therefore, Hattie was promptly dismissed for the night, and they aided one another as they prepared for bed. With a passion brought on by the fears of the evening, Darcy wasted no time in affirming Elizabeth was his, not releasing her even as they slumbered. She remained in his embrace for the entirety of the night.

The dowager was seated at the head of the table when Elizabeth entered the dining room the next morning. She was exhausted, but the modiste's appointment would not be cancelled due to her fatigue.

Fitzwilliam's grandmother was cheerful as she greeted her. "Good morning, Lizzy."

"Good morning." She took her seat and selected some toast off a tray on the table while the dowager poured her tea.

"Is your stomach upset?"

"I am a tad queasy, but such instances are rare, and toast is an effective cure."

The elder lady gave her a reassuring pat of the hand. "You are fortunate. I was bilious the first few months I carried Henry. Some days, I felt as though I could keep nothing down."

The knocker on the front door sounded and the dowager's expression became animated. "Right on time."

"You were expecting someone?"

Hobbes soon opened the door to let in a young lady, and Elizabeth stood. The visitor was dressed well in expensive clothes, but what drew her notice were the girl's looks. The chestnut brown hair and blue eyes were familiar.

"Georgiana?" she asked.

Georgiana beamed and stepped forward. "Hello, Lizzy! I hope you do not mind, but Grandmamma invited me to join you shopping."

"No, I do not mind at all; I just had not expected you." She walked around the table to come face to face with the young girl to whom she had been corresponding. "Grandmamma has been sly and not said a word."

The dowager gave a lift of her lips. "I was unsure if she would make it. After last night, I was even more doubtful."

"I did not want to miss today. I have been so looking forward to it."

"Have you eaten, dear?" interjected her grandmother. "Elizabeth had just come down to break her fast. She will need to eat soon if we are to make our appointment."

She led her new sister to the seat beside her. "I am so glad you have come, but I do not wish you to be in trouble with your father."

Georgiana situated herself as a cup of tea was placed before her. "Oh, he left at sunrise this morning. He was rather eager to return to Pemberley." She placed a muffin on her plate and glanced to her grandmother. "Papa was furious last night upon his return to the house. I was sure he was to come here, but he refused to speak of what occurred."

The dowager peered towards Elizabeth, her face mirroring her sense of wariness. They had no wish to ruin Georgiana's vision of her father. "I believe no one has any desire to revisit last night."

The elder lady nodded. "I apologise, but I feel it is best that you do not know, Georgiana."

The girl placed her hands in her lap and stared down at them. "It is not as if I do not have some idea of his schemes from the servants. I am aware that he wished to nullify your marriage to my brother in some manner, which I believe did not go as planned."

"It did not." Elizabeth covered her sister's hands with her own.

Georgiana lifted her head to regard her with a sorrowful expression. "In truth, he is really a loving father, yet I cannot understand why he behaves as he does. Last night, a man came late after he returned, and I heard them speaking in Papa's study."

"You should not eavesdrop," scolded her grandmother.

"I know, but I was worried about what he had done." A tear dropped to her cheek and trickled down to her chin where Elizabeth skimmed it away with her fingers.

"He was unable to do any harm. Please do not fret."

"I assumed his plan had not met with success. He told the man he would no longer require his services. The man asked about money Papa owed him, and I believe he was paid. I hid in the music room when he departed." Her voice lowered, and she eyed them with uncertainty. "He was not a gentleman."

Was this man the forger, and what else had Mr. Darcy planned if the falsified marriage license had not worked? At least, his schemes appeared to have been abandoned with her husband's threat.

The wary grandmother appraised her granddaughter. "Georgiana, what have you told Mrs. Younge about today?"

"She knows I am going shopping with you, but she will not tell Papa."

How could she be certain? Elizabeth noted the concern of the dowager as she turned to Georgiana. "How do you know?"

The young lady wore a smile that hinted of mischief. "Mrs. Younge no longer sees her family since she became my companion and has indicated she would keep my secrets if I wished to spend time with you. She rode with me here, but when the carriage pulled around to the stable, she walked down the street to find a hackney carriage. Her plans for today are to visit with an old friend."

It was odd that her governess was so ready to keep secrets from her employer. Hopefully, Georgiana would not find herself in trouble with her father.

Before she could be questioned further, Georgiana clasped her hands together. "I do not wish to speak of Papa anymore today. We are to go shopping, and you know that I dearly love to shop." She glanced between her grandmother and her new sister. "Where are we going and what are we to purchase?" The glow that alit her face coaxed Elizabeth to smile.

"We will visit the drapers and then take our purchases to Madame Lebrun. Lizzy also requires alterations on several gowns." The dowager glanced to Elizabeth. "I would not alter them all, my dear, just those you will require for now."

Georgiana grinned. "Good; Mrs. Younge and Papa both agreed that I require a few new gowns. I have quite outgrown my last. My maid had to add trim to the bottom of a few because they had become so short."

"Then we shall all have a gown made today," replied the dowager. "Lizzy, you should speak with Madame Lebrun, so she can plan your future gowns accordingly."

Her new sister gave her an eager glance after a sip of her tea. "Do you plan to attend a ball or the theatre whilst in town?"

Elizabeth turned to Georgiana. "I am not certain of any balls, but we may go to the theatre. Why do you ask?"

"Well, Aunt Elinor always tells Madame Lebrun if she has a ball to attend, so she can help her select the best fashion plates."

"Oh." A small grin tugged at her lips. How could she hide this from Georgiana? The poor girl was relegated to listening at doors and relying on gossip to hear news of her father's wishes and family's activities. The tidings of a new niece or nephew from a letter or from the London gossip mill would not do. "We have not told many people yet, because it is too soon to know for certain, but your brother and I believe you will become an aunt sometime in April."

"Really!" Georgiana turned to her grandmother as the older woman gave a chuckle. "That would mean that you shall become a great grandmamma." Her forehead crinkled and she took pause. "But you do not seem surprised."

"Dear, they did not have to tell me because I suspected as soon as Lizzy walked through the door."

"Is this why you are required to have your gowns altered?" Georgiana's hands reached out to clasp hers. "And why you are ordering new ones?"

She laughed in delight at the girl's enthusiasm. "Yes, some portions of my bodices have grown a bit snug for my taste, and I will require new gowns in a few months."

"You will also require a few items for winter," interjected the dowager.

With a quirk of her lips, she took a quick glance towards the elder lady. "I am certain I will."

Georgiana clapped her hands. "I am so excited—I am going to be an aunt! I hope I will be able to see him or her whilst they are still a babe." Her eyes suddenly widened and she grasped Elizabeth's hands once more. "You could come to Ramsgate during the summer! Papa says that once I am fifteen, he will allow me to go to the coast with Mrs. Younge!"

"You should be in school." The dowager placed her utensils down on her plate with a dissatisfied expression.

"Papa says it is not necessary since he can hire whatever governesses and masters I require." Georgiana turned back, missing the roll of her grandmother's eyes. "Perhaps Grandmamma could come, too. We could spend the summer together at the seaside!"

She nodded as she acknowledged both the grandmother and her granddaughter. "We will have to mention it to Fitzwilliam and see what he says. Please let us know if your father continues to plan this for you, and I am certain your brother will do what he can to meet you there." Fitzwilliam would wish to go, if for no other reason than to keep a watchful eye on his sister.

"Of course!" exclaimed Georgiana. "I know Papa plans to accompany me for my birthday in June, but he says he will pass no more than a few days at Ramsgate with me before his return to London."

"Ladies, if you are finished with your breakfast," interrupted the dowager. "We should depart, else we will not make it to Madame Lebrun's on time."

Much to his disappointment, Elizabeth was gone when Darcy opened his eyes, but upon peering at the clock, he understood why; she would have already left with his grandmother.

The morning's planned activities would include a visit to his Uncle's to ascertain Anne's condition. Because her daughter had been removed from her care, Lady Catherine was not expected to be in attendance, but he almost wished she would make an appearance.

Sooner or later, he would have to deal with her, and why not be done with it!

As he was shown into the family drawing room, Aunt Elinor leapt to her feet to embrace him. "Fitzwilliam, we are so happy to see you. You do look well. How is Lizzy?"

He took great pleasure in her inquiry after his wife. "Elizabeth is fine, thank you. She is shopping with Grandmamma."

"Oh, I wish mother had informed me. Grace and I would have enjoyed joining them."

"Hello Fitzwilliam," said Grace, who stood just behind her mother.

Uncle Henry followed by both his sons, entered the room, striding over to greet him.

"Darcy! We wondered when you would venture to town." Richard stepped forward, the last to shake his hand.

"Georgiana arrived last week, and we timed our arrival with when she suspected my father would depart."

Huntley chuckled in amusement. "So, the two of you have conspired to visit with one another behind your father's back. I have always admired my little cousin, and this makes me even prouder of her."

"You are proud of her for defying her father?" questioned Grace. "She is but fourteen years old since early June! You would not be pleased if your child committed the same sin."

Huntley shook his head as he took a seat. "No, dear sister, but she is not my daughter. Uncle George is erroneous in this instance, as well. I am proud of her for not blindly following her father's dictates in this situation."

"She favours her mother," added Uncle Henry. "She is a caring, loving soul, and she cannot bear to be separated from a family member with whom she is so close."

Richard laughed and pointed at Darcy. "I remember when I found you in the nursery playing dolls with her. She must have been five and you were seventeen. You were horrified at me discovering your secret, but I soon learned not to tell a soul."

Grace wore a puzzled expression as she tilted forward in order to see her brother. "Why? What happened?"

"I teased him once—*once*—and he thrashed me for it." Huntley and Uncle Henry guffawed as Richard reddened. "I had not realised how he had grown since the last time we had fought."

"I remember that summer," snickered Huntley. "He blackened your eye, but you told mother and father you had been hit in the face by a tree branch whilst riding."

The humour of the memory elicited a grin as he sat in a chair near the fire. "I believe you could beat me with rather little trouble these days, Richard. Do not let that one loss vex you."

Richard took a place on the sofa. "I have not, cousin. I admit it nagged at me when I was younger. I had fantasies of revenging myself upon you for that one defeat. Eventually, I decided one loss in seventeen years could go without being avenged."

Grace chuckled and rolled her eyes. "You are too kind, brother."

Uncle Henry's amusement subsided, and his air became serious. "I would imagine you are here because you heard of Anne."

"Yes, my father paid us a call last night and Anne's condition was… well, discussed."

"The visit did not go well." Uncle Henry's definitive look told him it was a statement and not a question.

"I would like to ask your advice later, if you have the time?"

"Yes, of course," his uncle replied. "Would you care to visit with Anne?"

He was taken aback by the offer. The possibility she might not have been well enough for visitors or that Lady Catherine might be around to prevent it had been a concern. "Yes, I would. Do you think she can tolerate company? I would not wish to cause her undue fatigue."

"Not much can be done now," commented Grace in a remorseful tone. "She is too weak to last much longer."

Aunt Elinor stood and took a place beside her husband. "She is resigned to it and wants nothing other than to enjoy what time she has left. I am thankful Henry acted to remove her from Catherine, and wish we had done it a long time ago."

His uncle took his wife's hand. "I do as well, dear. Though she has absolved us of blame, I wish I had listened to Mother much earlier. I did not want to rile Catherine, and I had no knowledge she was part of the problem."

"Anne was never healthy, even when she was a child," said Richard in a reassuring tone. "Our interference may not have helped."

"Now _you_ are trying to absolve us," said Aunt Elinor. "We should be allowed some guilt over this, son. We should not have cowered away from the subject just because Catherine is a tyrant."

Uncle Henry shook his head as if to clear it. "Enough! Darcy, follow me."

The evident self-reproach Uncle Henry harboured was obvious in his demeanour; his downcast spirit, the sadness in his eyes, all were proof of the weight upon his shoulders. However, Darcy was not without fault in the matter, either. He could not regret Elizabeth, but if he had wed Anne, perhaps…

"You can end those thoughts you are having straight away, son," his uncle interrupted as they climbed the stairs. "Even had you married her, Anne still might not have survived. As Richard said, she suffered from fevers or maladies with great frequency, and if Catherine was the cause or exacerbated it, then the damage was already done."

"Then perhaps you should not bear so much guilt either." He could not witness his uncle's reaction, but he should not have the culpability of Anne's demise. "As you said, the damage could have already been done."

Uncle Henry shook his head, adamant in his view. "Mother has campaigned for Anne's removal since Lewis de Bourgh died. My father feared dissolving what little relationship remained with his eldest daughter, and I… well, as I said earlier, I did not want to deal with her diatribe." His uncle stopped before a door and took care to open it quietly.

The room was large, yet sweltering, due to the fire roaring in the grate. Anne's companion was reading aloud from her seat at the bedside, but the lighting was too dim for him to make out the figure in the bed, so Darcy stepped closer.

"Pardon the interruption," said Uncle Henry, "but your Cousin Darcy has come to see you, Anne."

"Fitzwilliam?" came a small voice from the bed.

He forced himself to move even closer, though it took all his restraint not to retreat. How pale and thin Anne had become; she was so small in comparison to her bed and the bedcovers! Mrs. Jenkinson stood to offer him her chair, and he braced himself as he took the seat. His hand enclosed her cool, damp fingers.

The corners of her lips twitched and she swallowed. "Do not be so shocked. I am certain I have appeared worse."

"I am sorry," he stammered.

She sighed and gave his hand a weak squeeze. "Oh Fitzwilliam, do not be sorry. I have heard those words too much the past few days from Uncle Henry, Aunt Elinor, Grandmamma."

A glance back showed his uncle had left the room. Anne was too fatigued for entertaining more than one visitor at a time.

"We all want the best for you." He covered their hands with his free one. The words were honest; all anyone in their family had ever wanted was her happiness.

A weak smile took form upon her lips. "I know. Aunt Elinor and I have conversed often since Uncle Henry brought me here. She told me the story of how you met your wife."

Those first memories of Elizabeth always brought him such happiness, even if it had been an emotional day. "Aunt Elinor met her the day after me."

She gazed upon him with concern. "You took quite a risk in marrying a complete stranger rather than forcing me into a marriage neither of us wanted."

"At the time, it seemed necessary for both Elizabeth and me."

"Have the issues with her family been resolved?"

He shook his head. "We have been unable to locate the uncle who was the cause of her problems."

"Hopefully, he is unable to cause more mischief."

As she studied his face for a moment, his eyes were drawn to hers. They were still bright, intelligent, caring; her mind was untouched by her illness, unlike the rest of her ravaged body. "Grandmamma believes you and Elizabeth have found love. Is this true?"

Heat suffused his face. "You are quite demanding for information."

"When you agreed to wed Elizabeth, you may have sacrificed your happiness because you thought you would save me. I only wished for reassurance of your felicity." Her voice showed the strain of their visit as it became weaker. It did not seem to take much to tire her.

"Elizabeth and I both are happy, Anne."

She smiled, and though it was not much of a smile, the gesture was as genuine and as full as her health could manage.

"Elizabeth is easy to love, and she professes to love me from time to time."

She chuckled, and he restrained his surprise. The sound did not resemble one he was accustomed to hearing, but after a moment of alarm, he leaned forward to press a kiss to her hair.

"Do not let Mama see you do that. She would contact everyone she knows to obtain your divorce." Anne's eyes betrayed her mischievousness, and he let out a bark of laughter. Her eyes fluttered a bit, and they dropped closed as she fell asleep.

Mrs. Jenkinson stepped beside him. "She pushes herself to converse with everyone until she is simply too fatigued, but she confided she would change none of it. These moments with her family are precious to her."

He observed his cousin as she slept. "Is she always so weak?"

"She had been awake for over an hour when you entered, so she had already used what little strength she still possesses. If you would like to spend time with her again, I will send word when she awakens.

With a nod, he rose and turned to face his cousin's long-time companion, who bore the dark circles under her eyes from the fatigue and strain of the last months. How difficult it must have been to care for Anne under the tight rule of Lady Catherine!

He took Mrs. Jenkinson's hand from where it rested on the chair and encased it between his own. "I would like to thank you for your care of Anne. If you require a letter of reference for your next position, I would be pleased to pen one."

She appeared flustered, but by no means displeased. "Thank you, Mr. Darcy. Your uncle and grandmother have also made similar offers, and I am grateful since Lady Catherine was quite angry with my desertion." With tears in her eyes, she gazed over to the frail figure in the bed, removing her hand from his to tuck a bit of the bedclothes in place. "I have cared for her since she was four. I started as her governess. Did you know?"

"No, I was not aware she had been in your care for so long."

She folded her arms around herself. "My husband disappeared about three years after we were wed. It was somewhat of a scandal in the small village where I grew up as the daughter of the local clergyman. When my husband did not return, my husband's brother claimed the small estate, and I sought employment as I could not bear to remain where I was pitied."

Her gaze returned to him, and he did his best to offer her a warm smile. She wiped her cheeks with her handkerchief and moved past him to the seat where she could resume her vigil. "Miss de Bourgh became the daughter I was not allowed. I wish I could have done more for her."

Her voice was soft, but he heard her clear as a bell. Everyone harboured some guilt over Anne's life and eventual passing.

"I believe you did all you could. Lady Catherine would have released you from service had you challenged her too strenuously, and then you would have been unable to help Anne at all. Her mother would have, no doubt, employed someone more biddable to her wishes."

Mrs. Jenkinson nodded, and he excused himself to return to his family in the drawing room. His foot had no more than stepped through the door when he heard the loud, familiar sound of a walking stick as it struck the floor.

"YOU!"

Chapter 18

Darcy's eyes lit upon Lady Catherine, who stood in the midst of his uncle's family, giving him a murderous glare.

Uncle Henry regarded his sister with great caution. "Catherine, you will not abuse my nephew in my home. If you wish to see Anne, you will not start the tirade you have no doubt fantasised about since you learned of his marriage."

"Uncle, Anne was asleep when I left. Mrs. Jenkinson indicated she would send word when she awakened."

"*You* have visited Anne?" Lady Catherine spat out with venom. "You did not care enough to make her your wife, so why would you wish to see her now?—unless it was to ensure your inheritance of Rosings."

"Lady Cath…"

"You filthy, greedy Old Mr. Grim! Waiting for her to die so you can claim Rosings and her money! You should be ashamed of yourself!"

He suppressed a growl as he stepped further into the room. "Neither Anne nor I wished to marry one another. I was doing her a favour."

"A *favour*? By making her a laughingstock of society?"

His restraint worked to rein in the anger threatening to bubble to the surface. "Anne does not care of the gossip. Why should you? She never wished to wed anyone and asking her to produce an heir would have been a death sentence. Your demands, madam, were both unfair and unfeeling."

The imperious lady sniffed. "My daughter would have been mistress of Pemberley and Rosings. Few would have rivalled her standing."

He was rueful as he shook his head. "For how long? If our betrothal and marriage could have extended her life, which is doubtful, how long would she have lived? Her constitution was never hardy."

"You would have lived at Rosings," she demanded.

He was courting a tirade, but he would not dissemble. "No, I would never reside where I must deal with you. You are not the master of me, and I would not wish to spend every day evicting you from the master's study."

Aunt Elinor bit her lip to avoid laughing while his uncle's eyebrows rose up his forehead.

Lady Catherine's nostrils flared and her lips tightened to a thin line. "You have come every Easter to check the books and to confer with the steward; I have never done more than offer my frank advice."

He took a deep breath and exhaled in another attempt to remain calm. "Yes, for which you have told me quite often you are celebrated. You must also remember when I would tell you that I planned to walk the estate. Your housekeeper and butler knew what I was about and allowed me back inside through the kitchens. I would then use the servants' hallways to reach the study, where I would lock the door."

Uncle Henry was shaking in silent mirth, until he released an accidental snort, which garnered his sister's attention.

"So, I see you take his side in this matter, too?" Her voice was still strident as well as indignant. "You are just as soft as my father was."

Uncle Henry began chuckling again in response, this time, out loud. "Thank you. I take it as a great compliment to be compared to Father."

"I will not remain only to be made a fool! Have someone show me to Anne's chambers. I wish to have a word with her."

"No one will wake Anne," Aunt Elinor stated firmly.

"You will not keep me from my daughter!"

"We will do what is best for Anne's health," interrupted Uncle Henry before she could utter another word. "You may have done irreparable harm with the treatments you subjected her to before we took her from your care, and despite the physician's prognosis, *we* are still praying for her recovery."

"You may be, but he is not!" She pointed her walking stick towards Darcy.

He saw no point in dragging out any argument with her, so he remained quiet. Hopefully, Uncle Henry would show her the door soon!

His uncle stepped forward and pushed the bottom of her walking stick down towards the floor. "Catherine, you are welcome to call to see if Anne is awake and wants to see you, but you will not abuse anyone under my roof."

"*If* Anne wants to see me?" She screeched in tones he had never heard before. "Why would my daughter be unwilling to see me?"

Aunt Elinor closed her eyes and sighed while Uncle Henry motioned his footmen forward. "I will be as frank as you are celebrated to be. Anne has not expressed any desire to receive you, and has voiced her relief at your absence. In the future, we will take Anne's wishes into account before we bow to yours. She will live for no one but herself from this day forward."

"You will not exclude me from my daughter's life!"

Uncle Henry nodded and his men stepped to either side of Lady Catherine. With a swift bow, he gestured towards the door. "On second thought, we will send word if Anne indicates she is receptive to your visit. We do not want her rest disturbed when she is in such dire need of it." Lady Catherine's mouth opened to speak, but his uncle never gave her a chance. "Maxwell, Dennis, please show Lady Catherine to the door."

The two footmen revealed their experience with Lady Catherine when each reached out to take an arm. She whipped away from both men as she turned on her heel. "I can find my own way out."

The footmen followed her to the doors of the sitting room where she turned towards her brother one last time. "I plan to consult a solicitor and will not remain silent until my daughter is returned to my care."

With a shake of his head, his uncle stepped forward until just out of striking distance of her cane. "Sir Lewis de Bourgh named me Anne's guardian in his will, and you are a woman. It is improbable you will do naught but bring speculation to your own parenting abilities by making this public knowledge; however, if you insist in the endeavour, I wish you luck."

Lady Catherine's face became pinched as she listened to every word. She made to open her mouth a few times as though she had thought of a response, but in the end, she strode from the door.

The front door soon slammed shut, and the sound reverberated through the house, indicating she had reached the hall on her own.

"I never thought she would leave," said Aunt Elinor, breaking the silence.

Darcy made his way to a chair and took a seat. "She was here for a while, then?"

Aunt Elinor rolled her eyes as she resumed her spot on the couch. "She arrived not long after you left to visit Anne, so we did our best to delay her. We were about to send Grace to see if Anne even wanted to speak to her mother and hoped to give the two of you more time."

"I appreciate your consideration."

"Did you speak of Rosings?" asked Uncle Henry.

"No, we did not have long before she became too fatigued. She desired to know about my marriage to Elizabeth. After the tales she was told of our betrothal, I believe she wished to ensure I am happy."

Grace wiped a tear from her eye with a sniff. "She asked what we know of you and your wife, and your life together. She was concerned you may have sacrificed your happiness for her sake."

"I supposed matters could have ended so, but Elizabeth and I have found ourselves content with our situation."

Every one turned at the sound of Richard's heavy snort. "You make it sound as if you merely like her. The two of you are so besotted. I am amazed a moon-calf expression is not permanently etched upon your face."

Huntley laughed and slapped his brother on the back. "I am glad you are here to tell us the truth of the matter."

He was insulted at his cousin's assertion. "We are not without decorum."

Richard lifted his eyebrows. "The two of you touch a mite more than is acceptable in public, but no, you do not grossly breach propriety." The smirk on Richard's lips told him any indication his cousin would side with him had disappeared. "However, the two of you were on occasion unable to be found during the day, often retired early, and sometimes even remained abed late."

Uncle Henry grinned. "I am pleased to hear it, son. I knew Lizzy would be good for you."

"And since Darcy has not mentioned it, she has proven herself to be an accomplished rider."

His proud expression could not be helped as he nodded. "My wife is quite competent on horseback."

"You are praising a woman's riding abilities, brother," asked Huntley, surprised. "I do not believe I have ever heard you compliment a woman on their horsemanship—not even Grace."

Richard turned to his sister. "Forgive me, Grace, but Lizzy gets along well in the saddle."

With a giggle, Grace shook her head. "She must be exceptional for my exacting brother to praise her."

"Richard joined me and Elizabeth once," clarified Darcy, "but a few days later, Elizabeth, whilst riding, had an encounter with an adder." He proceeded to tell the story, his face brimming with pride when he spoke of how Elizabeth managed to stay seated for as long as she did.

Huntley's eyebrows rose. "I have never understood how women remain in the saddle when a horse gives them trouble. I remember when Grace was learning, and she dared me to ride side saddle."

"She did not!" exclaimed Richard. "Where was I for this? I would have wagered a great deal of money that your rear would hit the dirt."

"I think you were visiting Darcy at Pemberley." Grace smirked at her brother's embarrassed expression. "And, he did indeed fall off."

With a bark of laughter, Richard shifted to the edge of his seat. "I would also wager that was when he ceased to tease you about riding side saddle?"

"There was that," she said with the same mischievous grin. "I believe the final straw was when I slipped a few garden snakes into his bed." They all knew of Huntley's fear of snakes, and a few snorts with some laughter were heard about the room.

Aunt Elinor tilted forward with an amazed look upon her face. "Why was I never told of this?"

"It was after Richard's return, and he helped me get rid of them," grimaced Huntley. "He only agreed to be of aid if I swore not to tell on Grace."

His aunt's finger raised to her three children. "I trust no more snakes will come into my houses."

Her daughter gave a mischievous grin. "No ma'am."

"Thank goodness." Aunt Elinor reached over and placed a hand on her nephew's arm. "Fitzwilliam, you must join us for tea. Mother plans to bring your wife along once they finish shopping."

His brow furrowed. "Grandmamma had not mentioned the stop last night."

Uncle Henry moved to a seat. "Anne wishes to meet Lizzy, and we sent a note this morning requesting mother bring her by."

"You may as well stay, otherwise you would spend the afternoon on your own." Aunt Elinor wore a hopeful expression and he laughed.

"Very well, I will remain. Mrs. Jenkinson offered to send for me when Anne awakens, and I would like to speak with her again."

Richard rose and adjusted his sabre. "Unfortunately, I cannot remain. I am expected back at the barracks." He gave Darcy a slap on the shoulder as he passed. "I am certain I will see you again whilst you are in town." He kissed his mother's cheek and rushed out of the door.

Fitzwilliam's shock was evident when Elizabeth entered with not only his Grandmother, but also Georgiana, a few hours later.

"Georgie!" he exclaimed. He jumped from his chair and hurried over to embrace her.

"Did you go shopping with Elizabeth and Grandmamma?"

Georgiana's face was animated as she nodded. "I was unsure after last night if I would be able to join them, but Papa left this morning."

"What did you tell Mrs. Younge?"

"Mrs. Younge does not tell Father all that takes place."

Her husband's eyebrows furrowed as he frowned, making it clear Elizabeth was not alone in her concern.

"Have you told her you are meeting me and Elizabeth?"

"Yes," answered Georgiana. "She does not have a care who I visit so long as they are family."

Fitzwilliam eyed his sister in a sceptical manner. "But, why would she take such a risk? If Father found out, she could lose her position."

"I do not know." Georgiana gave an unconcerned shrug. "She claims it is because she misses her family. To be honest, I do not care much why. I am just pleased I get to see you! Are you not pleased as well?"

His expression transformed into a brilliant smile, yet he still had a bit of uneasiness in his eyes. "I am very pleased to see you, but I am disquieted by Mrs. Younge's willingness to go along with this deception."

His sister shook her head. "And in all honestly, I do not believe we have reason for misgivings."

Elizabeth had to garner her husband's attention before this got out of hand, so she wrapped her hand around his arm, giving a small shake to her head. An argument was useless. They were unsure how much time Georgiana would remain in London, and what little time they had together should not be spent in a disagreement.

They took seats with the family, and Aunt Elinor ordered more tea in the event anyone needed refreshments. Their conversations made for a noisy group until everyone had caught up on one another's news.

How she enjoyed once more being a part of a large, boisterous family! Everyone chatted and made plans for the coming week. This sort of interaction had been missed.

As Elizabeth finished her tea, a maid entered to inform them that Anne was once again awake, and Fitzwilliam stood, offering his hand to her.

"Anne has a great desire to meet you."

"Me?" she asked, a bit stunned. While pleased to have had a letter from the young woman, she had not expected to have an audience with her.

The dowager smiled and patted her hand. "She is quite eager to make your acquaintance. Since we removed her here, her primary focus has been questions about you and Fitzwilliam."

"Oh," she said softly.

She stood and followed her husband through the corridors until they reached Anne's suite of rooms, where he knocked. An older woman answered and let them inside, where two chairs sat beside a bed containing, perhaps, the frailest young woman she had ever seen. Anne's face was almost colourless, the pallor pronounced by her dark hair and wide eyes. Her dry lips almost cracked as she smiled.

"Fitzwilliam, you have brought your wife?"

Her voice was almost as weak as her body appeared! How could someone treat—no mistreat their daughter in such a fashion? It was unthinkable.

Upon making a swift decision, she stepped to the seat closest to Anne's upper body. "I hope you do not mind my impertinence, but after your letter, I am counting on your forgiveness." She sat, took Anne's frail hand in hers, and leaned forward, so she was closer. "I am glad to meet you at last. I hope you will call me Lizzy, as the rest of your family does."

She held her breath for a moment as Anne appeared to take in all she said. After the passage of a few moments, she was just about to begin apologising when Anne's face broke into a grin.

"I believe I was the first to be impertinent with my letter, so I do not mind a bit in return. I would also be honoured to call you Lizzy."

"Good." A hand rested upon her shoulder, and she turned to where Fitzwilliam stood, watching with amusement.

Anne's weak voice drew her attention. "Grandmamma has told me of how your marriage came to be. I was sorry to hear of your family."

She swallowed in an attempt to control her emotions. The year of mourning had healed her immensely, but it was still difficult to speak of those she held so dear. "Thank you. I do miss them terribly, but I have also been blessed with a new family, who are wonderful. All of you have been most welcoming."

"You have not met my mother then, I take it?" Anne gave a raspy laugh, and Elizabeth reached over for a glass of water on the bedside table, giving Anne a sip before replacing it. "Thank you."

"No, I have not met Lady Catherine, but I hear she is a force to behold."

Despite her weak constitution, Anne's eyes were animated and full of humour. "She is, for the most part, a great deal of wind."

The frank statement made her giggle as she moved a lock of hair away from Anne's eyes.

"I imagine, since Fitzwilliam is to inherit Rosings, you will be forced to make her acquaintance one day—just do not give what she says much importance."

"I am accustomed to her vitriol, Anne," came Fitzwilliam's voice from behind her. "I will protect my wife."

Elizabeth raised one eyebrow. "You do not think I can manage Lady Catherine?"

His laugh joined Anne's weak expression of humour as he placed his hand on her back. "I believe you would handle her admirably, but do not fault me if I would prefer it not be required of you."

She returned her gaze to Anne, whose lips quirked to one side as she watched them interact. "I will be pleased to have Rosings belong to you. I know you will not live there, but your children will be raised with love and bring that love to Rosings. That is what I want for my father's house."

"We will appreciate the gift," said Fitzwilliam, "even if we do have to deal with your mother."

A smirk appeared upon Anne's face. "I do admit to a certain satisfaction in knowing that Mama is angry it is your inheritance."

All of the talk of death was unsettling! She shook her head as she rearranged Anne's bedclothes. "You will live many more years, so let us abandon this discussion."

Anne's frail hand dragged across the coverlet until it covered hers. "I am happy to do this for the two of you, Lizzy. I will not live much longer, and my wish for Rosings was to find someone who will appreciate it and care for it. I know Fitzwilliam will take care of the estate for his child. I know it will prosper, and the idea pleases me."

Tears began to stream down Elizabeth's face, and her husband placed his handkerchief in her hand. "I am sorry," she mumbled, as she tried to dry her eyes.

Anne gave her other hand a gentle squeeze. "You have just come out of mourning for a tremendous loss. I can understand why the subject would stir your emotions."

Fitzwilliam's arm came around her shoulder, and he hugged her to him. "Being more emotional is another sign of being with child," he whispered near her ear. "Would you object to my telling Anne? I believe it would make her happy to know there will be an heir for Sagemore and Rosings soon."

She nodded, as she tried to stem the flow of tears running down her cheeks.

"We have some news we would like to share with you, Anne."

The young woman's eyebrows lifted and an expectant expression came over her face.

"Grandmamma knows, of course, but we have not shared with anyone else as of yet."

"I will not tell anyone until you do," said Anne.

Fitzwilliam stepped forward and knelt beside Anne's bed. "We have reason to believe Elizabeth is with child."

Tears welled in Anne's eyes. "I hoped that was your news." Her face shone of her happiness, and she was a bit more animated. "I wish to be here long enough to have your suspicions confirmed. How long do you think it will be?"

"From what Grandmamma has said, I think sometime in the next month or so," she replied. "I promise that other than Fitzwilliam, you will be the first to know."

"I look forward to it."

A brisk knock sounded about the room, and they all turned as Mrs. Jenkinson opened the large, dark oak door to reveal Georgiana.

"I hope you do not mind my intrusion," she said tentatively. "I wished to speak to Anne as well."

She rose to stand with her husband, so Georgiana could take her chair. "Of course."

Once seated, her sister leaned towards Anne. "You look well."

A glance at Anne did reveal a small amount of colour she had not had earlier.

"I am more than content, Georgiana. I am so grateful Uncle Henry and Aunt Elinor brought me here."

As Elizabeth took Fitzwilliam's arm, he tensed. "Anne." His wariness on the subject illustrated by the trepidation in his voice. "Your mother was here earlier, wishing to see you. Uncle Henry indicated it is your choice. You do not have to allow her visit."

Anne's eyes shifted down, giving her the appearance of feeling ashamed. "I know it must seem like I am an undutiful daughter, but she has become more difficult than usual as of late. She tells me how much of a disappointment I am, and I fear she will only come here for no other reason than to tell me again. I could not bear it."

The despair upon Anne's face pained Elizabeth, so she took a seat on the edge of the bed and placed her hand over Anne's. "She has no one to blame for her disappointment but herself. Do not let her bitter words hurt you." She nodded towards her husband and Georgiana. "Everyone here loves you, and I am certain all of us consider her words untrue."

"She is correct," said Fitzwilliam from behind her. "We have never expected you to be more than yourself. We want you to be happy."

"I do not wish to see her," she whispered.

"Then you shall not." Elizabeth's words were spoken firmly as she used her handkerchief to dry a few tears that had fallen from Anne's eyes, then leaned forward to kiss her on the cheek. "We should give you some time to visit with Georgie."

"You will return, will you not?" Anne asked full of hope.

With a squeeze of Anne's hand, she smiled. "I will visit daily, if you wish."

"I do. I do wish it. I have missed so much being closeted away at Rosings. Do not think I dislike Rosings, but..."

"We understand," reassured Georgiana.

She rose to join her husband. "I will call on you tomorrow, so ensure you rest well tonight."

Anne's eyes conveyed her amusement. "I look forward to it."

Mrs. Jenkinson walked them to the door, stopping them before they could leave. "I could not help but overhear much of your conversation with Anne. Thank you for telling her of your suspicions." She spoke in a soft tone as she glanced back towards her charge. "I cannot remember the last time I saw her so happy. She has spoken often of her desire to have a family at Rosings. Through you, she is seeing her dream fulfilled."

"Her generosity will make it possible for a second son to have a home rather than seeking employment," said Fitzwilliam. "She gives us a gift we could never repay."

The older woman nodded and smiled as she closed the door behind them.

After a few steps Elizabeth stopped. She could not hold in her tears, and Fitzwilliam took her in his arms.

"Perhaps you should not visit her every day if it causes you such upset."

"I cannot deny her when it brings her such joy." She sniffed and dabbed at her eyes. "I always pictured a thin perhaps pale young woman behind her letter. I never dreamed she was so frail and wan."

"You must have had quite a shock when you first saw her."

"Grandmamma tried to warn me, but I could not imagine such a dire situation as was evident today. She will not live long, will she?"

Fitzwilliam held her close to his broad chest as he shook his head against her hair. "The doctor does not believe she will last the month, but perhaps anticipating the babe's quickening will give her what she needs for the will to live."

"I am glad we confided in her. If she passes, she knows that her home will continue. It brought her such joy when you told her."

He nodded. "I had hoped it might. Rosings will be a wonderful estate for a second son."

"What if we have only daughters?" Her voice was low and unsteady. She knew he would love any daughter as much as he would a son, but her parents' relationship had deteriorated as each respective girl was born. What if it happened within her marriage, as well?

He chuckled and kissed her hair. "Then I will be in terrible trouble."

She drew back and regarded him inquisitively. "Why is that?"

"Because if they resemble their breath-taking mother in even the slightest way, then I will be unable to say no to them, and they will give me a headful of grey hairs."

She stood on her tiptoes and brushed her lips against his. "I love you."

"I love you, too, Mrs. Darcy."

Chapter 19

Darcy stood and shifted his weight from foot to foot while he waited alongside Richard and his grandmother. Tonight's excursion to the theatre was a part of the celebration of his grandmother's birthday, and Elizabeth was late in joining their party.

She had spent the last month honouring their social obligations, visiting Anne almost daily, and spending time with Grandmamma and Georgiana. The babe had quickened at the end of October, and in their excitement, they had told Anne the same day, which brought tears to his ill cousin's eyes—and to his own.

That morning, Elizabeth had awakened early, as was her wont, but she bore signs of fatigue from their hectic schedule. So, rather than meeting his uncle and cousins at White's, Darcy sent word he would be unable to join them, and spent the day with Elizabeth in their rooms, ensuring she napped.

He set down his empty glass of port. "Did you visit Anne today?"

"I did, and I am afraid her rally is at an end. We suspected she was in decline, and this morning confirmed our impressions. She has precious little energy. The physician suspects she will not last much longer."

"The poor dear," lamented his grandmother. "I have always had a great affection for Anne. I do wish we had removed her from Catherine's care years ago."

"Father is of the same opinion. Of course, the solution is clearer now than when she was a child."

Darcy shook his head adamantly. "No one is more culpable than Lady Catherine for her daughter's present condition. We could all find some way to blame ourselves, but in the end, Lady Catherine's decisions caused the most irreparable damage." He ensured he caught his grandmother's eye. "Anne was never hale. I can recall my mother's observations about her fevers when she was yet a young girl."

His grandmother sighed as her shoulders dropped. "I remember those, too, but I do wonder if a proper physician and a loving home could have altered the outcome."

Richard took her hand and clasped it between his own. "Darcy is correct. We do not know if it would have changed her future, and if Anne knew we all felt to blame, she would not be happy."

When Elizabeth entered the room, the others present stood, and the dowager approached to take Elizabeth's hands, holding them away from her body so she could view her dress. "You look lovely, Lizzy! That colour of green is a becoming compliment to your complexion."

Elizabeth bestowed upon Darcy an exquisite smile, and his breath caught in his throat. God he loved her! She was handsome, intelligent, and witty. He was a fortunate man to have won her regard!

He had admired the deep, forest green gown when she had first worn it in Bath, and to him it was obvious that Madame Duparc had altered it: the bodice fit certain areas better than it had prior to their trip to town, and the skirt still hid the slight swell of her abdomen, provided she did not protectively cover it with her hand as he often caught her doing. She was radiant as she made her way to him and took his arm.

His grandmother glanced at the clock and took her seat. "We still have some time whilst we await the carriage."

"You never told me about your call on Lady Tabitha Dawkins," he observed. A few days prior, the dowager had taken Elizabeth to call on Sir Gabriel's wife, who had just borne his heir.

"I believe I told you enough." His wife's disgusted expression brought a smile to his face, and his grandmother let out a girlish giggle.

"You only informed me that you had no wish to call on Lady Dawkins again."

"Precisely! That alone should indicate it was a miserable visit." The sour expression upon her countenance was diverting, and he chuckled along with the others.

His grandmother was still giggling when her eyes returned to him. "I fear Lady Dawkins did not impress our Lizzy with her maternal nature."

Elizabeth snorted. "Maternal? I doubt she has ever touched the poor child."

"Knowing her, I would say you are correct," commented Richard. "Whatever possessed you to call upon that woman, Grandmamma?"

"Her mother's bragging of Sir Gabriel's heir has not ceased since the child's birth. I planned on calling out of courtesy, but I thought Lizzy might find the experience enlightening."

His wife's free hand moved to cover the swell. "You thought I might need lessons on how not to be a mother, then?"

He chuckled and bestowed a tender kiss to her temple. "I am sure that is not what Grandmamma intended."

Her condition ceased to be a source of worry for her not long after they arrived, and the quickening had awakened something protective within her. Since that time he had happened upon her speaking or singing to the babe in her womb when she thought she was alone.

"No, I just wanted you to be aware of the Ton's expectations of care for their children. What you do is your choice. Neither I nor Elinor adhered to what society expected. My daughter Anne did not either."

"I remember sitting on the floor before the fire in my mother's study as I played with my soldiers," reminisced Richard. "She often took us for walks herself, and when father would not be home for dinner, she took her meals in the nursery."

"My mother did much the same." Remembrances of his mother never failed to cause a tremor in his voice; he cleared his throat. "I do not have many memories of her study, though. She did much of her work whilst I was with the governess or my tutors. I do remember she had a cradle for Georgiana that was moved from room to room with her. I had a nursemaid, but I do not think her duties were too taxing."

His grandmother smiled lovingly as Darcy spoke of his mother. "As Georgie became older, the nurse would keep her occupied so your mother could finish her duties. I also recall Georgie playing on the floor much in the same manner as Richard did, but the nurse was nearby so she was always minded well."

"Did you have a nurse when you were young, Lizzy?" asked Richard.

She crinkled her forehead as she caught the corner of her bottom lip in her teeth. "I do not remember one being at Longbourn. Funds were always too tight for such an expenditure."

The dowager tilted her head and appraised Elizabeth. "Your mother must have been in great demand with five girls born in six or seven years."

"Hill, our housekeeper, was there to help, and when I was a bit older, I was often with father in his library while Jane helped Mama with Mary, Kitty, and Lydia; however, Mama changed when Lydia was born, and did not hold her and Kitty to the same standard she did Jane, Mary or I."

Richard looked perplexed. "Why was that?"

"I know Mama was told she would not have any more children after Lydia, and with no heir, nothing was ever the same. She insisted Jane and I were out at fifteen. We were to find suitors so we would wed and not be a burden when Papa passed."

"Your mother feared for your future," he observed.

"And hers as well." Elizabeth's voice was soft as she faced him.

"Excuse me, ma'am," came Hobbes' voice from the door. "The carriage has pulled to the front when you are ready."

The ride to their destination was swift, yet they remained in the long queue until their carriage pulled to the front of the theatre where both Darcy and Richard stepped out. As they straightened their topcoats and waited for the ladies, Richard motioned behind them where a beggar leaned against a wall near the entrance. As usual, women milled about the entrance selling fruit and programs, but this man had no occupation other than to stand and watch the quality enter the building.

"I am surprised they have not had him hauled away." Darcy shook his head in disgust and pivoted back to wait for the ladies.

The two men kept a watchful eye on the vagrant until Elizabeth and his grandmother were ready to alight. Darcy was ill at ease with the man's presence, and wished he would not loiter so close to the entrance. The beggar must have been doing well for himself if he remained.

Once they were all on the pavement, they strolled towards the theatre doors. Elizabeth's hand rested on Darcy's arm, and he covered it with his own. The shimmer from the lights of the busy theatre in her eyes, the glistening highlights in her hair, the softness of her soft skin under his fingers—everything but Elizabeth disappeared around him. She occupied his every thought and his every attention until reality reappeared in the most unexpected and disturbing of happenings.

266

Elizabeth's expression became bewildered and her grip upon him was fierce. His arm smarted where she dug her fingers into his sleeve and his shoulder throbbed as she clung to him. She was being pulled from his protection! Elizabeth's head pivoted in the direction she was being drawn, and she cried out, her eyes returning to him, wild and terrified.

When his field of vision widened, he repositioned himself to clutch her in his embrace in an attempt to dislodge the filthy beggar who had latched onto her other arm. Did Elizabeth's alarmed expression mean she recognised the man, or was she startled by his haggard appearance? Darcy had yet to free her from the grip of the intruder, who muttered and swore boisterously as he wrenched her towards him.

The topic of the man's ranting was not discernible; therefore, he tightened his arms around his beloved wife's body as he bellowed out Richard's name, his heart pounding so hard it was painful.

When his cousin did not appear straight away, he roared Richard's name a second time. An eternity passed before his cousin responded, and when the colonel appeared and strode towards the assailant, the unbearable pain in his chest began to subside.

One of Richard's hands went to the beggar's throat, while the other grasped his wrist, digging the tips of his fingers into the man's exposed flesh until he released his prey.

Without a backward glance, Darcy rushed Elizabeth into the theatre where his grandmother stood just inside the door.

"Go help your cousin," ordered the dowager as she took Elizabeth by her forearms. He followed for a moment as she brought his wife to a corner and began to speak to her in hushed tones.

His voice cracked. "Elizabeth?"

She shook all over but attempted a smile. "Go help Colonel Fitzwilliam. I shall be fine with Grandmamma."

A curious crowd had begun to gather, and he hesitated before he rushed back outside the entrance where he found Richard restraining the beggar against the wall by his neck.

When his cousin saw him, he motioned him closer. "Guess who we have here!"

A long look at the man did not reveal anything familiar about him. Where would he have ever met him?

"Go on, tell him your name." The hardened soldier's voice his cousin employed was downright terrifying; he was thankful Richard always took his part.

"Tell him," he growled.

"Ed… Edward… Gardiner."

Darcy's eyes bulged, but the man did not seem to notice his shock.

"You will get me killed with this spectacle," hissed Gardiner.

"You created this scene. Why could you not leave Elizabeth alone?" Darcy's sudden fury prompted him to clench his fists in order to refrain from pummelling the pathetic man before him. How dare he intrude upon Elizabeth's comfort and security!

Gardiner grimaced as he manoeuvred a bit of space for his neck in order to breathe. His Adam's apple bobbed as he gulped. "Lizzy and Philips made a fool of me, so when I recognised her, I wanted to frighten her. She has put me into hiding for the last few months, fearing for my life. I figured she should feel the same fright for hers."

"Your situation is no one's fault but your own, sir." His palms itched to take the position of his cousin, to convince this man to never touch his wife again, but Richard would never allow it.

"She would have freed me!"

Richard clamped down on Gardiner's throat until he choked and heaved. His cousin spoke in low tones. "Now is not the time, Darcy. You do not want this aired to all of society."

Sure enough, people were watching the display rather than entering the theatre. "Richard, can you take him to Ashcroft and lock him in the attic?"

His cousin's eyes bulged. "What would possess you to help this bag of rubbish?"

Darcy pivoted to Gardiner and leaned in so the nosy crowd could not hear. "If you will accept, I shall pay for your passage to the Canadas with two hundred pounds."

The haggard man stared with his mouth agape. "Why would you do this?"

"Elizabeth has little family left, and I know that despite your actions, your death would pain her. I am of the opinion that whilst you remain in England, you are a threat to her. By sending you where

Grayson cannot find you, I ensure Elizabeth never feels guilt for your death whilst at the same time I ensure her safety. It is a worthy investment, if you ask me."

Richard was not pleased with his cousin's proposal to the piece of filth, but nodded to indicate he understood Darcy's reasoning.

"Will you accept my offer?"

Gardiner studied Darcy's eyes before he gave a rough bob of his head. "I may as well. I have nothing to lose."

"You are too soft, cousin," muttered Richard.

Society would invent a multitude of gossip if they departed directly after the attack. Elizabeth needed to be well enough to attend the performance regardless of the circumstances. "I may be, but Elizabeth, Grandmamma, and I must remain for the play. Can I trust you to take him to Ashcroft House?"

"Of course, but I must remove him now."

Darcy peered behind them to see the carriage had not moved since they arrived, and both the driver and footmen stood near the equipage, staring. He and his cousin bustled Gardiner to the carriage and shoved him inside while Darcy stepped close enough to the driver so he could hear as he spoke to him in low tones. "Take them to Ashcroft house and then return for us."

The driver seemed bewildered about the goings on but obeyed without question.

When Darcy returned to where he had left Elizabeth, neither she nor his grandmother remained, but a glance about the room revealed that she was in the company of his grandmother near the stairs. As he drew closer, his grandmother gave him a small nod and both his shoulders and back relaxed. Could his wife truly be safe and sound?

He groaned to himself when the voice of the woman to whom they spoke reached his ears. Why did it have to be those cloying Dashwoods?

"You must have been terrified, my dear. The theatre should never have allowed a common beggar to remain so near when a performance is scheduled. It is a threat to all good society."

"Oh! Mr. Darcy!" Mrs. Dashwood cried upon his approach. "I was just saying what a travesty it was that the theatre allowed *that* man to remain near the entrance." She paused and donned a look of affected sincerity. "Poor Mrs. Darcy!" The last was said in such a way that even the most dim-witted individual could have ascertained her false concern.

"Mr. Dashwood." He gave a slight bow. The husband reciprocated the greeting as Mrs. John Dashwood curtsied. "Mrs. Dashwood. I thank you for your care for my wife. As for the vagrant, my cousin Colonel Fitzwilliam volunteered to escort him to the magistrate, so he could do no further harm." He stepped beside Elizabeth and she took his arm. Her hands still quivered, but she appeared composed, which was the most pressing issue.

"Lady Matlock, you have such gentleman-like grandsons!" Mrs. Dashwood fawned to his grandmother. "But, it will be such a shame for the colonel to miss the play."

Darcy covered Elizabeth's hand and entwined their fingers as she ever so slightly leaned into him. "The colonel will return if it is possible, but he decided our safety was paramount to his entertainment."

Mrs. Dashwood nodded, acknowledged someone behind him with a raised hand, and addressed her husband, "I see Lady Selwyn has arrived. We should greet her."

Mr. Dashwood gave a brief nod. "Yes, of course, dear."

"Please excuse us, Lady Matlock, Mr. Darcy, Mrs. Darcy."

A breath left him in a whoosh as his shoulders relaxed. He then held out his hand to direct both his wife and grandmother. "We should make our way to our box."

The ladies agreed, and he led them up the stairs. They did not speak as they strode through the theatre, and managed to avoid most of their acquaintance, reaching their seats with haste. Darcy seated himself to Elizabeth's left while his grandmother was situated on his wife's other side, which allowed them both to offer her comfort.

He leaned towards Elizabeth and took her hand in his. "You are well, are you not?"

"You sent him to the magistrate?" Her eyes bulged and her mouth was agape. She was aware of the identity of her attacker!

"No," he whispered. "He has been taken to Ashcroft House where he will be locked in an attic. Tomorrow, I shall arrange for his passage to the Canadas where he can live out the remainder of his life without fear."

"You would do that?"

He squeezed her hand and bestowed a kiss to her knuckles. "It is the most sensible solution. He will be safe from Grayson's men and no longer be a threat to you."

Tears welled in her eyes, but none fell.

"Thank you."

He passed her his handkerchief in the event she needed it. "Would you like to try a glass of wine? I am sure it would do you good." He continued his caresses to her palm, careful to keep the action low enough so most of the crowd would not see.

She scrunched her nose. "No, thank you. Just give me some time for the shock to subside."

"Go fetch an empty glass." His grandmother directed as she pulled open her reticule and drew out a small flask.

"Pardon?"

"Wine has been turning her stomach, so perhaps a little brandy would be of use."

"Grandmamma! You carry a flask of brandy?" He glanced around. His voice had not been loud, but just in case, he assured himself that no one had heard him.

"For times like these, Fitzwilliam. Now, she can drink it from here, or she can appear more of a lady and society will think you obtained a glass of wine for her, which would not be unusual under the circumstances."

"With the exception of the colour." He leaned towards his wife's ear. "You will be well?"

She pursed her lips in an obvious effort to restrain her laughter. "Your grandmother will protect me. I would much prefer to drink from a glass if possible."

Elizabeth watched him as he rose and departed the box. He was such a dear to be so worried. Her fingers twitched as she tried to rub some warmth back into them.

"Let me know if he begins to mother you too much. I can set him straight."

She giggled and took the dowager's hand. "Thank you for earlier. You prevented me from losing my composure." She rubbed the back of his grandmother's hand with her thumb, which stopped when it passed over the third finger of her left hand. The jewel that adorned it was different! She verified it with her eyes, in the event her fingers were mistaken.

"Grandmamma, this is not your wedding ring. When did you begin wearing this?"

"Several months ago. It was a gift from my husband on our twentieth wedding anniversary."

She continued to scrutinize the sapphire and then considered her own wedding bands. "You gave your rings to Fitzwilliam for me to wear!" How had she never realised before? "They seemed so familiar when we were wed, but I had thought it a coincidence. How stupid of me!"

The dowager grasped Elizabeth's hands and stared her directly in the eye. "I wanted you to have them, Lizzy. Of all my family, I felt those rings belonged on your finger first."

"But why?" She was overwhelmed and confused as to why his grandmother would insist on passing her wedding rings to her. Grandmamma spoke often of her husband, and the love she had for him was evident to anyone whenever his name was mentioned. Why would she allow such a precious keepsake to leave her finger?

The older woman smiled warmly as she took Elizabeth's hands. "Because you remind me of myself. My father was a gentleman of modest means, much like yours, and I had little dowry and no connections of consequence. My uncles were also country squires, but were no more affluent than my father."

"And your husband did not care."

"He had married Lady Celeste Gillingham for money, connections, and his parents' approval. He refused to marry for those concerns again. One of our neighbours had a house party and a ball one summer, and Gerald was there." The elder lady gave a wistful sigh as she recounted the memories she so evidently cherished. "He stood up with me twice during the ball, and was by my side so I could not dance with other gentlemen. He was very benevolent and gentle for such a large man—much as your husband is."

"You should have your rings," she argued. "You must miss them."

The dowager shook her head and halted Elizabeth's attempts to remove the rings. "A part of me does, but I have my memories, which are my most treasured possessions. I think Gerald would agree that those belong on your finger, and he would not disapprove of my using this ring in their stead."

Elizabeth removed her hands from the dowager's and was able to once again consider the bands encircling her finger. She adored them, but she would have never wanted his grandmother to part with so special a keepsake.

The elder lady covered the rings with her hand. "I know you like them, and I want you to wear them. I cannot think of anyone more deserving."

Her eyes met the dowager's, and she acquiesced. "I do not just like them—I love them dearly, yet I dislike the idea of you missing their presence.

"I shall not allow you to return them." Grandmamma's expression was resolute, and one side of Elizabeth's lips quirked upwards.

"Very well. I will argue no longer, and instead, thank you for passing them on to Fitzwilliam. I am honoured you chose me to receive them."

They sat in silence for a few minutes while she held the older woman's hand.

A dry voice from beside her mumbled, "I did not think *she* would be back this season."

A glance across the theatre revealed Caroline Bingley entering a box with a group Elizabeth did not recognise. The haughty woman surveyed the guests around the expansive room and paused when she espied Elizabeth and the dowager. She did not acknowledge them; rather, she spun around when a man offered his arm to escort her to a seat beside his. Louisa Hurst was seated behind her sister.

"Mrs. Hurst…"

"Is behind her sister. I do hope they will not seek us out this evening."

"Fitzwilliam told Mr. Bingley that he would cut his sisters should they attempt a public conversation with us."

"He did?" His grandmother whispered with genuine surprise. "Oh, to be able to witness the conversation Mr. Bingley had with his sisters over that dictate! I would imagine the shrew had a right fit over it."

She grinned and tilted her head closer. "You should not say such things, Grandmamma!"

"Why? Because it is what all and sundry thinks, but will not voice aloud?"

Miss Bingley was not worth her attention, so instead, she allowed her eyes to roam the rest of the boxes. Several ladies she had met during calls were in attendance, as well as some of the gentlemen from trips about town with her husband. She was about to lean in to ask her companion a question, when Fitzwilliam startled her by taking his seat.

"I apologise for the wait. I ran into Bingley at the refreshments." He took his grandmother's flask and poured some brandy into the empty wine glass he had procured.

"How is Mr. Bingley?" asked Elizabeth.

"He is well and nothing less than ecstatic. Miss Bingley is being courted." He sniggered as he handed Elizabeth the goblet.

His grandmother leaned forward. "I hate to question good fortune, but is the gentleman quite sane?"

With her hand covering her mouth, Elizabeth made an effort to stifle the burst of laughter threatening to escape her lips. She then attempted a stern look, but it became a spectacular failure.

"I know what you are trying to do, Lizzy, but it *is* a pertinent question."

Fitzwilliam stifled his laugh with his fist. "He is quite sane, but could not marry without attention to money it seems."

"It is a good match for both of them then," commented the dowager. "He is a gentleman, and she has a substantial dowry."

Fitzwilliam nodded towards the Bingley's box across the theatre. As Mr. Bingley took his seat, he broke into a broad grin for Elizabeth and the dowager. "I do not believe she has ever wished for a love match, so it should have been her objective long ago. Bingley expects that a proposal should be forthcoming. He has been courting her for two months now."

After taking a sip of the brandy, Elizabeth contemplated the gentleman she assumed was Miss Bingley's beau. He was not an unattractive man, but he lacked a certain warmth that appealed to her; however, Miss Bingley lacked the same intangible quality, so she doubted either would miss what they never had themselves. In her opinion, such a relationship was still a sad fate!

"My love?" She turned at the sound of her husband's endearment. "Is something amiss?"

She shook her head. "I suppose I was wool-gathering."

His forehead wrinkled in silent question, and she smiled. "I was studying Miss Bingley and who I assume is the man who is courting her. I would not wish for such a marriage for myself. I always dreamed of marrying for love."

"I suppose our felicity was a bit backward, but you have a husband who loves you dearly."

She grinned and entwined her fingers with his. "And I love him just as dearly."

"And I love both of you," came the dowager's voice from beside her. "Now hush and forget about Miss Bingley. The play is beginning."

Chapter 20

After his abrupt departure with Mr. Gardiner, Richard never did join them at the theatre. He was not even at Ashcroft House when they returned. Instead, they found a young officer standing guard outside of an attic room, who was relieved the next morning for a fresh, rested sentry.

At long last, Richard made an appearance while they broke their fast with a document of some sort in his hand. "I have found a ship!"

His grandmother eyed his rumpled uniform. "Have you been home to sleep, Richard?"

"No, I have not. Instead, I have made much better use of my time, and went down to the port where I found our guest transport! It leaves at the beginning of the week for Nova Scotia."

Darcy took the paper in his cousin's outstretched hand. "I told Gardiner the Canadas. What if he disagrees?"

With a resonant snort, Richard plopped into a chair. "The point was to remove him from England, which this accomplishes with haste. He should not look a gift horse in the mouth!"

He scanned the document, which detailed the ship's name and certain particulars including when it would disembark and crew. "How did you manage it?"

"Do you remember Randall Babcock?"

"From Eton? Did he not attend Oxford?"

"He did," continued Richard, "but we remained good friends after Eton. His father owns ships that sail between either Southampton or Liverpool and the colonies, but they just bought a new ship from a builder near London and it is at the port as we speak. They plan on sending it to Southampton where it will take on its crew and cargo before it sails on to Nova Scotia."

He tensed and sat forward in his seat. "To begin with, what information did you provide him, and moreover, what will the passage cost?"

"The captain has been informed of an acquaintance of mine, who has come into some difficult times and wishes to start a new life. He does not often take passengers, but if Gardiner is amenable to work as part of the crew until they reach their destination, he will not charge a fee for passage. Babcock was intent Gardiner keep what little funds he might possess."

He nodded, concerned that Edward Gardiner might regard himself as above menial work. "We shall have to ask him. He may not agree."

Richard took a seat and began to shovel food onto his plate. "He would be an imbecile to refuse this offer. It will provide him an escape from England, and Babcock indicated he could live on the ship until it disembarked."

"Richard, this is not the barracks. Please eat with some decorum." His grandmother's face showed the evident distaste for his cousin's lack of manners.

With a sheepish expression, Richard stopped chewing. "Sorry, Grandmamma." His mouth was full as he spoke, and the others rolled their eyes as he attempted not to display the food within.

"Perhaps if *I* explained the offer," broached Elizabeth.

"Absolutely not!" The ladies stared at both Darcy and Richard, who in unison slammed down their utensils.

"I do not see why not! I have known him longer than either of you, and I wish to speak with him anyhow." Elizabeth's tone was defensive and matched the ire in her eyes.

He remained adamant. "I shall not have him upset you or worse, cause you an injury."

"He would not harm me since I am the reason you are sending him from the country. If he were to injure me, you might turn him over to Grayson."

"Why do you wish to see him?" The idea did not have much merit, but Elizabeth would continue to work on him until he relented.

"You can accompany me, but I wish to speak with my uncle one last time before he is gone forever. Despite all that he has done, he is still a part of what little family I have remaining."

With a sigh, Darcy ran his hands up and down his face in frustration. "Very well, let us be done with it!" He leapt to his feet, and offered one hand to Elizabeth, who rose to follow him towards the stairs.

Elizabeth continued behind him until they reached the door, which he requested to be unlocked by the young soldier Richard had posted. Once they were within the room and the door locked behind them again, an uneasy Edward Gardiner stood from the trunk where he had been seated. He shifted from foot to foot and appeared angry.

"Uncle Edward." Elizabeth's voice held a tremor as she took a tentative step in her uncle's direction. "How are you?"

A sarcastic bark erupted from Gardiner's mouth as he clenched and unclenched his fists. "I have been living in the slums of London. Do you think I am well?"

With a step forward, Darcy placed a hand on his wife's back; Gardiner must understand she was by no means unprotected. "You would do well to mind your tone." He refused to allow this man to abuse his wife, regardless of their previous relationship.

As Gardiner eyed the two of them, his lips were drawn tight and his stance was haughty, indicating his anger, but his shoulders dropped as he attempted to quell the display of his ire. "When did the two of you become acquainted? Were you already betrothed when I came to Meryton to retrieve Lizzy, or was your marriage the work of my brother Philips?"

Darcy bristled. How did Gardiner deserve any sort of explanation? "I was at the inn the day you told Philips you would take Elizabeth." Gardiner's eyebrows furrowed as he made an evident attempt at remembering Darcy's face. Could her uncle place him? It seemed doubtful since he was sitting behind Gardiner and Philips. "I heard your entire argument and offered marriage as a solution to their problem."

"And Philips drew up the paperwork and you took her with you that night." He did not ask, but stated the obvious progression.

Elizabeth nodded. "Yes, we were wed within the week."

"So instead of allowing me to sell you to someone to save myself, you whored yourself to escape."

How dare Gardiner speak to his wife in such a fashion! She was a gentlewoman and not some common prostitute! Darcy's shoulders tensed as he made to raise his hand in the man's direction, but Elizabeth's voice prevented him from intervening on her behalf.

"You are delusional if you believe I would have accepted your wishes." Her vehemence and refusal to show a hint of shock at her uncle's accusation were astonishing. "I met Fitzwilliam and found him to be agreeable—someone I could respect. I would not be sold to a stranger who would treat me as a servant to their whims."

She paused, providing him with an opportunity to reiterate his warning. "I would advise you to be careful of the manner in which you address my wife. I have had investigators watching Grayson's men, and I could turn you over to them with very little effort." A glare was Gardiner's response.

"They have been merciless. I have been unable to find work since I returned because they are always in Cheapside." Gardiner was still angry, but he kept his temper under better regulation. His eyes rested on the swell of Elizabeth's waist, and he clenched his fists. "I assumed your marriage would be legitimate from the start. It made you less valuable to me—Grayson wanted you untouched. Now you are worthless to me."

He had to remove his wife from the room! Her uncle's restraint on his ire was limited, and he would continue with his hurtful words as long as she remained. They would accomplish nothing of use until she could be convinced to leave. His hand grasped Elizabeth's arm, but instead Elizabeth thwarted his plans by shaking off his hand to step closer.

"You did not find me worthless when I was young." Tears in her eyes threatened to spill over her lashes as she spoke, and her voice quivered. "You would bring gifts when you travelled to Longbourn. I remember the wooden pony you brought when I was ten. Do you?" She gasped back a small sob. "I never left the house without it. Mama claimed I would be the death of her because I would set it on the table beside me at dinner."

"Your mother's nerves were legendary in Meryton." Gardiner's voice was devoid of any warmth, and Darcy wondered if her uncle had any feelings other than the selfish ones he had exhibited thus far.

"They were, as was the kindness you bestowed upon us as little girls. I remember when you brought Miss Margaret to visit us. She was so handsome, and it was obvious how much the two of you loved one another. I know she would be heartbroken to see what you have become."

"Elizabeth!" The direction she steered could anger Gardiner more. She was too kind-hearted, and it was unsurprising that she wished to change her uncle; however, she would not obtain the transformation for which she hoped.

"She is not here to see what I have become." Gardiner's voice was almost a hiss and menacing. "She left me because her father and I lacked the funds to pay for more than the apothecary, who claimed her illness beyond his capabilities."

"So you allowed her to depart this world with your heart? I think that she loved you and would want you to keep it for yourself!"

"I vowed I would never be in that position again." Gardiner moved towards the window, but stopped in the sunlight that streamed through the panes. "I took part in several ventures, which brought me half of what I paid for the first ship. I made a significant profit on that first run, but Philips was correct. I was not buying fast enough ships. I wanted a profit and could not afford the necessary transport, which allowed the second shipment to be seized. I still owe Grayson ten thousand pounds."

Elizabeth did not attempt to draw closer to him, but remained rooted to her spot while she continued. "And now my husband shall ensure you leave Grayson behind, so you can begin again. If I had not escaped you, you would still be paying your debt."

"I would have had a reprieve, and my debt would have been lessened."

Elizabeth shook her head. "I believe I shall return to Grandmamma. I hope someday you let go of your bitterness, Uncle Edward. I know the man I grew up adoring is still there somewhere, but mired in guilt. I miss him a great deal." She observed him for a moment as if she hoped he might reciprocate some kind of feelings for her, but her uncle remained silent. "I wish you good luck and a happy life."

She turned and walked towards the door, but had not managed to open it before Gardiner called her. "Lizzy!" A certain amount of his haughtiness had disappeared, and instead, an almost defeated man stood before him. He did not throw out accusations or bitter words. "Goodbye," was all he said.

After a cheerless nod, his wife departed. Darcy stared at the door for a moment to ensure she was gone before he returned his attention to the ragged man, yet when his eyes set upon Edward Gardiner again, the humble visage had disappeared—the bitterness had returned.

"How long before I can depart?" His voice was harsh.

"My cousin has arranged your passage through an acquaintance of ours. A short time ago, he purchased a new ship and is willing to take you on as one of the crew for the voyage."

Gardiner's eyebrows rose. With luck, he would not be above the terms of the deal. "One of the crew?"

"It is not his usual practice to take on passengers, so he asks that you work on board during the crossing. Do you know anything of sailing?"

"I can manage it, if it frees me from Grayson. I have no doubt he will kill me if he finds me."

Darcy gestured towards the sparse room where Gardiner was staying. "Mr. Babcock has offered to let you join the small crew already aboard, until Monday, when you will sail for Southampton. There, the ship will collect its cargo and the remaining crew before it sets out for Nova Scotia. I know it is not Upper or Lower Canada, but it was the swiftest way for you to depart England."

"The destination is irrelevant. I just do not understand why you would do this for me? Especially, after the deal I made with Grayson for Lizzy."

"Disguise of every sort is my abhorrence, so I will not pretend to think well of you or to even like you; however, had you not put Elizabeth in danger, she would not be my wife. I have no wish to reward you, and if you were not one of her last remaining relations, I would see you handed over to whoever this Grayson is for frightening her." His lungs drew in a deep breath, but his attempt to calm was futile and his anger began to simmer. "Do you have any concept of what you put her through? You, sir, terrified her with your unspeakable plan!" Darcy ground out the words, leaning towards the scoundrel. "A lesser woman would have broken under the weight of your threat."

Gardiner made to say something but Darcy held up his hand. "Regardless of my wishes in the matter, I will not have her feel guilt for your death, nor will I allow her to fear you or your fate. This is the best solution I have found. So—will you accept the terms?"

Her uncle regarded him warily, as if unsure he could believe him, but nodded.

"Good, I shall attempt to arrange for some decent clothes, and I shall check with the housekeeper about a bath, if you would care for one."

"I would, thank you." When he uttered his thanks, his face puckered as though he had sucked on a lemon, but at least, he appeared to realise they were not his enemies.

"In addition, I have decided to add the cost of a passage to the funds I shall provide you upon your departure. For Elizabeth's sake, I hope you find a good life wherever you happen to settle."

He made to leave the room, but was stopped when his name was called from behind him. When he turned, Gardiner had approached so he was no more than a few paces away. "You should be aware of Grayson's identity. He may still be a threat to Lizzy, and if he discovers you were of aid to me, he may be a threat to you as well."

"Why would you want to be of help to us now?" Her uncle's sudden willingness to be of use was off-putting, and any information the man might offer was certainly suspect.

"You and Lizzy did not have to arrange for any of this, particularly after all I have done. I do not know Grayson's plans, but he has a lofty position and ample funds to arrange things as he likes."

"Are you saying he is a peer?" Darcy's tone was incredulous, but the notion of a peer that would take a young woman as payment for a debt seemed dubious.

"He is, but he uses the name Grayson for his dealings in trade and smuggling. He is also known as Lawrence Grayson, Viscount Carlisle."

"I find that difficult to believe. His family is known for their aversion to dabbling in any form of trade."

Gardiner exhaled with a gravel growl. "They are; but I happened to arrive early to the apartments he uses to conduct his business, and overheard him discussing an investment with one of his men, who addressed him as Lord Carlisle. I had heard of Debrett's Peerage, so I checked a booksellers that afternoon and found him listed."

"You bought a copy of Debrett's Peerage?" This was as suspect as his other claims.

"No, I acted as though I was looking for a different book. His name did not take long to locate."

In order to consider the information, he strode over to stare out of the window. Why would Gardiner give him this information? What if his accusations were true? He shook his head with vehemence. "I cannot comprehend how Grayson could keep his identity so well hidden."

The other man shrugged. "Grayson is a common enough name, and he seldom conducts his criminal business himself, using the name

Thomas Grayson for investments. I am certain if another peer heard the name, they would not link the viscount, due to his reputation and the difference in forenames."

"I find it difficult to credit, but I shall remember. Elizabeth will not be alone if he is nearby." Darcy doubted her uncle was too concerned since he was so eager to trade her for his debts, but he could tell Gardiner believed his assertions—even if Darcy did not.

He did not look back as he rushed from the room, searching out Mrs. Henderson to request a bath for their guest upstairs as well as for the clean clothes he would require. Once she assured him she could find something suitable, he sought out Elizabeth, who was reading in the conservatory.

"There you are."

Her smile warmed him. "Here I am."

He took the seat beside her and wrapped an arm around her shoulders. "Are you well?"

"I am. I did have seven months to mourn the uncle I lost." With a sigh, she rested her head against his shoulder. "He is the man I remember from my childhood."

"I know you do, but that man became lost in his own misery. Perhaps one day, he will find his way back."

"Thank you for helping him. I know you would much prefer to leave him to his own devices." Her eyes did not leave him, but there was no sadness, or even gratitude to be found in them. Instead, her adoration was written there, clear for anyone to read. He drew her against him and held her close.

"I would hate for you to lose more of your family."

She drew back and placed her hands on his cheeks. "The man I knew died long ago, but I appreciate that you feel he might be reborn. I am also grateful you will provide him with that chance."

Elizabeth's lips claimed his and she deepened the kiss until he groaned and pulled back. "You cannot do this to me outside of our chambers," he whispered.

"So take me to our bed, Fitzwilliam. I believe I am in dire need of a nap."

Her command set his heart racing, and he aided her to stand. They managed to maintain decorum as they ascended the stairs, but once out of sight, the servants below were sure to have been startled by a loud shriek, followed by gales of laughter, as he chased her down the hallway to their rooms.

"A safe departure, then?" Darcy examined Richard's expression. He had no reason to think his cousin would defy his wishes, even though Richard did not approve of him helping Gardiner.

"Yes, and Babcock said he would contact me if something goes wrong." Richard reclined in his comfortable seat at White's with a snifter in his hand.

"Good riddance!" Darcy raised his glass, overcome with relief that Gardiner was gone.

Richard tipped his own glass forward in acknowledgement. "I still say you gave him too much money."

"If it keeps Elizabeth safe, then it is worth every shilling."

After his cousin took a sip of his brandy, he blew out a heavy breath. "I suppose you have a point."

"What did I miss if you are conceding that your cousin is correct?" They both turned to find Uncle Henry, who laughed as he approached their table with another gentleman.

"Nothing of importance, or I would not have surrendered."

Darcy rolled his eyes as he and his cousin stood to greet the earl.

Uncle Henry chuckled and gestured to the man beside him. "Lawrence Grayson, Viscount Carlisle, I would like to present my nephew, Fitzwilliam Darcy, and my son Colonel Richard Fitzwilliam."

"I have heard much of both of you." Carlisle barely dipped his head. "I believe I remember my wife speaking of your marriage a few months ago."

The expression on Carlisle's face had a certain quality that did not sit well. Could this man and Gardiner's business partner be one and the same? As he had told Gardiner, the Carlisle earldom was known for their adherence to living strictly from their assets and not investing in trade.

He nodded. "Yes, we were wed in May."

"Aah, still early enough for me to wish you joy." Carlisle reached into his coat pocket and pulled out his watch, opening it to check the time. "I apologise, but I am to meet someone. I hope you will not find me unforgivably rude if I excuse myself so soon?"

"Of course not." Uncle Henry reached out and shook the viscount's hand. "After all, our meeting at the door was happenstance. It is not as if we had plans."

Carlisle's grin was wide, and Darcy flinched as Richard's boot dug into his toe. He spun towards his cousin, who almost imperceptibly shook his head, then he turned back in time to find the viscount's hand before him.

"It was a pleasure." They shook hands, and Carlisle then offered his hand to Richard.

Once he had excused himself, they both watched as Carlisle disappeared through the exit in the direction of the private rooms.

"I heard of Lizzy's run in at the theatre. I hope she is well." Richard had informed Uncle Henry of the entirety of Gardiner's attack and flee from London in private while he arranged Gardiner's transport, but they had decided to keep the secret within the family.

"She is well. Nothing more than a bit of a fright. Grandmamma's brandy was all it took to set her to rights."

Uncle Henry and Richard began to laugh. "Yes, I am sure it did," his uncle agreed. "I'm assuming she had her flask."

He nodded. "How long has she had that? I have never seen her use it before."

Uncle Henry's lip quirked as he sat back and made himself comfortable. "Father purchased it as a gift about five years before he died. He even had her initials engraved on the side. The shopkeeper's face was entertaining when he realised whose name was represented by the engraving."

"Grandfather bought her a flask?" asked Richard with disbelief.

Nodding, Uncle Henry continued to beam. "Who do you think introduced her to brandy?"

After one last round of laughter, Uncle Henry began the conversation they had planned. His entire body shifted and he spoke a hair louder than was his wont. "Have you discovered what became of the vagrant who grabbed her?"

For the first time in his life, Darcy desired to attract the eavesdropping gossips, so they did not modulate their voices as this performance was their entire reason for venturing to the club this afternoon. They did not want the beggar linked to Elizabeth's uncle, so the man at the theatre had to disappear in some manner. Since Uncle Henry did not attend that evening, he was the most obvious person to ask about the encounter.

Richard nodded as he continued the charade. He explained how he brought the beggar to the magistrate, but the fellow was released the following morning. Of course, Uncle Henry would not agree, but Darcy would indicate it was Elizabeth's decision and she wished to return home. He would not insist she remain in town to prosecute a vagrant.

"I do not think we need worry ourselves over him," commented Richard to finish their performance. "I daresay the blight learned his lesson."

Darcy then changed the subject, and lowered his voice since they no longer desired to be overheard. "Speaking of blights, I contacted the investigator and called off the investigation of Gardiner's location."

"What reason did you give for terminating the search?" Uncle Henry rested his forearms upon the table.

"I told Simms I found it improbable he would be found alive, if we found him at all. I did not wish to waste additional funds on what I felt was becoming a fruitless endeavour."

"Good," agreed Uncle Henry. "I shall indicate much the same when I send him a note in the morning."

Richard leaned over so he could whisper to his father. "How long have you known Carlisle?"

Uncle Henry furrowed his brow and regarded his son with a puzzled expression. "For some time. I am also acquainted with his father. The family has an impeccable reputation, and I find them both to be amiable men."

"Not so impeccable if you consider his name is Grayson?" Again, Richard spoke in a low voice, but his father jerked back.

"No," he whispered. "I am certain it is a coincidence. How could he keep such an identity from becoming public knowledge?"

Darcy drew closer to his Uncle. "Perhaps because he has men who represent him and do the not-so-gentlemanly work."

286

His uncle stared without emotion for a moment. "No, I do not believe it possible."

"It may not be him," whispered Richard, "but Gardiner himself named him as the infamous Grayson. Be wary of what you say when the two of you are in company together."

"I will consider it." It was evident Uncle Henry was still sceptical, but then there was no guarantee that Gardiner's claim was fact.

With the business they had planned concluded, they discussed other ventures and family issues until Darcy excused himself to visit the water closet. He made to return through one of the hallways when he heard a low voice from one of the rooms. "You owe me, Carlisle, and I expect whatever you find me will make up for the cockup with this one. I shall expect her at a discount and unscarred."

He stopped short of the doorway. He had been so willing to dismiss Gardiner's claims while Richard had been more inclined to believe the accusations, and yet, now he was listening to the proof!

"The scars were supposed to be minimal, and how was I to help it if an interfering relative married her off before she was turned over to me? From what I was told about the girl, she was perfect. She had been untouched and had spirit."

The man's voice was slick, and it would be easy to imagine him persuading almost anyone to do his bidding. What rendered Darcy ill was the understanding that this was the real Grayson, and that they were discussing none other than his wife.

"I want what I was promised. I turned out my last whore not long after you gave me word that you had found a replacement. I broke her long ago, and you are aware by now how they lose their appeal once they are broken. I only kept her until I had a new plaything."

Swallowing the bile that rose to his throat, Darcy clenched his fist in an attempt not to barge into the room and strangle both men. Who they were was of no consequence, only that they had planned this for his Elizabeth.

"I shall find you something," Carlisle implored. "Just give me a bit more time. I do not know if it will be a gentlewoman, but I shall locate a suitable replacement."

"I prefer them gently bred," the man objected. "They are more fun to break than those waifs you find who roll over and part their legs at the first sight of food. They are too simple for my tastes. I want some fight."

"I know what you desire, but your preferences can be difficult to come by. As I said earlier, I require more time."

"Very well." The voice growled in such a manner that it sent a shiver down Darcy's back.

He darted back to the end of the hall in order to prevent detection, then began to walk as the voice, who he recognised as the Duke of Cumbria, exited the room, followed by Viscount Carlisle. The duke had never been an acquaintance, but his atrocious reputation was well-known.

Carlisle spotted him and held out an arm to invite him into the room. "Ahh, Darcy. I hoped to speak with you in private."

"I do not understand why." He attempted to modulate his voice, to sound nonchalant, but Carlisle did not appear convinced. Carlisle led him near the fireplace where he offered him a seat. "What business do you believe the two of us have because I am at a loss as to what you would wish to discuss with me?"

"It is simple, Darcy," he replied with a worrisome smile. "I wish to discuss your wife."

Chapter 21

"I do not believe you are acquainted with my wife." Darcy's voice was cold, but he maintained some distance from Grayson, lest he be tempted to strangle him.

"No, I have never had the pleasure of an introduction, but I know her uncle, Edward Gardiner, well. Have you ever made his acquaintance?"

He shook his head. "No, I have never cared to meet him, and furthermore, I hope to never have the man grace my doorstep."

Carlisle tilted his head as if studying him. "I understand the sentiment. The man has caused me nothing but grief since I was first introduced, yet I must find him. Do you know where he might be hiding?"

Once again, he shook his head while concentrating on his composure. "No, I hired investigators to search for him, but he is exceptionally well-concealed. I am unaware of his whereabouts."

The statement was not a full-out lie. He had no idea where Edward Gardiner's transport was at that moment and would have no update until they left Southampton. How tiresome was this deception! And Carlisle had scarcely begun his interrogation.

"The man has caused my wife a tremendous amount of grief. Her family perished in a horrific accident, and they believed him to be a loving uncle. She was dismayed when she discovered that his plans for her future had nothing to do with caring for her. My sole interest in Gardiner is to prevent him from harming her further."

The viscount studied him for a few moments before he nodded. "Since you listened outside of this room, I am certain you now realise my connection to Edward Gardiner." Carlisle paused and watched Darcy for a reaction. The viscount must have recognised he would get nothing, since he crossed his arms over his chest and leaned against the table behind him. "I must request your secrecy in the matter. I do not want all and sundry aware of my other business ventures."

"It seems there are already a few who are familiar with your dealings."

Carlisle smirked. "I am very careful to limit my business to those who have more to lose than I; keeps my reputation safe."

Darcy glared and joined his hands behind his back, clenching them together, the only clue to his anger and tension. "Why would I desire to protect your reputation?"

The viscount stepped forward, so they were almost nose-to-nose. "You dislike Gardiner, so I can assume you know the plans he had made for your wife." Darcy held his breath as he waited for the direction of Carlisle's conversation. "As long as I have your utmost discretion, I assure you your wife is in no danger from me. After all, Gardiner promised her untouched, and, as I understand, most of society believes her to be with child. She has no value for my purposes, and is therefore safe."

"I am relieved to hear it," he said through clenched teeth. The man was despicable! Carlisle spoke of Elizabeth as if she were merchandise for the taking; however, he bit back any further retort, as his loss of temper would be detrimental. Carlisle would cease this discourse at some point, would he not?

"I do ask that you contact me if you hear from Gardiner. He still owes me a great deal of money, and I intend to collect."

"Do you think him still in the country?" asked Darcy. "The man has been missing for so long that he could have made his way to a port and taken a ship to anywhere."

Carlisle gave a nonchalant wave of his hand. "It is possible, but I am assured he lacked the funds for such a journey. He could not have made it to Oxford much less Liverpool." Carlisle lifted a half-empty glass of brandy from the table and downed it in a swift movement. "I must be off. I promised my wife I would be home for tea."

Darcy's eyebrows lifted of their own accord, astonished the viscount spoke of his wife with such warmth.

A menacing chuckle came from the viscount. "You should not appear so shocked. I am not entirely without heart, and I do have certain principles." His voice lowered as he stepped closer. "For example, I do not bargain over women often. I have an exclusive clientele for whom I procure a specific product, along with a few other ventures. It shores up the accounts on our estates.

"And, despite what I do, I find that a happy wife creates a pleasant home to return to in the evening. It also does not hurt when I wish her to warm my bed."

Darcy's face burned at the blunt nature of Carlisle's last statement. Some men spoke of their wives or mistresses in such a fashion or worse, but he could not abide the habit.

Carlisle guffawed and slapped him on the back. "Come now! Your wife is with child. You know what it is all about."

"And I prefer to keep the matter between my wife and myself," he said with affront.

"Very well." The viscount nodded as he shrugged into his coat. "I can respect your wishes. After all, my life revolves around secrecy and concealment."

Carlisle strode past him towards the door, and Darcy kept his eyes upon him as he walked by, calling his name before he could leave.

"Carlisle, may I ask you two questions?"

"I may not give you the answers you seek."

If he could just beat the smirk from the viscount's face—but the idea was a dangerous one.

"Do you not feel remorse for what you have done to the women you have sold?"

The viscount lifted an eyebrow and then shrugged in a casual manner, as though his actions had not ruined innocent lives. "I have two clients who request maidens from me. One has only a few specifications whilst the other has very precise demands. Most are from the slums and the parents are most willing to take the amount I offer in return for their daughter. The others are more difficult to procure, but I am able to obtain them through debts and impoverishment. I come to their aid."

Bile burned the back of Darcy's throat and he swallowed hard. He had no desire to delve any deeper into Carlisle's dealings. How could he continue to look the other way—even if it were a necessity? "Your family has a reputation for their upstanding characters and never dabbling in trade. How do you maintain that?"

"I would imagine you also wonder if I am the first of my family to use nefarious activity to maintain our lifestyle."

Nodding, Darcy took a step closer. "That is correct."

"I learned my business at my father's knee, as he learned from my grandfather before him. The earl has his own business interests as I have my own. We also attempt to keep our full name only known to a small selection of our most trusted men."

"Which is why most people call you Thomas Grayson?"

"Yes," he replied. "Lawrence Archibald Thomas Grayson." He took out his pocket watch and checked the time. "Now, I must head for home. Thank you for speaking with me, and please do send me an express if you happen to locate Gardiner." He turned and exited the door, pausing just outside. "Also, please give my regards to your wife."

Carlisle strode away. As soon as the cur was gone, Darcy dropped into a seat and took a deep breath. He leaned his head back so he stared at the ceiling and remained in that attitude for at least a half hour as he contemplated all he had learned.

What if Carlisle discovered he had helped Gardiner? Perchance, the man would never return from Nova Scotia! His heart settled knowing Elizabeth was safe, yet what of those other women. It rankled him to sit by while they were enslaved and abused, but he had no choice. His first loyalty was to Elizabeth and their child. He could not put them in harm's way.

With a frustrated shake of his head, he had begun to rise to return to the others when Richard peered around the doorframe.

"There you are. Father and I wondered where you had disappeared. We are ready to leave for home." He turned his head back and forth to study the room. "But why are you in here alone?"

He stood and made his way closer to Richard. "I do not wish to speak of it at the moment."

His cousin observed him in a concerned manner. "Carlisle?"

He nodded and followed Richard to where his uncle waited by the door with his hat and coat. "I believe your wife was to come visit Anne this afternoon. Would you care to return to the house with us and join her?"

"I had hoped to, yes," he replied. After they climbed inside the carriage, he looked over to where his uncle was seated across from him. "Has Anne shown any signs of improvement?"

"No, she has not opened her eyes in a few days. The doctor has indicated we should prepare ourselves for the worst." Lord Matlock gave a weary sigh. "Catherine has been relentless to call on her, but Elinor is insistent that we will adhere to Anne's wishes; thus, she refuses to allow her entry to even the house. On the other hand, Lizzy has been a godsend. She has spent most of the last week with Anne."

Well aware of the time his wife was spending with his cousin, he had been touched by her willingness in the beginning; but, due to Elizabeth's ability to love without reserve, it had become difficult. "Yes, but she returned to Ashcroft in tears yesterday, and was so upset, I almost forbade her from going today."

Her anguish was heart wrenching, and the idea was to prevent her further pain, yet he had hesitated. Elizabeth's temper was terrible when provoked, which had resulted in their first row two months after they were wed. They had engaged in trifling disagreements; however, Elizabeth Darcy was not to be underestimated.

"Why did you change your mind?" A smirk crossed Richard's lips.

Darcy raised his eyebrows. "I did not wish to stoke her ire."

Uncle Henry began to chortle. "She has let you have it then?" He rubbed his hands together as he inhaled through his teeth. "Good for her! I was wondering how long it would take before she settled into your marriage and told you off."

Laughing, he shook his head. "Elizabeth's manner was a bit teasing when we first met, but she was even-tempered. I never imagined she could become so impassioned when angry."

"I am willing to bet it was over something absurd," ventured his uncle.

"Yes, she wished to have her sitting room redecorated whilst we were in town, so she would not be subjected to the mess on a daily basis, but I thought it would be better for her to oversee the work." His uncle and cousin both chuckled. "I had no idea she would oppose my plan with such vehemence."

Uncle Henry tilted his head and peered over his spectacles. "Those sorts of arguments are more common when a woman nears confinement. I would learn to agree with her more often than not."

Richard guffawed. "I am appreciative that I am not to be henpecked like the two of you besotted fools."

"Your mother's companionship and love are worth it in the end, son. You could have the same if you wished."

In complete agreement with his uncle, Darcy slapped his cousin on the back. "When the time comes, I would be happy to let you have the use of Rosings for as long as you require. You could even keep the profits in order to purchase your own estate."

Shaking his head, his cousin placed a hand on Darcy's shoulder. "I appreciate what you are trying to accomplish, but it is not the life for me. Besides, Anne is not yet in her grave."

"Despite how much we wish Anne would recover, it is plainly a matter of time. Your father and I have been reviewing Sir Lewis' will, as well as Anne's, in preparation for the day."

Richard turned to stare at him, incredulous.

"It was Anne's idea."

"Anne asked this of you?" his cousin clarified.

Uncle Henry leaned forward with his elbows on his knees. "Anne wishes us to know the terms both she and her father had set out for Catherine because she does not want her mother to give any argument that may delay the execution of the will. Catherine will be furious and recalcitrant. We have to know what we are about when we deal with her."

"Anne understands that Elizabeth wishes to return to Sagemore," explained Darcy. "Elizabeth's condition has become apparent, and so she is no longer joining Grandmamma during calls. I still insist on us walking together in the park each morning, but she prefers to walk around the estate and not London."

"She is preparing for the babe," added Uncle Henry.

Darcy's lips curved, and he nodded. "She is." His happy expression disappeared as he turned back to Richard. "Anne has known from the beginning she would not survive long. I believe she rallied as we all waited for Elizabeth to know for certain she was with child. Our cousin enjoyed the excitement, and an heir is the fulfilment of her wish to have a family at Rosings."

Uncle Henry gave a snort. "Goodness knows, it has never been that way whilst Catherine resided within its walls."

"If you do not wish to take me up on the offer, Richard, then I shall lease Rosings until it has an heir ready for its management."

"You intend to hold it for a second son, then?" asked Uncle Henry.

"If we are blessed with one, then yes, if not, then perhaps a daughter."

Richard's expression was wistful. "Anne would like that."

"I believe she would, too. I shall have to look into the legalities of such a venture, but it is not worth pursuing for now."

His uncle resumed his upright posture. "Will you turn it over to a solicitor to handle the lease?"

"I will require my solicitor to draw up the papers, but I have someone in mind. I intend to send word to him within the next few days to ascertain if he is interested."

All conversation stopped within the carriage, and they disembarked to make their way inside. They were still removing their gloves and hats when Lady Elinor happened upon them, her eyes awash with tears.

"I am so glad you are here!" Her breath hitched, and she sniffed. "Anne's breathing changed a short while ago, and we have sent for the physician. Elizabeth and I both agree, she has taken a turn. We do not expect her to make it through the night."

Darcy sighed as he handed his gloves to the footman. "How has her condition changed? Perhaps it is a fleeting alteration."

"Her breathing is slowing. She also sometimes pauses between breaths and has even gone as much as a minute without inhaling. I think poor Lizzy holds her breath whenever Anne does, but she refuses to leave her."

Aunt Elinor choked back a sob as she took his hand. "She has begun reading her Psalms." She stopped for a moment to give a distorted chuckle. "Although, Elizabeth leaves out the parts about casting enemies into the pit. She says she does not wish to read Anne anything about her enemies or casting people into pits whilst she is dying."

Uncle Henry gave a sad smile and pulled his wife into his arms. "We could only do so much for her. She always insisted she must stay with Catherine."

Aunt Elinor once again stifled a sob as she drew back, but her husband kept his arm around her waist. "That is because she did not wish for Catherine to start a war with the family. Anne knew she had no loyalty to mother or to us and would not hesitate to try to ruin us."

"Lady Catherine would have been the one ruined," said Richard. "If you will excuse me, I wish to sit with Anne one last time before she passes."

Darcy, amazed at Richard's calm and composed demeanour, stared as he exited the room.

"He has dealt with more death than any of us will in our lifetime." Uncle Henry's concern was evident when he turned towards him. "I doubt he will have much more of an outward reaction than what we observed during the carriage ride here.

Darcy ran a hand through his hair. "We should sit with Anne before the physician arrives. He may not allow us entry again for some time, if we do not."

With a turn, he led the way through the quiet halls. His uncle's house was never a noisy or boisterous place, but the atmosphere was never this calm; the stillness gave an eerie aura. Upon reaching Anne's chambers, the door was ajar, and he placed a hand near the opening to make his way inside.

Elizabeth sat upon the bedside with a Bible resting in her lap while Grace and Richard stood to the opposite side, Richard's arm around his sister's shoulders. Darcy made his way behind Elizabeth and placed a hand on her back, but she did not flinch or give any indication she was aware of his presence.

He made to speak, but a gasping breath drew his attention to his cousin in the bed. Elizabeth's shoulders began to shake, and he trailed his hand across her back as he watched and waited for Anne to take another breath. Her next was delayed and it was the same gasp, followed by an extended exhale.

Elizabeth brought herself under control, placed a hand on Anne's cheek, and waited. If only she would breathe again. But then how could she be so selfish as to hope for Anne's continued suffering? She had sat with Anne all day and had been the first to notice when the poor lady took a turn for the worse.

Aunt Elinor had attempted to persuade her to take some time for herself, but Elizabeth had refused and remained by Anne's side. They had become close over the almost two months she had been in London, and she was loath to lose someone who had become another sister. She had lost so many—Jane, Mary, Kitty, Lydia, her father and mother, and now she was forced to say goodbye to Anne.

Dear, sweet Anne, who, like Jane, never had a cruel word for anyone. What had Anne done to deserve this?

Elizabeth waited and waited for another breath as she heard Grace and Elinor begin to cry from the other side of the bed. Another breath would not come, but she still waited, until she heard her husband's voice break through the sounds of the others tears.

"Elizabeth... my love?"

Her hand moved from Anne's face to her arm as she became aware of his large, warm palm between her shoulder blades and turned her head in Fitzwilliam's direction. When had he entered the room?

"She is gone." Her voice was soft, and her eyes burned as tears pooled in her eyes.

He nodded, helped her stand, and took her into his arms. As she met with the safe harbour of her husband's embrace, she could no longer control her emotions like before, and began to sob uncontrollably.

"Shhhhh, Anne would not want all of these tears." His voice was gentle and low, but it did not calm her. As she poured out her grief, she became more insensible of her surroundings than ever before.

Later, she would discover she had not heard the dowager's entrance into the room, or her advising Fitzwilliam to take her to a bedroom down the hall; she had not heard the physician enter and suggest to her husband that she should be given laudanum before she harmed herself or the baby; and she had not heard Fitzwilliam's angry rebuttal as he refused the physician's advice, nor his insistence that his wife was not so feeble-minded that she would cause herself an injury.

Her surroundings came into focus once more when she awoke, ensconced in a strange bed with Fitzwilliam curled around her back. Her stomach gave a resounding rumble. How long had it been since she had eaten? How long had it been since Anne had passed?

The baby rolled within her womb, and she had a dire need to relieve herself. Pulling herself up in bed, her husband was startled and sat straight up.

"Elizabeth?"

She placed her hand on her lower abdomen and winced. "I require a chamber pot."

Darcy pointed towards a door in the corner, and she hastened through, taking care of the most necessary business before returning to the bedroom. She fingered the folds of the unfamiliar nightshift she was wearing.

"I changed your clothes after you cried yourself to sleep."

She peered up to where he stood donning his dressing gown. "It is not one of mine."

"No, it belongs to Grace. The whole household was occupied yesterday afternoon, and there was not a servant to be spared to be sent to Ashcroft house."

"Please do not think that I mind." She glanced at the clock—it was half-two. How long she had slept? "How long has it been since Anne…?"

"Yesterday," he responded. "Grandmamma suggested this room, so I brought you in here and remained, holding you. You cried for the better part of an hour before you fell asleep. I had my meals brought up and have not left."

"Please forgive me for worrying you so."

He approached her and cradled her face in his palms. "You have spent so much time with Anne during the past fortnight. I have been concerned because you were overwrought and exhausted, but I thought if I allowed you to rest, you would be well." He touched his forehead to hers. "Are you hungry?"

"Famished," she said with a small smile. "Do you think the cook has enough food to feed us both?" Fitzwilliam chuckled when she placed her hands on her belly.

"She has been cooking since daybreak. I am certain she can manage to put something together for my beautiful wife and the child she carries." Ringing the bell, he made arrangements for a meal to be brought up while she waited on the sofa by the fire. He spoke at length to the servant, gesturing often with his hands.

After he closed the door, Darcy settled himself in the corner of the sofa beside her and enfolded her in his arms as she rested against his chest. "I was thinking whilst I waited for you to wake."

"About?"

"I know you wish to go home, but I must travel to Rosings to attend to Lady Catherine and install the new steward. I thought perhaps you might want to journey ahead to Sagemore, and I could follow when I conclude my business in Kent."

Elizabeth drew back and began to shake her head before he even finished his suggestion. "I will not be without you, Fitzwilliam Darcy, so you can rescind your offer at once. Your business at Rosings could take a few days or it could take a fortnight. We have no way to know, and I do not wish to be on my own." She was on the verge of tears and spoke with anger. Separation was not an option, and she was furious for him suggesting it.

"You need not become so upset, Elizabeth. I offered you a choice..."

"A choice I have neither requested nor desire."

He massaged her back with one hand and placed his other over hers. "Shhh... I always prefer to have you with me."

Fitzwilliam began to smile, beam, in fact, and she narrowed her eyes. "Why are you so happy when I am upset?"

"Several reasons," he said as his grin widened. "I love you, and I am pleased you wish to remain with me rather than returning home. I also find your ire rather humorous."

"Why is my anger humorous, may I ask?" He began to chuckle, which made her more furious. "Laughing is not helping, sir."

"Sir?" He pressed his lips in a tight line, but his endeavour to suppress his mirth was unsuccessful. "I do not think you have called me sir since we first met." He shook his head. "You have become angry—more than reasonably angry over an idea I would have never forced upon you. I do not mean to offend you further with my laughter." His warm kiss on her temple was welcome, but did nothing to alleviate her distress. "I love you, dearest Elizabeth. I shall always want you with me." His palm moved to the swell of her waist. "Both of you."

Elizabeth turned and met his lips with her own as she attempted to convey her deepest feelings with a tender moment, yet when she pulled back, his smile still unnerved her. "Why are you still smiling in such a fashion?"

Fitzwilliam laughed and shrugged. "I thought of something Uncle Henry told me yesterday."

"Which is?" she asked testily.

"That you would have more of these unreasonable fits as you come closer to your confinement?"

She gasped. "You think I am like this for no other reason than the babe?"

"I do not think you would be as angry if you were not with child."

He may have thought he could reason with her, but she was not ready to be reasonable. She rose, took a seat in an armchair, and folded her arms across her chest. A knock came from the door and Fitzwilliam called for the person to enter.

"I am so glad to hear you are awake, Lizzy," exclaimed Aunt Elinor, as she entered the room. "You must have been exhausted to sleep most of the day away. I feel responsible for allowing you to sit for such long hours with Anne. I had no idea the toll it was taking."

Elizabeth shook her head. "I would not have left Anne's side. The sole reason I departed at night was due to a promise that I would. Anne insisted."

"She told me. She was as concerned for you as you were for her."

A warm tear trailed its way down Elizabeth's cheek, and she swiped it away. "Will you accompany Uncle Henry to Kent?"

"He insists upon it, so yes; although, I would have gone, even had he not insisted." Aunt Elinor's eyes darted between her and her husband. "Will you travel with us or return to Sagemore?"

"She has chosen to go to Rosings." Fitzwilliam still wore that insufferable grin. Elizabeth responded with a small snort.

"Perhaps I should leave the two of you to whatever it was you were discussing before my arrival." Aunt Elinor patted her shoulder. "Someone will be up soon with some nourishment. I know cook wished for you to have something special when you awoke. Apparently, the servants have spoken of your care for Anne, and she was touched."

"That is charitable of her. I will have to go down and thank her before we return to Ashcroft."

"I am certain she will be delighted." Their attention was diverted when a footman and a maid appeared at the partially open door. "Ah, please bring those trays inside and set them on the table." Aunt Elinor gestured to a small spot set between the fireplace and the sofa before turning her attention back to them.

"Now, I do not know what transpired prior to my visit, but given my nephew's ridiculous expression, I am certain it is nothing but pure nonsense. Fitzwilliam, I would apologise to your wife, and Lizzy, I doubt it is as bad as you imagine. Accept his apology and be done with it. We do not need strife amongst us at this time. Catherine will bring enough."

Aunt Elinor looked to her nephew. "Henry says we leave at first light tomorrow. Is that your wish as well?"

Fitzwilliam agreed. "Yes, we should install Anne in the family tomb as soon as possible, and I see no reason to delay the inevitable taking possession of Rosings. Uncle Henry offered to send letters to the vicar at Hunsford to arrange for the funeral, as well as a man he suggests to replace the steward at Rosings."

"He sent them express before dinner."

"Good, I wish to have it all concluded without delay."

Aunt Elinor gave a wry smile. "I cannot fault you for that. She leaned over to kiss Elizabeth on the head. "Enjoy your meal, and I shall see you in the parlour before you depart for Ashcroft." They both thanked Aunt Elinor before she bustled back out of the door, closing it behind her.

Her husband's eyes returned to her, and she lifted her eyebrows. "I apologise for finding humour in your testiness and in Uncle Henry's remark. Would you forgive me *and* join me?" He patted the cushion beside him and motioned her over with his head. "Come, my love. You know you would rather cuddle with me than sit there by yourself."

The sensation of his arms around her would be of such comfort, but he had been so insufferable! Aunt Elinor's words came to mind, so she rose and took the seat at his side where he enfolded her in his embrace.

"I am sorry if I am moody. I do not wish to be."

His lips caressed her hair while his hand covered her abdomen. "I do not mind since it is due to this little one here." Fitzwilliam leaned over and kissed the growing bump as she cradled his head in her hands. "The two of you are what mean the most to me in this world."

Tears burned as they again flooded her eyes, which caused her husband to chuckle and pepper soft kisses to her cheek. "We should eat so we can return to Grandmamma's and pack for tomorrow."

Elizabeth's stomach rumbled from hunger and Fitzwilliam smiled. "See, the babe agrees and demands food now." He leaned forward, took a plate, and placed a roll and a cup of chocolate on it before handing it to her. "We must not keep our little one waiting."

Rolling her eyes, she took the dish and leaned back. "You will spoil him if you never keep him waiting. He must learn patience."

Fitzwilliam ran his fingers down her back. "I intend to take care of him as I take care of you."

"Then he will most definitely be spoiled," she laughed.

"Then so be it."

Three carriages, carrying the entire Fitzwilliam family and the Darcys, pulled away from Ashcroft House as the sun's first rays began to peek through the streets of Mayfair. When they passed the road that would take them to Sagemore, Darcy gave a sigh and repositioned the curtain for their privacy. He pulled Elizabeth a bit closer, grimacing as his eye caught the black of her gown.

She once again wore mourning colours. He had been so insistent that she not even purchase grey at the modiste in favour of colour, but at least, this time, she would not be without that luxury for a year. Hattie had shown the good sense to choose one of Jane's finer gowns and dyed it before they returned to Ashcroft, so Elizabeth would have proper attire for their arrival at Rosings. His wife had been upset at ruining one of her sister's belongings, but after giving the matter further consideration, she saw sense in her maid's choice.

Elizabeth took a deep breath and exhaled it in her sleep and he smiled. She had drifted off in next to no time upon their departure!

He loved her so much. She would require protection from Lady Catherine's vitriol upon their arrival—if the lady was even there. Uncle Henry had sent her notice that her daughter had passed, but they had not had any response. God only knew what awaited them!

Leaning into the corner, he pushed away the worries of what would happen that afternoon—they would arrive soon enough. Instead, he would rest with Elizabeth after the harrowing week. With one last soothing inhale of her orange blossom perfume, Darcy surrendered to his dreams.

Chapter 22

Considering Elizabeth's condition, neither Uncle Henry nor Darcy desired to rush the trip to Kent, so when they had need of a change of horses, their party took tea within the coaching inns. The journey, as a result, was a little longer than usual, arriving at Rosings approximately six to seven hours after they departed London.

While they waited for the footman to open the door, Darcy gazed at Elizabeth from across the carriage. He had swapped seats just prior to their arrival to a more proper arrangement, and was now tapping his fingers against his leg as he waited for the moment he could hand his wife down. He ached to touch her.

Oblivious to his stare, Elizabeth tied her bonnet, only to catch his eye as she pulled the ribbon tight. "Is something amiss?"

"No," he said with a smile, "I was just thinking how fortunate I am to have such a wife." He enjoyed the wide grin that accompanied a pair of pale pink cheeks, yet a more serious question could not be helped. "Are you certain you wish to confront Lady Catherine with the rest of us? You and Hattie could walk the grounds until we are certain she will not be a problem."

Elizabeth shook her head. "No, I will be there to support you. Lady Catherine will disparage me whether I am present or not, and her opinion will have little effect on me. I do not care for the petty judgements of a woman who mistreated her own child."

With the confrontation that awaited him inside, it would not do to press the matter lest he have an argument with his wife. "Very well, but if I request you leave the room, I expect you to do as I wish."

Her expression displayed her dislike of his demand, but to his surprise, she did not argue. "I do not see why it would be necessary, but I will agree."

The familiar thump of the step being set sounded and the door opened, allowing him to exit. Darcy held out his hand for his wife, who stepped down and took his arm. His stomach roiled, but Elizabeth's touch alone helped him suppress his anxiety by reminding him of his purpose. She required him to be strong both for her and for their child.

"According to the footman, Catherine returned last night," confirmed Uncle Henry, as he straightened his coats. "I hope you are geared up for a battle royal, for that might be what awaits us."

"She will not be reasonable, but she has no choice in the matter."

"No, she does not." Uncle Henry peered from the tip of the cupola, to the clock, and finally to the arched entrance beneath them, took a deep breath, and looked back to him. "Shall we go in and best the beast?"

His grandmother gave a small snort while Elizabeth and Aunt Elinor chuckled.

"Once more unto the breach[1]," exclaimed Richard, who drew his sabre and pointed it forward.

"I do not believe it will be once more, and put that thing away." Aunt Elinor slapped her son's arm. "I have no doubt Catherine would send for the magistrate to delay matters if she spotted you drawing weapons."

"That might make matters easier." Everyone's attention was drawn to Huntley, and they stared at him in surprise. "What? We would have a witness who is not family to the enforcement of the will."

Uncle Henry shook his head. "I do not believe that would make her easier. Catherine has no sense of shame for her actions because she believes she is above those around her."

"I agree with Richard," groused the dowager. "Let us get inside and eliminate the business portion of this visit. I have no desire to stand in front of the house for the remainder of the afternoon. I would much prefer to go inside, or I should have toured the garden with Grace and her maid."

They passed through the arched entrance to the small court and the ornate front door, flanked by columns and overset by gargoyles and a relief of the de Bourgh coat of arms. Higgs, the butler, was waiting at the door when they stepped forward.

"Good afternoon." He addressed Darcy and Lord Matlock. "You should be aware that Lady Catherine expects me to refuse you entry."

He donned his most official manner. "I take it you and Mrs. Langton received my express?"

"Yes, sir." The aged butler gave a nod. "We have carried out your instructions as written. Lady Catherine's maid would have been a problem, but an errand was found to keep her busy after her duties this morning."

His grandmother chuckled. "So Lady Catherine's belongings are being moved to the dower house?"

"As we speak ma'am."

Darcy leaned forward just a bit. "My wife and I will want to meet with you and Mrs. Langton in regards to the staff. I shall not have anyone informing Lady Catherine the business of this house; any staff remaining loyal to her must be released."

"With the exception of her maid," interjected Elizabeth. She shrugged her shoulders. "She should be allowed to trust the person who cares for her so intimately."

He agreed and returned his attention to Higgs, who extended his arm to gesture them inside. "I will notify Mrs. Langton of your request to meet with us. I am certain she will be available at your convenience, as will I."

"Thank you," replied Darcy. Uncle Henry was expected to lead the way as was his wont, but instead, he demurred and held out his arm.

"This is now your property, and we are here to help and support you."

Darcy glanced back at the butler, who waited with his usual patience, took a deep breath, and forged forward, taking Elizabeth with him.

He did not turn to see if his family followed. The sound of their feet as they strode along on the black and white tiles of the entrance hall, as well as the tell-tale clank of Richard's sabre against his leg was proof they had not abandoned him. Without requiring him to ask, his family had travelled with him to ensure he had their support. He was fortunate to have such relations.

Elizabeth's hand squeezed his arm, and he sought her face, seeking comfort in her eyes as Higgs stepped around them to open the door. The elder man did not enter before them to announce their arrival, but instead gestured into the room to indicate that Darcy and Elizabeth, followed by their family, should precede him.

"Higgs!" Lady Catherine bellowed as she rose to her feet. "I advised you most strenuously to refuse entrance to *these* people! I will not tolerate such insubordination from anyone! Even you!"

"As you say madam," Higgs replied evenly before turning to his new master. "Do you require anything further, sir?"

A small snort emanated from Richard's direction before Lady Catherine stepped forward. "How dare you! You can find yourself a new position! You will not remain at Rosings!"

"You are mistaken, Lady Catherine." Darcy straightened his spine in order to appear more imposing. "I am in possession of both Sir Lewis de Bourgh's will as well as Anne's."

"I am well aware of the contents of those documents, and I intend to challenge the validity of them both! Anne was of a weak mind." Her volume dropped just a bit and she gave a dismissive sniff. "She did not know what she was about when she named you her heir."

"That challenge is easy to refute, Catherine." Uncle Henry stepped forward until he was beside Darcy. "We spent a great deal of time with Anne in her last few weeks, and she remained lucid until the end. Her mind was not addled in the slightest."

"My physician will attest to her condition! I knew Anne better than anyone! She was *my* daughter!"

"Which physician?" asked the dowager. "Your physician here? Or one of the numerous physicians who bled her in London?"

"I only wanted the best treatment for my daughter!"

"I find that difficult to believe." Aunt Elinor emerged from between her sons. "We interviewed several physicians who treated Anne during the last fortnight she remained with you. Each said you were determined to have her well, so she could marry high and above Fitzwilliam Darcy. You may have killed your daughter for vengeance not love."

"Marrying above the Darcys was best!" She punctuated her claim with a heavy stamp of her walking stick. "She had no idea what was good for her! Rosings required an heir!"

"She would have died in an attempt to bear a child," lamented Elizabeth. "She had neither the strength nor the fortitude to bring a babe into this world. Anne understood this…"

"You have no right! You know nothing of my Anne!"

"That is enough!" yelled Darcy. "My wife has spent the last weeks of Anne's life seated at her bedside! They had conversations for as long as Anne's constitution would allow, and when she was fatigued, my wife would read to her and on occasion sang to her." He raised his hand and pointed at the imperious woman. "She proved herself a better relation to Anne than you ever were, and I will not have you treat her in such a cruel manner. Anne would not wish her to receive this abuse, either."

Spittle flew from her mouth as she cried in fury. "*You* allowed *this* woman to pollute my daughter's mind! She was far above you by rank and circumstance! You had no right…"

"*Enough* Catherine!" bellowed Uncle Henry. "Anne took great comfort in the time she spent with Mrs. Darcy. We believe the sole reason she lived as long as she did was due to Mrs. Darcy's confession that she was with child. Anne was enlivened by the prospect, and eager for the day she was told of the quickening."

Lady Catherine turned an appraising eye towards his wife's abdomen, and Darcy tucked her behind him.

"I sent instructions yesterday for the dower house to be opened and cleaned for your use."

Lady Catherine's face began to turn a brilliant shade of red. "I will not reside in the dower house! *This* is my home!"

Darcy attempted to remain unperturbed despite Lady Catherine's vitriol. The bellowing, aside from being deafening, would not accomplish the matter at hand, and the situation would be better controlled if he was under good regulation. "No, Rosings, as well as the house in town belong to me—which includes the dower house. I am offering you the opportunity to live there, but I am not required by any legal document to offer you any form of housing."

"My marriage contract…"

"Leaves you your portion—your settlement of twenty-thousand pounds and no more. I can arrange for an establishment for you in London where you can reside for the remainder of your days."

Her nostrils flattened and whistled as she sucked air through them, and her eyes bulged as she held it in. "You would not dare! You would see me put up in Cheapside if you had your way."

"That notion is tempting," interjected Uncle Henry. "I have a friend who owns a small home near Mayfair—a street or two over from the more fashionable addresses— that will be inexpensive to lease. It is not what you are accustomed to, I am afraid, but it would be sufficient to your needs."

Her eyes shot back to Darcy. "So, I am expected to remain in the dower house whilst Rosings stands empty?" Her voice was strident and demanding. "That will be a waste!"

"I never indicated Rosings would remain empty." His shoulders tensed and his jaw clenched in apprehension of the explosion that would occur as soon as he put his match to the kindling. "I have a friend who wishes to lease Rosings until such a time he can purchase his own estate."

"*You have what?*" She advanced forward and hurled her walking stick out in front of her, shaking it in Darcy's face. "You would lease my home to that friend of yours who is in *trade!*" Her face screwed in concentration. "Bingham… Bingtree… Bingbee…"

"Bingley is his name, and yes, he sent an enthusiastic response to my offer of a lease on Rosings. My solicitor is arranging the paperwork as we speak. Bingley hopes to take possession before the New Year."

The changes in colour on Lady Catherine's face were more pronounced than earlier and became worrisome. She went from red to almost purple as she began to sputter. "You… you…" She gave an abrupt swallow and thrust her stick forward, almost knocking his nose. "You would defile my home with the stench of trade!"

Richard reached forward, grasped her cane, and ripped it from her bony fingers.

The manoeuvre only distracted Lady Catherine for but a moment, since she drew herself up much as Darcy had earlier, so she appeared taller than was her wont.

"Rosings belonged to Anne, and now it belongs to me. As to Bingley, his sisters will accompany him, and I believe Miss Bingley's betrothed will join them for a time. I know they intend to spend a month complete before they return to London for the season."

Lady Catherine continued to appear an unnatural colour, and he glanced to his uncle, who did not appear concerned at all by her complexion or the fact that at that moment, she again held her breath.

"The staff," began his uncle, "has unloaded our trunks and by now, brought them upstairs. Anne's body will be delivered later this evening, and she will be laid out in the blue drawing room until the funeral on the morrow. I am expecting your vicar, Mr. Thacker, to join us for dinner, so we can finalise the arrangements for the service." He cleared his throat and gave a nervous tug to the bottom of his jacket as if it required straightening.

"It pains me to say this Catherine, but we have tried for years to have you a part of the family, and you have spurned us at every effort. It has come to a point where Darcy now owns Rosings, and due to your actions, you are no longer welcome in this home."

"You were acknowledged as my brother when your title made it necessary," spat Lady Catherine.

"I have been aware of your feelings for some time, dear sister. Your spite and unwillingness to recognise your family has always saddened me. I believe the sole reason you accepted my sister Anne as you did was due to her marriage to George Darcy. You took notice of Pemberley and the wealth of the Darcy name and used your own sister as a means to further whatever social ambition you possessed."

Lady Catherine sniffed and brushed some fluff from her sleeve. "I saw potential. I hoped for a male heir, but there were of course, no guarantees. Just as there are none in regards to this child."

She attempted to point around him to Elizabeth, but Darcy moved each time, so his wife was always shielded.

"So, you befriended my Anne in the hopes of betrothing a child of yours to a Darcy heir." The dowager's ire was evident in her eyes as she stepped towards her husband's eldest child.

"My son could have married Anne's daughter." She gave a haughty sniff. "It still would have been a marvellous match. "Without an heir, Pemberley could pass to their first-born son."

"Except for the fact that Pemberley is entailed."

Lady Catherine's eyes darted back to Darcy and narrowed. "George never mentioned an entailment."

He was rueful, yet chuckled as he shook his head. "No, my father is rather secretive regarding his business affairs and Pemberley, and shares his business with no one but his solicitor. If I had not been born, Pemberley would not have been held for a son from Georgiana."

His uncle approached his sister while she was calm. "Nothing will change, Catherine. Despite any blustering and bellowing you do, Rosings will still be the property of Fitzwilliam Darcy." She huffed, but did not begin ranting or raving. "Anne wanted it to be this way, and so it is."

"I wish you had seen her face when my wife told her of our child," said Darcy with caution. "Her smile was the widest I had ever seen. The thought of a new heir to this house brought life to her for a short time, and she held on for longer than we ever thought possible."

"Anne was too soft-hearted." Her voice was cold, but a sadness appeared in Lady Catherine's eyes that shocked him. Could she have had some distorted sense of love for Anne? He searched for that hint once more, but the emotion had since disappeared.

"Anne had compassion," his grandmother interjected. "She wished to find happiness on her own terms, but knew you would never allow it. In the end, it is what drove her from you. You can blame us for your misfortunes, if you like, but the sole person to blame is yourself."

"I do not have to listen to this idiocy one moment longer!" Lady Catherine's voice elevated as she spoke, and she began to search the room for someone to come to her aid. When she realised no servants were about, she pointed towards the door. "You shall see yourselves out! I take no leave of you! You do not deserve such condescension!"

She strode straight towards Darcy, and he sprang to the side, keeping Elizabeth behind him until after she passed. He then followed her until she reached the two footmen, who blocked the foot of the stairs.

She was resolute, and not at all polite. "You will remove yourselves at once!"

The smaller of the two men flinched, but stood fast as Darcy and Uncle Henry came to address her.

"Your belongings have been moved to the dower house, and as soon as your maid returns from wherever Mrs. Langton has sent her, she will join you. One of the estate carriages should be waiting in front of the house for your use. We bid you a good day madam."

"I shall not leave Rosings! This is *my* home!"

"You do not have a choice. You can depart Rosings on your own, or I can have these two men escort you to your carriage." Higgs entered the room, followed by two additional servants, which ensured enough men were present to remove her.

Lady Catherine espied them and gave a great huff. "I have never been thus treated! I will tell all of society. You will be spurned for what you have done—for your lack of feeling!"

"I beg to differ," disagreed Aunt Elinor. "I find it more believable that our nephew will be applauded for his actions."

One of the footmen placed a hand on Lady Catherine's elbow as his other arm stretched before him, beckoning her forward. She did not move, but instead, whipped her arm away from his touch. "How dare you place a hand on me!"

Uncle Henry's voice remained calm. "They will all touch you if you do not remove yourself from this house at once." Two more men stepped forward and she began to stride in the direction of the entry.

She did not fight, but continued to screech as the servants trailed behind her. "I will carry my point! You will pay for what you have done!"

Upon reaching the carriage, Uncle Henry stepped forward. "Your settlement money will be dispersed through Darcy; I would not attempt anything against him. He could make your life a misery if he wished."

Her face was pinched as she climbed into the plush interior. The walking stick Richard had confiscated was placed on the seat opposite, the door closed, and the driver given leave to proceed. The two of them then stood on the steps and watched until the horses turned the corner.

"Well," commented Uncle Henry with a smile. "That was easier than I expected."

"You thought it easy?"

"When you have known Catherine for as long as I have, any argument which ends with her departure in under an hour is considered painless." The men laughed as his uncle gave him a slap on the back. "Shall we go inside? We have the ladies awaiting us."

"Huntley did not open his mouth once during all of this."

His uncle guffawed. "Have you never known that he is terrified of Catherine?"

Darcy chuckled and shook his head. "He has never mentioned anything of the sort to me."

Uncle Henry beamed as he enlightened Darcy about his cousin's foible. "She gave him nightmares as a child, and he still would rather avoid her if given a choice."

"Then let us pray you outlive your sister."

"Indeed!" His uncle snickered as they returned inside.

Elizabeth could not explain the foreboding feeling that they had not heard the last of Lady Catherine, but upon mention of her suspicion, the dowager and Aunt Elinor revealed they were of the same opinion, which was not too much of a surprise.

Based on her limited knowledge of Lady Catherine, it was improbable for the termagant, as Richard called her, to concede with such apparent ease; nevertheless, she was proud of Fitzwilliam for remaining steadfast and not surrendering to her arguments.

Once Lady Catherine had been shown the door, their party all adjourned to their rooms to refresh themselves, which gave Elizabeth a chance to see more of the house. The décor was gaudy and useless. Large, dark tapestries adorned most of the walls paired with heavy dark stained wood and upholstery. A fleeting hope that perhaps their chambers were not as dreadful as the remainder of Rosings passed when she entered, and a disappointed sigh rose from deep within her.

"Do you find nothing attractive about Rosings?"

She chuckled at her husband's perceptiveness and shook her head.

"I am certain that once it is redecorated, it will be a beautiful home." He scanned the room as he ran his hand along the mantel. "But it will be quite an undertaking, one I assumed we would begin while we are here."

Her vision was drawn to a portrait of a beady-eyed man over the fireplace and then back to her husband. "You are in earnest? It could take years to overhaul this house!"

"Why do we not begin with the removal of that painting?" He stepped closer to the mantel to glance at the nameplate beneath. "I do not believe Mr. Jonas Preston de Bourgh has the face for a bedchamber."

She covered her mouth as she giggled. "I would not want him to watch whilst we sleep."

"Whilst we sleep?" He took her hand and pulled her into his embrace. "Him spying on our slumber is the least of my concerns." His head dipped to her neck and his lips brushed against the sensitive skin, causing gooseflesh to ripple across the back of her neck and shoulders. "I love it when you do that."

"Do what?" Her voice was breathy and soft to her own ears. He drew back with a broad grin.

"I see your shiver and those little bumps break out across your skin when I touch my lips there. I rarely close my eyes anymore because I do not want to miss it." A knock at the door brought an immediate frown to his face, and she laughed. "Why do you make sport of my disappointment?"

"You remind me of a little boy when you wear that expression. I fully expect one of our children to don that look during a scolding one day."

He beamed and placed his hand over her increasing belly. "I would rather see your pout cross her lips."

Elizabeth bit her lip and grinned. "I suppose we shall see, but in the meantime, Hattie is waiting." Darcy began to depart as she opened the door to reveal Hattie with a jug of water.

"I have your water to be cleanin' up with, ma'am. I can redo your hair if you like. I know a long trip in a carriage can take its toll…"

Fitzwilliam had paused by the door, and interrupted before she could continue. "I believe Mrs Darcy's hair is just as handsome as it was after you styled it this morning." Hattie flustered and stuttered her thanks as he glanced back to Elizabeth. "Shall I return in a half-hour?"

"I will be waiting," she said as he disappeared through the door.

A basin of warm water and a fresh gown from Hattie did much to restore her humour. The dust from the road had been as much a cloud over their arrival as had the confrontation with Lady Catherine. As her maid finished her hair, Elizabeth stroked a hand over her abdomen and smiled.

"I'd imagine the little one has been movin' a great deal." Hattie placed a hairpin as she watched at Elizabeth in the mirror.

"More and more every day. He is very persistent, just like his father."

Hattie chuckled as she surveyed her work. "If you will forgive me for sayin', not so unlike his mother."

She gasped in indignation. "Hattie!"

"I may be no more than a mite older than Miss Lucas, but I remember when you were born. And I remember the wail you let out when Mr. Trevor christened you." They both began to giggle as

Hattie placed her last pin. "Your poor mama was beside herself tryin' to calm you down, but your father just laughed. And when the service was over, he took you for a walk around the chapel."

"Did he?" Her mother had told her many times about her tantrum during her christening, but never her father's part.

"Indeed he did. I remember him speaking to you as he pointed out birds and different flowers. I recall my mama being very impressed with Mr. Bennet that day."

Hattie glanced for loose pins and then touched Elizabeth's shoulder as she did when she was finished. She then began to tidy the dressing table, placing the box of hairpins in a drawer.

"Hattie?" Her maid glanced up with a questioning expression. "Thank you."

"You are welcome, Mrs. Darcy."

She gave a chuckle. "Mrs. Darcy."

A confused look crossed Hattie's face and Elizabeth smiled. "Can you imagine if my mother heard me addressed by such a name?" She picked up her handkerchief and clasped it to her chest.

"Ooooh, Mrs. Darcy! How well that sounds!"

"How well it sounds indeed," came a deep voice from the door. Hattie curtsied, grabbed Elizabeth's travel gown, and departed with haste to the dressing room.

"Are you accustomed to entering a lady's bedchamber without knocking?" She offered a playful arch of her eyebrow over her shoulder, and he answered her gesture with a laugh.

"Only when I am particularly acquainted with the lady."

She turned to face him, but could not resist the temptation of being impertinent. "And are you *particularly* acquainted with many ladies?"

He extended a hand to pull her into his arms. "Just one."

She placed her hands upon his chest and ran a finger along the edge of his lapel. "Just one? She must be very special."

"She is unique. She challenges me with her wit, she teases me incessantly, and her love has made me the happiest man on earth."

Elizabeth scoffed and rolled her eyes. "I do not know how I could ever do all of those things, Fitzwilliam. I believe you exaggerate my accomplishments, and you should be aware excessive flattery will get you nowhere."

He chuckled and touched his lips to her forehead. "We should go meet with Mrs. Langton and Higgs before it is too close to dinner."

She groaned and wrapped her arms around his torso. "I suppose we should. Is it terrible I wish to order a tray and spend the evening in our chambers—once we rid ourselves of Mr. de Bourgh, of course."

Fitzwilliam smiled and brushed his lips against hers once more before he offered her his arm. "I desire the same, my love, but we must take care of the staff first."

Elizabeth took his arm and sighed. "I know you are correct. I just do not relish this meeting."

"Neither do I," he replied as they departed through the doorway.

Elizabeth closed the door behind her and leaned all her weight against the solid oak panel. "Thank you for having us retire early."

"Our family understands if you are tired. You should not push yourself until you become so fatigued. Aunt Elinor and Grandmamma are here to help you, if you allow it." She exhaled with exhaustion and turned, so he could unfasten her gown.

"You do not wish to wait on Hattie?"

"I am exhausted and content to sleep in my chemise. I do not require Hattie for a simple disrobing."

When she had removed the garment, Elizabeth placed it on a chair. Her husband then helped her with her petticoats and corset while she removed the pins from her hair. As soon as she was clad in her chemise, she kicked off her slippers, and climbed into the bed, where she settled on her side.

"My love, you are still wearing your stockings."

"They will come off while I sleep," she mumbled, as the bedclothes were peeled back from her body.

She did not attempt to discover what he was doing since she was certain what he was about, and was soon proven correct when her husband's strong hands untied the delicate ribbon on the top leg. His agile fingers stroked down her knee and calf as he removed the stocking, tossed it away, and began to massage her foot from heel to toe.

"Ooooh." He chuckled at her low groan. "That feels wonderful."

When he stopped for a moment, she glanced up as he shed his topcoat and waistcoat. His cuff buttons clinked into a cut glass dish on the side table, and he began the same process with her garter on her other leg. Fitzwilliam had just begun to rub her foot as he had the other when a loud knock interrupted them.

He placed a soft kiss in her hair. "Give me a moment."

She rolled over as he cracked the door open enough to see who was there. "I am sorry for disturbing you, sir," came the voice of Higgs. "But Lady Catherine is outside and is insistent she cannot sleep in the dower house."

Fitzwilliam ran a hand through his hair. "And what is it she feels is amiss?"

"The mattress in her room is too hard, but, if you will pardon me for speaking my piece, that mattress was just installed—new."

Elizabeth stood, wrapped a rug around herself, and took a spot beside her husband. "New?"

"Yes, ma'am." Higgs averted his eyes. "Miss de Bourgh replaced it a few months before her mother took her to London. One of her biggest concerns when she became mistress was to ensure the dower house was in good repair."

Fitzwilliam began to speak, but she stayed him with a hand to his arm. "Forgive me, Higgs, for requiring this of the staff so late at night, but is it safe to assume Lady Catherine has never had issue with the mattress in her former chambers?"

The older man smiled. "No ma'am, she has never complained."

"Then would you please have several footmen load it into a cart and exchange it for the mattress Lady Catherine feels is inadequate. She then should have no further complaints about the bed at the dower house."

"If you give me a moment," interjected Fitzwilliam, "I will accompany you down and give her the news myself."

"No, sir." Higgs held up his hand to stay Fitzwilliam. "I will be pleased to deliver the message." With a trill laugh, he rubbed his hands together and gave a quick bow. "I hope you have a pleasant evening, sir, ma'am."

The butler's chuckles echoed as he made his way down the corridor.

"I almost wish I had gone down to deliver the message." Fitzwilliam's voice was low as he complained, but it was obvious he was more amused than angry. "We will pay for this on the morrow. You do realise?"

She returned to bed and nestled back into the bedclothes. "Well, we shall just have to sleep well, so we can meet whatever challenge Lady Catherine presents with our wits about us." She could hear him as he removed the rest of his clothes. "Are you going to join me or keep me waiting? I am cold."

The bed dipped as he slid behind her. His arm circled her waist and his hand opened to splay across her belly. "How is this?" His warm breath tickled her ear, and his bottom arm slipped underneath so she was in his embrace.

"Much better," she mumbled.

"I love you, Elizabeth Darcy." A soft kiss grazed against her shoulder.

"I love you, too."

The room was so dark you could not see, but Darcy smiled at the sound of her voice as she drifted to sleep. He felt something poke his palm, and he forced himself to remain quiet and still, realising it was his unborn child. The babe had never made a movement he could feel before, and a part of him wished to wake Elizabeth. He wanted to celebrate and wake the entire household!

The single matter that prevented him from bolting up and out of bed was his wife. She had been fatigued with their schedule in London and caring for Anne, and she required rest if they were to continue to tackle Rosings together. After all, the morrow would be a trying day if Lady Catherine had any say in the matter.

1 *Shakespeare, Henry V, Act III*

Chapter 23

The morning of Anne's funeral was a beautiful day with the most brilliant blue sky. A part of Elizabeth felt such a solemn day should be at least a little dreary, but at the same time, it could be said nature was celebrating Anne's life and her spirit, which made the day perfect.

Everyone had breakfast together before the men left for the service, leaving the ladies behind to oversee the servants as they put together refreshments for anyone who wished to offer their condolences after the funeral. Lady Elinor and Grace offered to take charge of the impromptu gathering, so Elizabeth could see to other duties, above all, the meeting with Mrs. Langton in regards to the furnishings and ornamentation.

Contrary to what was expected, she opted to begin in the more public rooms. "I simply wish to reduce some of this clutter," she stated, as she scanned the walls and furniture.

The dowager laughed and crinkled her nose. "Rosings has been this way since my first visit years ago. Some of these are de Bourgh family pieces. It might be a nice gesture if Fitzwilliam contacted them and offered to return these heirlooms to them, since I can tell you there were more than a few ruffled feathers when Anne was named heir."

Her eyebrows rose. "They felt it should have been entailed?"

"Sir Lewis was the oldest of five brothers, and the second brother, Mr. Preston de Bourgh, had two sons of his own. He was very put out that he was overlooked."

Mrs. Langton strode over to the escritoire in the corner and pulled out some paper, ink, and a quill. "I will catalogue whatever we take down so a list can be included within the offer."

"That is an excellent idea," praised Elizabeth. "I think we should begin with the large tapestry in the middle. I hope the coverings are not so faded that the wall appears dreadful."

The housekeeper loaded her quill with ink. "Lady Catherine did not open the drapery often, ma'am. If there is sun damage, it should be minimal."

"Good! Then that will be the first thing to come down."

Elizabeth and the dowager spoke for a moment as the servants worked. When her attention returned to their task, the tapestry was down and the hanging fabrics still in reasonable condition—ugly, but not faded.

"We will need to do something about these fabrics," she remarked. "Grandmamma, would you be willing to send me samples from London. I could pick what I like, and we could have them sent here to be installed."

With a step forward, Mrs. Langton held up her first finger. "Before you do that, Mrs. Darcy. I have something I would show you first."

Elizabeth pointed to two paintings for the footmen to take down before she and the dowager followed Mrs. Langton to a supply closet below stairs.

"Miss de Bourgh attempted to redecorate several times, but her mother always complained her tastes lacked sophistication and would instruct her to throw away the items we had ordered."

The dowager's shoulders dropped. "Poor Anne! I do wonder how she managed to exert any control over Rosings."

"Lady Catherine had no interest in the day to day running of the estate," chimed in Mrs. Langton, "as long as she was allowed to run the household, but Miss de Bourgh capitulated when her mother would become angry at her attempts to have any influence within the house."

Mrs. Langton stepped over to several trunks and lifted the lids to reveal fabrics for the walls as well as furniture and drapery. "I always told Lady Catherine I disposed of Miss de Bourgh's orders, but I could not. I hoped one day perhaps they could be used."

Elizabeth fingered a fine Chinese floral patterned wall covering. "These seem as though they were expensive. I cannot believe Lady Catherine would order them away as if they were scraps from the kitchen."

"I certainly can," remarked the dowager. "She could be petty when she wished, and I am certain she resented what she considered Anne's interference."

She stood tall and placed her hands on her hips. "Well, I will not dispose of them. The former mistress of Rosings wished them to be used and so they shall." She pivoted to face Mrs. Langton. "Do you know of anyone we could hire to pull down the old papers and install these?"

"Yes, ma'am. I believe a local furniture builder in Hunsford can take care of the upholstery. I will send out inquiries today." Mrs. Langton choked back a tear. "I do wish Miss de Bourgh were here to see her plans carried to fruition. She picked such lovely colours and fabrics."

Elizabeth placed her hand on the housekeeper's shoulder. "Thank you for showing them to us. I am happy to carry out Anne's wishes, and it will leave us with extra funds to redecorate a few other rooms as well."

After sorting through the papers and other materials, they returned to continue their original task, and managed to render the drawing room almost tasteful for anyone who would call.

Upon the men's return, Fitzwilliam surveyed the entry with his eyebrows raised. "What mischief have you been up to today?"

Elizabeth grinned. "We thought to remove some of the clutter. I believe the green drawing room will fit a few more people and this hall is not so suffocating."

Uncle Henry glanced into the drawing room and then to the ladies with a surprised expression. "The draperies are open and light is coming into the house!"

His wife slapped his arm. "The room almost seems inviting, but I am afraid until the fabrics are removed, it will still feel small and dim."

"Well, as soon as Mrs. Langton can procure someone to do the work, it will be done." Everyone regarded her as if she had forgotten something, and she suppressed the urge to roll her eyes.

"We still need to order the materials, dear," Aunt Elinor informed her gently.

The dowager chuckled. "Anne took care of that matter for us."

Fitzwilliam placed his hand on Elizabeth's back with a furrowed brow. "I do not understand."

After a brief explanation of Anne's purchases for the house, the dowager shook her head. "I must say Anne had lovely and expensive taste. Chinese wall coverings and the most exquisite fabrics for new drapes and furniture."

"That does explain a question I had after going over the books this morning." Fitzwilliam shook his head sadly. "Anne did not touch her pin money, with the exception of several extravagant expenditures noted to a drapers in London."

"The materials." Elizabeth took the handkerchief her husband held out and dabbed her eyes. "I intend to use them."

"Of course you do." He kissed her temple and hugged her closer. "We are expecting a few callers from the service, including several people from the village, Anne's physician, and the apothecary."

The dowager gave a sigh. "Do you believe they are sincere or attended because they were sad to lose the business?"

Grace turned to her grandmother appalled. "Grandmamma!"

Huntley gave a sour grimace, which prompted Elizabeth to giggle. "Mr. Thacker is to attend, and I suggest we all have a brandy before he arrives." He poured the men and his grandmother a glass, and then, gave Elizabeth, Aunt Elinor, and Grace each a small amount of wine.

When everyone had their drinks, Richard raised his snifter. "To Anne."

"To Anne," they all chorused and took a sip.

After dabbing her eye with a handkerchief, the dowager cleared her throat. "Did Catherine attend the service?"

Uncle Henry gave a low harrumph. "Unfortunately. She noticed where Anne was to be interred and became irate."

"For what reason?" Elizabeth was appalled.

With a shake of his head, her husband sighed. "She claimed Anne, as the mistress of Rosings, deserved a more esteemed placement within the crypt."

"After a rant of some duration," explained Uncle Henry, "she departed in a huff, which suited our purposes. We were able to conclude the funeral."

They sat in silence for a few minutes until Higgs appeared at the door. "Mr. and Mrs. Thacker."

Everyone stood as the toadiest little man Elizabeth had ever seen entered the room. After the initial greetings, he offered excessive praise for Lady Catherine, Anne, and Fitzwilliam. Elizabeth was certain she saw Huntley grimace.

The evening would be a long and arduous—nay Herculean, task.

The next fortnight at Rosings was busy and productive. Darcy replaced the steward and set to work with the replacement to ensure he was well aware of his master's expectations. He was fortunate to find the man well trained, and pleased to discover that minimal alteration to his current practices was required.

Elizabeth, with the help of the dowager and Aunt Elinor, replaced what little help they lost with the change from Lady Catherine and managed to transform Rosings from a cluttered jumble of antiques to at least bearable. Anne's contribution included four sets of decorations, recovered from storage, which Mrs. Langton had arranged to be installed over the next few months.

Darcy glanced up from the ledger to Elizabeth, who spoke in an animated fashion to Grace about some topic of interest as they walked across the great hall; she paused at times to place a hand on the side of her belly.

"Elizabeth!" he called before they could turn the corner. "Where are you going?"

Both ladies stopped and faced him. "Mrs. Langton sent word that the furniture for the drawing room was delivered this morning. Grace and I wished to see how it all looks."

"May I join you then?"

Elizabeth beamed in pleasure. "I would be happy to have you join us as long as you do not mind a discussion on embellishments and fabrics."

With a chuckle, he stepped forward, offering each lady an arm. "I believe I can bear it for a short time."

The sofa and chairs were back in their places when they entered the room, and Elizabeth grinned. "It looks wonderful!"

"She did not mention he brought the drapery as well," remarked Grace.

"Mrs. Langton indicated he brought in some help due to the size of the task. I believe he plans on the removal of the furniture from the music room next."

"I suppose it is a good thing Bingley's sisters will not join him. I suspect they would complain about the inconvenience." He appraised the room, pleased with the result. "Bingley will not care."

"I will not care about what?" An abrupt pivot revealed his friend standing just inside the door with Richard.

His cousin chuckled and slapped Bingley on the back. "I found him riding up to the front of the house and thought I would play the part of butler."

Darcy stepped forward and held out his hand. "Bingley? You did not indicate you would be here so soon."

Bingley shrugged. "I have had enough of my sisters at the moment, and I wished to get away. I hope you do not mind."

"I extended the invitation for you to join us at your leisure. You are welcome, of course."

"Excellent!" Bingley surveyed the room; his gaze paused on Grace to whom he offered an unabashed grin.

Darcy could barely suppress a roll of his eyes. Bingley always gravitated towards the prettiest unmarried girl in the room, and he appeared to have found her.

He gestured to Grace as she stepped forward. "Bingley, I do not believe you have met my cousin and Richard's sister, Lady Grace Fitzwilliam." His friend bowed with a wide grin as Richard circled around to stand beside his little sister.

"Grace, this is my friend, Charles Bingley. I believe you are more familiar with his sisters Miss Caroline Bingley and Mrs. Louisa Hurst. He will be leasing Rosings for the next year or two to learn about estate management."

Grace's expression was one of interest. "You hope to purchase your own estate?"

"I do. I had hoped to find one to lease next year, but when Darcy mentioned he had a property, I decided to begin straight away."

Elizabeth proceeded to quit the room. "If you will excuse me. I need to notify Mrs. Langton of our guest."

Before she could depart, Bingley caught her attention. "Do not go to any trouble. Just put me in a cupboard somewhere and I will be content."

"I think I can do better than a cupboard, Mr. Bingley," remarked Elizabeth drily, then left to locate the housekeeper.

Darcy suppressed his laughter at her remark, but his attention was yet again drawn to Bingley, whose eyes had returned to Grace.

"How long do you intend to reside here?"

"I hope to remain for some time," he answered, as he glanced back Darcy and Richard. "At least long enough to understand the workings of the estate."

"That could take years."

Darcy nodded in agreement to Richard's remark, while he regarded Bingley with a serious mien. "He is correct. I would not mire myself down in everything at once. I am certain Mr. Barrow will be pleased to help you along, and your experience in your father's business ventures will be to your advantage as you learn what is required."

Bingley positively radiated joy. "I am pleased that my background in trade will be beneficial!"

"You should not find such fault with your past, Mr. Bingley." Grace wore an almost scolding expression as her brother regarded her in surprise. Darcy raised his eyebrows and her cheeks pinked. "I meant nothing more than any business experience can be considered an asset. Father comments often how much he must handle the accounts and financial considerations for the estate. I believe Mr. Bingley's proficiency should lend itself well to that portion of the endeavour."

Bingley rolled up on his toes and back down as he continued to appear happy and eager. "I thank you for the vote of confidence, Lady Grace. I do hope I can live up to your expectations."

Richard failed to disguise a bark of laughter as a cough. In all probability, his cousin was considering Bingley's painful demise should he hurt his sole and younger sister.

The clock on the mantel chimed, and Richard looked to see the time. "I had not realised the hour. Grace, will you accompany me to the library, so I can tell mother and father I am departing."

Elizabeth re-entered the room. "I wish you did not have to leave us so soon."

"I am afraid I must. The regiment expects my return." He held out his hand, shaking Darcy and Bingley's hands. "If I do not see you before your confinement, I wish you well." He leaned over to kiss Elizabeth's cheek.

She nodded as she reciprocated the gesture. "You are welcome at Sagemore whenever you wish."

Chuckling, he pulled back. "I know.

"Now, little sister, I need to deliver you to our parents."

Grace gave him a quizzical look, but did not object as he led her from the room.

Darcy gathered Elizabeth's hand in his while he attempted to level a merciless stare at Bingley. "Mind your attentions to my cousin. Richard and Huntley will not be merciful if you excite expectations you do not intend to fulfil."

Bingley's eyes widened. "I was enjoying the face of a pretty woman, nothing more. They cannot fault me for that!"

"I request one more thing: that you consider your actions. If you decide you wish to call on her, then discuss it with my uncle, but do not give my cousins reason to call you out."

Elizabeth placed her free hand on her husband's arm. "Perhaps now would be a good time to mention we have a room awaiting you, Mr. Bingley."

"I am aware my behaviour with the opposite sex is sometimes rather forward," confessed Bingley. "I will check myself often, Darcy; I assure you."

"I ask nothing more."

Bingley clasped his hands and then, rubbed them together. "Well, Mrs. Darcy, do you have someone to show me to my room? I believe I would like to remove the dust and horse smell before I am tossed into the pond down the road."

A footman was summoned to escort Mr. Bingley to his rooms, leaving Darcy and his wife quite alone.

"You promised we would not remain much longer," she scolded in a modulated tone. He drew her into his arms and pressed his lips to her temple.

"And I shall keep my vow. We will remain a week, and not a day longer. Mrs. Langton has proven herself capable of carrying out your orders on the renovations, and Barrow is very capable of teaching Bingley how to run the estate."

He fingered an errant curl at her neck. "We shall return home where we will remain until we meet Georgie in Ramsgate."

"I suppose now we only need worry about Lady Catherine." She buried her head in his chest.

Darcy stroked her back as her shoulders lifted against him and dropped in an audible sigh. "She has not shown herself since Anne's funeral. Why do you believe she will cause trouble now?"

They had been fortunate Lady Catherine had remained so silent! The lack of response from her was out of character, but the peace had been too wonderful to question.

His wife's arms stole around his chest with the firm bump of their child between them. "She is not the sort to disappear without a word. You should warn your friend, then you and Uncle Henry should take a trip to the dower house to ensure she is not up to mischief."

Darcy drew back and regarded her with an alarmed expression. "Why would we want to venture into a pit of vipers?"

"She is not an entire pit of vipers," she said with amusement. "Only one; but if you do not seek her out, she will come here. I am certain of it."

Groaning, he wrapped his arms around her shoulders once more and pressed her close. "We scarcely have a se'nnight. I do not want to get her riled."

Elizabeth buried her head in his chest again and exhaled. "She has been riled since you married me in Anne's stead. Leaving her to her own devices will not change matters."

Lady Catherine had indeed been silent, but Elizabeth was proven correct when the woman presented herself at Rosings a mere three days later. Higgs, despite a scowl that betrayed his misgivings, showed the former mistress to the newly-decorated drawing room where she was guarded by a footman until the master, who was going over his ideas and plans with Bingley and Barrow, could be notified.

"What brings you to Rosings, Lady Catherine?" asked Darcy as he strode into the room. Bingley followed with Uncle Henry who had happened upon them as they were on their way to the front of the house.

Her eyes lit upon catching her first glimpse of Bingley. Darcy had given him the option to remain behind, but his friend felt there was no time like the present to put their initial meeting behind them.

"I see you still intend to pollute the shades of Rosings by allowing this *tradesman* to reside within its walls." She spit out the word tradesman with such distaste he expected Bingley to frown but instead was shocked to see him tilt his head and smile.

"I do not expect I will cause too much of a stench, and I do hope we can be agreeable neighbours."

Lady Catherine's eyes bulged. "Me? Be friendly with you? I think not."

Bingley chuckled and held out his arm. "Perhaps you would care to have a seat? I believe Darcy received some nice sherry from London last week, if you would care for some."

Darcy peered over to his Uncle, who appeared to be holding back laughter, then back to Bingley. When had he become so confident with someone so domineering? He had never been so with his sisters.

With a sniff of disdain, she turned to Darcy and ignored his friend. "I see Mrs. Langton showed your wife Anne's terrible choices in decoration. I am not surprised she was sentimental enough to use them.

"Although, I suppose your friend would not know the difference if something was dreadful or not."

Uncle Henry took a step forward and crossed his arms over his chest. "What is it you want, Catherine?"

"I heard you had redecorated, and I hoped to procure some of my belongings."

"Your belongings?" asked Darcy. "Every item you possess was packed and moved to the dower house."

She released a growl and pointed to a side table. "A gilded box once sat on that table; you have no doubt put it in storage. I want it returned to me."

He shook his head as the reason for her visit became clear. "That box had a small engraving that listed a de Bourgh ancestor. It is no more yours than it is mine."

"It has been mine since I was mistress of this house. If you are not using it, then it should be restored to me."

"It was returned to its rightful owner." He gestured around the room to indicate some of the paintings and the tapestries. "As was everything that was removed from the rooms that have been renovated."

"What?" shrieked Lady Catherine, but recomposed herself in an instant. "I never received the box. To whom did you give my belongings?"

"Mr. Preston de Bourgh came to retrieve them within a few days of our letter. I was very impressed with his prompt answer." He smiled at his Uncle Henry's agreement.

"He was elated our nephew contacted him." His uncle clasped his arms behind him and rolled back and forth on the balls of his feet. "Mr. de Bourgh was deeply obliged to acquire pieces that once belonged to his parents and grandparents."

Lady Catherine's expression was pinched, but to his astonishment, she did not yell. "He was not heir to this estate; my husband was the heir and had the right to leave it to whom he wished. Those pieces no longer belonged to the de Bourghs."

Darcy's hands clenched at his sides. "They were de Bourgh history; no one is more suited to maintain the legacy. We are not part of that family, and therefore, have less appreciation for those pieces. Mr. de Bourgh was the ideal choice.

"He had already contacted a few of his brothers, and they planned to split the heirlooms between them. Mr. de Bourgh even helped us sort through the attics and took a great deal of what was stored there, as well."

Uncle Henry glanced back and forth between Darcy and Lady Catherine. "I felt it a wonderful and caring gesture that our nephew restored their heritage to them."

Darcy waited for the explosion. They had been throwing sparks at the kindling for a while—a rather dangerous occupation—but Lady Catherine's livid face *was* rather amusing.

She opened her mouth, and he braced himself for the anticipated volume of her voice; however, the assault never came. Instead, the door opened and the ladies all filtered into the room.

"Catherine!" exclaimed the dowager. "Why do you appear as though you have been sucking on a lemon?"

His grandmother had an expectant, almost eager countenance, and he could not help but chuckle.

Elizabeth made her way beside him as she bit her lip, attempting to hold in her mirth. He took her hand, kissed it, and entwined her fingers with his.

"You should see the progress being made on the west drawing room." Aunt Elinor situated herself in an armchair near the fireplace. "The work is coming along well. Anne's choice of colour was an inspired one."

The lady sniffed but refrained from making a critical remark. What was happening? Why was she so reserved?

"Lady Catherine, would you care to join us for tea?" asked Elizabeth, much to his dismay.

His grandmother motioned to the seat Lady Catherine always occupied when she resided at Rosings. "Have a seat, Catherine. Lizzy needs to get off of her feet, but she would never be so rude as to do so while you still stand."

Lady Catherine opened her mouth as if to speak, but no sound came. Instead she peered around at everyone, ending with Huntley, as he strode through the door.

He flinched when he noticed her presence, averted his eyes at once, and took a seat next to his mother. "The servant you sent informed me we were having tea, Mother, yet I arrive and there is no tea, or even a cake, of which to speak. Are you having sport with me?"

The last was spoken at almost a whisper, and Darcy began to cough in order to hold back his laughter.

Grace giggled. "Sit, please, and give the servants a few moments. The refreshments will arrive to your satisfaction soon enough."

His grandmother was still watching Lady Catherine with an unrecognisable glint in her eyes. "You may as well have tea with us before you return to the dower house."

Why was she insisting Lady Catherine remain for tea? Her arguing was enough to ruin anyone's appetite.

But his unspoken wish was not to be granted, and he was forced to be polite when the imperious lady gave a small huff as she seated herself in her favourite chair.

"I suppose by the time I return it will be too late for tea."

Darcy glanced down to Elizabeth, who smiled without a hint of surprise. What did she know that he did not? They were aware of something, indeed!

Several servants entered with the tea service, and the family began to chat while they had their repast. He kept an eye on Lady Catherine, who remained haughty, but different somehow.

Bingley had seated himself to her right, and attempted to initiate a conversation. Leave it to Bingley to attempt the impossible! Darcy's attention was then called back to Uncle Henry, who asked his plans for the holiday, and so, forgot to check back and ensure Bingley was not being drawn and quartered.

Elizabeth's wide grin in their direction was the impetus that returned his attention to Lady Catherine, who now spoke with Bingley. She appeared to be doing her usual pontificating, but he interjected his points and held his own.

Lady Catherine remained for an hour complete after tea, and rose when the clock struck. "I should return," she announced to the room.

Elizabeth stood and motioned to a servant posted near the door. "We are pleased you could stay. I shall call for a carriage to drive you back."

The old woman's face appeared incredulous. "You will?"

After the remainder of the family stood and bid Lady Catherine goodbye, a smiling Elizabeth held out her arm for Lady Catherine to precede her towards the door, and Darcy sprang from his seat to follow. He did not trust his wife to a woman who had been so angry with her in the past.

The servants brought Lady Catherine's outdoor garments as Mrs. Langton stepped forward with an ornately-carved wooden box in her arms. Elizabeth took the item and presented it to Lady Catherine.

"We found some correspondence you must have saved in a desk in the library. Mrs. Langton commented that your husband had purchased this box for you as a gift when Anne was born, so we placed anything we felt belonged to you within."

"As you should." Lady Catherine's voice was imperious, but not condescending. "I will notify Mrs. Langton should I notice any of my correspondence is missing."

Elizabeth exhibited very little reaction; she smiled and nodded.

Good Lord! He would have to increase the housekeeper's wages should Lady Catherine become too demanding!

His wife attempted small talk as they waited for the carriage, and the elder lady gave a few curt answers. At the sound of the horses, Lady Catherine did not say goodbye or wish them well; she simply climbed inside and rode away.

"I do not understand what just happened."

"The footman, who took the job as butler in the dower cottage, told Mrs. Langton that Lady Catherine has not had a visitor in the last fortnight. She has dressed each day and waited for someone to call, but no one has shown."

"Do you mean to tell me she sought us out for company?"

She could not be serious! The idea that Lady Catherine would seek companionship amongst her own family was preposterous, but Elizabeth bobbed her head up and down to indicate he was correct.

"I assumed she had come to argue over something! I never would have imagined that was her purpose."

"Which is why we joined you when Mrs. Langton informed us she had called. From what I understand, even Mr. Thacker has abandoned *her* to pay court to *you*."

"Pay court?" He could not stand the obsequious little toad of a man, and he despised the way the parson would sidle up and agree with everything he said.

He could not help but smile when a small giggle erupted from her. "He wants you to love him. And how could you not?"

Darcy shook his head, took her hand, and drew her closer. "I should make you pay for such a remark." Her eyes widened as he grinned.

"Servants are about, and we should join the others."

He wrapped an arm around her back to steer her in the direction of the drawing room. "I shall have to have obtain my retribution when we retire, then."

She stopped and pressed a finger to his chest. "No tickling, Fitzwilliam."

He grinned, and led her through the doors of the drawing room where Bingley was seated beside Grace. Huntley was in a chair across from them, staring Bingley down over the edge of his book. Darcy released an exhausted exhale. He had managed to eject one worry from his house and in exchange, was confronted with another.

Bingley had best know what he was doing!

Chapter 24

Darcy stared unseeing at the account books he had worked to complete since his return to Sagemore. He despised the time involved to finish the work that collected while he was away, but he had enjoyed his time in London, and later at Rosings, with Elizabeth. Her performance at Rosings had been admirable, and with Bingley's help, she would have the house prepared for him to take residence.

Bingley was another matter. It had become apparent that Bingley had decided he was more than a little interested in Grace, and before their departure, requested Uncle Henry's permission to court her. However, since Bingley was spending Christmas at Sagemore, they would begin their courtship when he returned to London for the season.

He glanced out of the window in the direction of the river. Where would his wife be at that moment? His old business had been completed, and it would not hurt matters to delay his current business for one day. Smiling, he rose and made his way to the entrance hall where he met Mrs. Green.

"Do you happen to know where I could find Mrs. Darcy this morning?"

"The mistress insisted on walking out, sir. Her maid and I both prevailed upon her to remain within the house and walk the halls, but she would hear none of it." She lifted a hand to point at him. "Mark my words! With all of the rain the last few days, her petticoats will be six inches deep in mud!"

He was amused by her chastisement rather than affronted, since it was well known that his housekeeper liked his wife; her outspoken behaviour in this instance was due to concern rather than spite.

"I am certain she does not intend a lengthy walk. The weather is too cold today for a long ramble."

His housekeeper's eyebrows lifted along with her tone. "I would not be so sure. She changed into one of those older dresses she owns—the one Hattie added the extra material to the hem. She has already been gone nigh on half an hour."

"I hoped to spend some time with her this morning." He motioned to a footman for his coat. "I shall hunt her down and ensure she has not overdone it."

Mrs. Green's eyes lit up, and her face erupted into a wide smile. "Oh! Bless you, sir! You would put my mind at ease for certain. And, when you return, I shall have a warm bath awaiting the mistress along with tea, chocolate, and some of the biscuits cook baked this morning."

"I am certain she will be most appreciative, Mrs Green." The housekeeper nodded and bustled for the servant's stairs.

He shrugged on his great coat and chuckled as he headed out of the door. Mrs. Green had been ecstatic when she noticed Elizabeth's condition, and had been very solicitous of her mistress' needs. Her initiative had been appreciated, but after three days of rain, Elizabeth had been cooped up far too long and began to chafe at the restriction of the indoors. The showers had not been heavy so, while everything was still wet, the mud would be no hindrance to her escape from the confines of the house.

Elizabeth had almost never strayed from the island since their return unless she was visiting Page. He surveyed the property from the front of the house and did not find her, so with a brisk step, he set off for the stables.

When he entered the front doors, Johns was standing to one side, speaking with a groom, but he motioned towards the back where Page was housed.

Nodding, he made his way in that direction but slowed when he heard the soft sound of Elizabeth's voice.

"I have missed you, boy. Yes, I have."

Her tone was better suited to cooing to a baby rather than speaking to her sizable horse, and he had to bite his lip to refrain from laughing.

"Mrs. Green was trying to keep me indoors, but after three days of rain, I had to take a walk to come see you. Did you miss me?"

He stepped around the corner and expected to see her, but she was not in his view. Instead, he found her just inside the stall door where she scratched Page up and down his large white blaze and under his chin.

"If I had known you wanted a dog, I would have found you one small enough to fit in your lap."

She started and placed a hand to her chest. "I do not require a dog, thank you. I am perfectly content with Page; I will have enough in my lap when the baby is born."

He opened the stall door. "Mrs. Green is very concerned. She all but shoved me out of the house to search for you."

Elizabeth gave an unladylike growl. "She was none too happy with the idea of me out in this weather. I believe she stated it was positively glacial outside."

"She wants nothing more than to ensure you and the babe are well."

"I doubt the babe is aware of the weather from inside my body, and though it is a bit nippy, it is not unpleasant."

"The barn does help with the temperature outside."

"Of course!" she exclaimed, as she placed her hands on her hips. "I walked around the house for a quarter hour and then came to see Page before I walked a bit more. She must think I am quite insensible."

Page nudged her back, and Elizabeth pressed a kiss to his nose before she exited the stall.

"Elizabeth, she cares for you very much." He could not help but feel she was being unfair. "I have it on good authority she has had nothing but the highest praise for you."

"And whose authority might that be?"

"My steward has heard it mentioned when he ventures into the village. She feels fortunate to have such a mistress."

"She is bound to be relieved you did not wed Miss Bingley."

He laughed and drew her forward by her hand. "I am certain she is, and I am also certain her knowledge of that lady has made her all the more appreciative of you." His wife sighed and allowed him to draw her into his arms. "It is not in your nature to be so unforgiving. What is the matter, my love?"

She shook her head and snuggled herself a bit closer. "I just wanted to escape the house, and she and Hattie kept trying to persuade me to stay inside. I became so frustrated, so when you took up her cause, I became angry."

"I knew why you wished to take a walk." With a finger under her chin, he tilted her face upwards so he could see her eyes. "When I

335

found I had time, I decided to seek you out, so we could walk together."

Her eyes lit up, and she began to grin. "That would be delightful. I hoped to make another circuit around the island on the river path before I returned to the house." He took her hand, entwining their fingers, and led her out of the stable and across the bridge. They had just veered off onto the trail when a carriage pulled up behind them and Bingley alighted.

"I say, Darcy. I had not expected to find you taking a walk through the muck."

He peered at Elizabeth just as her shoulders dropped. "Elizabeth needed some fresh air after three days of rain. We thought to take a ramble around the island, but we will make our way back to the house. I am sure you would like to refresh yourself."

Bingley lifted a hand before Darcy could step forward. "No need to abandon your stroll for me. I am capable of showing myself to the house, and I have every faith your servants will rise to the occasion.

"The trip was rather arduous, and I will require some time to put myself to rights anyhow. You do not have to wait on me."

Elizabeth shook her head. "But it would be rude of us not to accompany you."

Bingley laughed, stepped forward, and bowed over Elizabeth's hand. "If we were at the house, we would greet one another, and I would be whisked upstairs by your housekeeper before I could muddy the floors. This is no different. Please continue your walk."

"You are certain?" asked Darcy.

"I am no child, and I am in no way offended."

After they shook hands, Bingley climbed back into his carriage for the short trip to the front entrance.

"I feel as though I am being rude by not accompanying him."

He smiled and tugged her along with him on the trail. "Bingley has become more like family over the years than a friend, and he may very well be family soon. He meant what he said, so let us take our stroll before we return." With one last glance at the departing carriage, she wrapped her hand around his arm, and fell into step beside him.

Darcy adored the intimacy that arose as they walked. Sometimes they spoke of the household or their family, sometimes of books or music, but their usual practice was to immerse themselves in the views around them and only to speak on occasion.

Today, Elizabeth commented more on the few animals present along the way, but did not say much else. He hoped she was not still upset with Hattie and Mrs. Green, and that she would not be cross with either upon their return.

In the end, he had no reason to fret. His wife did not utter a single sour word to the housekeeper, even if she did catch the older woman scrutinizing her petticoats and muddy boots, the latter of which they were made to remove before they ventured to their chambers.

He escorted his wife to their rooms, but she paused within his to kiss him with ardour. "Do you wish to bathe together?"

His surprised reaction prompted a giggle. "I would by no means suspend any pleasure of yours, my love, but I will dismiss James first. I would not like him to be present as is his wont when I bathe."

"I will have Hattie help me remove these muddy clothes, and I will meet you in your dressing room."

She disappeared through the door leading to her room while he marvelled at his luck in his choice of wife. Grinning, he departed to find his valet in order to dismiss him until he was called.

"I must thank you for inviting me for Christmas." Bingley rested his glass on his leg as he took in the library. "I was not anticipating the return to London and Hurst's home."

"I should think not," commented Darcy. Elizabeth had fallen asleep after their bath, and he had dressed to return to his study until Bingley appeared, which was about an hour later. They decided to catch up over brandy, allowing his wife the much-needed rest.

"I do feel a bit de trop. You must be sure to inform me if you and Mrs. Darcy wish for time alone. I can make myself scarce with ease."

Darcy smiled as he situated himself in the comfortable chair. "We are quite capable of secluding ourselves within our rooms if we wish for solitude. You will not disturb us."

Bingley took a sip of his brandy. "Your aunt ventured to the house a few times after your departure. She is an entertaining old cat."

"I believe the family consensus is harridan, but I suppose cat would work."

"She may have been once," observed Bingley, "but she took tea with us twice the week after you departed. She does not strike me as manipulative like Caroline."

"I would have you take care. I have never known her not to have some manner of agenda."

"But what does she have to gain anymore? Her daughter has passed. You have made it clear she is not to interfere in Rosings, else she will be banished to a 'respectable' neighbourhood in London." He shook his head. "I think she is defeated and lonely, but I will keep her past behaviour in mind."

Darcy examined his friend. "To be honest, I was amazed with how well you handled her. Why have you never behaved as such with your sisters?"

With an amused smirk, Bingley gave a shrug. "I suppose because they *are* my sisters. Louisa was not always catty, but was a loving older sister when we were children.

As for Caroline, she was always alone when she was young. Louisa cared for her, as well, but they attended different schools. I think father viewed it as an opportunity to obtain wider social connections.

"Whilst she was away, Caroline changed. I have maintained hope that she might say or do something to indicate she is still the same person as when she was young, and I suppose is why I have given her such a free rein."

Darcy placed his glass on the side table. "When does she wed?"

"Before the New Year, but she is angry with me for pressing her to choose; thus, I am not invited." Bingley's eyes expressed his pain, and Darcy pitied him.

"Perhaps one day, she will realise it was as much for her own good as yours."

A wry chuckle escaped Bingley's lips as he became fascinated with his empty glass. "I doubt it. I suspect she will attempt to reconcile once she has heard of my courtship with Lady Grace, but I will not allow her to manipulate the situation for her own gain."

"Good!" Grace knew Bingley's sisters and was not fond of them in the slightest. Darcy was relieved Bingley acknowledged the possibility

338

they might attempt to elevate themselves through her if the courtship led to marriage.

"I do not know how your finances stand, but if you are interested, you could lease Rosings Place."

"Lady Catherine's house in town?"

"Anne's—now mine, but yes, Lady Catherine claimed it as if it were her own.

"Should you marry Grace, you would have a place to live when you are in London, rather than at my uncle's."

Bingley gave the matter some thought, staring out of the window at the rain-soaked garden.

"I believe I will take you up on your offer. I know Caroline will try to insinuate herself back into my life, but I wish to distance myself from her as much as possible." He shook his head as he adjusted his cuff. "I had enough of her scheming prior to Bath, but her manipulations there were the straw that broke the camel's back."

Darcy agreed, and they spent the remainder of their time in a discussion of the lease and Bingley's plans, until Elizabeth appeared an hour later.

Early Christmas morning, Elizabeth woke with a start due to the unceasing movements of the baby, which also prevented her from falling back to sleep. She did not wish to disturb Fitzwilliam, so she moved to the sofa beside the fireplace. With her feet tucked under her dressing gown, she settled in to read her book until she found herself being kissed awake some time later.

"Why are you sleeping on the sofa?" he asked between kisses. She opened her bleary eyes and shifted closer to him.

"The baby would not allow me to sleep, so I came over here to read." The open book in her lap was only a page or two further than her last stopping point. "I must not have read for long."

He placed his warm hand across her stomach, his fingers splayed and his palm pressed flush against her shift for a few minutes before he began rubbing in circles.

"Very quiet now."

"Seems to be." She spoke in soft tones as she relished the look of adoration he bestowed upon her belly. He leaned in and grazed his lips against hers.

"Happy Christmas, my love."

She grinned as she wrapped her arms around his chest. "Happy Christmas."

"If you let me rise, I will fetch your present." Fitzwilliam had the boyish grin on his face she found so endearing.

"You wish to exchange gifts now?"

"I am certain Bingley has a gift for us, just as we bought a gift for him, but I thought we would not want to bore him by making him watch us exchange our presents to one another."

He disappeared into his dressing room for a few moments, and returned holding a rather large package, which he placed in front of her.

"What could I ever require that is so large?"

"Open it and I will explain." He placed a hand on her back as she leaned forward and pulled the ribbon binding a length of fine muslin.

"I thought you could embroider it for a shawl or a gown for the baby."

"It is beautiful, thank you." She released the last bit of the knot, which held everything together, and eased the fabric off of a large, carved wooden box.

"I found a gentleman who makes these in London. I told him your love of nature and he described this." He pointed to the intricate flowers inlaid upon the lid. "I have seen you with letters from your family, locks of their hair, and a few other keepsakes, all scattered around in different places. I thought you could keep them together in here."

"It is beautiful." She wiped a tear from her eye and ran her fingers along the details on the lid. "How did you think of it?"

"I offered to have mourning jewellery made for you, if you recall." She nodded and squeezed his hand.

"I did not want you to go to such an expense. Charlotte was kind enough to gather the locks before the funerals, and I am content to have a small part of them. I also had not wanted to be covered in mourning jewellery."

He lifted her hand to kiss, but she placed it on his cheek and drew him down to press her lips to his.

When she drew back, she opened the lid to examine the different compartments. "It is exquisite. I just do not know where I will put it."

Fitzwilliam pointed to a place on the sofa table behind them. "I thought here, so when you want to view its contents, you have all the privacy you could desire."

He drew something out of his pocket, and placed it in her palm. "Your Uncle Philips enclosed this in his last letter to me and asked me to hold it for today."

She closed her fingers around the folded paper and held it for a moment, tracing her finger along the seal before she broke it and unfolded the page with care.

14 December 1811
Meryton, Hertfordshire

Dearest niece,

I hope you have not waited long for this letter. After I read your latest missive to your aunt, I felt the need to tell you how pleased we are to know you are happy and well.

Putting you in the carriage with Mr. Darcy was one of the most difficult things I have ever had to do, and I berated myself for weeks after your departure. Had I done what was best? Would you have been better off journeying to one of the Canadas? Those questions were nothing to the sheer panic I felt at times wondering whether Mr. Darcy was as good a man as he seemed. Those weeks we were in Brighton and did not correspond were the most difficult. I felt so helpless—what if you should have had need of our aid?

Despite how well these schemes appear to have succeeded, I owe you an apology for my inability to protect you as I should—for waiting as long as I had to inform you of your uncle's machinations. I have felt guilty for allowing you to be forced into a decision that should not have been made with such haste and for you to be compelled to marry a man you did not know and did not love.

I have come to know your husband through my correspondence with both you and him since our return to Meryton, and I am impressed with his character and intelligence. I am even more impressed with you, dear niece. Your strength, compassion, and kindness are shown in all your actions and words. I feel your father looks down upon you with a proud smile much like my smile when I read your letters.

You did what was necessary at the time and proved yourself an incredible young woman and wife. It is not difficult to discern the love and pride your husband has for you and his excitement for the arrival of your child. He is positive you will be an excellent mother, and I can only echo his belief.

Your aunt and I pray for a safe confinement and a healthy baby. I am certain my wife will write you before the end of the week, but I am also positive her letter will be nothing but gossip.

All our love,
Bertram and Edith Philips

Elizabeth wiped a tear that had fallen to her cheek. She would need to pen a letter to Uncle Phillips when she managed a free moment; she wished to thank him for his words and to absolve him of any guilt he might retain. The decisions that had brought her such happiness should no longer bring him pain, as they were made and made for the best. Her husband pressed a handkerchief into her hand and she chuckled.

"Perhaps I should begin to carry them in my dressing gown."

He wrapped an arm around her. "If your letter was similar to mine, tears are warranted. He has harboured a great deal of guilt all these months and is relieved to find things as they should be."

"He says as much." She held out the page for Fitzwilliam, and gave him enough time to read it in its entirety.

"He is correct. I am very proud to be your husband. I also feel we have been remiss in not paying them a visit for so long. After all, they are all the family you have remaining."

"They understand why we have not been to Meryton," she soothed. "Uncle Gardiner seemed a risk in the beginning and then, once we had him sorted, there was Anne's death."

"But we could go now, before your confinement."

She frowned and shook her head. "I want to see them, but I do not wish to travel until after the baby is born. We have been away from home so much since we were wed, and I just wish to remain where we are until we are forced to leave."

"Perhaps on our trip from Oxfordshire to Ramsgate, we can break our journey in Meryton. They would be pleased to see the baby."

"Aunt Philips would be thrilled to have us visit with the baby. She and Uncle Philips were never blessed, and she has fawned over every baby born into our family. We all had special shoes, hats, and gowns she would sew for us."

"Then it is settled," he agreed in a triumphant tone. "We will venture to Meryton this summer. Would you like to pen them a letter and ask if they have an objection or should I?"

She drew his face down to bestow a lingering kiss upon his lips. "I will write them." She then placed a small peck to his nose. "Thank you."

"Why do you thank me?"

"Your care for me and my family. I would imagine some might wish to ignore the connection."

He frowned. "I would be heartless to commit such an offense against a beloved wife."

"Which you are not." She put a hand to her back and made to stand. "I should retrieve your gift from my dressing room."

"Do you require any help? Books can be rather heavy if there are many in the package."

She turned and regarded him with curiosity. "Books?"

"Yes!" Her husband was far too smug, and she waited for the explanation that was certain to be forthcoming. "I found a very large number of books in your dressing room at Ashcroft House. I assumed they were my Christmas present, so I let them be; however, I have no wish for you to hurt yourself or the child lifting something so heavy."

"How kind." Her voice dripped with sarcasm, and she had to bite her bottom lip to hold in the gales of laughter threatening to escape. He could be so haughty when he wished! "I am certain I can handle the weight, but thank you."

He frowned, and she waddled to her dressing room, smiling to herself; however, the trunk she had used to store his gift proved to be awkward.

"I may require your hand after all."

Fitzwilliam leapt up, grabbed the handles, and carried the small trunk to where they were seated.

"Elizabeth, this is your small trunk. I do not understand."

"I thought it would be more attractive than the wooden crate in which it was delivered. Hattie and I also found it easier to conceal in the luggage on our trip to Rosings and return to Sagemore."

He made no move to open the clasp, but instead, stared at the trunk with an odd expression.

"Will you not open it?"

"There are no books inside, are there?"

Her teeth bit her bottom lip once more as he studied her reaction. "Why do you assume so?"

"The trunk is far too light for the number of books I espied in your dressing room." He appeared so confused, and a giggle escaped before she could swallow it back down.

"As I said before, will you not open it?"

He started and gave a quick smile. "Oh… of course." With a release of the clasp, he lifted the lid. His eyes widened, and he reached inside to stroke the object within with reverence.

"Where did you purchase this?"

She beamed and pressed herself to his side. "In London. Richard found a man who *he* claims makes the finest saddles in England. Whilst you were at your solicitors one day, he accompanied me to the man's workshop, and assisted me in making the order."

He fingered the skirt of the saddle where a small Darcy crest was hand carved into the leather, and then grasped it around the pommel and the cantle to lift from the trunk to his lap. His hand stroked across the rich leather of the seat before returning to the crest.

"I have never seen someone put their family crest or shield on their saddle in such a manner."

"The man who made it learned to carve leather in Spain in his youth. Most gentlemen purchase the saddles he has on display, but I requested this one be made for you. He asked if I wished to embellish it as it was made."

"It is wonderful." He reached over and claimed her lips with passion. "I cannot believe you went to so much trouble."

She laughed as he set the saddle aside and shifted her onto his lap. "It was really no trouble. I only asked Richard and Huntley if they had any unusual ideas for your gift, and placed the order."

344

He scattered kisses over her eyes, nose, and finally her cheeks. "Thank you."

"You are welcome." She gave a small giggle. "May I ask why you were so certain the books in my dressing room were your Christmas gift?"

He put a hand over his face and groaned. "I am ashamed of my pride earlier. I was so certain, was I not? You must have thought me insufferable."

She held her fingers about an inch apart. "A mite bit conceited perhaps."

With a self-deprecating shake of his head, he hugged her a bit closer. "What were those books if not for a gift?"

"They were for your grandmother, aunt and uncle, and your cousins. Did you not peek at the books I had hidden?"

"I confess I had not. I only glanced at the two on the top of the stack before I heard Hattie, and hurried back to our chambers."

"Then you missed the copy of *Cecilia* for Grandmamma.[1]"

"Most definitely! I must have seen your gifts for the men since I am sure Grace would be receiving another novel."

"Perhaps I bought her Wollstonecraft's *A Vindication of the Rights of Woman*."

His eyes bulged and his jaw dropped, eliciting a round of giggles from her. "Alas, I did not."

His shoulders dropped and he exhaled in relief. "Grace has enough notions from Grandmamma without adding more fuel to the fire."

She began to laugh outright, and he regarded her with a wary eye. "Why are you so amused?"

"I may not have purchased the Wollstonecraft, but your grandmother did."

He let out a bark of laughter. "At least Uncle Henry will not write me a scathing letter for giving her such a book. Poor Bingley!"

She pinned him with a furious look despite the fact she was not at all angry. "Do you imply a woman cannot be as intelligent as a man or they should not be educated to the full extent of their abilities?"

His face lost all traces of humour. "Elizabeth, you are fully aware that one of the things I love most about you is your intelligence, and

I have always encouraged you to expand your mind through extensive reading. I would never treat you as inferior, as you well know."

She allowed a hint of a grin to show, and he exhaled heavily. "You are too unkind! On wrongs swift vengeance waits.[2]"

"A man should never be ashamed to own he has been in the wrong.[3]"

"Most unfair! You have selected the portion of the phrase useful to you and disregarded the remainder." He became smug and quirked his lips upward. "A woman, especially if she have the misfortune of knowing anything, should conceal it as well as she can.[4]"

She gasped with mock affront and replied with a smile and arched eyebrow. "What are men to rocks and mountains[5]?"

With a laugh, he leaned in for a kiss she bestowed willingly, allowing her lips to cling to his for a moment. When he drew back, his forehead remained pressed to hers. "I suppose we should dress for church, so we do not leave poor Bingley waiting."

"He is not so poor," she whispered.

He picked her up and placed her feet on the floor. "No, but he will be poor for company if we abandon him."

"We would not be all that late." She stood on her toes and caressed her lips against his neck.

"Why must you be so irresistible?"

George Darcy sat alone in his study long after Georgiana had retired for the evening. He stared at his glass of port as well as a letter he held before him.

Catherine was now aware of the entail, which bothered him. He did not care to have his personal business bandied about as gossip, and Catherine's mouth was far from silent; however, her knowledge of his financial affairs was not what put him in such a melancholy mood this evening, rather it was her revelations about his son. Fitzwilliam had taken control of Rosings, and the boy had not been timid in the slightest.

For all his disappointment, he found he was proud of his son for his stand against the formidable Lady Catherine, yet he could not tell him. Fitzwilliam would be in Oxfordshire with his wife.

His wife! He lifted a spare copy of the false marriage license he had retained after their confrontation in London. He had thought to find a different scheme, but after reading the letter, he could not do it.

Catherine described his son as bewitched and besotted. She still proclaimed her dislike of the young lady, but in reading between the woman's diatribe and disparagement, he detected a bit of a grudging respect. The new Mrs. Darcy had stood her ground with Catherine as well.

The ultimate revelation was Elizabeth Darcy was with child. His son would be a father come spring, if Catherine's calculations were correct. He would be a grandfather!

Yet, he would *not*. He would not be welcome to be of service to his son during such a time nor would he be allowed to see his first grandchild. What sort of grandfather did that make him?

What would they tell his grandchild about him? Would that child come to resent him in the same manner Fitzwilliam had?

Georgiana already regarded him with such sadness. He was certain she was aware of most of the disagreement, but of how much, he had no idea. He was thankful for her continued care and love despite her knowledge of his transgressions. He did not deserve her forgiveness.

Christmas at Pemberley had been celebrated as the holiday always had—with the exception of Fitzwilliam's absence. His son might not exude the liveliness of George Wickham, yet the elder Darcy missed his son's quiet, yet thoughtful presence. Until this year, Fitzwilliam had never missed a Pemberley Christmas; the day was not the same without him.

He picked up the forged marriage license, stared at it for a moment, and then tossed it into the fire. He would bestow the only Christmas present Fitzwilliam would desire—no further interference in his life.

---

1 The title of Pride and Prejudice is said to be from a line in Cecilia, "The whole of this unfortunate business," said Dr. Lyster, "has been the result of pride and prejudice."

2,3 Alexander Pope

4 Jane Austen, Northanger Abbey

5 Jane Austen, Pride and Prejudice

Chapter 25

Darcy looked up from his work to take in the bleak, bleary day outside. Winter had passed with a wet chill that never abated; yet Elizabeth still insisted on walking whenever the weather was passable enough to venture out of doors. Her determination to exercise could not be deterred; yet, his concerned appeals ensured she remained within the confines of the island. Her visits to Page were not as often as she wished, so he always took the time to accompany her when she walked as far as the stables.

Elizabeth's waist expanded as the time flew by. The initial swell had not been of excessive size, but since Christmas, the bulge had gradually grown until her gait was more of a waddle than her usual graceful stride.

She never complained of discomfort, yet the additional weight had to be taking its toll. The girth of her ankles and feet had expanded along with her waist until the sight of her once shapely legs made her husband wince. They had to hurt!

Today, they expected his grandmother, who would remain with them for the next few months. He was grateful for her offer to aid them through this time. Elizabeth would require a motherly figure in the birthing room, and his grandmother's willingness to fill the role pleased him; the two ladies had developed such an intimate bond since their initial meeting almost a year prior.

He never dreamed he would meet his wife in such a manner; however, he was thankful for the crises that led them to save one another. It was still difficult to credit that in May they would be wed a year!

Elizabeth emerged from a cluster of birches and, satisfied by her appearance, his attention returned to his ledgers. She would walk the gardens closer to the conservatory now that she had made a circuit around the house.

Darcy stared at the books without seeing the numbers before him for a while before he closed the book, grabbed a letter beside him, and left his study to search out his wife. When he came upon her, Elizabeth had not moved far from the birches and was meandering through what would be a bower of roses trimmed with lavender come May.

Her face lit with joy as she noticed his approach. He could *never* question her love for him when he was welcomed with such happiness. She was beautiful and had such a softness about her in her present state.

"You came to accompany me?"

"I did," he responded. "I could not concentrate on the books any longer. I had to join you."

She strolled underneath an arbour and peered around the edge in a flirtatious manner. "Am I such a distraction, Mr. Darcy?"

He laughed in delight, and dashed behind her to wrap her in his arms. "I would prefer to spend all of my time in your company, but alas, I do not have that luxury. Someone must oversee Sagemore and Rosings lest we be relegated to the hedgerows."

A joyful giggle erupted from her lips as she turned to face him. "I hear Mr. Bingley does well with his courtship."

He held a letter he had received this morning before him. "I received this express just after you departed for your walk."

Elizabeth bit her bottom lip and took the missive from his hand. "It is unopened!" she exclaimed, surprised.

"I thought it may be welcome news; I planned to save it until your return." He stroked the velvet softness of her rosy cheek with his knuckles. "But, I could not abide waiting. Shall we go to the library and read it before the fire?"

"I must appear cold." Her eyes narrowed with suspicion. "Or, has Mrs. Green pled her case for my protection from the unforgiving elements?"

He shook his head. "No, I plead my own case. Your nose is quite red, and your cheeks are a lovely pink hue…"

"If they are lovely, then perhaps we should remain out of doors a little longer." She wore his favourite mischievous expression, which would, no doubt, captivate him for the rest of their lives.

His palm stroked over where their child was safe within her womb. "I could rub your back and your feet whilst you read the letter aloud."

"Are my feet and ankles truly so dreadful?" She leaned forward as though she were attempting to catch a glimpse of her toes and giggled. "I cannot see them, so they must not be there."

He took her hand, and then led her to the terrace and through the doors to the library, where he rang the bell. Mrs. Green bustled in and collected Elizabeth's outdoor garments, but not before expressing her relief that Mrs. Darcy was once again indoors and away from the frigid chill of the outdoors.

"I will have some refreshments sent in right away, sir," said the motherly housekeeper, as she exited the room.

After Elizabeth settled herself on one end of the plush sofa, Darcy lifted her feet to set them in his lap. He handed her the letter, and then set to work removing her boots, which he placed on the floor beside him.

Deep red lines were pressed into the turgid skin from the seams of her half-boots. His fingers grazed the angry flesh as he wrapped his hands around her feet and began to knead his thumbs into the arch.

She rested the side of her head against the back of the furniture and sighed. "I will be unable to read if you put me to sleep."

He chuckled. "Then perhaps you should hurry."

She broke the seal, unfolded the page, and turned it in several directions as though she could not read it. "His handwriting is atrocious."

"He smudges and blots many of his words, does he not?"

"He does! How do you decipher this mess?" She drew the paper back and then brought it closer.

"If you can make out just a few words, sometimes his meaning becomes clear." Her doubtful expression made him grin.

"10 March 1811
Rosings Square, London"

"He has moved into the house in London, then?" The paper was folded down, and she peered over the top.

"Bingley installed himself not long after his return to town. His sisters have been banned from the home, so he does not entertain."

"He banned them?" she asked, incredulous.

"Miss Bingley, rather Mrs. Harper, is a married woman now, and her husband has his own home in London. Bingley has made it clear neither she nor Mrs. Hurst will impose upon him there. They will not be allowed to use Grace to forward their social ambitions."

"Grace would not tolerate them, but I am glad to see Mr. Bingley standing up for himself in such a fashion." Her attention returned to the letter as she squinted her eyes and bit her lip. A sudden lift to her eyebrows indicated she made out Bingley's poor penmanship, and she began to read.

"Darcy,

"You are to read the ramblings of a happy man. Grace has finally done me the honour of accepting my hand. I know I am ridiculous—as if I have been waiting years rather than months—but my angel has said yes!

"Your uncle had a bit of sport with me when I asked his permission, but I suppose it was to be expected. I look forward to becoming a part of your family. Huntley still views me with a wary eye, but I believe once Grace and I are wed, he will accept me as you and Lord Matlock do already.

"I hope you will not be offended when I say, I do not wish to wait any longer than necessary to make Grace my bride. We have set a date for two months hence, and we would wish for you to come, yet we understand your presence may not be possible. Please do not feel obligated should it still be too early to travel, or should Mrs. Darcy feel uncomfortable leaving the babe at Sagemore.

"I look forward to bringing my bride home to Rosings—at least until I purchase an estate of my own. I must thank you again for the lease of Rosings, as well as the house in town. I would not be in a position to marry without them.

"Best Regards,

"Charles Bingley, Esq."

He set down one foot and proceeded to begin with the other. "He sounds in his cups."

"Can you blame him for imbibing when he is so joyous? He was likely drinking brandy with Uncle Henry and Huntley and wrote this as an afterthought." She pressed her palm to the side of her bulge. "Would you care to travel to London for the wedding?"

He started from an image of Bingley drinking brandy with Huntley and Uncle Henry. "Oh… no, we will be travelling soon enough when we journey to Ramsgate. I do not wish to unsettle the babe too soon. Bingley and Grace will understand."

Elizabeth tilted her head as she observed him. "You could always go without us. The staff… "

"No!" he exclaimed. "I will not."

With an earnest expression, she reached out to barely touch her fingers to his shoulder. "I did not intend to upset you. It was merely a suggestion."

He placed her foot down upon the cushion and shifted forward to cradle her face in his hands. "I have no intention of parting with you unless it is necessary. Do you understand?"

"I do." She leaned her cheek into his palm. "I do not want you to go, but I also would not wish to hold you back."

Darcy rewarded her statement with a short but passionate kiss. Mrs. Green's return prevented him from repeating the gesture and forced him to return to his previous position. Once their refreshments were set on the small table before them, he handed his wife a cup of chocolate and a biscuit.

"My place is by your side," he affirmed. "I would not be happy travelling without you."

"I love you, too."

Her willingness to have him travel without her was a sacrifice he appreciated, but she needed to understand that he had no desire to leave her. He could not leave his life and world behind in Oxfordshire.

Elizabeth studied him as she took a sip from her cup, and he gave a shuddering sigh. "Are you well? I did not want you to have regrets over missing the wedding of your friend and your cousin."

"I do appreciate the gesture, but please understand my unwillingness."

"I *appreciate* your unwillingness." Her smile was not forced, but more amused. "I desire nothing more than to have you by my side."

Their disagreement solved, they partook of their refreshments and then Elizabeth received her long-awaited back rub. She fell asleep long before he was finished so he made a quick trip to his study to retrieve his books and papers. The library had a perfect spot for him to work as she slept nearby.

The sun's rays came in at an angle through the windows as the afternoon progressed, and he accomplished the work he set out for the day while Elizabeth remained on the sofa covered with a warm rug.

Darcy closed the journal where he kept track of his plans and the items he had completed and gazed at his wife, who was lightly snoring. The sound brought their first carriage ride together to his mind, and he smiled at the remembrance. He continued to stare until a familiar voice startled him from his reverie.

"I do not imagine you get much work done in such an attitude." His head snapped around to where his grandmother stood with an amused expression on her face.

"I did not wish to leave Elizabeth whilst she slept." His voice was low so as to not wake his wife. "I have completed my work for today."

She entered the room, and he embraced her. "You were not greeted by anyone at the door?"

"No, I was, and I was informed that you and the sleeping Mrs. Darcy were in the library. I did not wish to be announced, as I was certain the noise would wake Lizzy, and she requires the rest." She drew back, tiptoed over to Elizabeth, and carefully moved a curl from her face. After studying her for a few moments, his grandmother returned with a pleased expression.

"She appears hale and happy, even whilst she slumbers."

"She has been very well. The midwife was pleased when she visited last." A chuckle escaped his lips and his grandmother looked at him askance. "The midwife said Elizabeth was not like most of the fainting ladies of the house and should weather the birth well, as long as there were no unforeseen complications."

Her lips formed a thin line. "I see the fear in your eyes, Fitzwilliam. Do not begin fretting now. Otherwise, you will do her no good when her time comes."

He swallowed hard and then cleared his throat in a futile attempt to dislodge the lump that had arisen. "I know you are correct."

"Yes, I am," she affirmed. "Now, pour me a brandy. I have been cooped up in a carriage all day and could use some refreshment." She sat in a wingback chair and took her glass when it was offered.

He took a seat near Elizabeth's head as his grandmother sipped her drink. Had his grandfather ever introduced her to cigars? A small snort escaped at the thought.

"What amuses you?"

"It is nothing, Grandmamma. I assure you."

She gave an exasperated sigh. "I am in no mood to speculate, so out with it."

One lip tugged upwards as he shifted in his seat. "Did grandfather ever teach you to smoke cigars?"

The dowager countess scoffed. "Of course not! I am a lady and would never smoke such a vile thing." She brushed a bit of fluff from her skirt. "Besides, he said he did not want me to smell of the dining room after the ladies left."

He chuckled, but eyed her with suspicion, assuming there was more to the story than she was divulging.

"I will not tell you more, so do not stare so!"

Chuckling, he took a sip of his drink. "Yes, grandmamma."

"You should know I brought your cousins with me. They wished to refresh themselves before greeting you." She spoke in a casual manner, not as though she had brought unexpected guests. "Huntley was not having much luck this season, and their mother has lost all patience with him. Richard only has a fortnight away from his regiment, but he does hope to be here for the birth. He wishes to be of assistance to you."

"The midwife believes the end of the month or the beginning of April."

His grandmother peered at Elizabeth's bulge and lifted her eyebrows. "Another three weeks?" she asked sceptically.

"Yes, why?"

She shook her head and took another sip of her brandy. "No reason. No reason at all."

Elizabeth sat across the table from Darcy at dinner. It had been five days since the arrival of his grandmother and cousins, and she had borne their company well. Tonight, her appearance was not out of the ordinary, except that she was quiet—too quiet. Not so much as a word had left her lips during the first two courses, and she pushed the food around her plate as though she were attempting to discern the most appealing arrangement. She was not eating.

His grandmother appraised her from the seat to her left. "Lizzy, you are rather dull this evening."

A forced smile resembling a grimace appeared upon his wife's face. "I apologise, Grandmamma. I do not feel well. Perhaps I should excuse myself. I do not wish to be rude."

"Dearest, I was not intimating you should leave." The elder lady took Elizabeth's hand. "However, if you would feel more comfortable in your chambers, I will accompany you and aid you in becoming settled."

"That may be for the best." Her pale countenance and easy acquiescence made his stomach clench.

His concern rising to the fore, Darcy began to stand, but Elizabeth stayed him. "I am well. I simply have no appetite, and my back aches. Be assured that Grandmamma will be of great assistance to me, whilst you remain as host to your cousins."

"Are you certain?" He glanced to Huntley and Richard who were both attending to the conversation. "They *are* able to amuse themselves."

"We *are* in the room," interrupted Huntley.

She grinned, but again, the expression was not genuine. "I am well aware of the fact they can amuse themselves, *and* that you are within the room."

Darcy rose to help her to her feet. "Richard, Huntley, I will return in a moment." It did not matter whether they agreed or not, he would escort his wife to her rooms.

With his grandmother trailing behind, he led Elizabeth from the dining room. They came to a halt at the foot of the stairs when she bid him pause. "You are not well."

"I hurt." She placed her hand to her back kneaded her fingers into the flesh. "My back usually aches, but not like this."

With a touch to Elizabeth's abdomen, his grandmother's expression changed to one of concern. "How long have you been in such pain, Lizzy?"

"Since late this morning."

"Why have you not said something sooner?" The urgent tone of her voice brought Darcy's stomach into his chest.

A tear made its way down Elizabeth's cheek as she looked to the older lady in alarm. "I did not think it was anything out of the ordinary."

Mrs. Green bustled in from the servant's hallway, and the dowager turned to her. "Please send for the midwife."

His eyes widened. "Do you truly think?"

The dowager shook her head. "I do not know, but I do not want to deliver this child if it is." Using her thumb to work upon Elizabeth's lower back, she asked, "Lizzy, is there no pain in your belly at all?"

Elizabeth peered between them. "The pain in my back wraps around to my stomach, but it is not as the midwife described." She put her hand to her abdomen and flinched.

With a firm grip on his wife's elbow, his grandmother gave him a significant glance. "I think it is time to get you upstairs."

Darcy wrapped an arm around her back and walked Elizabeth towards their chambers. They reached the door and, suddenly, his wife bent over with her hand again at her abdomen, sucking a breath between her teeth. When her distress passed, he helped her straighten, but she wore a strange expression.

"Fitzwilliam?" She lifted her skirt a few inches to reveal her now wet slippers.

His grandmother's strident voice commanded his attention. "Do not faint, Fitzwilliam! Return to your cousins and allow me to handle this."

The lump in his throat bid a hasty retreat as he gulped it down. "But... I cannot leave her."

"You paled at the sight of her waters. We do not have time to attend you, should you swoon."

"Elizabeth?"

Her weary eyes locked with his. "I love you."

"I love you, too."

"Good," she replied breathlessly. "Then leave me with Grandmamma and return to Richard and Huntley."

"But they do not need me..."

A weak chuckle escaped her lips. "Grandmamma brought them to keep you busy whilst I laboured, so allow them to be of use." She took a deep breath and exhaled. "You turned ashen upon seeing my wet slippers. I do want you with me, but I know Grandmamma is correct."

An unforced wry grin appeared upon her face. "Think upon it as me saving your reputation. What would your cousins say if you fainted?" His grandmother began to chuckle, and he shook his head.

She reached up and bestowed a sweet kiss upon his cheek. "I love you, but I cannot remain in the corridor." Her expression was hopeful when she drew back. "I will see you when he arrives?"

Darcy nodded as he once again swallowed down the bile that had risen in his throat; his wife had disappeared through the door.

His grandmother stepped forward. "You must remember she will be well—she and the child."

With a slight tremor, his voice cracked as he tried to speak. "You will not leave her?"

"I swear to you, I will remain by her side for the duration."

His grandmother followed his wife into her bedchamber, and closed the door behind them. The solid oak panel remained closed and did not reopen though he remained, rooted to the spot, for several moments. Why should he not be allowed inside? His relegation to the dining room or the library with his cousins was maddening! Those were the last places he wished to be!

Despite his upset, he did make his way back to the dining room, where he was received with a hearty welcome.

"Thank goodness you have returned!" exclaimed Richard. "Knowles would not allow the next course to be served until you were back."

A plate was set before him, but he did not see what was placed on the fine china. His physical being was in the dining room with his cousins, yet everything within him remained in the corridor outside of his chambers.

Huntley waved a hand before his face to garner his attention. "I heard Grandmamma sent for the midwife. Is it time?"

Richard glanced in Darcy's direction and snickered. "I would take his preoccupation as a confirmation, brother. I must say, I am relieved. Lizzy has looked miserable as of late, and I had begun to worry she might go longer than I can remain."

"Do you think I cannot keep him distracted enough on my own?"

A snort erupted from Richard and he began to shake with mirth. "You would drown him in port and brandy until he was rendered unconscious!"

Huntley became affronted. "I most certainly would not! Why do you always paint me as such a disreputable character? I happen to know many of your unsavoury exploits!"

"As I know yours, brother dear. I am sure we could paint one another with a most unflattering brush."

"But I do not accuse you of behaving with dishonour!"

Richard balked and stood. "I never…"

"Enough!" boomed Darcy. "If this is how you plan to distract me from Elizabeth, then you may leave me to my own devices! I do not intend to pass the next day listening to you both bicker as boys in your short pants!"

Both cousins had the sense to appear ashamed, and Richard returned to his chair. "I apologise, Darce. I will wait to lump my brother's jolly knob until after the child is born."

He sighed and glanced down at the dish. "I cannot eat."

A look of concern crossed Richard's face. "She could labour through the night. You must eat something."

With a grimace, he pushed the plate away. "Please tell cook there is nothing wrong with the meal. I am certain it is wonderful, but I lack the appetite."

The footman removed the dish. "Yes, sir."

Huntley held his fork aloft. "You will not mind if we eat our meals, will you? We would like to carry out our duties with aplomb."

Darcy's lips quirked up at his cousin's absurdity. "Please finish your meal. I shall not be offended." He reached for his glass of wine and took a sip. "As you said, it will be a long evening."

Five hours later, Darcy was pacing the library while he awaited word on his wife's condition. Mrs. Green had been down several times to inform him all was well, and that Elizabeth was progressing as expected. Yet, Elizabeth's health could not be confirmed with his own eyes, so he fretted.

"You will wear a hole in the rug if you continue," remarked Huntley. He was not yet in his cups, but he had made a concerted effort to become so over the last five hours. Richard had enjoyed his liquor but had not imbibed to the extent his brother had. Darcy could feel his eyes upon him as he continued to stride back and forth.

After deciding he had waited long enough, he began to move towards the door but an arm dragged him back. He turned to glance behind where Richard had grabbed hold of his arm to tug him towards the chair he had occupied earlier.

"Release me." His voice was harsher than he intended, but he would not be restrained.

"Grandmamma will fetch you when you can see her. In the meantime, you must remain with us."

"I will ask you once more to release me, Richard," he growled as he yanked his arm away from his cousin. "I do not wish to harm you."

Huntley sniggered and took a swig of his port. "My wager is on Richard. Sorry, Darcy."

Richard grasped his arm, this time around the bicep, and pulled. "You will not hurt me. Sit down, and I will get you a glass of port."

He tried to remove his arm from Richard's grip, but his hold was too firm. His cousin pivoted to ascertain why he had not moved when Darcy clenched his fist and delivered a brilliant blow with his right hand to Richard's jaw.

His cousin hit the floor with a thud, and Huntley began to guffaw. "I did not think he had it in him!"

Darcy was free and therefore not concerned that Huntley rose from his chair in an attempt to aid his brother who was rising from the rug. He made to return to the door when Mrs. Green entered with haste.

"I apologise for the interruption, but sir, we are in need of your assistance with the mistress."

Something within his chest lurched with fear. "Is she well?"

"She is, sir. The midwife asked her to rise to take her place in the birthing chair, but the pain in her back is so intense, she cannot stand. You are the only suitable person to request for help in this instance."

He gave Richard a smug expression as the man rubbed his jaw with a grimace. "I am that, Mrs. Green. Please lead the way." The housekeeper preceded him to their chambers and through to the sitting room where she glanced inside. Why had she not continued?

"I thought I was needed?"

"You are, sir, but the midwife was insistent that I not bring you in whilst your wife was having a pain."

The room ahead quieted with the exception of his grandmother's voice, which was soft and full of praise. When he entered, Elizabeth was curled onto her side, pale and drenched with sweat. Without waiting for instructions, he made his way past Mrs. Green and dropped to his knees near the edge of the bed.

"Elizabeth." He spoke softly and caressed her arm to gain her attention.

"Oh! Fitzwilliam!" Her arms wrapped around his neck as the damp from her hair wet his cheek.

Darcy's arms engulfed her in a fierce embrace, yet he remembered his task and moved one arm under her knees in order to lift her. With a gasp, her body tensed when he stood. Her eyes fluttered with exhaustion and the lines upon her face spoke of her pain. How could she take any more?

He peppered numerous kisses on her crown and curls while he carried her across the room to the birthing chair. He murmured in her ear, "I love you so much."

"I love you, too," she sobbed. "I am exhausted. I do not think I can do this."

He pressed another kiss between her eyebrows. "You are the strongest woman I know, Elizabeth Darcy. You *can* deliver this baby. I have faith in you." Before he could place her in the seat, her body went rigid and her hands gripped him with a force he had not expected.

"Hurry, sir." The urgency in the midwife's voice carried through the sound of Elizabeth clawing his coat and the blood pounding in his ears. "Place her in the chair and then you *must* leave."

With great care, he set his burden in what appeared to be the most uncomfortable wooden chair he had ever set eyes upon, but she refused to release him. Instead, she began to cry out as she grasped and pulled at his cravat.

The midwife stepped forward with her arm outstretched towards the door. "It is time you left, sir."

He gestured to his throat where Elizabeth had not relinquished her grip in the slightest. "I cannot."

"That is it, Mrs. Darcy!"

His wife's face contorted in pain as she twisted his cravat, restricting his breathing. He glanced up to seek help but instead, his grandmother chuckled.

"You are laughing?" he choked out.

With a snort, his grandmother shook her head. "You are not even blue yet." She reached across, removed Elizabeth's hand from his cravat, and began to speak to her over her cry.

"Mr. Darcy!" The midwife glared, and he reluctantly drew himself up from Elizabeth's side.

The room was entirely too hostile! He removed himself with all due haste and strode straight to the library, where Huntley and Richard watched as he made his way to the crystal decanter to pour a full snifter of brandy.

"Darce?" said Huntley with reticence. The brothers both stood and came to stand to each side of him.

He took a deep breath and brought the glass to his lips in an attempt to drink the entirety of its contents. After three gulps, Richard wrested the brandy from his hand, which then spilled down the front of his cravat and waistcoat.

Huntley leaned forward and placed a hand on his shoulder. "She must be close if they needed help to move her to the birthing chair?"

A loud cry echoed from the direction of the stairs and Richard's eyes widened. He then brought Darcy's glass to his lips and took a large swig. "We should have James bring you a change of clothes. You cannot meet your child stinking of liquor."

James appeared soon after with the much-needed change of clothes and had Darcy dressed and returned to the library with haste; a new glass of brandy was clenched in his hand as he posted himself by the window, staring out into the darkness.

The wait felt like hours, but according to the clock, he only stood before that window for another hour complete before his grandmother entered the room. He attempted to ascertain the outcome by her expression, but she revealed nothing.

"You are wanted in your chambers, Fitzwilliam."

Chapter 26

Darcy did not wait but a second before he tore out of the library as though something chased him for dear life. He took the stairs two at a time and raced down the hall until he reached the outer doors to their sitting room, where he halted and took a deep breath.

How was Elizabeth? His grandmother surely would have said something had the birth not gone well!

He had discarded his topcoat soon after he donned it, but gave his remaining waistcoat a shaky tug before he opened the door. The room was empty, so he moved to the entry to his chambers, giving a tremulous breath as he turned the knob.

The dark oak of the door swung open, and his gaze was immediately drawn to the bed, where a radiant Elizabeth lay with a swaddled bundle in her arms.

Mrs. Green approached and gave a swift curtsy. "Congratulations, Mr. Darcy. Please ring if you require any assistance."

He nodded as he continued to stare, entranced, at his wife. Despite her damp hair and her exhausted appearance, she was beautiful. Her hair was drawn back into a plait, but a few unruly curls had escaped the confines of the arrangement, framing her face. Her skin glowed and her cheeks were rosy, which confirmed her immediate health.

She peered up and beamed with happiness. "Will you not join us?"

His shoes were kicked into the corner, and his waistcoat discarded as he rushed to the bed. Eschewing the chair placed to one side, he sat upon the edge of the mattress as she stroked the babe's cheek with her finger.

She winced as she leaned in his direction, and he tilted in to meet her. "I would like you to meet your son." His eyes darted down to the child and back to her. She grinned and nodded as if to confirm her words.

He held his breath as the baby was deposited into his arms with care, and he peered down upon the small bundle, which was a bit larger than he had anticipated. He stared without a word, unable to remove his gaze from the marvel before him, until Elizabeth's voice brought him back.

"Fitzwilliam?"

He caught her eye and broke into a smile as his frantic heart calmed and his eyes stung with tears. "It is no wonder you were miserable, my love. He is considerably larger than Georgiana when she was born."

"He is handsome, is he not?"

His gaze traced his son's eyelashes, his nose, and his lips. His son favoured him. "I believe he resembles me far too much to be considered handsome."

Elizabeth shook her head and chuckled. "And I believe he is so very handsome due to his resemblance to you." She patted the spot beside her. "I would like you to hold both of us in your arms if you are able."

With great care, he adjusted himself beside her and wrapped his arm around her shoulders, so she could cuddle to his side; her head rested against the side of his chest with one hand touching the precious bundle in his other arm.

"Have you given thought to a name?"

Elizabeth had been adamant that she would not choose a name until she laid eyes upon their child. How else would they know if the name suited?

"I thought to ask you the same question. I would be pleased to call him Fitzwilliam."

He lifted his eyebrows as his eyes widened. "I have never cared for my name. Please do not insist upon it for our child." He peered down to his son's angelic little face." I felt we should name him for your father."

She tilted her head so it would be easier to observe him. "But you never met my father."

"That hardly signifies." He frowned. He need not have made Mr. Bennet's acquaintance to respect him! "He raised and educated you; he created the woman I love and the mother of my child. That alone deserves my respect and admiration."

A tear dropped to her cheek as he pressed his lips upon her loose curls.

"I was so worried whilst you laboured." His eyes burned and his voice cracked with emotion as he pulled her closer.

"I believe it was better you were not at my side. After all, you were here only a short time, and I attempted to strangle you." She blushed and bit her lip. "Please forgive me."

A tiny bark of laughter escaped his mouth. "You were in terrible pain and not responsible for your actions. Do not feel as though you should apologise."

She drew his head down and claimed his lips. "I love you, and I am sorry you had to wait in suspense."

"I will admit to not being so averse to the idea after helping you to the birthing chair. I attempted to drown myself in brandy when I returned to the library."

Her eyes were wide and her jaw agape. "Did you really?"

"I did." He pulled her a bit closer, prompting her to wince. "Richard wrested the glass from me and spilled brandy down my suit."

She giggled and gazed at him with an adoring expression. "I thought I detected a slight smell of brandy, but I thought you drank it—not wore it."

He closed his eyes and laid his head atop hers. "So, what about a name for this not so little man? I still wish to name him for your father."

"Thomas Aaron Bennet was his name," she replied. "We could use a portion if you wished rather than the whole?"

"I believe Thomas Aaron Bennet Darcy suits him well. Do you not think so?" He gazed at his son's face, taking in the chubby, dimpled cheeks, the dark swath of hair that adorned his crown, and his little lips that moved as he suckled in his sleep.

His attention was diverted back to his wife, who sniffled beside him.

"I imagine it will, once he has grown into it."

"You miss them today, I am sure."

"When he was born, my first thought was of you and how excited you would be, but my second was of my family. I had a fleeting thought of who would notify them."

"Oh, my love!" His arm gave her a gentle squeeze. "They know and are joyful for us. I am certain."

"I miss them." She gave a shuddering breath and wiped her cheeks. "Please do not think I am unhappy with you, but I do miss them."

"It is natural to long for them. They were your family." One side of his lips lifted. "Even when you mimic your mother, I know you loved her and it is part of how you remember her."

His wife gave a quavering laugh. "I do miss her. She was silly, loud, and sometimes embarrassing, but she was still my mother. I remember how she held me in her arms when I broke my ankle. She did rant and rave that I had no compassion for her nerves, but when Mr. Jones wrapped my leg, she held me close. Of course, she began her complaints again when he was finished."

His arm could not release the possessive hold of her shoulders. If only her mother could have been there for her today. "I know they are not the family who raised you, but there is an entire clan of Fitzwilliams and three Darcys who adore you."

"And I adore them. The two Darcy men in particular."

She yawned, and he relaxed, relieved she was exhausted but well. "You should rest. You were adamant you would feed this little man yourself, and I am certain he will be punctual in regards to when his meal is due."

Her grin was still evident as her eyes drooped. "Perhaps a short nap," she murmured as she drifted off to sleep.

Elizabeth jolted awake at the sound of Thomas' loud complaints, and rolled over to find him in his great grandmother's arms as she walked about the room.

"How long has he been awake?"

"He woke a half-hour ago, but I think he desired someone to fuss over him for a while. After all, every man wishes for a woman to fuss over him, do they not?" The dowager cooed as she said the last to the baby.

Elizabeth held out her arms and her son was passed into her embrace. He sought out the nipple offered and was soon nursing steadily, producing a rhythm of even gulps as her milk let down.

The elder lady took a seat upon the edge of the mattress. "His appetite has increased since he was born."

"It has. I can scarcely believe it has already been a fortnight."

"You seem more assured than you once envisioned." The dowager settled an appraising eye upon her, and Elizabeth nodded.

"I am. Everything is much simpler than I imagined it would be."

Thomas' great grandmother looked with pride at her newest grandchild. "He is a good baby."

"I am a very fortunate mama." She turned her gaze to the dowager and reached out for her hand. "I am very lucky to have you as well."

The dowager attempted to wave off her praise, but Elizabeth was adamant. "I have always called you grandmamma, but in my mind you were always Fitzwilliam's grandmother. Whilst I laboured, I came to realise that I had ceased thinking of you in terms of my husband, and had come to think of you as my grandmother too."

Her grandmother's eyes flooded with tears as she reached over to hug her, minding the babe between them.

"How dare you make me cry! I have a reputation to uphold." She withdrew and used her handkerchief to wipe her damp cheeks.

"Thank you for being of such help to me the day Thomas was born. I love you, Grandmamma."

"I was happy to be of service to you, dear. With the difficult time you had, I was relieved you had a woman you knew—even if I have not known you for years."

"You were of immeasurable aid. I was aware that the process would be painful, yet I had not expected it to be as severe as it was."

"My sister's birth was much the same, and she braced herself for the next labour, which turned out to be a pittance in comparison."

A corner of her lips lifted. "So the next child may not be the trial that Thomas was?"

"Precisely!" Grandmamma grinned. "However, I am certain you find him worth the pain and effort."

She laughed and stroked his downy cheek. "If you had asked me whilst I laboured, I might have given you a different answer, but now that he is in my arms, he was worth every bit of misery I endured. I suppose I understand a bit of my mother when she said we knew not how she suffered."

Her grandmother chuckled and leaned forward. "I will now come to your aid if you wish to escape your confinement."

Elizabeth shook her head. "I should be thankful to leave this room for a short time, but Mrs. Green would be apoplectic, and Fitzwilliam would fret."

"Finish nursing Thomas, and I will help you dress. Then you can sneak down the servant's stairs and take a short walk around the gardens. The sun is shining in a near cloudless sky, and it is a warm day for April."

She bit her lip and studied her grandmother. "Very well, but if I am caught out, I will blame you."

The dowager beamed. "I have large shoulders. Do not worry on my account."

After Thomas' back was patted, and he returned to sleep, she rose from the bed and stretched. Her grandmother helped her put on one of her simplest gowns, styled her hair, and aided her in slipping on her boots since she was still a tad sore.

She tiptoed down the servant's hallways undetected until she startled the cook at the door to the kitchens. With a finger to her lips, she brought her hands together as if praying, begging for her silence, to which the heavy-set woman responded with a giggle and a bob of her head.

The freedom of walking in the garden was wonderful after being cloistered in her room for so long. The feel of the cool breeze on her cheeks, the sound of the birds chirping, and the warmth of the sun radiating upon her skin all lifted her spirits; however, she did remain close to the house, taking a path behind a stone wall to shield her presence from Mrs. Green.

Her fingers grazed along the petals of a rose as she strolled around the corner and startled at Fitzwilliam, who leaned against a tree before her.

"Have you made your escape?" His brows were drawn over his narrowed eyes.

"Only for a short time whilst Grandmamma minds Thomas."

"I thought she had something to do with this rebellion against the midwife's instruction."

"I cannot remain abed in that room for a month complete, Fitzwilliam! I would die of boredom." He raised his eyebrows in a silent challenge. "Very well! I would not die, but I needed to stretch my legs. I never planned to go any further from the house.

"I would have brought you out of doors had you asked. I knew I would be forced to spring you from your captivity soon, but I did not imagine you would venture out on your own."

"Please do not be upset! I only walked here from the kitchens."

He drew her into his arms. "I only ask that you do not leave our rooms by yourself. I could not bear it if something happened, and you were outside alone."

"I feel stronger every day, and despite what the midwife says, I need to walk. I ache so when I am confined to the bed."

"Then allow me to escort you, my lady." She placed her hand upon his proffered arm, and they fell into step as they continued along the path.

"I had a letter from Georgiana this morning."

"I noticed it in the stack of post. Did she impart any interesting information in this missive?"

She smirked at his question, but shrugged. "I am uncertain what to make of her letters as of late. Have you noticed anything amiss?"

His forehead furrowed, and he paused a moment to ponder the query before answering. "I cannot think of any reason to fret. What alarms you?"

"Her letters are brief, which is unusual as they are usually lengthy, and she does not seem as open—as if someone is monitoring her correspondence." She paused and placed her other hand on his bicep. "Is it possible your father discovered our friendship?"

"I do not believe so, else we would have had a letter from him, and Georgiana's correspondence would have ceased. Is that all you have noticed?"

"She has not mentioned us meeting in Ramsgate in the last few missives."

"We have planned our arrival and have given her the dates. Perchance she does not see a reason to mention it."

"Fitzwilliam." She pulled on his arm to stop him. "She has been so excited that she has mentioned at the closing of every letter how she looks forward to Ramsgate. I do not think that would change, yet it has."

"Would it ease your mind if we arrived at Ramsgate a few days early as a surprise? We could plan our arrival for the day my father departs."

"I do," she affirmed. "I cannot suppress the feeling that something is wrong."

"I will attempt to elicit a confession of what the problem may be in my next letter, but there is little else we can do until June."

She sighed and leaned against his arm as he continued towards the house.

"Can I tempt you with our comfortable bedchamber?" He waggled his eyebrows, eliciting a giggle from her lips, but when he opened the door, Mrs. Green stood just inside with one of the maids. The housekeeper turned and her eyes bulged.

"Mrs. Darcy!"

With a start, the muscles in her back stiffened. "So much for a successful escape," she muttered under her breath.

"Not to worry, Mrs. Green." He passed over his hat and gloves, and took Elizabeth's hand. "I will have her returned to bed immediately."

The housekeeper disappeared into the servant's corridor, and Elizabeth's shoulders lowered. "She did not have an apoplexy as I suspected she would."

"Let us return to our son; I will keep you company for the remainder of the day. You may laze about in our sitting room if you like, and I may challenge you to a game of chess."

"I did not think you ready to lose again so soon."

His resonant laugh carried down the hallway. "I might surprise you by winning this time, Mrs. Darcy."

She rolled her eyes with a grin. "I doubt it, Mr. Darcy. I sincerely doubt it."

Darcy gazed across their carriage as his wife nursed their son, who was greedily suckling at her breast, while she hummed a soft melody and stroked the soft curls that peeked out from beneath his bonnet. Nothing was more beautiful than the two people he loved most in the world!

Two wonderful months had passed since his son's birth. Those months had possessed ups and downs that they had navigated as best they could. The deprivation of sleep some nights taking its toll on his work during the day; however, Grandmamma had been correct when she said most new parents bungle through it to the best of their ability. One question was taken and solved at a time as they forged the road they wished to take.

One obstacle had been Elizabeth's inability to produce enough milk to meet Thomas' growing demand. She approached the problem with as much logic as she could muster, but, while she gave the impression she was at ease with the solution, she had not borne it well at all.

Yet, they had been fortunate. Tenants, whose wives were still nursing their own children, stepped forward to offer their help until a wet nurse could be obtained. Elizabeth continued to feed their son and was able to produce enough for three good feedings a day, so the tenant's wives each ventured up to the house at their designated time to help.

For Elizabeth, the plans were easier to make than implement, and he had to console her when she could not bear to watch Thomas feed from another, holding her as she sobbed. With time, she became accustomed to their new situation and, after a fortnight of inquiries, a permanent wet nurse was procured. Elizabeth still wished to do her share, and he could not deny her what gave her such happiness.

"Your Papa has such a serious stare," she said to Thomas, as he watched her intently. "Do you think he looks to find fault?"

His lip quirked into a crooked smile. She once confided she had misunderstood his stare when they were first acquainted. She had thought he observed her to find fault, and now took great pleasure in teasing him about it. "I can assure you I do nothing more than take in the beauty before me."

"Flatterer!" Her eyes twinkled and her smile was radiant; his heart warmed at the sight. God, he loved her—her and their son! There was nothing he would not sacrifice for their happiness.

Her gaze dropped to Thomas as she unlatched him from her nipple and brought him to her shoulder, his head lolling to the side as he slept. "He has taken the carriage ride better than I expected. I was worried he might cry the entire journey to Hertfordshire.

"I do hope he does not keep Aunt and Uncle Philips awake all night since he has slumbered the day away."

He chuckled as she put her chemise, corset, and gown to rights, so she was covered before she began to pat his back.

"I do not expect they will mind." He pulled out his pocket watch and checked the time. "We should be drawing close to Meryton. If you pivot to the side, I can help you button your gown."

"You would make a proficient abigail," she teased.

"Not too proficient." He laughed as his fingers trailed up her back between buttons, and she gave a small shiver. "I would be more suited to aid you undress than to say, prepare you for dinner. I much prefer to disrobe you than to see you hidden beneath all these layers."

"Behave, Mr. Darcy."

He pressed his lips to the juncture of her graceful neck and shoulder. His last feather light kiss grazed the curve of her ear. "You prefer it when I misbehave." He grinned at the gooseflesh that erupted down her shoulder and back as he whispered in her ear.

She turned back into his arm, enabling him to claim her lips. "Do you think he had his fill?"

He smiled at the lax bottom jaw and the milky drool, which escaped onto a rag on Elizabeth's shoulder as the sound of her steady pats to his back reverberated around the cabin.

"I am certain he would make us aware if he were not satisfied."

The tips of his fingers skimmed along Thomas' pudgy little arm, and he leaned down to bestow a kiss to his tiny fist. "I want to have your portraits painted."

Elizabeth's brow drew together with a small crease between them. "Thomas is so young. Do not expect him to be content for the time it would take an artist to capture his image."

"I know you are correct, but I do not want to forget the two of you as you are now. He will grow, much as he has the last two months, and one day he will be a man—long before we are prepared for such an event.

"He has already grown so." Her voice was wistful as she sighed. "I do wish him to be healthy and to grow, but I want to savour this time with him."

His heart swelled with pride at her caring nature. He was a fortunate man indeed.

The carriage passed a familiar building, and with a swift peck on his wife's forehead, he moved to his seat across from her. She passed Thomas to him while she donned her gloves and her bonnet, and when she was finished, he shifted their son back to her arms.

They made a turn before they reached the village and small creases formed on Elizabeth's brow. "Where are we going?"

"You will see."

A loud gasp sounded from her as they took the fork in the road, and she stared down over the edge as they drove by. "Fitzwilliam, you cannot mean to go to Longbourn? Mr. Collins would not welcome us there. He once had a feud with my father over some matter or another, and the two never spoke again. I fear that is why he was so unreasonable when he took possession of the estate."

They rounded a slight corner, and the grey stone house came into view. Elizabeth had described her childhood home in detail, but his insides quivered at seeing a place so close to her heart. The equipage came to a stop, and short squat man exited the door, bowing in a grovelling fashion.

Elizabeth's brow furrowed. "He is not Mr. Collins."

When the door was opened, Darcy stepped out and helped Elizabeth alight, a hand at one elbow and another poised at her hip should she require help as she held Thomas, and brought her to stand before the man.

With a polite bow, he then was forced to wait as the stranger rose from his obsequious and overdone gesture of greeting. "You are Mr. William Collins, I presume."

"Mr. Darcy! I am excessively pleased to make your honoured acquaintance!"

Poor Elizabeth still had a crease between her brows as she stared at the man before them, but Darcy continued as if there was nothing amiss. "Mr. William Collins, I would like to present my wife, Mrs. Elizabeth Darcy."

"Ahh! Yes, my dear cousin. I am inordinately pleased you could stay at my modest estate. I am in great anticipation of hosting you whilst you visit the area."

Her head whipped to Darcy and back to Mr. Collins, who she regarded with wide eyes. "Your estate? But I made the acquaintance of a Mr. Isaac Collins, the heir, before I left Meryton."

"You have met my esteemed father." The pitch of Mr. William Collins' voice rose as his hands made a sweeping gesture to his chest. "I am afraid he is no longer with us, bless his soul. He passed away—not long after you departed Meryton as I understand it."

Philips had mentioned it in his letters, but the information had not been passed along to Elizabeth for fear of upsetting her. Darcy had also begun the plans for this surprise months ago, and his wife would have questioned why Isaac Collins was hospitable all of a sudden.

"Oh, I am sorry for your loss. Please forgive me if my questions upset you."

"Not at all," he gushed, again bowing his head as he spoke. "I understand your stay here was to be a surprise from your esteemed husband, so he likely withheld the information in order to increase the effect of his gift."

Darcy bit his lip as Elizabeth gave a nod. Her gaze turned to him, and the merriment that danced within expressed her amusement without words. She found Mr. William Collins as foolish as he did.

"I must express my satisfaction in your condescension upon my humble estate, but of course, what am I thinking? I should first invite you inside, should I not? Forgive me for such a grievous oversight! By all means, please follow me to the parlour. I am certain Mr. and Mrs. Hill have made arrangements for your servants."

An older woman approached them both to take their hats and coats, but she did not give more than a welcoming dip of a curtsy to him while she bestowed a brilliant smile upon his wife. Elizabeth grinned and greeted Mrs. Hill, who discreetly tried to peek at Thomas before she gave a swift curtsy and departed.

They were then shown into a small parlour where Elizabeth scanned the room with an eagerness he did not see often. They both took a seat, and Mr. Collins eyes set upon the baby.

"Do you not have a nurse for the child? I have been told by several amongst the highest circles of society that the only proper way to raise a child is a competent nursemaid and governess." He backed himself into a wingchair by the fireplace. "I was ordained as a clergyman and was considered for several lofty positions before my father passed. I have even made the acquaintance of your aunt, I believe, Mr. Darcy."

"My aunt?"

"Why yes! The estimable Lady Catherine de Bourgh! I will be forever grateful for her benevolent condescension."

A peek to his side revealed Elizabeth to be biting the inside of her cheek, while Thomas was fast asleep and blissfully unaware of the idiotic little man who was too fond of his own voice.

"Her benevolent condescension?" Elizabeth's voice gave a slight crack, and she cleared her throat.

"What was I thinking? Of course, you would desire refreshments after such an arduous journey! Hill!" He rang the bell, but Hill had anticipated him by arriving with a full tea tray before he could return to his seat.

Once she had arranged everything to suit, Mrs. Hill approached his wife. "If you will pardon me, Mrs. Darcy, but when we heard there was to be a babe, we prepared the nursery for him. I would be pleased to lay him down for you whilst you take your tea."

Elizabeth smiled with a warmth usually reserved for him and Thomas, and stood to hand their son to Mrs. Hill.

"Have Mary and Hattie arrived?"

"Yes, ma'am, and I will ensure the nursemaid is aware he is in the nursery."

She gave a last caress to the baby's head. "Thank you, Hill."

The housekeeper made her way from the room, and Elizabeth resumed her seat. "I apologise for interrupting you. You were saying Lady Catherine had bestowed condescension?"

Mr. Collins startled. "Well yes, she did! I was a candidate for the living at Hunsford, and she was a most gracious host."

Elizabeth lifted that one brow. "Lady Catherine allowed you to stay at Rosings?"

"I was given an exceedingly comfortable room within the servant's wing." He wore a smile ridiculous as he was. "The room was more than a humble clergyman such as myself could ever hope to deserve from one of her sphere."

374

With a suppressed cringe, Darcy took a deep breath, praying for patience. Thank heaven they were not staying longer than a few nights!

They would be forced to dine with the master of Longbourn one of those evenings, but the little man had decided to use the visit of his cousin to his advantage. Mr. Collins had requested Elizabeth act as hostess for a dinner party on their final evening at Longbourn. Since they were residing at Longbourn as his guest, Darcy did not feel he could refuse.

Mr. Collins appraised Darcy. "I understand you were Miss Anne de Bourgh's heir when she passed—God rest her soul."

"Do you correspond with Lady Catherine?" It was doubtful, but since Mr. Collins had so much knowledge of the lady, the question was logical.

"Oh no! I would never expect one as magnificent as her to correspond with the likes of me! Mr. Thacker and I were good friends as we pursued our studies. We exchange letters often." An air of concern overtook Mr. Collins' features as he paused for a moment. "I am grieved by her ladyship's present situation, but perhaps it is better to remain silent."

"You are too good."

Darcy's head whipped around to his wife, whose lips quirked up on one side. "I do hope we will not inconvenience you during our stay."

"Of course not, my dear cousin! I should thank you for acting as my hostess for the dinner party! I have wanted to entertain, but without a wife or sister to fill the post of mistress, I felt it should not be attempted."

Elizabeth's eyes widened, but Mr. Collins never noticed. "Not that much will be required of you. Whilst I am certain you are an able hostess, Mrs. Hill has planned the menu and arranged every detail."

She regained her aplomb and peered to him before her attention returned to her cousin. "Mrs. Hill is a competent housekeeper. I do not doubt her arrangements are satisfactory."

Mr. Collins gave a supercilious nod. How could one be so arrogant yet so subservient at the same time?

"Mr. Collins, do you think we could have some time to refresh ourselves before dinner?" A reprieve would be a blessed occurrence!

"Oh! How inconsiderate of me not to take into account your long journey! Hill!" He rose to his feet and made his way with haste to the bell pull.

Hill rounded the corner within a few minutes, and curtsied.

"Please show Mr. and Mrs. Darcy to their rooms." Mr. Collins' attention redirected back to the Darcys. "Dinner is with a strict adherence to my schedule. We dine promptly at five o'clock. I believe dining at a later hour is bad for the digestion."

Darcy gave a small bow before the man could continue. "I give you my thanks, Mr. Collins."

Mr. Collins bowed at the waist with an arm across his chest and the other outstretched. "It is I who should thank you for condescending to stay in my modest dwelling."

A sound much like a hiccup came from Elizabeth, and before she lost her composure, Darcy hastened her from the room with a hand to her back. They followed Mrs. Hill up the stairs to the corridor where she halted.

"Mr. Collins asked for the best two guest rooms to be prepared for your arrival, but I thought you might wish to stay in your old bedchamber. There is a door between Mrs. Darcy's old bedchamber and that of the one next door. Mr. Darcy could use that room if you so choose. I took the liberty of readying both, so you would have the choice."

Elizabeth reached out to take the older woman's hands. "I appreciate the trouble you have undertaken. My old bedchamber sounds wonderful. I never thought to set eyes upon it again much less..." Her voice cracked and the housekeeper was no less effected.

"It was no trouble, miss... ma'am... pardon me." She stepped forward and opened the door.

His wife entered, and though she was emotional, she beamed as she bit her bottom lip. He excused Mrs. Hill and followed, closing the door behind him.

"This was where you slept?" With a slow pivot, he absorbed everything: the furniture, the dressing table, the window seat, and the view of the small apple orchard behind the house. All were items she had once described, but he was now able to commit the actual scenes to memory.

"The room that connects," she explained as she turned the knob and passed through the doorway, "was Jane's."

His trunk was placed in the far corner, and he glanced back where Elizabeth's was in a similar position. Mrs. Hill was a sly one! She had known all along where Elizabeth would wish to stay.

"Do you think we will both fit in your bed?" He reached out and pulled her back to his chest. Her hands covered his on her stomach, and she sighed as she leaned back into him.

"You will have to hold me for the entirety of the night."

"That will be no hardship, Mrs. Darcy. No hardship at all."

The morning dawned with a beautiful blue sky splashed with a few clouds. The roads were nice and dry, so Darcy and Elizabeth eschewed the carriage for the short walk to Meryton as Thomas voiced his occasional approval of the weather from the safe haven of his mother's arms.

His wife pointed out trees and landmarks, which held fond memories and told him numerous stories of her youth until they reached the village, and the inn where he had overheard the life-changing conversation between Gardiner and her Uncle Philips.

The Bird in Hand appeared no different than it had the first time he laid eyes upon it, despite the passage of over a year. Its half-timber frame and white plaster facade had undergone much less alteration than he had in that period of time.

Elizabeth gazed in his direction with a knowing look. She, no doubt, knew where his thoughts lie; the turn of her mind was likely much the same.

They made their way to the small house behind Mr. Philips' offices, and the door opened before they could lift the latch to enter the garden.

"Lizzy! I noticed you from the window!"

Elizabeth's joy was apparent as she stepped forward and wrapped an arm around the lady. "Hello, Aunt. Did Uncle Philips tell you we would call?"

"He most certainly did! I was never so shocked in my life. That you would return to visit—and that baby!"

His wife handed over Thomas, who regarded his great aunt with a wary eye and expression to match. "I cannot believe it has only been two months since his birth. He is enormous!"

A hand to Mrs. Philips' elbow directed her towards him. "Aunt Philips, I would like to present my husband, Mr. Fitzwilliam Darcy. Fitzwilliam, this is my aunt, Edith Philips."

He bowed and she gave a quick curtsy. "And this little one must be Thomas." She gazed at their son until her face snapped back to them. "Oh! You must come inside! How rude of me to continue prattling on without a care as to whether you would be in want of some tea."

He gave a wide grin to his wife, who laughed with her eyes as she took his arm. Elizabeth's imitation of her mother began to make a great deal more sense.

Two long days were spent with Elizabeth's aunt and uncle as they visited and caught up on the news of both families; however, they opted to remain at Longbourn the final day of their visit to Meryton. The Philips were invited to the dinner party that evening, and Elizabeth wished Thomas to have a less disrupted day before they travelled on to London.

Her stomach clenched in trepidation when Mr. Collins requested her presence in what was once her father's book room. He gave no indication of why he wished to speak with her, and while his manner was his usual obsequious fawning, what could he desire that required privacy?

Fitzwilliam accompanied her at her request. His even composure and relaxed posture indicated he knew the reason behind the summons but he would reveal naught of what he knew. Mr. Collins' motives were unclear, and she was wary of him due to the actions of his father.

"Mrs. Darcy," he began in his usual snivelling manner. "When I acquired Longbourn from my esteemed father, I began to sort through many of the books in what was once your father's library, and whilst I do not wish to speak ill of the dead, I find some of the works within this library distasteful and immoral. I had thought to burn the offending books, but your husband has offered to compensate me should you care to have some of them." She pivoted her head towards her husband as her jaw dropped.

"I suggested, but I did not know he would agree until now."

Mr. Collins motioned in the direction of several stacks of books set in a corner. "I have no wish to retain any of these. Please select what you would like, and I will discard the excess."

Her husband's gaze followed her as she moved to the precious books her father had adored. How could she only select a few and leave the rest for Collins to treat as rubbish?

"Elizabeth?"

Her trembling hand reached out to rest upon the top of the stack. The cover was familiar as she had read Homer and discussed his works many times with her father.

"Mr. Collins, if you will have a servant crate them, we will take the lot. I will have them sent on to Sagemore once we arrive in London."

Her head swung to where her husband stood, observing her with concern. "Are you certain we have the space?"

He strode beside her, surveyed the stacks with a quick glance, and gave her hand a reassuring squeeze. "They should only take one or two crates, so we should be able to fit them between the two carriages. Hattie, James, and Mary do not travel with much, so there should be plenty of room on the top of their equipage."

She removed the volume of Homer and flipped through the pages until she found one of her father's handwritten notes in the margin. What Mr. Collins could find so objectionable to Homer was a mystery, but it was not of significance. Her fingers sought out and traced the delicate lines made by her father's pen. A sob caught in her throat.

"Thank you." Her voice was tremulous and came out as a whisper.

She closed the book and held it to her chest. "Thank you, Mr. Collins. Words cannot express our gratitude."

The toady man appeared inordinately pleased with himself, and he gave a bow as she spoke.

Her husband steered her towards the door with a gentle touch. "Why do you not check on Thomas? I will arrange matters with Mr. Collins."

With a nod, she made her way to the nursery. Thomas was sleeping, while Mary knitted as she rocked in the chair beside his cot. She spent a moment stroking his back to ensure he was well, but since she was not needed, she went to her former bedchamber for a moment to herself. The window seat was still a welcome spot to read, and she curled into her favourite niche as she opened her father's book. Little time passed before the sound of the door drew her from the pages, departing Odysseus' quest, as her husband stepped forward to take her in his embrace.

"Are you well?"

"I am very well," she said with a smile. "I owe you a large debt of gratitude for purchasing my father's books from Mr. Collins. I hope he did not request a large sum."

He chuckled and perched himself on the opposite end by her feet. "You owe me nothing, my love. Mr. Hill came in shortly after you departed to crate them, and I had a chance to peruse a few. There are several volumes I have sought for some time, but have had little luck in finding. They are no longer in print, and difficult to come by. Mr. Collins was unaware of what he possessed; the entire exchange was quite the bargain."

"I am so pleased!"

When he continued to chuckle, she frowned. "What amuses you so?"

"I hope I am incorrect, but I could have sworn I witnessed Mr. Hill place an extra book in the crate. He wore a vicious scowl directed at his master whilst he did it, too."

She raised her eyebrows. "I cannot claim to be shocked. I ventured to the kitchens the night we arrived. I wanted to ensure I was not needed for any of the dinner arrangements for tonight. Mrs. Hill has little love for either the elder or younger Mr. Collins. She said the first was miserly and mean, whilst she called the younger leather-headed."

His warm laughter filled the room, and he laced his fingers with hers. "So, they do not care for your cousin either."

"I am afraid Mr. William Collins never stood a chance. Mr. and Mrs. Hill were furious with his father for his appearance within a fortnight of my father's death. They felt he should have waited a short time out of respect. Instead, he swept in, claimed everything, and purged what he felt was rubbish."

She tilted her head, leaning it against the frame. "Mrs. Hill informed me how she and Mr. Hill packed our trunks with our clothes and any other items he wished to discard, and Mr. Hill delivered them to my uncle's. Mr. Collins was apparently unaware of how much they had packed. They were only supposed to send my trunk, but I received Jane's as well. Both burst open when my aunt opened them due to the amount they had squeezed inside."

"Mr. Collins gloated this morning about some of his plans for the estate." Her husband's voice was low as he spoke. He must have had concerns of being heard from outside the room. "He has spent a great deal of the estate's capital since he has become master. I expect he shall exhaust his funds within the next two years."

"So fast?" She sat forward in her seat. "What sort of improvements does he intend to make?"

"He indicated that one of the peers, who he met when he was seeking a living, insisted no estate was truly great unless it had an orangery, so rather than seeking land in the area to increase his income, he has chosen to add to what the existing property must support."

Her eyes closed in horror. "So he will ruin Longbourn in order to puff up his own self-worth?"

"He has already contracted with an architect, which, no doubt, required a hefty sum."

"It was bad enough when Longbourn was entailed to his father, but I dread what will become of it when Collins fails."

Her fingers received a slight squeeze. "I intend to meet with my solicitors when we reach London. If he fails, as I believe he will, I will authorise them to make him an offer. If he is desperate enough, he may just agree."

"You would purchase Longbourn?"

"My investments have fared well, and we do not spend our funds freely. We could afford it, and Longbourn is a fine situation; however, my main motivation has nothing to do with this estate's prospects or whether we have sufficient funds to purchase the property."

"You would acquire it for me?" Her voice cracked as her heart swelled and felt as though it might burst.

He smiled and pulled her to his chest. "It would be all for you."

Chapter 27

The faint sound of the waves and the noisy gulls roused Darcy from his slumber. They were two houses from the sea wall, but still close enough to hear the sounds from the beach and smell the sea air.

Elizabeth was curled into his side, her head on his shoulder and her leg thrown over his hip, as she mumbled in her sleep. Her slumber had become increasingly disturbed as her worry heightened in regards to Georgiana, but she should calm now that they were in Ramsgate. She would see that his sister was well with her own eyes.

Their short trip to Longbourn helped dispel some of her anxiety, but only lasted for the short duration of their visit while she was preoccupied with family. Once they travelled to London, his grandmother decreed his wife's concerns were not without merit, which caused Elizabeth's unease to return—and with that disquiet came the nightmares.

While in Meryton, they had returned to the scene of the fateful carriage accident, where Elizabeth left flowers. She even summoned the courage to recount what she remembered in great detail.

He and Richard often discussed his experiences in battle, and how some soldiers could not recall a terrible event in which they were injured. The two of them together formed a theory that somehow the mind protected the individual, yet Elizabeth remembered with great detail. She was a strong lady indeed!

Her mental fortitude made her concern over Georgiana more disturbing. What if his wife was correct? What if there was something amiss with his sister?

They had only arrived in Ramsgate the night prior. Bingley, who had arranged the lease of the house through a friend, had inquired if they could perhaps advance their stay by a few days, and the owner had agreed since no one else required the home.

As the arrangements now stood, George Darcy would depart Ramsgate that morning—he may have already left—and they would call on Georgiana in a few short hours to surprise her.

While his grandmother would never withhold information vital to Georgiana's safety, the knot in his stomach indicated she knew more than she divulged.

Elizabeth started, and he grazed his hand up and down her back. "The accident?" he asked softly."

"No, someone attempted to take Georgiana. I held tight to her hand, but she slipped from my grasp in the second before I awakened." She lifted her head, resting her chin upon his chest. "Do you think it possible your father has already departed?"

He drew back the thick bed curtains to bright daylight streaming into the windows. "I would imagine he set off at daybreak."

She shifted and groaned. "I need to go feed Thomas. I hope he has awakened."

His eyes followed her figure as she rose, admiring the curves illuminated by the sunlight through her shift. She was a bit curvier than before the birth, but he had no complaints! Her wider hips and heavier breasts only increased her appeal.

When she had bustled through the door to see to their son, he ran a hand through his hair, stretched his legs, and willed his erection to subside. Some days, Elizabeth would return after feeding Thomas, and they would remain in their rooms late into the morning. This morning would not be one of those times, much to his chagrin.

He rose, dressed, and made his way to the dining room, where his grandmother was already seated with her tea.

"I see we are all awake early this morning. That is just as well. I would like to call on Georgiana as soon as the hour is decent."

He pinned his grandmother with an insistent stare. "What is it you have not told me? It is evident there is more reason to be concerned than mere suspicion and supposition."

She gave a heavy sigh and returned her cup to its saucer, never relinquishing her grip upon the fragile china. "Georgiana and I were both concerned of your reaction if I shared with you what occurred in London upon my return from Rosings."

"My reaction now will not be pleasant if you do not inform me directly, Grandmamma."

She watched him with worry for a few moments and nodded. "Very well, but I beg of you to hear the entirety before you become angry."

His eyes closed as he groaned. "I do not care for the way this sounds."

"You will care for it even less when I tell you—I assure you." She glanced to the footman awaiting their orders, and caught his eye. "We will summon help if you are needed, thank you."

The servant bowed and exited as Darcy poured himself a cup of coffee. Something stronger might soon be a necessity, but for now, it would have to do.

"I called on Georgiana when I returned from Rosings. I wished to inform her of the goings-on and the lovely visit we all had once we had dispensed with the sad formalities."

He took a sip as he waited and listened.

"Your sister was not your usual cheerful young lady, and I found it odd that Mrs. Younge did not depart the room upon my arrival. I requested time alone with my granddaughter, and she left, levelling a nasty look in my direction before she closed the door behind her. I suspect she did not think she had been noticed."

"I have never cared for that woman. I told father I thought her a bad choice, but he dismissed my advice."

"Georgie did not say much, but I obtained her agreement to call on me the day after. She arrived before the formal callers, as I requested, and I informed Mrs. Younge that as my granddaughter would be receiving callers with me, we would not have need of her. I would escort Georgiana home after dinner."

He chuckled. "I do not imagine she cared for her dismissal. She has always fancied herself above her position."

"She appeared livid, and your sister gasped at my audacity. You are aware of how she is polite to a fault.

"I did not receive callers that day due to the extended period of time I spent cajoling the truth of the matter from Georgiana."

The more his grandmother revealed the more pronounced the knot in his gut became. They had never been required to cajole anything from his little sister, as she was always quite animated amongst family. She possessed a certain reticence in large public gatherings, but he could not blame her for it as he and his father both possessed that same characteristic.

"Please just come out with it. I cannot manage the suspense much longer."

"George Wickham." She spoke without elaboration—not that it was required. The name alone was cause for him to swallow in an attempt to prevent himself from becoming ill.

A low groan escaped his lips, and he placed his elbows on the table, cradling his forehead in his hands.

"What has the blackguard done now?"

"Whilst we were all at Rosings, he appeared in London, and insinuated himself at Darcy House. He made a point of accompanying Georgiana on her walks, and was present at every meal. By what she confessed to me, he sounded to be courting her."

"What!" His heart was beating with force against his rib cage. "Please tell me you did something! That you did not simply send her back on her own!"

"Of course I did, Fitzwilliam. What kind of person do you think me to be?"

"I apologise, Grandmamma, but he is dangerous. Father has overlooked some of his debts as the folly of youth, but you and I both know the extent of his depravity."

"We do," she agreed, "which is why I accompanied Georgiana back to Darcy House to remove her trunk and her maid. She had requested her maid sleep in her bedchamber for the duration of his stay, but I could not allow the situation to remain as it was. I informed Mrs. Younge her charge would reside with me until her father collected her at the end of the next fortnight. Mrs. Younge was welcome to spend that time as she saw fit."

"Did you write to my father?"

"That is part of the problem." She clasped her hands in front of her. "Do you remember how accommodating Mrs. Younge was when you were in town?"

His brow furrowed. Oh no! He closed his eyes and clenched his hands into tight fists. "Mrs. Younge has used my and Elizabeth's visits with Georgiana against her."

"She has, and your sister refused to allow me to inform him of the situation.

"George blustered in upon his return to London, and I described Wickham's behaviour, which he disregarded. I had no proof, no witnesses. He insisted Georgie was as a sister to Wickham."

Darcy slammed his fist upon the table. "He is after her dowry. I would bet my life on it! I can only suppose that hurting me would be an added benefit."

His grandmother agreed as she straightened the napkin in her lap. "If Georgiana is cryptic in her letters, it is out of necessity. She is desperate to see you, Elizabeth, and baby Thomas. I suspect she writes them with Mrs. Younge nearby."

"I want to have the ability to visit with my sister, Grandmamma, but I will not sacrifice her safety or her future for that privilege. I will expose Mrs. Younge for what she is, and I will return Georgiana to father."

The dowager nodded with downcast eyes. "I have spent the last week considering every alternative, and I admit it is the best way to end Wickham's scheme."

"This is why you contacted Bingley about us arriving a few days early?"

"Elizabeth wrote me with her concerns, and I penned a letter to my new grandson. I desire to beat Wickham at his game. If George departs this morning, I doubt Wickham will have sufficient time to call on her, much less abscond, if that is his plan."

He rubbed his hands up and down his face as if to scrub the worry from his mind. "Why did you not tell me of this sooner?"

"What could you do?" She speared him with a steady gaze. "Your father would not listen to me, and he would not listen to you. All you could do with the knowledge is worry, which would not do you, Elizabeth, Thomas, *or* Georgiana much good."

He sighed. He hated that she was correct, but she was. "Elizabeth should be down soon. I promised her a walk, and then we will call on Georgiana. You do plan to join us?"

"Of course," she responded swiftly. "Never will that scoundrel harm one of my grandchildren again. I will see to it he is drawn and quartered first."

He chuckled as Elizabeth entered. "We should ring the bell. I am certain Elizabeth will require some fresh tea."

The morning was warm and breezy by the water, but as it was still early, people were not out in abundance. Darcy walked with Elizabeth on his arm while she took in her surroundings.

He winced at the dark shadows and the subtle lines that framed her fine eyes. Her lack of a smile was also evidence of her concern for his younger sister.

"I enjoy watching everything awaken. Sometimes, I would venture into Meryton early on an errand for my father—usually to the bookshop. I liked to leave early and watch the village come alive whilst I waited for Mr. Hervey to open."

"There is not much business down by the water, other than perhaps a few fisherman."

"No, but there are more people about than when we began."

He checked the position of the sun. "We should return. Grandmamma and I hoped to call on Georgiana early."

"Fitzwilliam, Georgiana is not at home."

"Pardon?" How could she be aware of his sister's whereabouts so soon? He turned to her in puzzlement as she pointed in front of them. His gaze followed her finger to his sister walking in their direction with George Wickham. His teeth clamped and gritted together with a vengeance as Elizabeth's hand gripped his arm.

"Georgiana!"

His sister smiled, although it was subdued as her teeth remained hidden. Her hand lifted to wave, but Wickham grabbed her elbow to steer her in the opposite direction. Darcy began to open his mouth, but Georgiana yanked her arm away from Wickham and strode over to them.

"Fitzwilliam! I thought you were to arrive near the end of the week."

"We decided to push forward our plans." His sight remained steady on Wickham, who smirked as he sauntered towards them.

Elizabeth took his sister's hands, and drew her aside. "I am so pleased to see you! You will return with us to see Thomas, will you not?"

Darcy gave the ladies a quick glance before he returned his glare to Wickham. "Why are you here?" he growled. "You have had no interest in Georgiana in the past. Do not pretend you are suddenly concerned with being a brother."

Wickham gave a snort. "Why are *you* interested? You have left Pemberley and made your own life. One that does not include

Georgiana *or* your father." He leaned in to Darcy menacingly. "Do not interfere with my plans, Darcy."

He stepped closer and looked down upon Wickham. His extra bit of height being to his advantage at that moment. "Your plans do not include my sister. She will be joining us for the summer."

A snide laugh grated at Darcy's ears as Wickham peered around him to ensure his prey was still present.

"Your father would not approve. One note to him, and he would remove Georgiana from your care and put her in my path once more."

"But she would be safe with my father, which is what matters. Return to the slums of London and wreak your havoc there where you belong."

"I belong in Grosvenor Square and Belgravia—not St. Giles or even Cheapside. I will not be relegated to the mews and forgotten!" He sounded as if he was trying to convince himself rather than state his conviction.

"And how does Georgiana grant you access to those places? She is not your relation, and the Ton will not accept the son of a steward."

Wickham gave a malicious chuckle and Darcy's eyes widened. "My God! You do intend to wed her! I hope you know my father would never approve."

"He does not have to approve. We will be wed in Gretna Green and there is little you can do to prevent it."

"I can certainly try!"

Wickham grinned with his teeth bared as though he were growling. "Your father would never believe such aspersions on my character. He has always taken my part in the past, and he will continue to do so in the future."

Wickham again peeked to the side, but his eyes widened, causing Darcy to turn. Elizabeth and Georgiana were gone!

"Where did she go?" His voice bellowed down the waterfront, prompting several people to look in their direction. "Where did your slut of a wife take her?"

His back stiffened at the insult of his wife, but he remained silent. People were milling about; if a physical altercation erupted, Wickham had to throw the first blow. He grinned as he turned to face his adversary. "She has ensured Georgiana is far away from the likes of you."

"You do not want to interfere with my plans. I will not only find a way to ruin you, but I will ruin your precious sister." Wickham's lips twisted into a nasty sneer as he stepped closer, the putrid smell of stale liquor from his breath mingling with the air Darcy inhaled. "Her virtue will be a distant memory by the time I am through."

"With what proof? One walk on the waterfront does not a ruined reputation make."

Wickham snickered. "Since when does society require proof? The right rumours placed in the right ears could do more harm than the truth within the drawing rooms of the Ton."

He shook his head and gave a bark of laughter. "Do your best, Wickham. Your ruination of Georgiana would result in the loss of your only means of support. Without my father, you are homeless—no, you are penniless. Your actions have repercussions, and in this instance, dire repercussions. You had best consider your schemes before you implement them."

"My plan was progressing as it should prior to your arrival. You always ruin everything, Darcy."

"I do not consider myself as being the ruination of anything. In this case, I am the means of preventing a catastrophe. You would destroy Georgiana's life and her spirit."

"Spare me your dramatics! Once I put her in the family way, I would find other amusements. Your little sister would probably be as dry and boring in bed as you are just existing."

To hell with the onlookers! Darcy took one step forward crossing Wickham's jaw with a crushing blow, the force of which brought him to his knees. He took one disgusted look at Wickham, who was upon all fours on the cobblestones, and began to walk in the direction of the house. He had not made it far when a hand grabbed his arm and whirled him around.

He managed to grasp Wickham's shoulder as he dodged his blow, slamming him face down to the ground. Wickham continued to fight, but Darcy placed a knee in his back and pinned him to the hard stones.

"My cousin the colonel took me under his wing some time ago. I will no longer allow you to hurt me or anyone who falls under my protection. As Georgiana's brother, I *will* protect her whether my father has banned me from Pemberley or not."

Despite being face down to the ground and stuck there, Wickham attempted to rise and lash out at Darcy. "Return your sister to her house within the next four hours, and I will not harm her reputation. Yours I cannot guarantee. You should not have struck me!"

"Do your worst, Wickham. I am not afraid of you." Pressing his knee a bit firmer into his nemesis' spine for leverage on top of spite, he stood, stepped back, and strode away with a firm tug to the base of his topcoat.

A glance back revealed a few bystanders; however, they did not aid Wickham, and continued on with their business. He walked at a brisk pace past their street to ensure no one trailed behind him, before returning to the house.

When he entered the front door, Elizabeth's voice mingled with his sister's from the drawing room; he handed off his gloves and hat to the butler and followed the precious sounds.

"Fitzwilliam!" Georgiana exclaimed when she noticed his presence. She rushed over to embrace him, and held fast to him as he returned the gesture. "I was so worried. I did not want to leave you with Wickham, but Elizabeth insisted."

"Elizabeth was correct. I am glad you listened to her direction." He drew back, caught her eye, and held her gaze. "He lost any power he had to hurt me when you departed."

Her forehead creased. "But he could have injured you."

"I can defend myself, Georgie, which is easier done if I do not have you and Elizabeth as distractions. If Wickham chose to revenge himself on me by hurting one of you, I would be devastated. It was preferable for you to be gone."

She sniffed and brought her handkerchief to her eyes. "I had not thought of it so."

"I did not wish to leave either," confessed Elizabeth. "Did the footmen I sent find you?"

"No, I never saw them, but I walked down the waterfront past the house to make sure Wickham did not follow." He led Georgiana back to her seat and leaned over to press his lips to Elizabeth's temple.

"I am relieved you have returned in one piece."

"I have learned a great deal since I left Pemberley. He cannot inflict the damage he once wrought."

He took a place beside Elizabeth and examined Georgiana, who shrank back into the cushions under the scrutiny. "I need to know if you have ever been alone with Wickham."

"Other than this morning?" asked Georgiana softly.

"Yes, other than this morning. What about when he came around in London?"

She shook her head. "No, he did try, but I demanded Mrs. Younge remain. She once insisted she could not walk in Hyde Park with us, but I summoned my maid to replace her."

Elizabeth reached out and took his sister's hands in hers. "I bet neither Mrs. Younge nor Mr. Wickham were thrilled."

"No, Mr. Wickham was displeased. He did not say as much, but it was evident in his expression."

"Georgie! I heard from Sarah you had arrived with Elizabeth." His worried grandmother strode into the room to greet her granddaughter.

"We happened upon her as she walked out with Mr. Wickham," explained Elizabeth.

His grandmother's nostrils flared and her hands clenched at her sides. She turned to Darcy with narrowed eyes. "Where was Mrs. Younge?"

He shrugged. "She was not present."

"Mrs. Younge professed to feeling unwell and insisted that she remain behind." His sister's gaze darted back and forth between them.

"I must go make arrangements for your trunk to be delivered." His hand rubbed the back of his neck. "We must leave at first light."

Elizabeth made to speak, but it took more than one attempt for the sound to emerge. "Thomas has done very well with travel thus far, but he must have a few days at least before we set out again. He sleeps so much in the carriage that Mary and I have a difficult time when we arrive. Must we depart with such haste?"

"I wish we could delay, but Wickham has threatened to write my father. He has also threatened Georgie's reputation should I not return her to her establishment." His sister's eyes welled with tears. He should not have been so blunt. "I apologise, Georgie, but we must contact Father. He is the only person who can prevent Wickham from speaking."

"But he is returning to Pemberley and will be difficult to reach until he arrives."

"I am aware of that. I also believe a hasty departure from Ramsgate will give the appearance of you having left with him."

"We could make her stay with us very public." His grandmother lifted her brow. "No one would give Wickham's stories any consideration if she has been seen with us for the remainder of our stay."

"There is still the possibility of Wickham contacting my father." He stood and began to pace. "He would spin his own tale and win father over. We would never convince him of Wickham's scheme should he precede us to Derbyshire."

He continued to stride to and fro until Elizabeth's voice broke through the jumble. "How long has Mr. Wickham been in Ramsgate?"

"Pardon?" He halted at his spot and stared.

"From what you have told me, Mr. Wickham often amasses large debts beyond what your father's allowance covers. Did you not say he is no longer welcome in Lambton?"

He nodded and took a step towards his wife. "Yes, when I paid off his last round of debts, I informed the Lambton merchants I would no longer cover Wickham's future spending. They refused to extend him credit from that day forward."

"Is it not possible that he has amassed some debts here already— particularly if he has resided here for a week or so whilst he awaited your father's departure?"

A light beamed from his grandmother's eyes as her face broke into a wide smile. "That is an excellent idea, Lizzy."

"You wish me to have him imprisoned for his debts?"

"Yes," she replied. "It would afford us some time before we journey to Pemberley. We could give Thomas the few days he requires, and take our time as we travel north."

His grandmother's expression read of steely determination. "Fitzwilliam, take James and search out where Wickham stayed or is staying. He would not have wished George to be aware of his arrival, so he would remain at an inn. His dissolute habits would no doubt give him a substantial bill."

"Very well, I will see what I can find. Georgiana, you are not to leave this house until I have solved the immediate problem, or we depart on the morrow."

She wiped her red-rimmed eyes with her handkerchief and sniffled. "Of course! I only wish I was not such a bother."

He rushed forward and kneeled before her, grasping her shoulders. "You are not a bother! It is Wickham who has caused all of this fuss—Wickham and Mrs. Younge." His father also played a part, but it was perhaps better to remain silent on that point. "Do not think I have forgotten her part! She will never work as a companion again!"

Elizabeth slipped from the room, but he remained. "Do you understand, Georgie? You are not to blame for any of this. Mrs. Younge has used you ill, and Wickham's scheme was to convince you to elope."

"Elope!" exclaimed his grandmother. "God forbid!"

"I would never!" Georgie gasped as she shook her head. "Why would he think…?"

"He can be very persuasive when he is motivated. A large dowry was his prize, and he will not relinquish it without a fight. He expects your return within a few hours, or he will ruin your reputation and send an express to Father."

His grandmother leaned forward in her seat as though she were about to spring from her chair. "Then you should find James and be on your way. You do not have a second to lose."

As he rose, Elizabeth came in bearing not only a huge grin, but also Thomas, who stared at everyone with wide, round eyes. "I brought someone to cheer up the conversation. No one can discuss such serious topics in the presence of a baby."

His sister bounded up and exclaimed over her new nephew. A loud kiss was placed on his forehead prompting a wide toothless smile.

His son was certain to enjoy the unceasing attention he would receive over the next hour.

He pressed his lips against his wife's cheek, and left the ladies to their cooing to search out James. His valet was not difficult to locate, and was not at all averse to the abandonment of his master's shoes for the morning. He could shine them later.

It took almost an hour to locate the inn where Wickham had resided for the past week. James had practically sprinted back to find Darcy after his initial conversation with the innkeeper, and they proceeded with all haste to return.

"He snuck out this mornin.' I am still tryin' to figure out how 'e got his trunk an' all past me. If 'e can do it, some other rascal could do it, too. I can't be affordin' tha!"

"So, he had not paid prior to his departure?"

"Nah, left quite a bill, 'e did—five nights, several day's worth a meals, and all tha' ale 'e done drank."

"I would like to pay for the debt, Mr. Clarke, if you would allow it."

"Well, I wouldn' be turnin' ya down." The innkeeper observed him for a moment while he rummaged for the appropriate payment. "He owes you money as well?"

"Of sorts." With a lift of his shoulders, he glimpsed at the tally placed before him. "I have often paid his debts, but more importantly, he has caused me and my family a great deal of grief over the years."

Mr. Clarke took the money Darcy handed him, and proffered the marker. "I hope you be findin' a way to get rid of 'im." The innkeeper leaned across the bar and pointed across the street. "He got 'imself a new suit. I suppose the one 'e 'ad wasn't good enough for what 'e 'ad planned."

James exited, headed to the tailor's shop Mr. Clarke had bobbed his head towards, while Darcy extended his arm to shake the innkeeper's hand.

"Thank you for the information." An extra crown was placed upon the counter and the man's jaw dropped.

"Thank you, sir. If you be needin' anythin.'"

With a curt nod, he exited the inn as James waved him over to the tailor's shop where Wickham had indeed acquired quite a debt, since he used the finest materials that particular tradesman stocked.

James frowned as he watched Darcy pay. "He always did put on airs, that one."

"My father did nothing to discourage the belief. It is as much his fault as it is Wickham's for wilfully deceiving himself."

James agreed as Darcy received the slip of paper, which increased Wickham's debt to a substantial figure for just one week. The constables, Mr. Poore and Mr. Barrett, were brought into the situation, accompanying him to his sister's lodgings, while James reluctantly returned to shining his master's shoes.

Without question, he and the constables were admitted to the front hallway where they handed the aged butler their hats and gloves.

He passed a slip of paper with the direction to the house. "Miss Darcy's belongings and her maid will be sent to this residence. She will be remaining with her grandmother, the Dowager Countess of Matlock, and myself for the remainder of her time in Ramsgate."

The elderly man balked and stared. "I beg your pardon, sir, but Mrs. Younge informed us that Miss Darcy is not to be in your company. She indicated it would result in the loss of our employment."

"You are denying her brother and her grandmother access on the word of a paid companion?" questioned Mr. Poore from behind him.

With a tilt down, so he was eye to eye with the butler, Darcy clenched his jaw. "Mrs. Younge will never have employment as a companion again after I am finished with her. She will be fortunate to find a position scrubbing chamber pots."

A snicker came from Mr. Poore as he stepped forward. "I would do the bidding of the brother—your loyalty to the companion will bring you naught but disappointment."

"Of course, sir." The butler's response was a mumble as he bowed and then, led them to a parlour where Mrs. Younge was having tea with none other than Mr. Wickham.

"See, I told you he would see sense." Wickham rose with a wide grin and stepped to the side to look behind him. "I say, Darcy, where is Georgie?"

The butler gave Wickham a distasteful look and departed the room.

"She will not return to this house. I have taken the liberty of paying your debts, Wickham. These two gentleman are here to take you to prison."

His complexion paled a notch, but otherwise, his visage was composed. "You had best give this more consideration. I will ruin your precious Georgiana and anyone else you deem important."

"Georgiana's ruination would hardly garner you any aid from my father, and one letter to my steward could ensure you are jailed for a very long time."

Wickham's face screwed into a nasty jeer. "You are bluffing."

"I have a record of all of your debts to me at Sagemore. I could easily have you transported to London and see you placed in debtor's prison there. The Marshalsea might teach you some humility—a quality you have always lacked."

As his plans crumbled before him, Wickham became furious. "You will regret this! I will not just disappear."

Darcy shrugged in a nonchalant manner while he roiled inside. Wickham could not know how anxious he was if this plan was to succeed. "Your disappearance is more than I could ever hope for, but alas, I know you will never willingly depart. I will find a way to prove to my father what you are, and he will deal with the leech he has created."

Wickham lunged for him. "You bastard! I deserve more after licking your father's boots for all of these years! I deserve to be counted as his son since you left him and your inheritance behind as if it were trash!"

The constables stepped forward and grasped Wickham by his arms before he could harm Darcy, but the miscreant continued to fight against their restraint. "You cannot do this! I do not owe anything of significance here in Ramsgate!"

"I'd wager one of those debts was for this fancy new suit you're wearing," mentioned the constable. "The tailor's bill alone for this rag would do, but you also ran up a large tab at The Bull. Mr. Darcy has enough—unless you have the funds to pay your debt in full; but then, you might want to consider keeping your money for food whilst in prison. There are no free meals to be had there either."

Wickham reddened. "You should consider what you are doing, Darcy. I cannot be held in there forever. Lettie will see me out as soon as she can manage it."

Mrs. Younge's eyes widened. "Yes, of course I will, George."

With a pivot in her direction, Darcy stepped towards his sister's companion. "You had best think of your own future, Mrs. Younge. Neither my father nor I will write you a recommendation as things stand, but we can blacken your name amongst the Ton. You would never be a paid companion again—not that you should have ever been in such a trusted position in the first place."

"I have spent the night in the same home as Georgiana," cried Wickham with desperation. "In London, I returned to the house when your father left for Pemberley."

Darcy shook his head. "And every servant in the house could testify that Mrs. Younge was there as well. Not only was Mrs. Younge in residence, but for the short time you resided in the same home, Georgiana requested her maid sleep in her bedchamber."

Wickham's face blanched as he jerked in an attempt to gain his freedom, and Mrs. Younge grimaced. "That was the reason for the cot beside her bed."

"Mr. Poole, I have nothing further to say to Mr. Wickham. I will be in touch in approximately a fortnight when I learn of how my father wishes to proceed."

The constable agreed, and he and his partner began to tug their unwilling prisoner from the room. Wickham hollered and fought with the authorities, but by the time they had wrangled him to the outer door, he quieted—likely to avoid a public scene. The man was always a schemer. Such a public display of him being taken to prison would not serve him well in the future.

Once the din had quieted and Wickham had departed, Darcy turned to Mrs. Younge, whose eyes bored into him.

"What do you intend to do with me?" Her voice was more humble than her expression would indicate.

"I would like you to pack your belongings and leave. I do not want to ever hear your name associated with a respectable family again. Do I make myself clear?" He pivoted to depart, but Mrs. Younge grasped his sleeve.

"But Mr. Darcy! I have nowhere to go!" Her once angry eyes filled with tears. He glared at her fingers, which released him with haste.

"You should have considered that predicament before you conspired with Wickham. I will do naught to help you now."

"But perhaps your father will, once he hears what I have to say."

Her hands fidgeted as she shifted her weight from foot to foot. Could she truly have information, which could sway his father?

"And what information could you provide to change your fate?"

She shook her head adamantly. "I will only tell Mr. Darcy."

With a step forward and a lean in her direction, he towered over her small frame. She shrank back only a bit, but it was the reaction he had intended.

"You will tell me, else you will not have an audience with my father. I will see to it."

She studied his eyes and brought her thumbnail to her lip to chew. "I have your word to promote my cause?"

"That depends on your information. There may be naught my father or I can do."

"He could come to my aid if he chose." She paused and then, nodded. "Very well, I will tell you."

He listened as Mrs. Younge told him of her predicament, giving a quick gesture of understanding when her lengthy explanation was complete. "I will tell my father. I cannot guarantee he will take action in regards to your situation, but you have my word he will hear it."

"I ask nothing more, Mr. Darcy."

Chapter 28

The familiar Derbyshire landscape passed as the carriage carrying Darcy, Uncle Henry, Huntley, and Georgiana drew closer to Pemberley. It had not been a fortnight since their arrival in Ramsgate, and Darcy's eyes were heavy from exhaustion. Elizabeth's desire to afford Thomas as easy a trip as possible made more sense than ever; although, the child seemed to be more well-rested than the remainder of their party.

They had recuperated in Ramsgate for three days prior to their departure for Derbyshire. Bingley and Grace had welcomed them at Rosings for one night, which allowed them to have a brief visit with the newlyweds and Thomas some time to adjust, so that he did not sleep the day away. They stopped the following night at Ashcroft house in London where they received word they would be welcomed at Matlock—an easy distance from Pemberley—for as long as was necessary.

After three long days of travel, Uncle Henry and Aunt Elinor greeted them with open arms. They were excited to see their new nephew, and Aunt Elinor secured the child as soon as he was safely out of the carriage, citing he was as close to a grandchild as she had at the moment. Huntley grimaced at her barb and chastising look.

The journey then continued with Uncle Henry and Huntley, who had invited themselves along upon learning Wickham's scheme. Both had been justified in the fury Wickham had incited in them, and by extension, their ire towards George Darcy. The elder Darcy's belief in the upright character of his godson had almost cost the family Georgiana, and Lord Matlock made his stance clear upon the recitation of the incident at Ramsgate—he would not lose another family member due to his inaction. The loss of Anne still weighed heavily upon his uncle. Darcy appreciated his uncle's support regardless of the reason.

Huntley had indicated a desire to accompany them in order to aid in setting George Darcy to rights. In his opinion, Wickham should have never had the access nor the opportunity to influence Georgiana. The elder Darcy had been negligent when he hired Mrs. Younge and lackadaisical when he allowed one such as Wickham near an impressionable girl.

Georgiana was given the option to remain at Matlock with Elizabeth, Thomas, and Grandmamma until the initial explanations were given, yet opted to join the men in the hopes she could assist. She had confided that she dreaded a confrontation with their father, but saw no other alternative than to reveal all.

At present, she sat beside Darcy, her hand around his arm and her head against his shoulder. There was a distinct possibility they would be separated by that afternoon and both were rather subdued as a result.

With a quick glance out of the window, Uncle Henry closed his book. "There is the marker. We are now within the grounds of Pemberley.

His sister's head darted up to peer out of the window. She turned to him with wide eyes and a tear trailing down her cheek. "I am sorry."

"Why are you sorry, Georgie?" asked Huntley. "You have done nothing wrong. Mrs. Younge and Mr. Wickham both used you quite ill—Mrs. Younge especially. I find her blackmail unforgiveable. She took advantage of your family's estrangement and her position for her own gain and to further Wickham's schemes."

"He is correct." Darcy tipped her chin towards him. "I am touched you were silent in order to visit with Elizabeth, Thomas and me, but none of us wishes for you to be put in danger. I hope you have learnt a lesson and will consider our feelings should something of this nature ever occur again."

"Of course, I have. I just never dreamt either would create such a vile plan."

Huntley's doubtful gaze studied Georgiana. "You are very well informed in regards to the servant's gossip. Had you never heard any tales of Wickham?"

"I imagine the servants would not have told her much as many of his exploits are not appropriate for a young lady's ears. Should father have discovered, the servant would have been dismissed."

"All servants talk…"

Georgiana turned to her cousin with a smirk. "Pemberley servants may gossip within the kitchens and hallways, but should a rumour surface in the village, the servant who spoke of the family outside of the home would be dismissed."

"Obtaining the identity of the gossip monger is never difficult," explained Darcy. "I was witness to my father's dismissal of a maid five years ago. She did not spread anything dreadful, but it was the principle of the matter. He dismissed her before the entirety of the staff."

A whistle from Uncle Henry drew their attention. "George was always an excellent master to his tenants and servants. I knew that inspired a certain amount of loyalty, but I now understand why there is so little gossip about the Darcys. The only source is what occurs outside your homes."

They passed over a rise and out of the woods where he took his first glimpse of Pemberley in over a year. The house was unchanged as it came into view in its situation on the opposite side of the valley, backed by a ridge of high woody hills, and a stream that wound through the front of the park.

He had not been gone for many years, but should it not seem different somehow? There remained a part of him that would forever consider it home, despite his love for Sagemore—but then home was now with Elizabeth. There was no home without her and Thomas.

The carriage descended to the front entrance, where they disembarked, and ascended the steps to the butler who awaited them.

"Lord Matlock, Lord Huntley, Mr. Darcy, Miss Darcy. The servants were not informed that you would be arriving today. Is the master aware of your visit?"

"My father is not expecting us, Howard, but it is of vital importance that we speak with him."

The butler considered him and stepped aside, holding out his hand in an invitation to enter. Then he began to lead them towards the library until a voice bid him to halt.

"Georgiana, why have you returned and with your brother?" came their father's strident voice from the stairs.

She faltered, so Darcy took her hand in a silent show of support. His father did not miss the interaction and stepped down until he was directly before their party.

"I asked you a question, Georgiana. Do I not deserve an answer?"

"Y… y… yes, sir," she stuttered. "I… I had… had a problem in Ramsgate. Fitzwilliam aided in my removal."

"What sort of problem?" His inquiry was made in a forceful tone, and Georgiana visibly shrank back from her father.

"George, we should conduct this conversation behind closed doors," interrupted their uncle. "I have no doubt in the discretion of the Pemberley servants, but it would not do for any portion of this tale to become public knowledge."

His father's jaw clenched and unclenched several times as he studied each member of their group before finally conceding with a curt nod. "Very well, would you *all* please join me in the library?"

Once the doors were closed behind them, Georgiana sank into a chair and began to cry. The stress of the entire situation still distressed her, and she would be of little help in relating the tale.

George Darcy ascertained that fact and turned to his son. "Would you please explain why you were in Ramsgate at the same time as your sister and why you have removed her from her establishment?"

Darcy took a deep breath and released it. He did not wish to cause trouble for Georgiana, yet there was no other way to explain the situation other than to divulge everything.

"Georgie and I have been frequent correspondents since I last departed Pemberley."

His father's face bespoke of his irritation as he pivoted to face his daughter. "You expressly defied my wishes?"

To everyone's surprise, Georgiana lifted her face from her handkerchief, looked her father in the eye, and responded, "Yes."

"Yes? And this is all the reply which I am to receive?"

Uncle Henry stepped forward and placed a hand on the elder Darcy's shoulder. "Perhaps it is best if we save *this* discussion for later. It is imperative we get to the point and a decision made as to how to proceed."

His father regarded his uncle with confusion. "I do not understand."

"You will."

"As I said," continued Darcy, "we have been corresponding. We met in October when Georgie was in London, and then made arrangements to spend time together in Ramsgate.

"Grandmamma and I both had concerns in regards to the suitability of Mrs. Younge whilst she was in residence in London."

"Your grandmother removed Georgiana from Mrs. Younge's care." His father frowned and clenched his fists. "I was displeased with her officiousness in the matter. She gave no reasonable explanation for her actions, other than she wished for a visit without interference."

"Because I begged her not to tell you, Papa."

The elder Darcy furrowed his brow and kneeled down beside his daughter. "You begged her not to tell me what, pray tell?"

"George Wickham arrived in London a week after the family departed for Rosings."

His father shrugged his shoulders. "I would prefer he not stay at Darcy House due to the possibility of harm to your reputation, but he has his own chambers and was unlikely to interfere with your plans."

"But he did," she whispered. "His behaviour was unlike in the past, and he was insistent he should accompany me on walks in Hyde Park."

"Explain to father what you mean by different." His father had to understand, which would not occur unless his sister related the story in full.

She glanced over and closed her eyes for a moment before she began to speak. "As I said, he was insistent he would accompany me on walks. He had the seating changed at dinner, so he was seated directly beside me.

"Then Mrs. Younge mentioned that he was such a handsome suitor."

"Suitor?" the elder Darcy boomed. "Surely, you jest?"

His sister began to cry, and Darcy stepped forward to take her hand, giving it a gentle squeeze. "Mrs. Younge threatened to notify you of my communication with Georgiana should my sister inform you of Wickham and her actions. Grandmamma managed a confession of the circumstances from Georgie and removed her with all due haste from Darcy House for her protection."

His father pinched the bridge of his nose as if fighting a headache. "Mrs. Younge indicated Rebecca wanted to spend time with her granddaughter. She felt your grandmother disapproved of her as Georgiana's companion, which was why she was relegated to remain at Darcy House."

Darcy gave a bitter chuckle. Mrs. Younge's lie was not so far from the truth. "But Grandmamma informed you of Wickham's behaviour."

"She did, but not to the extent Georgiana just did. She also did not mention Mrs. Younge's complicity."

"At my request," interjected Georgiana.

"She should have ignored your request and told me! Wickham was supposed to be making arrangements to study the law, not court my daughter!" He raised his voice and Georgiana startled. "You should have told me." The elder Darcy sighed and stepped over to kiss her on the head. "I apologise, Poppet. I am frustrated and unsure of what to believe."

"You should allow Fitzwilliam to continue," said Uncle Henry. "There is much more to the tale."

Georgiana grasped her father's hand, redirecting the elder Darcy's attention to her. "My brother speaks the truth. I feared you would prevent my communication with him, so I allowed Mrs. Younge to threaten me. Please believe me, Papa. Fitzwilliam came to my aid in Ramsgate. Without him, I would have been lost to you."

His father's eyes narrowed and his eyebrows furrowed. "I demand to know every detail of what occurred in Kent."

A tear dropped to her cheek. "Wickham came to the house the morning you departed."

"He was supposed to be in London." His father's voice reflected his disbelief, but his confusion was evident.

"That may very well be," cried Georgiana in frustration, "but he was not in London then, as he is not in London now."

George Darcy stepped back, shocked at his daughter's uncharacteristic display of temper.

"Elizabeth and I stepped out to take a walk along the coast when we spotted Georgie as she walked with Wickham—*without a chaperone.*"

"Where was Mrs. Younge?" His father glanced back and forth between his son and daughter.

Georgiana lifted her head from where she had been resting her forehead on the heel of her hand. "She claimed she was ill and could not accompany us. I attempted to demur, but she was insistent and suggested there would be nothing improper since we were to walk in a public place. Mr. Wickham made the intimation that I would be rude to refuse."

The stress of the situation was taking its toll on his sister. He would need to handle matters as much as possible. "When we spied them walking along the sea wall, Elizabeth drew Georgie away, so I could confront Wickham."

"You allowed your *wife* to chaperone your sister?" his father stormed.

Uncle Henry stepped between them and placed a hand to the elder Darcy's chest. "Settle down, George. Lizzy is intelligent and poised for one so young. I daresay she would have been a better choice of companion than that horrid woman you employed. Whilst Fitzwilliam spoke with that worthless ward of yours, Lizzy ensured Georgiana was brought to her grandmother, and did so without Wickham's notice."

"You only think Wickham worthless because he was the son of a steward."

Uncle Henry gave a derisive chuckle. "I think him an opportunistic little weasel, who will milk you for any farthing he can get."

Huntley stepped forward. "Those farthings would not last long, as he would lose more than he possessed at the nearest gambling establishment whilst he ran up a tab on ale he had no intention of paying. Oh! *And* let us not forget the barmaid or innkeeper's daughter…"

"That is enough," interrupted Darcy. "I do not relish a discussion of Wickham's more notorious exploits with Georgie in the room."

George Darcy glowered at the viscount. "I have heard yours and your father's opinions of Wickham prior to today, yet you have never had any proof he is as you say."

A scoff came from Huntley's direction. "You are a fool."

George Darcy reddened and stepped forward, but Uncle Henry again put a hand to his chest. "This is not conducive to solving our current problem." He turned to his son. "Arthur, perhaps you should take a walk."

"I only spoke the truth!"

"I know, son, but it is not of any aid at this point. We need to finish the discussion about Ramsgate, and dredging up the past is not helpful." Huntley sulked and strode from the room with a vicious slam of the door.

Without a pause, Darcy returned to the task at hand. "We know Wickham's motive was to wed Georgie in order to obtain her

405

dowry—Mrs. Younge confirmed as much. She also indicated that he believed I had been disinherited, and Wickham himself claimed he deserved my place as your son—as your heir. He had grand plans to somehow become master of Pemberley in the future through the marriage."

"I would never have sanctioned such a match," countered his father.

"He does not require your consent for an *elopement*." Uncle Henry stepped over to the brandy and removed the stopper as he raised his eyebrows. "Do you mind?" When no answer was given, he shrugged and poured a small glass.

Darcy glanced down to his sister, and then back to his father. "His plan was to take her to Gretna Green. After he told me of Scotland, he noticed Georgie was gone and became furious. He threatened her reputation as well as mine amongst society. He then made comments I will not divulge before my sister."

Her eyes bulged, and she sprang to her feet. "What was it he said?"

He shook his head. "No, it is too vile. I will tell father, but I will not upset you further."

She huffed. "I suppose I shall join Huntley on that walk." Her exit was similar to her cousin's, and as soon as she left, Uncle Henry took a seat.

"I suggest you have a seat for this next part, George."

George Darcy shook his head. "I do not require a chair. I require you to continue." He looked back to his son insistently.

"He accused me of the ruination of his schemes, and I told him I would not allow him to destroy Georgiana's life. Wickham then said, 'Once I put her in the family way, I would find other amusements. Your little sister would probably be as dry and boring in bed as you are just existing.'"

His father stared, and he began to doubt whether his father's faith in the matter could be attained.

"You should examine your son's knuckles. I imagine he put quite the wallop on Wickham to be so badly bruised." Uncle Henry gave a head tilt in the direction of the hand which Darcy shifted so what remained of the injury was hidden.

"It is of no importance. If it were not for Elizabeth's quick thinking, we would have never made it to Pemberley in advance of Wickham.

As it is, I informed the magistrate and the constables that I would make arrangements for Wickham within a fortnight."

"You had him jailed?" asked his father in disbelief. "How does that protect your sister's reputation?"

"He was jailed for debts; otherwise, he would have disappeared without paying, as he has done in the past."

"If he were as bad as you claim, I would have heard word of debts in Lambton by now." The elder Darcy wore a sceptical expression as he leaned against the desk behind him. "Rebecca and you," he said with a nod towards Uncle Henry, "have attempted to convince me of this for years. I have never seen evidence of him gambling or amassing large debts, rather he has remained a loyal companion as his father was before him."

After staring for a moment at a miniature of Wickham kept upon a shelf, the elder Darcy took long looks at both him and his uncle. "I cannot accept that Wickham would behave in such a fashion with Georgiana. Perhaps if Georgiana had remained, I might be more convinced…"

Darcy's head shook. Would his father never trust in him? "She was not present for that conversation. I had gone to make arrangements for her trunk. I only returned when I had the necessary papers, and in the presence of the constables, who I am certain would attest to Wickham's threats when he was taken away."

"And what debts did you pay?" asked his father. "I would not have left him without funds to pay his expenses."

Uncle Henry gave a snort. "He likely gambled away the bulk of his allowance."

Darcy stepped forward before his uncle and father could begin an argument. "Are you aware that he stayed for a se'nnight at an inn in Ramsgate? A bill he had no intention of paying as he departed the establishment without the owner's knowledge—which included an entire week's lodging, meals, and ale. He had also seen fit to purchase himself a new suit."

"No doubt, he wished to look his best when he courted Georgiana." Uncle Henry's glare towards the elder Darcy was thunderous. His uncle had always despised George Darcy's blind affection for the boy, and with the scheme against Georgiana, his anger for the situation had worsened.

"Uncle! You are not helping matters now."

"Whether it helps matters not, I am sick to death of your father's loyalty to a leech who does not deserve what he has been given. Wickham is an unappreciative little whelp!" He stood and slammed down the glass, breaking the stem.

"You have funded this boy for years," he yelled as he stood face to face with the elder Darcy. "You have called your own son a liar, and accepted the word of a worthless scab since you took the boy into your home. He has beaten your son, blackmailed him, and ensured you were never told of his exploits.

"Your stable manager attempted to tell you once, do you remember? Within a fortnight there was the accident within the stables and one of the horses was killed."

"Johns did not lock up as he aught."

Darcy shook his head. "I checked the stables that evening. Everything was locked tight when Johns was finished. We have never discovered Wickham's means of entering that night, so we could never prove his complicity."

"Have you ever questioned your servants? I would wager everything I own they have Wickham pegged." Uncle Henry began towards the door. "In fact, where is Mrs. Reynolds?"

He opened the heavy oak panel and peered out where a footman stood at the end of the hall. "You there, please ask Mrs. Reynolds to join us in the library."

The footman gave a bow and hurried off. "I will prove to you once and for all the worthlessness of that young man."

With a shake of his head, George Darcy closed the door. "This is not necessary. I will hear what you have to say, though I still insist that I would have heard of any debts he had in Lambton."

A frustrated exhale escaped Darcy's lungs. "When I discovered the amount of the credit given to Wickham by the tradesmen in Lambton, I paid them, but with the understanding that I would only cover his debts the one time. I do not believe any one has extended credit to him since. Last I heard, he no longer ventures into Lambton, and instead, rides to Kympton and Buxton."

Mrs. Reynolds hurried in and curtsied. "You wished to see me, sir?"

"Not me, Mrs. Reynolds. Lord Matlock has some questions he would ask you."

Her expression became puzzled as she pivoted to Uncle Henry. "Of course, Lord Matlock. How may I be of service?"

"Mrs. Reynolds, I would appreciate it greatly if you could give us your honest opinion of Mr. Wickham?"

Her eyes widened and her mouth opened without a sound escaping. Her gaze darted to her master as though she was requesting permission.

"Your honest opinion, if you please," continued Uncle Henry.

The elder Darcy's eyebrows furrowed. "Please, what do you think of Mr. Wickham?"

"But I could never speak ill of one of the household, sir." Her voice was tentative and worried.

George Darcy stood straight and took a long stride forward. "Now, I insist upon it. What have you to say about the man?"

She peered to each of them, her eyes betraying her anxiety, and cleared her throat. "We thought it a noble thing you did, taking the boy in and all, but he soon began to behave as though he owned the place."

"How do you mean?" His father took another step forward.

"Well, at first, he began to give orders. He would tell the maids he wanted clean sheets when it was not the day for it. He would insist the nightshirts the cook and I made him were not sufficient. He wanted ones identical to the ones the young master wore.

"After a year or two, he began to make advances towards a few of the younger maids."

"What?" exclaimed his father. "Why was I never told?"

Her eyes again darted back and forth between her master and his son. "By that time, sir, Mr. Johns in the stables had attempted to inform you of the problems he caused for young Master Fitzwilliam. You insisted it was no more than boyhood mischief, so I dared not broach it with you."

George Darcy retreated back to his desk and clenched its edge.

"Is there more?" asked Uncle Henry.

"Yes, sir." Her worried eyes remained on her master. "I solved the problem by instructing the maids to never be alone. They were to always work in pairs."

"Very industrious of you." With a quirk of the lips, Uncle Henry showed his approbation.

"Thank you, sir. Since then, I heard the tales of young Wickham's debts in Lambton as well as those of the young master when he paid the debts. I know the tradesmen there no longer extend credit to Wickham.

"I am also aware of children he has fathered in the local area."

The elder Darcy again pinched the bridge of his nose. "Am I aware of any of these children?"

"Yes, sir. Your tenants, the Smiths, have taken in two boys, which are both natural sons of Wickham's."

He groaned. "They were such a blessing to the family after they lost their own children in the fire. I never considered their origin."

"Their mothers are different girls." Her eyes darted between the three men as she continued. "The elder is the natural grandson of the butcher in Kympton, and the younger is the result of his seduction of the innkeeper's youngest daughter."

"The inn in Lambton?"

"Kympton, sir. Each arranged for relatives to take the girls in until their confinement. I knew of the Smiths' predicament, and put them in touch with the fathers. There was a third, but the young girl and the babe died in childbirth."

"Who was the girl?" asked his father.

"The vicar's daughter from over in Buxton. She passed almost a year ago now."

"Mrs. Reynolds, did you ever see evidence Mr. Wickham beat my nephew when they were boys?"

"I did. His valet desired my opinion on how best to treat the injuries." She looked to the younger Darcy with tears in her eyes. "Poor Master Fitzwilliam! The bruises to his ribs were just dreadful!"

"I do not understand…" George Darcy shook his head vehemently.

"Sir, if you will pardon me for speaking freely. Mr Wickham is a practiced liar. The boy and man I see around Master Fitzwilliam or the maids is a different animal than that who courts your favour. He simpers and fawns and pretends to be what he is not."

410

"I am grieved and shocked." His father's pale visage spoke volumes to his state. "I feel I owe you an apology, Mrs. Reynolds. I disregarded everyone. I wanted to believe Wickham was like his father, like my good friend, when in fact, he is as much an opposite as one can be." He shook his head and rubbed his face. "You should have felt you could approach me with the problem of the maids."

"What is done is done, sir. We cannot go back and change matters."

"But you can change how you deal with Wickham in the future, George. You must protect Georgiana before he damages her reputation."

Mrs. Reynolds gasped. "Please tell me he has not imposed himself on our Miss Darcy!"

Uncle Henry placed a hand upon her shoulder. "Not to worry. He has hoped for more than what he has received, but he will spread lies and tarnish her reputation if we do not act soon to stop him."

"Oooh, that boy! I have wanted to take him over my knee for years."

"It would have done him a great deal of good, I am sure." Under different circumstances, Mrs. Reynolds comment would make Darcy laugh, but instead he gave a small smile. "Thank you." He peered over to his father, who leaned over the desk supported by his arms. "We know where to find you should we require more information."

She gave a nod and departed, her keys rattling against her chatelaine.

"We need to make a decision in regards to him, and soon. I must pen a letter to the constable and magistrate." Darcy gestured towards the paper and quill upon the desk to garner his father's attention.

"There is also the predicament of Mrs. Younge."

"What of Mrs. Younge?" asked his father weakly.

"She is with child, and she claims Wickham is the father." Darcy's hand rubbed across his forehead as he attempted to stave off a headache, but the action, thus far, was not of any help. "I am reluctant to be of aid to her, but she did provide more information as to Wickham's motives after his arrest."

"Was not Georgiana's ruin enough?" His father slumped against the edge of his desk.

"If she is truthful, then it was not. He did wish for access to her dowry, which he intended to use to keep Mrs. Younge." His father winced. "But he was also of the idea that I was disinherited from Pemberley, and expected it to pass to Georgiana."

Uncle Henry poured himself another brandy. "He is mad!"

"Even had I the power to change its disposition, I would have never allowed Pemberley to fall into his hands. He is not a Darcy, and should his plan have succeeded, I would have had him put on a ship to New South Wales or a similar colony. It would be preferable to see Georgiana live with the shame of being deserted than with someone who duped or forced her into an elopement."

Uncle Henry took Wickham's miniature from the mantel and handed it to his father. "Perhaps that should be our plan to rid ourselves of him now."

Darcy's eyebrows raised in the direction of his uncle and father. "We could arrange for Mrs. Younge and Wickham to wed, and then banish them together; although, I do wonder where you got the idea for that scheme?" Darcy chuckled and Uncle Henry rolled his eyes.

"The plan has merit!"

"I believe they both have merit." His father was still ashen as he straightened and faced him. "I owe you an apology for a wrong for which I can never make atonement."

Uncle Henry nodded. "Indeed you do, and Fitzwilliam, you will not excuse the offenses away."

"Uncle, I believe this should be between father and myself."

"He is correct, son. I have taken Wickham's part over yours for far too long. I believed you were jealous of the time I spent with him when his father died. His father was such a good man, and Wickham had always been such a well-behaved boy. I never dreamt he had such evil propensities.

"Poor Johns!" His father rubbed his forehead. "I have wronged him as well, but I do not know why you allowed it."

With a heavy exhale, Darcy dropped into the nearest chair. "We both knew what happened that night, but we had no proof and Johns refused to let me vouch for him. He knew Wickham would revenge himself upon me, and he had seen me beaten too many times. I needed a good stable manager at Sagemore, so…"

"So you gave him a place rather than see Wickham punished?"

"Would Wickham have been punished without proof?" asked his uncle. "You never believed them in the past, so why would you have believed them then?

His father took a seat behind the desk and leaned his forearms upon it. "I have given matters a great deal of thought lately. I have heard the gossip of you in town, and I am aware of whispers of Wickham dallying with widows and a few card games, which I never bothered to correct. They were not maidens, and whilst I did not condone the action, it was not as though he was ruining innocents." He dropped his forehead into his palm. "Only he was.

"My abominable pride prevented me from taking other's opinions of him and determining the truth."

Darcy shook his head. "I am still amazed we convinced you today."

He sighed. "How could I refute it? Georgiana insistence you told the truth, compounded with the gossip, and finally, Mrs. Reynolds' confirmation of his character. I made a promise to his father, and as I just said, I have been convinced the son was of the same ilk."

A glance between his father and uncle gave the indication they were both of a mind to make a final resolution. "We should make this decision now, so I can leave on the morrow."

The elder Darcy shook his head. "No, I created this mess, and I will journey to Ramsgate to repair the damage I have wrought.

"I will see that Wickham weds Mrs. Younge. Assuming he was after my daughter's dowry, he will be unable to scheme against another with similar intentions. Mrs. Younge will have a child and be a married woman. She will not again seek employment as a companion with such a situation."

"You will see them wed and then leave them to their own devices?" Uncle Henry's tone was incredulous.

"No, I will give Wickham three-thousand pounds and passage to one of the colonies. I will allow him to choose where. I hope by providing him with such a sum, I will have discharged my duty to his father."

Uncle Henry regarded the elder Darcy with concern. "You fulfilled your promise years ago, George. I do not believe the money is necessary, but if it assuages your guilt in the matter then we will not dissuade you."

His father gazed at him with an earnest expression. "Fitzwilliam, I will have to leave early on the morrow. Would you be willing to remain at Pemberley with Georgiana? I would be easier knowing she is well looked after."

"I appreciate your confidence, but Elizabeth is at Matlock. I will not be without her—without my family—for as long as it may take for you to conclude your business."

"Of course; your wife may stay as well."

Darcy stared at his father with a stunned countenance. "I will need to consult with her on the matter. I am positive she would agree since she has been concerned about Georgiana since Ramsgate, but I will not presume to answer for her."

"I remember well consulting with your mother on such matters. If you could perhaps send an express when you return to Matlock…"

"Georgiana would be welcome to stay with us," offered his uncle. "Though I do understand if you wish her to remain here."

His father shook his head. "It may be best to leave the decision to her. Mrs. Reynolds and the staff will mind her well, but after today, I believe I prefer her to have a member of the family until I return."

Georgiana and Huntley could be seen as they strolled through the formal gardens, and Darcy strode over to a set of French doors to call them both inside. Once his sister returned, she stepped before their father with an apprehensive mien.

"Please forgive me for not informing you of Mrs. Younge and Mr. Wickham."

"It is I who must beg your forgiveness." His father placed a kiss to her forehead and took her hands. "I should have not banished your brother as I did. You would not have sought him out in secret, if I had not behaved so. It was because of my actions—my greed—you were put in peril. I realised at Christmas how my demands alienated my own son, yet I was too proud to admit I was in the wrong."

Darcy stared at his father, his mouth agape. Had his father just admitted he should not have schemed as he had? Could he have truly seen the errors of his ways so long ago?

"Oh, Papa!" She threw her arms about her father's neck, and the elder Darcy held her to him. "I do wish you had listened to Fitzwilliam, but you did as you thought best. It was not what he or

Anne desired. Yet, everything has worked out as it ought. You will come to love Lizzy. I am certain of it!"

Uncle Henry gave a pleased chuckle. "We hope he will, but Georgie, let us take one matter at a time. Your father hoped your brother would stay with you here—at Pemberley."

"What a wonderful idea! I could take Lizzy riding and show her all of my favourite spots."

Darcy grinned and gestured to the sofa where he and his sister both took a seat. "Elizabeth would enjoy such a tour, I am certain, but I would also wish to show her Pemberley as well."

She gave a slight frown. "I had not considered that."

"I must also speak with Elizabeth before we make any plans. Despite father's invitation, she may not feel comfortable enough to accept. If such is the case, would you be willing to remain at Matlock until father's return? I believe we would all be more at ease to know you are with family."

"I would not mind in the slightest, although, I would wish to remain here until Papa departs."

"I will leave at first light in the morning," he interjected. "I dare not tarry, else what careful arrangements your brother has made will be for naught."

"You could send word of Lizzy's decision upon your return to Matlock?" She studied him with hopeful eyes, and one side of his lips quirked upward.

"You are determined Elizabeth and I come to Pemberley." The statement was not a question. Her wishes were apparent.

"I am! Mrs. Reynolds would be thrilled. She has wanted to meet Elizabeth since the beginning, and…"

"Enough!" he said with a laugh. "I will attempt to convince her, but I make no guarantees."

Georgiana Darcy beamed smugly as she glanced to everyone in the room. "I ask nothing more, dear brother."

Chapter 29

Elizabeth sang to Thomas as they continued their walk around the lake. He was a tad fussy, and she found a walk in the outdoors was of great benefit when he was in an ill mood. The happy gurgles he had uttered as they strolled had since subsided and his head rested upon her shoulder. He was certain to have drifted asleep, but she enjoyed holding him in her arms. He would not be so young forever, and this time with him was to be cherished.

As she rounded the last bend and exited the wood, Fitzwilliam stood in the path with a wide grin upon his face.

"Has Thomas enjoyed his ramble?"

"I will have you know that he gurgled and cooed every moment until he fell asleep."

He stretched out his hand to caress his son's downy hair. "I am glad to find him sleeping. Mary was quite beside herself when she could not console him this morning."

Elizabeth lowered him a bit so he was not on her shoulder but cradled across her chest. His little mouth gaped open as he drooled upon her gown.

"Here," said Fitzwilliam as he placed a handkerchief to soak up the mess, "so he will not ruin the fabric."

"I am unconcerned with him ruining the fabric. I can always embroider the bodice to hide it."

An arm snaked around her waist and they continued their walk. "I received a letter from my father indicating his return on the morrow."

"I am still amazed he escorted Mr. and Mrs. Wickham to Southampton himself." Mr. Darcy had been away for over three weeks, and had sent word several days before that he would begin his return.

"He will have employed several hands for the journey. He did not wish Wickham to escape and renege on the agreement, or even steal the money before they were to leave the country."

"So, he ensured the ship was to sail, before he handed Mr. Wickham the funds?"

Fitzwilliam nodded. "He has not written as such, but I am certain of it. I believe he had very little trust of Wickham before his arrival in

416

Ramsgate; yet he did not expect there to be other debts for him to pay.

"To think it!" she exclaimed. "He had purchased so many little trinkets in order to woo Georgiana. I thank God we arrived early."

"It was you who expressed concern about the alteration of the tone of her letters," Darcy reminded her.

They had gone over Georgiana's correspondence many times in the last few weeks, and her husband remained impressed she had noticed something amiss. He still could not see much difference between those letters and her usual manner.

"Grandmamma also knew there was a situation. She would have told us of Mrs. Younge and Wickham even if I had not had a bad feeling about it. Besides, Mr. and Mrs. Wickham are now wed and travelling far from us."

"I only wish father had not given him so much money," he complained. "What is to prevent him from purchasing a return voyage once he arrives? I would not be surprised if he abandoned Mrs. Younge as well."

"Which is why I gave half of the money to her." Their heads whipped around to where George Darcy stood at the opening of the trail to the stables. "After noting the amount you had paid and paying more of his debts upon my arrival to Ramsgate, I reduced the sum to one thousand pounds. I should like to know how much I owe you for the payment of all of his past debts. You should not have shouldered such a burden."

Her husband glanced around his father. "We did not expect you until this evening."

His father gave a smile that did not reach his eyes. "I rented a horse this morning and rode the remainder of the trip. I do some of my best thinking whilst I ride."

Her husband's head gave a curt nod. "I do the same."

The elder Darcy's eyes moved down to their son as he suckled in his sleep. "He looks as you did when you were a babe." He spoke so softly, as if in awe.

Mr. Darcy stepped further from the trees and looked to his son. "May I have the pleasure of an introduction?"

Fitzwilliam started, a reaction that bespoke of his surprise at the request. "Father, I would like you to make the acquaintance of my beloved wife, Elizabeth Darcy, and our son, Thomas Aaron Bennet Darcy."

The elder Darcy drew his eyebrows together as he studied the baby. "He is named for your father?"

"Yes, sir."

Was he upset or annoyed they wished to honour her family? He could not have expected them to name the child for him, could he?

"I have heard your family passed in a carriage accident. My condolences for their loss."

"Thank you," she responded in a bewildered tone. Her husband claimed his father's feelings were much the opposite as they had been, but it would take time to trust this new situation.

"I am afraid my question interrupted my son's introduction." He gave a slight bow. "I am George Darcy. I know we have been in company prior to today, but I would beg you forget my words then. I was wrong to behave as I did, and I have paid dearly for such a grievous mistake."

She curtsied as much as she was able with Thomas in her arms. He had been a large baby at birth, and had grown much since, making him a heavy burden when sleeping as he was.

"Here, why do I not hold him for a while?" Fitzwilliam carefully lifted the precious bundle from her arms and settled his son to his chest without disturbing his rest. "Perhaps we should make our way to the house. He is no longer fussy and will be more at ease in his bed.

"Of course," exclaimed his father, "I remember those days well."

They began to walk, and Elizabeth hooked her hand through her husband's elbow.

Mr. Darcy regarded her with interest. "I hope you have been well taken care of at Pemberley."

"Yes, Mrs Reynolds has been a godsend. She ensured we wanted for nothing. I assure you."

"Good. She has always been very capable. I am pleased you have found her accommodating."

"She has been thrilled to have a babe in the house." Her husband chuckled. "On occasion, I have found her in the nursery checking on Thomas and ensuring Mary is not in need of a break."

Mr. Darcy laughed, a sound that resembled her husband's low rumble. "She was much the same with Georgiana when she was a babe. She once confided to your mother how she had wished for children, but as she was never wed…"

"She was never blessed." A pang of sadness pierced her heart at the thought. Poor Mrs. Reynolds!

"Precisely. That is the reason Mrs. Reynolds would take Georgiana on walks from time to time. She is an impeccable housekeeper, and Anne allowed her to help the nurse and governess when her duties allowed."

"That was very kind of Mrs. Darcy." She glanced to her husband, who looked with pride at their son.

"Anne was always kind. I believe she made me a better man whilst she lived. I have become poorer for her lack of counsel since her death."

"But she is *here*." Elizabeth stopped and pivoted towards him. "My family may be no longer of this world, but I am aware of what they would want for me and my life. At times, it is as though I can hear their advice. Is it not possible you ceased to listen?" Heat rushed to her face and she took a step back towards her husband. "Please forgive my impertinence. I am afraid my mouth has run away with itself."

Fitzwilliam's arm came around her waist, and she closed her eyes in mortification.

"Please do not distress yourself." Mr. Darcy's expression held no anger despite the insensitivity of her words. "I have given much thought during my recent journeys as to what has transpired since her death and come to much the same realisation. I have long been aware of Anne's last wishes—without her expressly stating them— yet I ignored them due to the pain of her loss and in favour of family pride and greed. She would be ashamed of me."

"Disappointed, but not ashamed," interjected Fitzwilliam.

"I am unsure the distinction is an improvement." His father gave a rueful chuckle.

Fitzwilliam bestowed a loving glance in her direction. "I believe it is best to leave the past where it belongs in this case."

Mr. Darcy regarded his son with a puzzled expression.

"In the past." Her husband shifted their son in his arms. "You must learn some of Elizabeth's philosophy. Think only of the past as its remembrance gives you pleasure."

"There is not much of my recent past with you which gives me pleasure. I can never atone for the mistakes I have made." The earnest regret on Mr. Darcy's countenance was heart breaking, despite his previous behaviour.

"But it does not mean we cannot begin again. There would be new memories to replace those that are painful."

His father gazed at the son with hopeful eyes. "You could forgive my taking young Wickham's part over yours, and then the officious interference into your life?"

Her husband's foot shuffled against the ground as he considered his answer. "Trust will take time, but I am willing to try."

Mr. Darcy turned the same hopeful expression to her. "You have no reservations?"

"Sir, whether I have reservations or not is irrelevant. I merely want what is best for my husband and my son. If my husband is happier as a result of a relationship with you, then I cannot object, as long as your intentions are what they appear. Like Fitzwilliam, I cannot promise to give you my immediate trust."

His head shook adamantly as tears welled in his eyes. "I would not expect either of you to trust me after the manner in which I behaved. I can only express my gratitude for your willingness to accept me after the infamous manner in which I have treated both of you." He cleared his throat and straightened his posture.

"Georgiana mentioned in her letter you were to remain in Ramsgate until the harvest."

"Yes," answered Fitzwilliam, "we hoped to spend as much time as we could spare with her."

"She was so desperate to know Thomas." Elizabeth smiled as she reached to tuck the blanket away from her son's face.

"I cannot say as I blame her. I hope you will remain at Pemberley in the stead of your stay in Ramsgate." He peered around them and shrugged. "It is not the seaside, but I think it to be some of the prettiest land in Derbyshire."

"Your estate is beautiful." She turned to gaze over the lake, and then back to the father.

"Then you approve?"

A grin appeared upon her lips. "Very much so. I dare say there are few who would not approve."

"But it is you who must live here one day."

She took her husband's arm, and they began to stroll towards the house once more. "You are still so comfortably situated here with Georgiana that I have given the matter little thought. I am certain you will live on here for many years before you require Fitzwilliam's assistance."

When they entered, Mrs. Reynolds bustled forward while the butler took their hats and gloves. Fitzwilliam, with great care, handed Thomas to the housekeeper, who whisked him upstairs to settle him in his bed. They then followed Mr. Darcy into a drawing room where they all settled themselves.

"To answer your statement, Georgiana will be out in society in a few years, and I do not relish the idea of rattling around this house all alone whence she has wed. I hope you will consider visiting often, and when the time comes, you will join me here."

"We can promise to consider the matter." Her husband observed her reaction, but the idea did not alarm her in the slightest. "I do not mean to pain you, but we are very comfortable and at home at Sagemore. I would never force Elizabeth to leave her home."

Her hand reached out and settled on her husband's knee. "I do love Sagemore, but if circumstances required us to move, it does not mean I would not be amenable." She could not break his father's heart when he was making such an attempt to reconcile.

Mr. Darcy's face lit. "We should have chambers redone for you. You must pick whichever suite you wish, and you can make arrangements to have the rooms decorated as you choose prior to your departure. That way, you will have your own bedchambers when you return to visit."

"Mr. Darcy, our rooms are perfectly adequate. They are, in fact, very lovely. We do not expect you to spend money for rooms we might use but a month or two out of the year." Did he think her like most women of the ton? Did he expect her to make an immediate grab at his money, so she could indiscriminately spend his wealth? His attempt to make amends was honourable, but his intentions in this regard were not clear.

A maid entered to deliver their tea, and she set to work serving her husband and his father.

"I desire your comfort whilst you remain under my roof," he explained. "I believe it may make a transition easier should you need to reside here in the near future."

Fitzwilliam opened his mouth to speak, but his father held up his hand.

"Please, walk around the house and pick out a suite. If there are no changes you see fit to make, then I will not argue, but there is no room attached to your present bedchambers to convert to a nursery for Thomas.

"I thoughtlessly had not considered a child when I instructed Mrs. Reynolds as to which suite she should prepare. I do not think you the style of mother who is comfortable with your babe a floor above."

Her husband shook his head. "No, she is not. We will ask Mrs. Reynolds if there are suitable rooms for our use, but Elizabeth is not one to spend money unless it is required."

"All I wish is for you to make this home your own."

"Thank you, Mr. Darcy." She handed him his tea with a lift of her eyebrow.

Mr. Darcy chuckled and shook his head as he stirred his tea. "That expression makes me wonder what thoughts turn about in your mind."

Fitzwilliam smiled as she passed him his own cup. "I am particularly fond of her quirk of the eyebrow."

"Is that all you are fond of? My eyebrow?"

His grin widened and his teeth appeared with a low rumble of a chuckle. "Perhaps we should discuss my fondness for you later."

She pursed her lips and narrowed her eyes as she heard another low chuckle from his father.

"Do not mind me," he quipped. "I will drink my tea and pretend I have not heard a thing."

Elizabeth entered the family wing and opened the first door with Darcy just behind. He followed her inside as she gazed around the room, taking in her surroundings.

"Mrs. Reynolds suggested this suite. The chambers are near the beginning of the corridor, but they are the largest rooms in the wing."

"If they are so grand, then why did your parents not use them?"

"I would imagine for much the same reason we do not expel my father from the master's chambers. My grandparents still lived when they were wed, so my parents chose different accommodations. These were my grandparent's chambers."

Elizabeth glanced beyond the faded drapes to the scene outside. "The view of the garden is lovely. I adore the prospect of the pond near the edge of the trees."

"I thought you might." He smiled as he approached her from behind. "The rooms are rather out-dated. I know you did not wish to redo anything, but…"

"I will not prove myself to be what he expected when we wed."

"My love." He took her arms and turned her so she faced him. "I know it is difficult to forget, but I believe he has changed. In the last week he has gone to great lengths to prove himself. His request that you teach Georgiana how to run the house was a great vote of confidence."

"I know, but remember, I did not relish spending your money in the beginning, either."

He smiled and pulled her into an embrace. "I do not intend for us to live here. Sagemore is our home, but I do think it appropriate we have our own chambers—ones where we are comfortable and at home rather than feel relegated as guests."

She gave a heavy exhale. "I apologise. I spoke with Mrs. Reynolds as well, and I know she felt these were the most suited to our needs. My sensitivity is probably unwarranted, but I do not want to be the cause of more strife between you."

His hands cradled her face as he drew back to catch her eye. "You were never the cause of our strife. That began long before I made your acquaintance."

"I did not help matters."

"Whether I met you or not, I would *never* have wed Anne, and my father would not have been pleased. You know this, so why do you blame yourself?"

"I do not blame myself." Her forehead creased in thought. "I do not want to be the cause of further division after you and your father have reconciled."

"He can see how happy we are together. He made mention of it after dinner when we were drinking brandy. The regrets he has are not limited to Wickham or his anger over my rejection of marriage to Anne, they include his unkind judgement of you when he should have made your acquaintance."

"So you have come to trust him?"

A sigh escaped his lips. "Not as much as I wish; it is too soon. I have spent too long distrusting him and his motives."

She nodded and stepped from his arms in the direction of the mistress' chambers as he trailed behind, observing her reactions to the furniture and the room.

"Perhaps we could find a place for what is in the master's chambers, and once it is papered, this furniture could be moved into the other room. I suppose a sofa and chaise could be moved into here so the room is not bare."

"You mean to use this as a large dressing room of sorts?"

Elizabeth shrugged as she turned in a circle. "I would prefer it. Then the dressing room and abigail's room could be used by Thomas and Mary."

"I believe Mrs. Reynolds thought the next bedchamber could be used as a nursery. It is not a large room, and there would be room for several small beds. The dressing room would suit admirably for Mary as well."

His hand found hers and drew her back into his arms. "What if we decorated the rooms as they stand for us, but we sleep in here?"

"I suppose we could change rooms from time to time," she said with a mischievous smile.

424

"We could." He whispered near her ear and felt her shiver. "Perhaps we should try the beds." His lips found a particularly sensitive place beneath her ear. "Ensure the furniture is still durable."

She let out a burst of laughter. "Durable?"

His fingers began to draw up her skirt as a hand slipped in and around the supple skin of her thigh. He began to move her backwards until the backs of her legs were stopped by the mattress.

"Perhaps we should." Her voice sounded rough as he continued to trail kisses along her neck. "We would not want to sleep here later and find the bed did not suit."

The inspection of the rooms lasted a few hours, and young Master Fitzwilliam and his wife were not seen by most of the house until tea.

Their last evening at Pemberley, Elizabeth and Georgiana planned a larger dinner as well as entertainment. When the meal concluded, Darcy followed his father to the library where he settled himself in a chair near the fireplace.

"Your wife has a wonderful way with Georgiana." His father studied him as he spoke. "She has seemed to, by instinct, know the correct thing to say when your sister becomes upset over Wickham."

"Elizabeth was raised with four sisters. It makes sense she would be capable in handling a young lady of Georgiana's years. Her own sister Lydia was of a similar age when she died."

"She does not speak much of her family," observed his father.

He swallowed his drink and furrowed his brow. "She has gradually spoken more and more of them with those she trusts. I am afraid they will always be an emotional topic for her, so she is selective in whom she confides."

"I would like to know how the two of you wed… if you are comfortable sharing the tale."

His father's eyes were open with no apparent deceit, and he stumbled as he made to answer. "I… I suppose it could not hurt."

Trust would have to be tested sometime, and the elder Darcy would never desire the tale of their introduction to be spread about society.

The entirety of the story was divulged, from Georgiana's advice prior to his departure from Pemberley to the day of the wedding itself. When he completed his narration, his father stared at him agape.

"You wed a stranger rather than abide by my plan." It was not a question but rather, a statement made in an astonished tone. "I would never have believed it had I not heard it from you."

"I was taken with her from the moment of our first introduction." Why was he so defensive? It was not as if his father was accusing him of some dreadful deed.

A lop-sided grin appeared upon his father's face. "That much is apparent in how you relate the tale. You were remarkably observant in your first impression."

He reddened and peered down into his empty glass. "I believe I knew then… "

"You knew she was meant for you." The elder Darcy's smile subsided as he nodded. "It was the same with your mother."

"Grandmamma mentioned as much." A chuckle escaped his lips. "I almost ruined matters during the week in London, and Grandmamma set me straight. Elizabeth would have been well within her rights to refuse my hand, but she hoped I would become the man she met in her uncle's drawing room."

"She trusted you." His father tilted his head and caught his eye. "As she trusts you now. She is wary of me—I cannot blame her for being so—but she displays an unwavering trust in you. Few men receive such devotion from their wives. Do not ever take it for granted."

"I shall not," he affirmed. "I treasure her faith in me because I know what it took to earn such confidence."

"I hope to one day earn such a trust." The elder Darcy's gaze was steady and earnest.

"You have made an admirable beginning." He held his father's eye. "I believe you may find success in time."

"Thank you." His father's voice cracked as he swallowed hard. "I appreciate the opportunity more than you can know."

He cleared his throat as he set his glass on a side table. "We should hire an investigator to track down this Gardiner. I do not care for the idea of him remaining where he can still be of harm."

"I have it on good authority Gardiner has left England. He shall not return."

"That is a relief."

"Yes, Richard, Uncle Henry, and I were all relieved at the intelligence."

A light knock sounded upon the door. They summoned the person to enter

"Georgie and I are ready to begin, if you are quite finished with your brandy."

"We are, and I was going to suggest we join you." His father stood and made his way to Elizabeth, extending his arms to take his grandson. Elizabeth ensured he was tucked against his grandfather, and turned to Darcy with that blasted raised eyebrow.

"Are you going to join us for the performance?"

He chuckled as he stepped over to join them. "I would not miss it. I am certain it will be superior to many of the performances in Bath."

A small snort escaped her lips. "I suppose you feel that is flattery."

"Flattery corrupts both the receiver and the giver…[1] "

A spark flamed in Elizabeth's eye, and she smiled mischievously as she turned. "One may define flattery as a base companionship which is most advantageous to the flatterer[2]."

His father's lips quirked as he glanced to his son. "Sweet words are like honey, a little may refresh, but too much gluts the stomach[3]."

She giggled and shook her head. "I do not know whether anyone has ever succeeded in not enjoying praise. If he enjoys it, he naturally wants to receive it. And if he wants to receive it, he cannot help but being pained and distraught at losing it.[4]"

"You read sermons?" his father queried with surprise.

Elizabeth bit her lip as she reached the open door of the music room. "It is a quote the vicar in Meryton used often in his sermons. I have heard it enough over the years to remember it well.

"My sister, Mary, read sermons, and I believe she quoted it on several occasions."

She grinned again with a lift of her eyebrow. "My own sex, I hope, will excuse me, if I treat them like rational creatures, instead of flattering their *fascinating* graces, and viewing them as if they were in a state of perpetual childhood, unable to stand alone.[5]"

His father halted in place and peered to his son. "Wollstonecraft? It is no wonder Rebecca adores her as she does."

"Indeed," Darcy replied with a laugh. "Indeed."

1 Edmund Burke, *Reflections on the Revolution in France*, 1790

2 Theophrastus

3 Anne Bradstreet

4 John Chrysostom

5 Mary Wollstonecraft, *A Vindication of the Rights of Women*, 1792

Chapter 30

June, 2 years later

Elizabeth sat in her favourite, comfortable spot on the sofa as she embroidered in the morning sun from the window. The tiny gown, which was sewn by her grandmother, was set in her tambour frame while she stitched tiny flowers onto the bodice.

She paused a moment to run her hand over the swell of her stomach. Her intuition told her this child would be a girl, just as she had been certain Thomas was a boy. Fitzwilliam chuckled at her belief, but she could not shake the feeling this time was different.

"How are you?" asked Grandmamma as she entered.

"Tired but well. She is active again." Her hand rested against the movement to one side of her belly and the older woman chuckled.

"You are determined with this one as well?"

She lifted her chin defiantly. "I am. Fitzwilliam will have to become accustomed to my absurdity, I suppose."

"I daresay he does not disagree with your assessment, but enjoys teasing you rather than capitulating his agreement."

A commotion in the entry hall prompted her to rise and follow the dowager, who made her way towards a young messenger held in place by the butler.

"I was told to deliver this to Mr. Darcy himself! I have no time to lose!"

Fitzwilliam strode around the corner from his office. "I am Fitzwilliam Darcy. May I ask your name?"

"I am Adam Hastings," the young man said with haste. "I worked in the Pemberley stable with Mr. Johns when I was a small boy."

"I do remember you, Adam. He taught you to groom the horses as I recall."

"Yes, sir." He nodded as he held out a letter in his hand. "Miss Darcy asked me to deliver this to you. I rode as fast as I could. I even rode through the night!"

Fitzwilliam spared no time in taking the missive. "Thank you." His attention turned towards the butler and Mrs. Green. "Please see that Adam is fed and has a place to rest."

They led the young man away as her husband broke the seal and began to read.

Grandmamma stepped forward with worry etched upon her face. "Is Georgie well?"

"She is. It is father. He has suffered an apoplexy. My sister asks me to journey to Pemberley as soon as it can be arranged."

Elizabeth's hand covered her mouth. Mr. Darcy had appeared so healthy when he visited Sagemore two months prior.

Fitzwilliam looked to her and grasped her free hand. "I do not want to leave you, but…"

"What do you mean *leave me*, Fitzwilliam Darcy?"

His grandmother chuckled. "Perhaps, I should inform Mrs. Green that we will *all* require our trunks packed."

As Grandmamma made her way towards the kitchens, her husband turned back to her with pleading eyes. "You must see that I cannot take you with the babe due to arrive any day."

"I do not see anything of the sort. I told you before that you will not leave me behind, and you will not abandon me here to have this child without you."

He drew her into his arms and kissed her forehead. "I could not bear it if you were to become ill due to the rigors of the trip."

"My confinement should not be for another few weeks," she stated stubbornly. "I can weather the trip as well as anyone."

His eyebrows raised. "Thomas arrived a few weeks earlier than we expected your lying in would be." Fitzwilliam sighed and shook his head. "I know I should insist that you remain here, but I worry you will follow, dragging Thomas, Grandmamma, and Hattie with you."

She pulled back with a huff. "I would not have to drag them. They would follow willingly—I assure you."

Fitzwilliam gave a chuckle and ran his hands up and down her arms. "Very well. I will not depart without you."

Her arms wrapped around his neck and held him tight. "Thank you."

"Ensure Hattie and Mary pack everything with haste. We need to depart within the hour if we can manage it."

His lips found her forehead to bestow one last kiss before he strode to his study. He disappeared around the corner, and she let out a long exhale. The idea of a journey to Pemberley was not a pleasant one—the jostling of the carriage on her already uncomfortable body a dread she could not now avoid.

If Fitzwilliam would only be away for a few days, she might have remained, but his father's condition could necessitate a stay of a fortnight at least!

"I should side with my grandson and insist you remain," came Grandmamma's voice from beside her.

"He could be gone for weeks."

The dowager nodded. "He could, but I am certain he would hurry his return as soon as he learned your time was near."

"I cannot," she whispered. "I cannot wait here. I will not wait here." Her voice gained strength as she spoke. "The midwife did not expect the babe's arrival to be imminent when she examined me."

"There have been many women who go into their confinement with no warning."

"I am aware of such stories." She passed a hand over her belly. "I will endure this trip. I must."

The dowager smirked. "I will remind you of your words when you complain of a myriad of aches and pains due to the jostling of the carriage and the length of the rides. "You are aware he will push from dawn until dark."

"It is summer, and the days are long this time of year." Her hand pressed to her aching back. "I understand the duration of each day's journey."

"Do you?"

"Yes, Grandmamma," she responded testily. "We will be spending seventeen to eighteen hours a day travelling. I do understand."

Her grandmother raised her eyebrows at her tone. "Do not be angry. I needed to be sure, Lizzy. I would feel the same as you, but I wanted to be certain this was not borne of impulse and something you would later regret."

"I may hurt and be exhausted, but I will not regret my decision to remain with my husband."

Grandmamma nodded. "Then let us be off to Pemberley."

They did not leave within the hour but were on the road in just under two, which Darcy considered a veritable success. Hattie, Mary, and James were harried as they stepped into the servant's carriage with Thomas, yet Elizabeth began to doze a short time after the horses began the long journey. His grandmother sat opposite him the entirety of their travel, allowing Elizabeth to lay her legs across him when she felt the need.

Complaints of the long days in the confines of the coach were to be expected from Elizabeth, but she never uttered one. She was certain to ache by the end of their first day of travel, yet other than a few grimaces, she remained silent on the matter.

His watchful eye was trained on her throughout their journey as he studied her for any sign of distress or, God forbid, labour, yet she gave him no cause for such concern.

Their second day of travel began as the sun emerged just enough to give them some much-needed light. Their night at the inn had been mercilessly short, and Elizabeth gave a great sigh, tucked to his side as they neared the inn that evening.

"She has handled the trip better than I expected." Grandmamma spoke in a soft tone, so as not to disturb Elizabeth as she rested.

"Indeed she has." He glanced to his wife's swollen ankles and frowned. "But, the walks she insists upon when we change horses are not of aid to her poor feet."

"Exercise helps the aches and pains, and does her good. I remember well the desire to walk when I could no longer tolerate the soreness in my hips from lying or sitting for an extended period of time. The swollen feet and ankles are to be expected."

He sighed and gripped her to him as they hit a bump in the road. "I…"

"You are concerned, Fitzwilliam, which is warranted. Lizzy is an independent young lady, but I do not believe she would object to a bit of coddling after the rigours of this ride."

"Indeed, I would not," Elizabeth rasped.

"We did not mean to wake you." He arranged her curls away from her face.

"I was not in a sound sleep." She peered out of the window. "I do not recognise our surroundings, but it seems we are closer."

"We are about three hours from Pemberley, but only have about half the daylight required."

"Then we will arrive tonight." To his surprise, she stated it as if it were fact.

"I had not thought to push forward." He frowned. "I would never ask you to travel for so long."

Her hand rested upon his cheek, and he turned to bestow a kiss upon her palm. "You may not ask, but as long as Jones does not object, I believe we should continue. I can rest when we arrive."

"Elizabeth…"

"Speak to Jones when we change horses, and make your decision then. It is imperative you reach your father as soon as possible, and to stop at an inn for the night would delay your arrival."

He shook his head and made to speak, but a finger to his lips halted his words. "I am in earnest. Do not worry for me."

His hand pulled her forward as he drew her into his embrace. The babe gave a swift jab to his hand, prompting a smile. Everything was well. Everything would remain well. He had to believe it, else he could not concentrate on the task before him.

The passage of time dragged by until the change of horses, but upon their arrival at the inn, Jones indicated a willingness to proceed if the family were so inclined.

Elizabeth exercised and ensured she was prepared for the last leg of their journey, refusing to rest until they were comfortably ensconced within the coach. She propped her feet upon his legs, and once again, dropped to sleep.

She slumbered until they pulled before Pemberley less than two hours later. Mrs. Reynolds took one look at Elizabeth, and after an admonishing look in his direction, she and Georgiana hurried his wife upstairs for a bath and their comfortable chambers. His grandmother followed close behind.

He was ushered to his father's chambers, where the elder Darcy lay still alive in his bed. His father's valet explained the episode his father endured as well as the effects—his paralysis down the right side of his body and the speech problems that had arisen as a result.

The man who had always seemed larger than life was taken abed and suddenly seemed small.

He ran a hand through his hair as he sat by George Darcy's bedside. How would this affect his father on a permanent basis? Could he ever regain what he once was?

A muffled, slurred sound startled him from his thoughts to where his father reached for him with his good hand.

"Izsshe?"

He furrowed his brow as his father repeated the strange sound. The elder Darcy's valet, hearing the commotion, rushed into the room and took a place on the opposite side of his master.

"I believe he is inquiring of Mrs. Darcy, sir."

"You wish to know of Elizabeth?" he asked, surprised.

His father patted his left hand against the bedclothes, and the valet nodded. "That is his signal for yes."

"Elizabeth made the journey with me." The elder Darcy closed his eyes and gave a heavy groan. "She was whisked to our chambers by Georgiana and Mrs. Reynolds. I believe she weathered the trip better than I expected."

His father relaxed. "Grandmamma joined us. I hope you do not mind. She had just arrived to see Elizabeth through her confinement, and since the child will likely be born at Pemberley, Grandmamma invited herself along."

A harsh sound resembling a bark of laughter escaped his father's throat. He brought his good hand to his forehead and then looked to his son with tears in his eyes. "Ssssorrry."

"Are you apologising?"

His father struck his hand upon the bed in obvious frustration.

"You will not apologise. Do you understand?"

He began to wave his hand back and forth against the bed. The valet indicated that to be his father's method of saying no, but the son would not have it.

"Did you expect us to receive word of your illness and not ensure your well-being?"

His father closed his eyes.

434

"I intended to make a quick trip and return before the babe arrived, but Elizabeth would not have it. She insisted on accompanying me, and I will not drag her back to Sagemore before the birth. We will remain until you are well and Elizabeth is able to travel." He grasped his father's good hand and squeezed.

"You are sure to be better company than Richard and Huntley whilst I wait."

The elder Darcy gave a lop-sided grin.

"You see. It is done, and you will have to allow us to remain for the duration."

His father squeezed his hand. "Sank... sank..." he attempted and grimaced.

"Is that 'thank you,' sir?" Asked the valet, and the elder Darcy's hand patted the bed.

"There is no reason to thank me. I could not leave Georgiana alone to deal with such a situation."

His father appeared aggrieved, and stopped. What could he have said to cause his father such pain?

"I wish to be here for you as well, father. I believe we have made great strides over the last few years. Do you not think so as well?"

A relieved expression suffused the elder Darcy's countenance as his hand rapped the bed. A maid appeared with broth and tea as his father's valet began to fuss over his master.

"Perhaps I should peer in on Elizabeth to see for myself that she is well whilst your valet tends to you. If he will send word, I will keep you company until you fall asleep. Would that please you?"

His father patted the bedclothes, and he smiled. "Good, I shall return. I promise."

When he arrived at his chambers, James was laying out his nightshirt and dressing gown.

"I was unsure of when you would leave your father's side."

He held up his hand. "If warm water can be arranged, I should like to bathe and change. Then, I will sit with my father until he falls asleep."

James nodded. "I will leave your nightclothes out for when you retire." His valet's eyes shifted to the door that lead to the mistress' chambers and back. "I will have the bath ready as soon as you have ensured Mrs. Darcy is well."

He chuckled as he peeled off his topcoat and waistcoat. "Am I so predictable?"

"You are, but I do not feel it reflects poorly upon you, sir. Few are gifted the felicity in marriage you enjoy with Mrs. Darcy."

A smile lit his countenance as he handed James his cravat. "I tend to agree with you, but I give all the credit to my wife."

"As you say, sir." James gave a swift bow and exited through the dressing room while he made his way to his wife's chambers. He knocked softly and was not surprised when his grandmother opened the door. She was still in her travelling clothes as she put a finger over her lips.

"She bathed and fell asleep as soon as her head touched the pillows, despite her intentions to wait up for you."

A corner of his lips lifted, touched by her wish to wait for him. He had no expectations of her doing as such.

"Where is Georgiana?"

"She departed to check on her father. I suspect you will find her there when you return."

He stepped over to the bed and took a seat, careful not to disturb Elizabeth's rest. She was curled on her side with pillows cuddled down her front. He touched his lips with care against her temple. She sighed and began to murmur in her sleep. He kissed her hair and rose.

"I must bathe. I promised father I would return and sit with him until he fell asleep."

"Do not forget to rest yourself, Fitzwilliam. Elizabeth is not the only one who could use some sleep."

"His valet indicated father usually wasted no time falling asleep once he was tended to and ate. I suspect tonight will be no different. Elizabeth and I shall most assuredly sleep late in the morning."

"As will I!" His grandmother often spoke with conviction, but this was more emphatic than her usual speech. "I do not plan to travel in such haste again. These old bones do not agree with the pace."

"I apologise…"

"No," she interrupted. "I would not leave Elizabeth on her own to give birth, and I should like to be here for George as well. I just do not believe it to be in my best interest to attempt such a journey again."

He nodded. "I thank you for taking the trip, Grandmamma. I know Elizabeth will be more at ease with you in attendance during her confinement."

"I will be more at ease, as well." She peered over to Elizabeth. "I will return to my chambers now that I am assured she has weathered the trip. Mrs. Reynolds has posted a maid in Lizzy's dressing room to sit with her so she is not alone."

"I will remember when I return. Good night, Grandmamma."

"Good night, Fitzwilliam." She exited out to the hall and closed the door behind her.

He took one last look at the bed. How he wished to climb in behind Elizabeth and succumb to his dreams! Instead, he turned and made his way to his dressing room for his bath.

True to his valet's word, George Darcy did not remain awake long after his dinner, and after remaining with Georgiana until their father slept, Darcy gave in to his deepest desire by joining his wife in her bed. He did not rest well and rose early the next morning.

James was prepared when he entered his dressing room, and had him outfitted for the day with his usual efficiency. The elder Darcy was still asleep when he stopped by his chambers, so he requested he be notified when his father was next awake and made his way to his father's study.

The steward was taken aback at the son's insistence of handling his father's affairs for the time being but did not brook an argument. They discussed the few matters of importance that had occurred over the last few days, but with nothing further, the man went to tend to business, leaving the young master to peruse the contents of his father's desk.

The ledgers for Pemberley and three other properties were set in a stack to one side, and he opened each to ascertain where each account stood. Pemberley, Ellon Strath in Scotland, and Huntingdon were all financially sound, even if their numbers were not as high as he would have expected.

He reached for the final ledger, unaware of the identity of the property. The three prior estates had been in the family for generations, but what had his father purchased and when did he make such an expenditure?

The cover creaked like a book rarely opened, and he was stunned to see little in the way of entries, only the name of the property—Longbourn. He dropped back in his father's seat and stared at the page agape. He had been well aware the estate had been sold, but he had not known the identity of the new owner—until now.

Collins, as he had predicted, had spent from Longbourn's accounts until he could no longer pay his debts in Meryton. In the end, it was his debts to the butcher that broke him.

An offer from the Darcys of Sagemore was proffered through his solicitor, but his father must have been the individual who acquired the estate before their bid was presented. Fortunately, Elizabeth had been unaware until after the failed offer when he apologised for not succeeding in the endeavour.

She had not been angry or upset. Instead, she praised his efforts and led him upstairs to their chambers. She was too good!

He shook his head. His father had purchased Longbourn! But why?

"Fitzwilliam?" His wife's voice came from the door, and he peered up to where she waited for him to bid her enter.

"Please, come in." He held out his arm, so she could take his hand. "I was going over father's ledgers."

"Is something amiss?"

The account book in his hand drew his attention, and he stared at the page for a few more moments before he passed it to her.

"What is this?" She took the book with caution, but her eyes remained on him.

"Please look. I could use your insight on the matter."

Elizabeth's eyes drifted to the page and bulged. "Your father purchased Longbourn?"

He nodded in confirmation. "I am as stunned as you."

A maid entered with a tray and set it on a table in the corner. Elizabeth excused her and took a seat to prepare their repast as he returned to the account books for the other properties, discovering significant withdrawals from those accounts prior to the purchase date for Longbourn.

"He planned for it." He whispered it to himself, but Elizabeth heard and waddled around to look over his shoulder.

"I do not understand why he would want Longbourn."

"That is something I intend to discover." He shut the book firmly, and Elizabeth covered his hands.

"Do not become angry when you are unsure of his motive. He may not have intended anything untoward."

"I believe at times you and your description of Jane are not so dissimilar. You have a tendency to look for the best in people as well."

She squeezed his hand, drawing his eyes to hers. "I do not have reason to disbelieve his change over the last two years. He has never given us cause to think him false, and it would be a shame to destroy the relationship you have built on nothing more than suspicion.

"Do not allow your prior prejudices to ruin the relationship you now possess." Her earnest gaze prompted a nod.

"I will ask, but I am unsure what sort of answer I will receive. He has great difficulty when he speaks." His wife took his hand and led him to the sofa where he took his seat.

"I sought out Mrs. Reynolds on my way here, and we have an idea that may help."

"Really?" he asked as he took his teacup.

"She will need to find the necessary materials, but let us hope they will not prove too difficult to locate."

"You are being very mysterious."

"I do not want you to be excited if the attempt is unsuccessful."

"Very well. I will wait."

She handed him a plate as Thomas barrelled through the door and into his father's free arm. Elizabeth managed to grasp his tea before it spilled. "Papa!"

The long carriage ride had been excruciating for young Thomas, who missed his freedom while in the confines of the family carriage or travelling with his nurse. He would be a great deal to manage as he was sure to run his nursemaid ragged to atone for several days of restricted activity.

He lifted his son into his lap where he began to reach for the food on the tray. Elizabeth handed him a piece of toast as a winded Mary made it through the door.

"I am sorry, sir. I no more than set him upon the floor when he disappeared. I followed his footsteps as fast as I was able."

Elizabeth beamed at her son. "It is fine. We will send for you when we need you." Mary curtsied and closed the door behind her before they both began to laugh.

"Perhaps we should employ a new nursemaid to help with Thomas," he suggested, caressing his son's head. "The new little one will not make her life any easier."

"I suppose you are correct.

A knock at the door halted their conversation. "Enter," he called.

A footman opened the door and stepped inside. "Mr. Darcy, your father is awake." With a last cuddle and kiss to his son's head, he set Thomas beside Elizabeth and stood to go to his father.

"Fitzwilliam, you should eat."

He turned to find his wife regarding him with concern. "I shall. I promise, but I need to speak with him first."

She nodded, and he strode through the great hall and up the stairs to the family wing where he rapped upon the master's bedchamber door. The elder Darcy's valet allowed him to enter.

His father was seated, propped with pillows against the headboard with Georgiana seated to his right side on the mattress. His pallor was improved from the evening prior, and he gave his son a lop-sided smile.

"Morning." He was unsure of where to begin. How should he approach the matter?

"Fitzwilliam! How is Lizzy this morning? I hope she is rested from your journey north. She looked so tired when you arrived at Pemberley." George Darcy's eyes turned back to him with worry.

"She is much improved, thank you. She is with Thomas in the study if you wish to spend time with them."

"Oh, I should like to play with Thomas, but I would like to remain with Papa for a while longer."

With his good hand, George Darcy tapped on the bed and gestured towards the chair to his side. Darcy made himself comfortable as his father noticed Longbourn's ledger in his hand. His shoulders slumped, but he reached for a slate and slate pencil on the bed, which must have been the idea Elizabeth mentioned earlier.

He was right-handed so his left did not cooperate in the same fashion, but eventually he held up the board, which read, "*Tell Lizzy?*" as he pointed to his son.

"Did I tell Elizabeth?"

The elder Darcy rapped his hand against the bed with urgency as Georgiana looked on with worry.

"Yes, I showed her the ledger. I do not keep secrets from my wife."

His father swiped the slate clean with the arm of his nightshirt and concentrated as he put the pencil to the surface.

"*Gift.*"

His eyebrows furrowed. "You meant Longbourn as a gift?"

The elder Darcy's left hand patted the slate.

"For whom?"

His father exhaled heavily. "Iszzy!"

"You bought Longbourn as a gift for Elizabeth?" He was astounded. Why would he spend such an amount? His father appeared to care for Elizabeth, but he would never expect him to purchase the Bennet estate for her. "I…"

Georgiana placed a hand on her father's arm. "I believe I can answer your questions for Papa."

He looked to his sister with incredulity. "You were aware of this?"

A smile crossed her lips as she nodded. "I was. Papa spoke of his idea after the incident at Ramsgate. After his investigation of Elizabeth when you first wed, he was aware of the cousin who inherited Longbourn upon her family's death, *and* the son who succeeded him.

"He did not mention much after the two of you reconciled, but I accompanied him to Meryton several months ago. Papa was so excited when he spoke to me of his wish to purchase the Bennet estate, set matters with you to rights, and gift Longbourn to Elizabeth."

"Mr. Collins..."

"Mmbecile."

His head snapped up as the comment took him by surprise, then he chuckled. "I cannot argue with your assessment. I sent my solicitor to purchase Longbourn, but you anticipated me. I had made a promise to acquire her childhood home after we visited Meryton during our journey to Ramsgate."

"*Sorry.*"

"The gesture was not necessary, but Elizabeth will be ecstatic to know Longbourn is not owned by a stranger. When I discovered the property had been bought, she would not allow me to discover the identity of the current owner."

His father's one-sided smile reappeared.

"I suppose it suited your purpose, but now do you wish to tell Elizabeth or wait? She is aware you own the property, and I do not believe I will be able to deter her questions later."

The elder Darcy wrote on the slate, but angled it towards Georgiana who grinned and disappeared into the corridor. She was not gone for more than ten minutes when she reappeared with Elizabeth and Thomas in tow.

His father's expression lit when he noticed his grandson, and Thomas shyly agreed to sit with Grandfather on the bed.

Darcy explained his father's actions, which prompted tears to stream down Elizabeth's cheeks.

"For me? I cannot accept such an extravagant gift."

"Lizzy," interjected Georgiana. "Papa wishes for you to have Longbourn." She handed her a leather case she must have retrieved when she fetched Elizabeth.

With shaky hands, his wife opened the flap to reveal the papers placing her family's estate in her husband's name. The law combined with their marriage prevented her name from gracing the paperwork, but her eyes still welled with tears.

"I will have it added to your settlement when I amend my will to include the baby, or if I cannot, it will be left to you in my will." He stood at her shoulder as she nodded and still attempted to contain her emotions.

She handed him the folio and stepped to the side of the bed where she took the elder Darcy's hands. "I do not have the words to thank you."

His father tugged his hand from hers and waved it over the bedclothes. Darcy made to explain, but he did not have the opportunity since she grasped his good hand.

"You will not wave off my thanks," she argued. "I will have my say."

He began to laugh as she huffed and placed her hands on her hips. "Do not laugh at me, Fitzwilliam Darcy."

"You could not have expected us to ignore your use of one of Lady Catherine's favourite phrases! Father is laughing as well."

The elder Darcy made a valiant attempt to prevent his shoulders from shaking with mirth, but he could not suppress his amusement.

Elizabeth's lips quirked up to one side as his father grasped her hand with his. "amly."

She furrowed her brow, so he resumed his concentration on his slate.

"*Family*" was all it said, but if Elizabeth was unsure of his meaning, his insistent finger pointing in her direction would dispel all doubt.

A tear fell to her cheek, and she brushed it away. "Thank you."

Darcy swelled with happiness as he watched his wife and son with his father and Georgiana. At one time, he could not have envisioned a greater felicity than he experienced with Elizabeth, but Thomas proved him incorrect.

His father's acceptance of his marriage and family served to fill a void created when his mother passed from this earth. Perhaps they were meant to spend those years apart in order to discover one another again?

Only God knew the answer, but Fitzwilliam Darcy's heart was fuller than he could have ever imagined. That is until he held his newborn daughter, Rebecca Jane Margaret Darcy a mere five days later—and was besotted once again.

Epilogue

14 years later

Elizabeth Darcy stood before the drawing room window as sixteen year-old Thomas guided his younger brother George on Page. A smile graced her lips at the care her eldest took to ensure his five year-old sibling came to no harm on the aging horse.

"He is doing very well," came a familiar deep voice behind her. Fitzwilliam wrapped his arms around her waist, and she leaned back against his strong chest as they continued to observe the scene below.

"They are both doing well. Thomas is such a considerate elder brother, and George is terribly excited to ride Page."

He leaned his chin against her head. "Page's knees prevent him from being a proper mount for you these days, so it is nice he can still be of use. He will make an excellent horse for George as he learns to ride."

"I envy George's ability to ride him."

"I know you do, my love. But we shall find you a new mount that you will enjoy as much as Page."

She chuckled and pivoted in his arms. "I know you will leave no stone unturned in your search."

"I suppose not." He first skimmed his lips against hers and then pulled her closer as he deepened his kiss only to be interrupted by the sound of a door as it opened.

"I told you we should have knocked," hissed Rebecca.

Her younger sister Marianne pushed Rebecca aside. "Mrs. Gibbs said Mama was in here alone. Papa is supposed to be working in his study." Rebecca with a few quick strides overtook her sibling.

Elizabeth dropped her forehead to her husband's chest and giggled. "It is a bit late to argue over the matter now. Was there something you girls required?"

"Marianne claims you are to let Uncle Richard have Longbourn."

If Elizabeth had dreams of Rebecca resembling her beloved Jane in personality, they would have died a tragic death long ago. Her eldest daughter was a great deal like herself in so many ways. She was a

444

good elder sister, but she had an innate need to be correct that could be infuriating.

Her husband stepped back and levelled the girls with a stern expression. "Uncle Richard will reside at Longbourn for as long as he has need of it, but it remains your mother's property."

Richard had returned to the Peninsula several times in the quest to defeat Napoleon and withstood the rigors of war until the Battle of Waterloo where he was gravely injured. After almost losing both his leg and his life, he returned to England.

For years, he spent time in Bath taking the waters and frequenting the bathhouses for relief. After an offer from the Darcys, he was grateful to move to Longbourn. He was welcome to live out his life there in return for overseeing the property.

The biggest surprise came when the confirmed bachelor took none other than Charlotte Lucas as his wife in the fall of the previous year. They both cited practical reasons for their union—her age and his infirmity—but those who observed them closely enough could see they had a deep abiding friendship and love.

"Grandpapa bought Longbourn for Mama, did he not?" asked Marianne, who turned eleven this past winter. She was forever with a list of questions she wanted answered—also not unlike her mother at that age.

"Yes, your grandfather purchased Longbourn as a gift for your mother."

Rebecca glanced to her sister and then to her parents. "But Mr. Peele claims married women cannot own property."

Elizabeth closed her eyes and sighed. Mr. Peele, the children's tutor, had come with excellent references, but she detested his manner. He did not discuss or take exception. Every matter was yes or no: in-between did not exist in Mr. Peele's world.

"By law," began Fitzwilliam in a controlled voice, "your mother cannot own property, but Longbourn became a part of her settlement; she makes any major decisions in regards to the property, and when the time comes, it will be *hers* to pass down as she chooses. Do you understand?"

The girls both answered in the affirmative.

Elizabeth addressed her eldest daughter. "Is Nathaniel still attending his studies with Mr. Peele?"

445

Rebecca nodded. "Yes, ma'am, but he dismissed us to the governess."

"Mr. Peele said we have no need to learn Latin." Marianne's hands landed upon her hips. Elizabeth would wager anything that a question was coming. "Why is that Papa? I speak French, and I am learning Italian. I believe I should like to try Latin."

Fitzwilliam's lips drew to a thin line. "I will have a discussion with Mr. Peele. For now, the two of you shall do as he asks."

Elizabeth reached out and pulled Marianne into her arms. As parents, they attempted to have both their daughters and sons educated to the best of their abilities and inclinations. Thomas was on break from Eton, but Fitzwilliam and Elizabeth preferred tutors for the younger boys until they were old enough to join their brother. Both felt the girls received a better education as they were schooled with their brothers, and would remain with tutors rather than sending them to school.

"If you wish to learn Latin, we will do our best to see to it." She kissed her daughter's temple, brushed a curl from her face, and cradled her face in her hands. Whereas Rebecca resembled Elizabeth, Marianne favoured her father with her dark hair and blue eyes.

"You will find me a tutor for Latin?"

"We will if you truly wish to learn," interjected Fitzwilliam.

Marianne beamed and kissed her mother and father impulsively on the cheeks. "Thank you, Mama! Thank you, Papa!"

She bounded from the room as Rebecca turned to them. "You would hire a tutor just to teach her Latin?"

"As we would do for you if you asked." Elizabeth raised her eyebrows. "Is there something in particular you wish to learn?"

"I cannot think of anything at present." Rebecca gazed out the window as she pondered her choices before her regard returned to her parents. "Though, I should like to have more lessons with a music master if it can be arranged."

Their eldest daughter had learned to play from Georgiana, but when Georgiana wed the Earl of Bristol in 1816, Rebecca was left without a music teacher. She excelled at music and practiced the pianoforte much as her Aunt Georgie did—she played all day long if afforded the opportunity.

Georgiana was happy with her life, which made her absence bearable. Robert Digby had courted her for a year before she accepted his hand, but no one could deny it was a love match. They were well-suited.

"I will see what I can arrange." Fitzwilliam's lips gave a small lift. He loved to hear her practice and play. He was such a wonderful father! "Perhaps you should ask Aunt Georgiana for help when she and Uncle Robert visit in a fortnight."

"Thank you, Papa." Rebecca stepped forward with a wide grin and hugged her father tightly. "I love you."

"I love you, too, sweetling."

After Rebecca followed her sister out of the door, he turned to Elizabeth. "I wish my father were still alive. He had a way with finding excellent tutors for Georgiana."

George Darcy improved after his first bout of apoplexy and lived another eight years before experiencing another, this time fatal, episode. Fitzwilliam and Elizabeth moved to Pemberley not long after Rebecca's birth, and other than a month or two at Sagemore each summer, had resided at Pemberley ever since.

Fitzwilliam's father was not the only loved one to have passed. Grandmamma caught a trifling cold five years prior. The illness progressed to pneumonia within a se'nnight, and she passed a few days later, much to the dismay of those who loved her.

"What of the husband and wife we interviewed when last in London? He once taught at Oxford and had impeccable references, and she had a great deal of talent at the pianoforte."

Fitzwilliam eyed her with a smirk. "Have you been reading my correspondence?"

She regarded him in a bewildered fashion. Was he teasing, or did he believe she was peeking at his letters?

He chuckled. "I *am* teasing. I already sent them a letter a fortnight ago, and received word back this morning. They will accept the position and will arrive at Pemberley at the end of next week."

"When will you tell Mr. Peele?" She could not help the almost gleeful tone that escaped.

"I believe there is no better day than today. I do not appreciate his dismissal of Rebecca and Marianne's educational wishes. They have as much right to learn as Thomas and Nathaniel."

She stepped forward and placed her arms around his neck. "*You* are a wonderful father."

Her fingers traced his temple to brush his curls from his face. There were flecks of silver interspersed in those locks, but he was still as handsome as the day he stepped into her uncle's parlour.

He smiled and rested his head against her curls. "Well, I happen to adore my educated wife, so it only stands to reason I would wish to educate my daughters."

Elizabeth laughed and shook her head. "Still the flatterer."

He laughed and traced his fingers down her cheek. "I was not always proficient in the ways of flattery. Do not forget that Grandmamma had to show me how insufficient were all my pretensions to please a woman worthy of being pleased."

"She was only required to do so once, my dear. You proved you did not require further chastising."

"I should never have needed such a scolding in the first place! I was intimidated by what I felt and overwhelmed by your beauty. I found myself terrified I would love you and you would never love me."

"Were you really?"

Over the years, they had discussed their feelings and when they both began to recognise the love they had for one another, but he had never divulged so much about the time they were betrothed. "You had no reason to be concerned. I was already in a fair way of falling in love with you."

"You were?" He wore such a smug, infuriating grin.

"No." Her tone remained casual. He would pay for his pride! "I thought you insufferable and arrogant."

His face fell as he stared for a moment. He appeared as though he would release her until he tightened his grasp and began to tickle her sides.

She laughed uncontrollably until he halted. "You thought me insufferable?" His fingers sat poised to continue the assault.

"I thought you handsome, but I did not understand why you stared at me so. What I wanted was for you to behave as you did in my uncle's parlour. I desired your notice, sir."

448

He pressed a kiss under her ear. "I should go write the new tutors so they are aware I have received their acceptance." Another quick kiss was deposited upon her lips. "Did you read the letter I left upon your desk?"

"Yes, Uncle Gardiner has done well for himself."

"Well? He owns a large farm, is married, and has four children. He has done very well."

She was pleased her uncle had found such success, but she could not imagine a relationship with him after all these years, not after so much betrayal on his part.

The true relief had been five years prior when the Duke of Cumbria had challenged Carlisle to a duel, which Carlisle had won, shooting the duke in the heart; however, Carlisle received a wound to the shoulder. The wound festered, and within a fortnight, Thomas Grayson was no more.

Rumours abounded for months after the scandal. Viscount Carlisle's nefarious schemes were never unearthed, but those who were intimate with both parties indicated Carlisle had dallied with the duke's mistress. Fitzwilliam undoubtedly knew more, but she had no desire to unearth Carlisle and the duke's depravity.

"It was good of him to apologise." Fitzwilliam's voice pulled her from her memories.

"If you wonder whether I will return the letter, I have written a reply in which I forgive him. I wish him well, but I have no reason to believe he will desire a continued correspondence."

He held her in the solid embrace of his arms. "I love you."

She gave him a quick peck on the chin. "And I love you."

With a step back, he gave her hand one last squeeze. "Then I shall pen a letter to the new tutors, and another to a breeder to inquire after a horse for you."

His swift stride had him almost to the door when she called his name. He faced her with a questioning countenance.

"You need not hasten to find me a mount. I shall not be riding much for the next year anyhow."

She bit her bottom lip, examining his features as she awaited his comprehension.

He paused, furrowed his brows, and then his eyes widened. "You mean?"

She nodded and giggled at his elated expression.

"After all this time?" he said with wonder. "I assumed…"

"You assumed it was improbable we would be blessed again."

"I did." He pulled her forward into his arms and rested a hand on her stomach. "Do you have a preference for a girl or a boy?"

"In the beginning, all I wanted was to have a boy who resembled you, and now I have two." She shrugged with a smile thinking of Thomas and Nathaniel, who both bore such a strong likeness to their father, whereas George resembled his grandfather Bennet. "I do not have a preference this time. As long as he or she is healthy."

He held her close and stroked his hand up and down her back. "I want another little girl just like you."

She let out a bark of laughter. "Be careful! Rebecca and Marianne have you wrapped around their little fingers. A third little girl might put us into ruin."

"Did you think when I offered you marriage we would be where we are today?" He placed a kiss to her forehead.

"I did."

He drew back and studied her with a confounded look. "You did?"

"I had to trust in our decision—I had to trust in you. I would not have survived the experience otherwise."

"You never lost faith in me?"

She placed her hands on his cheeks and stared straight into his eyes. "Never," she said emphatically. "And I never will."

About the Author

L.L. Diamond is more commonly known as Leslie to her friends and Mom to her three children. A native of Louisiana, she has spent the majority of her life living within an hour of New Orleans until she vowed to follow her husband to the ends of the earth as a military wife. Louisiana, Mississippi, California, Texas, New Mexico, Nebraska, and now England have all been called home along the way.

After watching Sense and Sensibility with her mother, Leslie became a fan of Jane Austen, reading her collected works over the next few years. Pride and Prejudice stood out as a favourite and has dominated her writing since finding Jane Austen Fan Fiction.

Aside from mother and writer, Leslie considers herself a perpetual student. She has degrees in biology and studio art, but will devour any subject of interest simply for the knowledge. As an artist, her concentration is in graphic design, but watercolour is her medium of choice with one of her watercolours featured on the cover of her second book, A Matter of Chance. She also plays flute and piano, but much like Elizabeth Bennet, she is always in need of practice!

You can follow Leslie at:
Facebook: https://www.facebook.com/LLDiamond
Twitter: @LLDiamond2
Blog: http://lldiamondwrites.com/
Austen Variations: http://austenvariations.com/

Other Titles
by
L.L. Diamond

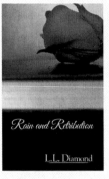

What if Elizabeth fled Longbourn?
When Elizabeth Bennet's parents attempt to force
her into a marriage of convenience for the sake
of her family, she flees to make her own future.
Will circumstances and their families conspire
to keep Darcy and Elizabeth apart or will they unite
to take them on together?

Darcy and the Deep South!
Single-mother and artist Lizzy Gardiner relied
on her sister, Jane, and her brother-in-law,
Charles Bingley, when she fled her husband.
However, when they introduce her to Charles' friend
William Darcy he doesn't make the best first
or even second impression.
Can the two of them leave not only their initial
prejudices, but also their pasts behind and find love
with each other or will the ghosts of the past return
to keep them apart?

452

Made in the USA
Columbia, SC
07 January 2018